Boogie House

A Rolson McKane Novel

T. Blake Braddy

A Jinx Protocol
Publication

*For Johnny Anderson,
the first reader*

Acknowledgements

The following people made this book more than just something I talked about to make myself feel smart: Zach Fishel, Josiah Shoup, Tommy Stubblefield, Jan & Bill Owens, Wallace Braddy, Leah Newman, Mary Coleman Palmer, Randy Cone, Roy Felts, Linda Wall, Jeanna Wheeler, Scott Sigler, Drew Wheeler, Bryan Center, Mike Swartzwelder, Justin Swartzwelder, Rick Gotwald, and – of course – Kate Blackmon.

First Chapter

I woke a little after midnight, gulped directly from the kitchen faucet, and tried to go back to sleep. Everything smelled like whiskey, and the gentle, watery tilt of the room kept me up, so I flipped to a channel I didn't want to watch and muted the volume. I thought about putting on music, but slide guitar was as appealing to me as fork tines on a dry dinner plate.

I tried desperately to become unconscious. I curled up on my stomach. Pressed my face to the cool side of the pillow. Stared at a show about dead celebrities. The screen's glow aggravated my looming hangover, so I killed the TV and padded through the house, looking for anything to distract me from how bad my head hurt. I tripped over a bag of clothes someone who used to live here left behind. The shirts and jeans still smelled like her.

I noticed a sliver of light peeking between the front door and the jamb. I had left it unlocked again. No real surprise. The bad dreams had started up again, ever since the accident, and they put me in a bad headspace, even when I was awake.

I sat on the porch in my boxers and smoked the last two cigarettes in my pack, watching the fireflies jitter and dance among the deflated azaleas. Every so often, the sky lit up and somewhere miles off a troubling crash split the darkness. The air smelled like coming rain, brought on by clouds black as spilled ink.

I stubbed the cigarette on the steps and flicked the butt out into the azaleas. (Which was probably not helping them.) I stood up, ready to go back inside, when an indistinct echo came out of the woods across the road.

I strained my ears toward the sound, which *could* have been a voice calling for help. Could have been a whole lot of things. Out in the country, sounds mutate and become something otherworldly.

Or it could have been my imagination.

The county where I live isn't big, and yet dirt roads cut through thousands of tree-lined acres, acting as cover for people who take driving sober as mere suggestion. Drunks occasionally flip their pickups winding a sharp curve and crush something vital. Usually they'll phone a buddy, though not always. I had sometimes spied grown men ambling like zombies down the road in search of sympathetic strangers, hoping aloud they weren't bleeding to death.

Such is the way of life in a small town.

There was desperation in that voice I heard. Or thought I heard. Reality had been inconsistent for me, of late. Too much drinking. Too many bad dreams. And there was also the thunder, which cut right through the silence, so I couldn't get a handle on what it was, exactly.

I grabbed my .45 from the house, put on some dusty running shoes and jeans, and headed in that direction.

I couldn't sleep anyway.

Across the road, I entered a dark copse of pines. Even under a full moon, the limbs, like old, gnarled fingers, obscured any trace of light, like walking into a windowless room at midnight. Occasionally, I stopped and listened, hearing nothing, smelling sap and tree rot in the air.

I went about my business cautiously, since I was trespassing on Leland Brickmeyer's property. This broken, forgotten patch of land wasn't even the beginning of their total holdings, but their laces were

2

tied a little too straight for them to abide me traipsing around like this after midnight.

The Brickmeyers had built their wealth on the backs of free labor during Reconstruction. Lumber Junction didn't really even become a place until the railroads were completed, but there had always been white people gracious enough to work poor and displaced minorities to death when it suited their interests.

Leland's father had bestowed on him a small fortune and a thriving timber business, but that last name was the old man's most important gift. Every town has a family like them. Local royalty, like the Kennedys with a country drawl. Most people who despised them just wanted a backstage pass.

Leland had used his last name to great effect, landing opportunities that would have otherwise eluded him. But reality is often harsher than perception. The mismanagement of this tract of land was just the tip of an ever-growing iceberg. He was not his daddy, and the stress fractures in the foundation were beginning to show. He had a bit of a political muscle he wanted to flex, and I'm sure he hoped it was more toned than his entrepreneurial one.

Brickmeyer and I had only spoken a few times, and only in an official capacity. Otherwise, I don't know that I could have stomached his glad-handing, empty charisma. He was transparent as a haint on All Hallow's Eve, but nobody seemed to care, so long as there was money involved.

A clap of thunder snapped me out of my thoughts. I descended a small hill and came to a man-made clearing.

I stopped in what used to be a gravel parking lot and watched in a sickened awe. The remnants of a smallish shack leaned to one side in the distance. What had once been a black-owned juke called the Boogie House was now just a rotten shell of a building, and though the doors had officially been closed for decades, tonight the Boogie House lived again.

And I'll be damned if it weren't *alive*.

The sound of piano and guitar swelled through the door, and silhouettes of women in knee-length dresses cut through the bright, even light within. I might have even smelled whiskey in the air if I weren't still fairly plastered.

A young woman stopped in the doorway, her lithe figure blocking the dance floor. She was light-skinned, beautiful. She bounced to the music, smoking a long, thin cigarette, a frizzy bob undulating atop her head. Her neck was wet with sweat, her red, flower-print dress whipping in a nonexistent breeze. She turned and looked in my direction but did not seem to see me.

I saw her, but only for a moment. She was blinking in and out, a light with a dimming bulb. A bad fuse box wasn't to blame; these were the spirits of the Boogie House. I had heard dark stories about this place but had thought it to be mostly old gossip gone wild.

The ghosts of decades past lingered there for a while, mixing together in a seductive dance. Dancing to music that wasn't really there. Showing out for me, I suppose. I was sweating despite the breeze, charged with a peculiar energy.

I approached the building, sneaking through the woods as if trailing spooked deer, hoping for something, but the whole scene flickered and died. There was a kind of beautiful flash, making blank silhouettes out of the patrons, and then the world went dark. Once again the shack was old and decrepit and condemnable. Just what it had been long as I'd been alive.

I stalked unevenly through the dark and pressed myself against the front of the Boogie House. Standing outside the entrance with a trembling finger on the trigger, I waited for my courage to catch up. The air smelled electric and burnt, like ozone but more raw. My nostrils ached from the burning.

I felt no immediate danger, but something jerked my instincts taut, and the dull throb of a hangover sharpened my senses. With the moon

4

blocked off by clouds, the Boogie House itself sank into the blackness. It was like staring into mud.

I turned into the doorway, pointed my weapon at nothing in particular. The voice itself had disappeared, leaving only the illusion of its existence in my head.

"Hello," I said, a half-question, "my name is Officer Rolson McKane. Lumber Junction PD. Come on out now, hear?"

It was a mostly untrue statement but gave me comfort anyway. I received only silence in return. The air and everything in it was still and silent. Another step forward yielded a patch of soggy wood. I tested my footing and placed some weight on it.

I must've been worried too much about myself, because I got caught unawares by what happened next. A human shape emerged from the far corner of the Boogie House, where the wall-length bar would have been. He fired before I could respond. The explosion of sound set off a series of reactions in me. I raised my weapon and dropped to one knee simultaneously, intending on returning fire. That was, until the boards holding me buckled, sending me off-balance and knee-deep into the ground below.

"Stop right there," I yelled, raising the weapon and struggling mightily to regain balance, but it was too late. The figure kicked out an old window and jumped through it, disappearing into the night in a single, graceless leap.

It was in that moment I saw his size. Beast could have been a pro ball player, maybe a wrestler or MMA fighter of some kind.

I pulled myself from the hole and backed out of that place. My heart kicked into a higher gear. Blood hummed in my ears. Chasing drunks down Highway 221 and kicking in the doors at suspected meth labs was as exciting as small-town cop life usually got.

I hoofed drunkenly through the rows and rows of pines, organized eerily like crosses in a long-forgotten graveyard. Ahead of me, footsteps sliding on loose straw drew me forward. I couldn't very well stop now. Fundamental fear and anger made my feet pump harder than I thought they could.

The hulk of a man slammed into a low-hanging branch, sending pine needles everywhere. He cursed, and I ducked just before he opened fire again. His accent was thick, country, but it wasn't a voice I readily identified, and the gun bursts erased my memory. The flashes from the muzzle gave me a brief view of his face, but the darkness obscured all but the most fleeting glances.

"Damnit," I said, firing two rounds at where he had been. I was sure I hadn't hit him, but I also didn't wait around to find out.

Taillights appeared out of nowhere, followed in quick succession by a slamming door and gurgling engine. White lights indicated the transmission slipping over reverse into drive, and then the engine roared, propelling the truck through the pines toward an undisclosed exit.

I fired two more rounds, hoping to hit something vital. I had to settle for watching the vehicle make its getaway.

"That wasn't a drunk looking for a lift at all," I said to the emptiness.

I returned home, constantly glancing about me and rubbing my arms. I had tied my t-shirt to a tree so I could find the spot in the morning.

The front door was open when I got back. The dreams that had dominated my psyche populated my imagination with all sorts of monsters. I went inside and put my face in every corner of the house before my heart began to slow down.

After I was sure I was alone, I sat on the couch in the dark. I used my ancient flip phone like a stress ball, flicking it open and shutting it repeatedly, compulsively. I couldn't force myself to call the station. The chief had made it clear my relationship with the force was to be of a "don't call us; we'll call you" sort of situation.

Tonight was making it not easier for me. Since I had trespassed without probable cause and had only jumpy hands as proof I'd been shot at, I decided to keep it to myself. For now.

Sleep was slow in coming, and my dreams unsettled me. Some I remembered in the morning, and a few revolved around my mother, standing in the kitchen amidst steamy dishes, her face smiling down at me through a haze of three decades.

Mostly, though, I dreamed of the Boogie House. One in particular, which dealt with the guy who owned the land across the way, sent me reaching for my .45, squinting into the doorway of my bedroom. I ended up pointing it at nothing but the vague apparitions spilling out of my head. Though I didn't have an indication that Leland Brickmeyer had anything to do with me getting shot at, I awoke in the dark with his face hovering over me, and I very nearly fired my pistol at it.

Second Chapter

The next morning I overcooked a pot of cheese grits and ate joylessly in the doorway, nursing a pretty vicious hangover as I stared at the woods. Made me feel like I was bickering with an upset neighbor. I guess I sort of was, only Brickmeyer didn't know what the quarrel was just yet.

In my head, as I thought about last night, I tiptoed around the word *ghost* (and also the word *crazy*). I wasn't some half-baked lunatic, but I also couldn't help but acknowledge what I had seen. I had been drunk but not high. I hadn't hallucinated the whole thing, but...shit, I didn't know. The whole thing reminded me of a piece of Gonzo journalism.

What I thought was out there made me more jittery than my two cups of coffee. And the weather wasn't helping. It was pouring down outside, like it does late in the spring, and the rain was busily erasing the truck's tire tracks from last night.

It almost hurt to believe it was the truth. Sometimes things happen to drunks, and they have to accept that reality, even if it doesn't quite measure up with what a sane, sober man might see. A drunk man's truth is still his truth, even if it isn't *the* truth.

Everybody needs something to convince him to get out of the bed in the morning.

I finished the grits and placed the bowl in the sink with the other grimy dishes before dressing for a muddy trek. I rescued a shirt from the bottom of the dirty pile and also a pair of jeans - tucking the .45 discreetly into them of course - and then I donned a jacket and slogged through the muck and the rain for the Boogie House.

The smell in there bent me over like a swift kick to the guts. I ran outside to be sick. Something had happened overnight. Being drunk makes you immune to some smells, but this was beyond even that. It wasn't hot outside, but the humidity had excited the decomposition of *something*. A four year degree wasn't necessary to identify the smell of something dead and rotting.

Once all my breakfast was on my shoes, I returned to the front entrance, weapon drawn for good measure, and scanned the inside of the juke joint. Nobody hiding here today. Couldn't take the smell, I'm sure. Not now. Not today.

It was then I found the reason the giant who tried to kill me had been here in the first place.

He - at least I thought it a he - lay sprawled in the corner, against the base of what used to be a serving bar. One arm stretched out above the body, giving the illusion of pointing, both legs screwed in awkward, rag-doll positions. *Dead* no longer accurately described his condition. He had gone to the far end of dead and then some. Georgia can be brutal on a body if the weather's hot and wet enough.

Medical examiner was going to have a field day. He'd probably had no experience with anything worse than a hunting or car accident in years.

"'Lo?" I said. No answer. Some birds fluttered in the rafters and flew away.

"Hello?" I repeated. Nothing. Outside, the rain played an improvised, striding rhythm on the partially caved-in roof.

I stepped inside, covering my mouth and nose with the front of my shirt, and approached the body. The stench seeped through the fibers of my tee. In eyeing the body, I tripped and nearly went waist-deep in the floor. Again.

One of the floorboards was loose. It wasn't like the others, which had rotted, so I had to be careful to get around it. No telling what kind of diseases and conditions were gestating on the ends of the old, rusted nails.

The victim was African-American. Young guy, maybe twenty or twenty-five, though I couldn't be entirely certain. Somebody'd given him the white sheet treatment, if I had to guess.

"Goddamn," I said. "That's a goddamn shame."

I leaned in, examining the face. Poor bastard had been knocked around pretty good, so that identification would be difficult. The two halves of his face looked mismatched. Could've been two different heads, so far as I knew.

A piercing sound made me jump, and I thought my skin would crawl off the muscle. I turned to find an old piano in the corner, swollen and rotted and incapable of producing sound of that caliber. But it had. Someone or something had played a chord of immense and simple beauty.

The tone suspended in the air for a few moments and then faded. A brief image of last night came back to me, but I shrugged it off. *Maybe a rat or something*, I told myself.

Haha. The lies we tell ourselves for the sake of self-preservation.

I returned my attention to the young man. He had suffered unimaginable torment. Not only that, but he had to endure the indignity of decomposing in an abandoned gin club. It was a fate befitting a child molester, or an abusive husband, not...whoever this turned out to be.

The Chief was going to have a fit when he found out I had turned up this body.

"No one deserves this," I said into my shirt, looking at the face, whose eyes stared at nothing. There was almost something knowing in them, a kind of death wisdom. And the lifeless orbs were staring directly at me. A fly lit upon one of the lids and then skittered across the open eye.

I shuddered. I felt myself being pulled into something against my will, but that could have just been the supernatural effect of the Boogie House.

The rain refused to slacken, but I poked around nonetheless, humming the melody to an old Elmore James song to keep the willies at bay. The old, rotten place carried a tune of its own, and that tune was harrowing, but there were no more shenanigans with the piano, so I was able to fail at being a detective in quiet solitude.

I was looking for a tree with a bullet lodged in it. Or bullet shards. All I got out of the deal was wet. There also were no footsteps in the corner where the stranger had shot at me, so it turned out to be a real bust for me.

Only, I guess it really wasn't. Coming out here had reinforced my belief that the Boogie House was haunted, though I didn't actually see any ghosts this time. A slightly supernatural piano chord would have to do for now.

At a certain point, I thought I heard slide guitar, but it was never definite enough for me to feel put off by it, not like what happened with the piano. This was something else. Could have just been me thinking about Elmore James again. Guy could play a slide guitar that made you not even want to pick up the damn instrument when you heard it.

By the time I was done puttering about, trying to do something miraculous with my less-than-stellar detective skills, the rain had soaked through my clothes. I walked back to the house and reluctantly called the police station.

I was told not to step foot in the station until the mess I had created blew over, and even though my first instinct is to ignore direct commands, my legs were still too shaky for me to even drive into town and face down my boss. (He might have described me as his former boss, but we have differences of opinion we're always trying to work out.)

"Lumber Junction Police Department," said a smoky, heavily-accented voice.

"Hey, uh, Dara. D.L. around?"

Dara Gibbons, not normally short for words, popped her gum. She wanted to dispose of me without me knowing. She started up chewing again. Too late.

"Mayor's in there with him," she said in explanation. "Can't have any phone calls. Take a message?"

"Mmm hmm," I replied. "Important stuff, or are they swapping bullshit back there?" I tried to make it known that it was most definitely the latter. It was *always* the latter.

"*Language*," she said. "He said not to let *anybody* through. That includes you. *Especially* you, and *especially* right now."

I rolled my eyes. "So does that mean D.L's not back there with the mayor, or he's making you lie because he didn't want to do his job?"

"And talking with you is his new job description?"

"Got nothing to do with me, D. I promise I won't give him a coronary. Just a minute. Sixty seconds. After that, you can transfer me back and pop gum in my ear until I hang up."

Her sigh could have curdled milk. I waited, holding my breath, until at last she said, "Oh, all right. Hold on a sec." There was a momentary pause, then, "You know, if you get him riled up, I'm gonna say you were posing as his golf swing coach or a *Guns & Ammo* editor or something."

"The only thing could help his golf swing is a gun." I thought of last night and cringed. Something sharp plunged through my guts. "It sounded funny in my head, right before I said it."

"I'm sure most things do, Rolson." I thought I sensed her smiling on the other end, but it could have been wishful thinking.

13

The line clicked over a moment later. Before D.L. could muster the breath to scream at me, I cleared my throat and said, "D.L., listen to me. I got something to tell you that has nothing to do with my case or how full of shit I am."

D.L. grunted, a hard, weary sound. "What is it? I actually *am* in a hurry, for once. Got lunch with the wife in ten minutes, and they dock her pay if she ain't back on time."

"Chief of Police should have influence over that stuff."

"You'd think that, but flower shops aren't intimidated by strong-arm tactics." I measured his voice. So far it was dry, non-committal. D.L.'s knack was for conversational banter of a certain kind.

I ignored the lie about the mayor meeting and dove right into an explanation. I said, "You know that shack that used to be a juke joint, over on the land the Brickmeyers bought some-odd years ago?"

"Not too far from your place? I s'pose I do. Brown Jug? Something like that?"

"The Boogie House. Brown Jug's the bar from that old Skynyrd song."

"Right, right. I get it. The *Boogie House*." He spoke quietly, in a measured tone. There was a question in his voice, but I wasn't about to answer it, not the way he wanted.

I said it bluntly.

"There's a body in it."

It was D.L.'s turn to sigh. I imagined his impossibly bushy eyebrows sliding up his forehead. "You drunk again, Rolson? Or did you run over somebody in the woods this time?"

I kept my voice level. "Nope. Sober as a judge."

"Round here, that's not saying much." It was a joke, but he said it distractedly, like he was also looking for a lost note on his desk.

He sucked his teeth and made that familiar *Mmmn-mmm-mmm-mmn-mmn* sound parents use when they are so incredulous that words fail them. "Jesus Christ. A body in the Boogie House. Sounds like an old blues number, doesn't it?"

He snorted, as if something horrible occurred to him. He paused again. "For a minute, I thought you were calling to tell me something had happened to Vanessa."

"D.L."

"Sorry. Wait until you have a child that breaks your heart like Vanessa did ours. And, as a wife, broke yours."

"Ex-wife," I said. Quickly changing the subject, I added, "Listen, D.L. In all the drama surrounding my...meltdown-"

"Let's be clear, Rolson: I did what I had to with you. These fucking - 'scuse my language - but certain people in town, well, they smelled blood in the water. They would have sent me out of town on a rail if they thought I'd shown you any preferential treatment. Far as reasons for calling, I figured it had something to do with Vanessa."

"I haven't seen her in forever."

"Don't suspect so. I keep waiting for the call, for them to tell me they found her face-down in a dumpster. Too bad you can't force sobriety on people." I could tell he resented the last sentence. "Anyway, Rol, I'll get a cruiser and ambulance out there. You sure it's a dead person? Not a squatter sleeping off a mean drunk?"

I readjusted the phone to the other ear. Shit, now that he mentioned it, I wasn't sure of much. "Pretty certain."

"I'll go ahead and call the medical examiner as well, then."

I waited, grasping for something to say. D.L. must have sensed it, because cut in with, "Take care of yourself. You ever need anything, you give me a call. Hear?"

* * *

Neither the cruiser nor the ambulance seemed to be in much of a hurry. Both vehicles crept along the road until the drivers saw me. The

15

faces of officers Bullen and Harper turned to scowls as I directed them into the woods. Spooner, the ambulance driver, didn't react one way or the other.

The path was just wide enough for vehicles, and I followed them to the Boogie House on foot and then went wordlessly inside after them. Above us, the clouds had given a respite from the rain, and in the humidity and rising temperature, the odor was particularly vicious.

Ronald Bullen stepped through the front door, spat. "Great fucking day to be out here," he said. "So goddamn great, the boss even refused to show up. Don't you think so, Harper?"

Harper, eyes averted, shook his head. "D.L. wanted to...keep his distance from, well."

He didn't say it, but Harper's eyes flicked in my direction, and I knew what he meant.

Unlike Bullen, a bearded, redneck John Goodman, Harper was slight, like a scarecrow with the stuffing all yanked out. And while Bullen should have been holed up in a biker bar with his fellow outlaws, Harper, on the other hand, could have just as easily been the store manager at a cheap department store.

"Body's been here for awhile," I said to the back of Bullen's head, ignoring the way he was sneering at the whole scene. "Laid up back in that corner. Think he might've been tortured something awful. There's trauma to the neck, but I couldn't make out much more."

"Hell, that sounds good. If you wasn't out of a job, I'd recommend you for promotion, Dee Wee." He was pleased with himself for the DUI reference, even if nobody talked that way anymore. His laugh could strip the bark off a tree, and he used it exclusively to get mean with people. I'd never seen the man smile when there wasn't something vicious behind it.

I backed off, raised my hands in mock surrender. I promised D.L. I'd play it cool, and D.L. was a man I wanted to keep in good with. I said, "You're right; it's your scene. Being the guy who discovered the

16

body, I thought it would be nice to help. Give a report like a normal citizen."

Bullen almost tripped over one of the loose floorboards but caught himself. Under the weight of the man, the juke almost seemed to bow inward on him.

"So this is the Boogie House, eh," Bullen said, ignoring me and stepping farther inside. "Somebody could have saved us the trouble of coming out here if they had just bulldozed this place years ago."

He sucked his teeth and grunted.

It was not in my nature to be conciliatory, but I was already treading on wet paper, so I needed to try another tack to keep from slipping. I said, "When I was real little, before I knew music, my mother told me Blind Willie McTell played *Statesboro Blues* in here, before this place had electricity. Just him and a couple people and an acoustic guitar, them all huddled around a bottle of whiskey and scattered candles. For this place, that's history, man."

The whole floor seemed to groan under Bullen as he crossed over to the body, and I could practically hear his brain working as he fished for a comeback. To himself, he said, "I reckon your mother, she'd know, wouldn't she?"

He turned and winked, not snickering really, but pretending to laugh nonetheless. His bloodshot blue eyes gleamed. The temptation to kick him in a hole in the floor was hard to ignore. Just kick him in and cover him up, let him rot under this place. I had to clench my jaw to keep from acting on the impulse.

Harper laughed thinly. His eyes darted between us, wide and scared but not happy, as his laugh might have implied.

"Men like you give the blues meaning," I said. Bullen raised an eyebrow but pretended to be looking at the piano, inspecting it.

"Fuck 'em" was all he said by way of reply.

It was a stupid, petty thing, saying that, and it certainly didn't hurt Ronald Bullen. The corner of his mouth twitched upward, the ghost of a smile. In that man was the representation of the south, mean and defensive and sweaty. Still, whatever racism and misogyny soaked him through, he was good at his job. Thankfully. Every man's got to have a redeeming attribute.

Bullen clopped the rest of the way through the building to the other side. He and I weren't on good terms - not that anybody ever got beyond 'asshole' distinction in his book - but we weren't really enemies. He just didn't like for me to talk or move or be in his line of sight.

Harper must have felt the heat coming off the both of us, because he was actively looking for something to say to bring the temperature of the room down.

"This ain't nothin' to get heated over, y'all," Harper stammered, looking nervously in the direction of the ambulance, behind which Spooner McCovey was futzing around with some brand of medical equipment. "Jeez, where the heck's Spooner with the body bag?"

Bullen hawked and spat again, laughing. "No matter. Sum-bitch'll need a ladle to get all of him up off the floor."

Third Chapter

People have learned not to bring up my mother within earshot of me. When I was in school, the first boy to make the mistake of calling her a 'nigger lover' had to get his nose reset and four teeth replaced. Since I lived most all my life in the Junction, I never really had to explain my displeasure about being teased on that subject to anyone else.

Occasionally the talk surfaces in conversation, I'm sure. Some think I blocked out what happened back in nineteen eighty-two, and so they give me furtive glances when they think I can't see them, but I know. The way I've lived my life has given plenty of people reason to run me down, but none as interesting as why I ended up getting raised by my great aunt Birdie.

What the town sewing circles don't understand is that my mother's death is not a secret to be kept, and the rumor mill is the rumor mill, so it can't be changed. I was a witness to some of what happened that night, so I have no reason to wonder why blue-haired church ladies sometimes treat me like wet plaster.

My mother lived - and, without protest on her end, died - under the weight of my father's thumb. He didn't kill her, but she would have, no doubt, lived a fuller and healthier life without him. It was a quick rise and slow descent, but out of their intense but flawed love came a son, so I guess it wasn't totally wasted time.

My father built relationships without foundations, so it shouldn't have been a surprise to him that they never lasted. He treated anyone he had a passing connection with as if he that person owed him something, as if giving a piece of himself were some sort of contract.

Eventually, it broke down. Sooner or later it was bound to happen. The old man didn't realize the arms he thought he'd been using to control others were instead wrapped around his own neck and slowly strangling him. And though he was a high school dropout, he wasn't a stupid man. He understood immediately why he hadn't been told about the pregnancy, why my mother had worn loose clothes to hide it from him, why she broke down crying when he confronted her about it.

My mother had finally called his bluff, and his response was to watch everything burn down around him, while he sat drunkenly in his recliner. He must have realized some dark truth about the pregnancy, though he never really said much of anything out loud about it.

I don't remember him actually hitting her, but my memories of the time - what little I remember - are punctuated by loud sounds and broken furniture. She didn't wear sunglasses and never wore makeup (never had to), so if he ever struck her, it wasn't in the face.

I was too little and too frightened by the old man to do anything about it except cry. I suppose I cried a lot, but that, too, could be me laying my own current feelings about the situation onto the past. It mostly feels like I'm watching the whole thing happen from a distance, like it's my own personal Christmas Carol, and I'm forced to think about what impact those nine months have had on the trajectory of my life.

When the baby came due, the doctor made a house call, trundling through the house with my father perched on his ear, demanding him to explain what had taken so fucking long, and, Jesus, aren't we paying you for a service and on and on and on. The good doctor, unaware of my father's interpersonal practices, offered a million apologies before readying the bedroom for delivery.

I wasn't allowed inside.

It was like an exorcism. I knelt on the floor at the end of the hallway and listened, pivoting over to the wall anytime I thought somebody might walk out and catch me.

There were loud sounds the whole time, but they changed, became something else entirely. Even at that age, I could tell they weren't what proud parents should be uttering.

Then there were screams of rage and then panic and then despair. I nodded off at one point and found myself, upon awakening, staring right at my dad, who stood in the doorway to their bedroom.

I couldn't read the number of emotions on my father's face as he pleaded with me to get the fuck into my room, *before something awful happens to you too, Rolson.* I was sent to my room when the complications became apparent to the adults.

It wasn't raw anger. He suddenly had the look of a man whose entire life has been one long series of Twilight Zone episodes. I tried to peer between my father and the door frame, but all I could see was my mother's body, still damp with sweat.

She was very still.

I couldn't hear my mother or the baby, and I couldn't be certain if they were both dead by then or not. To this day, the hours that followed are a strung-together mess of images.

It's like a collage. Part of me thinks I have included movie images and old, distorted dreams into my memories, but even then I can't quite put all of that night into a single narrative. I can piece together some things, but mostly I just remember sitting on my bed, picking at the shoelaces on my Keds. I would lie down and try to look up at the ceiling, but something about it just didn't feel right, so I sat up again. That felt like it was helping, somehow. It must have been the beginning of my weird sense of superstition.

It could have been a few hours I sat on that bed, or it could have been a few days. Either way, I didn't move, and it got so bad that I peed my pants instead of going out there. The thing my father became shortly thereafter was not unlike a monster, and I think the full transformation happened that night. I distinctly remember him banging drunk around the house, screaming, "You can hide from the devil, but you can't hide from God." Just like that. Over and over.

For the life of me, I can't remember if he came to check on me at all. Whiskey was his dark companion from then on, until that other thing happened.

Maybe the old biddies of the town are right. Maybe I have blocked some things out.

* * *

Watching what it took to get that young man's remains out of the Boogie House pried something loose in me I may never get back, something I did not realize I even had in me anymore.

Spooner proved ineffective at resuscitating the body, so Billy Margolee, the coroner, had to be called out, causing a series of setbacks. Margolee, a drunken, irascible sack of a man, complained nonstop. Not just about the stink, but about the bugs and the heat and the moisture and anything else that kept him from his daily pint of Old Bushmill's.

I stood around, mostly, and nobody seemed to mind. I kept one eye on the officials and another on the body, wondering if a chorus line of corpses would break out in an impromptu version of the Charleston for me. Nothing happened, though, and once the befuddled locals dispersed, so did I.

Back home, I drew a large glass of water from the tap, no ice, and drank down half before pouring it out and replacing it with something a little more amber-colored. Topping off the Beam with a shot of Coke and supplementing it with a High Life, I propped open the front door with a mud-caked boot and watched the uneven downpour of rain from my recliner.

Time passed. I finished the bourbon and three Millers under the impression that I'd get drunk. All that happened was the hangover returned. I slept until the rain stopped at dusk, at which time my cell phone rang. It was my lawyer, Jarrell Clements.

I flipped open the phone and said, "Run out of my money so soon? You know I'm on a cop's salary."

His voice was purely old school country. "Not anymore, you're not."

"Ouch."

"Ah, hell," he said, "ain't a damn thing, son. Even Thomas Jefferson died in debt."

"As long as *you* realize how broke I am."

He chuckled. His voice was low and refined but contained a slight drawl, like a verbal birthmark. "I came in fully understanding that. Can't make a silk purse out of a sow's ear."

"That's an old saying."

"I'm old school. Gimme a minute and I'll tell you firsthand about the War of Northern Aggression."

I rolled my eyes. "You got something?"

On his side of the line, I heard shuffling papers. "Sorry. My old ass is getting disorganized. The wires aren't firing as smoothly as they used to. I'm trying to get all my business settled for the day."

"That's all right. You're working hard."

The shuffling ceased. "Janita Laveau's made a turnaround in her opinion of you."

Now that was something. "What's that mean?"

"Means she's made it clear she does not want you prosecuted for ramming her with your car. Damndest thing I've ever heard of. You must have knocked something loose in her brain."

23

Even though I felt an extreme amount of guilt over the accident, I wasn't ready to bow out for a stint in lock-up. "Anybody listen to her?"

"Course not. Nobody's rooting for you in this situation."

"Nothing to root for, Jare. I got drunk, T-Boned a poor woman's Chrysler."

"Can't do anything about the DUI, but you already know that. That's a done deal. You were drunk, admitted to a breathalyzer. It would take a whole lot more than what you've got to be able to get that dropped down to reckless driving or some other nonsense. But if she clangs around enough, she might convince the DA to reduce or throw out the other charges."

"What are you going to do?"

"Me?" He made an incredulous *pfft* sound. "I'm gonna let her do it. You don't go-"

"Looking a gift horse in the mouth. That's also an old one."

"I'm an old man. A day older'n dirt and twice as gritty. You've got to have a little faith in the old man, though. I'm all that's keeping you from living the next six months in a box."

"You've got no bedside manner, do you?"

"Ask the people I lost cases for. They'd agree. Hell, ask my exes. They'd say the same thing. Have a good evening. I'll keep you posted on Laveau, see if she's using some kind of reverse voodoo on you."

"That's not funny," I said.

Jarrell was about to say something, but I cut him off. I hung up the phone and watched the rain sweep in large sheets across my lawn.

* * *

I proceeded uneasily inside. The Boogie House was dark, but it seemed to be made of bones or matchsticks or something. This was not the juke joint of reality, but a strange, otherworldly manifestation of it.

24

There was no moonlight to guide me, and clouds had blocked out the moon. I walked on, stumbling forward into the gaping holes of the building's floor in a strange, determined zombie-march. Each time I fell down, I almost lost consciousness, my eyelids trying to shut so I could rest. I persevered.

"He's not here," I repeated, unsuccessfully trying to convince myself that the dead body was gone. I don't know if you can break out in gooseflesh in dreams, but my entire body went cold. My stomach was engorged with ice water.

The ragged old piano situated behind him, the dead man stood at the room's center. Smiling broadly, one grizzled hand reaching behind his leg and tinkling random piano keys. Reality broke, and I was left hanging onto the jagged shards of what I hoped was a dream.

I lurched toward him, fighting to keep my eyes open. Getting closer, I saw that he wasn't smiling at all. His teeth and gums shone through ragged flaps of skin. His mouth had eroded almost entirely. It was a fleshless grin. His tuxedo, complete with tails, shoddily concealed the smeared blood and bile and mucus. There were other things on him, too, things that crawled and sputtered around at night on dusty wings, but I tried not to think about them.

I would say his eyes were fixed on me, but some predator had plucked them from the sockets, so all I saw was cavernous darkness. The body, even in dreams, was not immune to decay.

We stood across from one another, long-lost strangers. I wanted to scream - my skin wanted to crawl off to some other place when I saw him - but it was an empty, silly gesture. All I did was open my mouth and make a horrible choking sound. An astronaut lost in space.

"*Don't be frightened*," he said. He opened his mouth in what appeared to be a sigh, but no breath escaped him. "*I'm not here to hurt* you."

I stammered, searching for a reply. I looked down. The suit coat bulged below the final button, and I gawked at his paunch as I reached for something to say, but he didn't seem interested in the questions

25

circling my mind, which is where I felt his presence strongest. He was peering into my brain, checking my thoughts for...for something, but I couldn't quite know what at this moment.

He answered one of my questions before I could ask it. "*That's gas in my belly*," the body said. "*The gas will continue to accumulate until I'm embalmed. Don't you know anything 'bout the dead?*"

That was easy. "I know they don't tinkle piano keys or wear cheap tuxedos."

The lipless grin widened, and his shoulders shook in mock laughter. I say 'mock' because it was an impossible gesture. He couldn't laugh or sigh. How could he talk? Then he said, "*Maybe the dead that* you *knew didn't, but, then again, they don't have a monopoly on what we* all *do, now do they?*"

"I don't know," I said. "I never thought about it, I guess."

Simply being here opened up a whole new world for me. I had all sorts of new things to consider.

"*Seems like you should. I* am *here, after all.*"

"I'm not so sure about that. You're dead, and I'm dreaming. It's no more complicated than that, I don't think."

I tried to rationalize. This is not happening, not *happening* happening. This 'thing' is a hallucination in a dream, a dream you cannot control somehow. He's actually in a morgue, ready to be autopsied.

But I didn't believe any of that, no matter how fervently I tried to convince myself. I was utterly dumbstruck. The urge to ask the all-important question, not *how* but *why* he stood there, circled my mind, buzzard-like, but in the dream I didn't possess the faculties to pose the question. I could only gape stupidly at him and wonder.

Flies lit on his face, skirting in and out of grotesque wounds I honestly tried not to stare at. He seemed not to notice. He said, "*Don't forget about what you already know. Sometimes re-seining the pond will yield new fish.*"

I thought about men holding nets and walking the length of a drained pond. I thought about mud on the ends of sticks, and of a gross, dark net, and I had trouble keeping my stomach from rolling. It was then I looked down and saw I was wet all the way up to my waist, and I smelled the distinct odor of pond water.

There were more pressing matters for the moment, however. I said, "Are you telling me to go back to the Boogie House?"

I looked around. "I mean, I'm here, but – I'm dreaming, right? This isn't the *place* place, is it? The last two times I went there – or came here – all that came out of it were gunshots and dead bodies. I'm afraid of what I'd discover if I went back."

"*Fear isn't what motivates you, Rolson. The truth does. You're a seeker, and you are looking because you have something inside you that needs solving as much as my death does.*"

"If you want it solved, maybe you should. You're in the all-powerful business now, invading people's dreams and all." To put a finer point on it, I thought of something crude and mean, hoping he'd see it, but he gave no indication that he had peeked *that* far into my head.

"*It don't work like that,*" he said, and the resulting look, somehow, was saddening.

He breathed out, and I swear to God I smelled putrefaction, even though I knew it was a dream. My stomach lurched, and I leaned over to vomit. All that came out was dust and sand. It flowed out of me in a coarse, grimy jet. I closed my eyes to avoid looking, but my mind created the picture of it all, and in that picture, I saw more than just dead bodies and old memories. Flashes of situations, of things I had not yet seen but would, jumped in front of me in a continuous stream, pummeling my sense.

All of the answers I needed might have been present in those few seconds of torment, but I couldn't know. It seemed like I didn't exist on the right plane of existence for it, that - just maybe - I had to be in the same condition as the dead man to be able to understand it all, like a foreign language. I could catch clips but only clips, and I couldn't formulate them into a narrative of any kind. It was just data. Binary code. Ones and zeroes for those who had stepped beyond.

Did he somehow think I might be able to understand it, or was this just an unfortunate outcome of being privy to this world? Did all people who ended up on this side of the void have to experience the same kind of torture?

When I was done, I stood up and saw his face mere inches from my own, his eyeless sockets glaring into me. There was detail in the face, but it still looked like an oil painting in which the artist used thick, broad strokes. "Who did this to you?" I asked. I didn't expect an answer, and I didn't get one, but I couldn't walk away without asking it.

It just seemed like the easy way to go about solving this, getting the information directly from the source. I can be fucking silly like that, trying to use logic.

He reached two purplish hands out and placed me face-up in the hole at our feet as if I were a toy. A puppet. Ha.

Through eyes growing hazy and confused, I stared up at him, garbling nonsense words, trying to get at what I'd been trying to say all along: *What do you want me to do about this?*

Dirt poured from the cuffs of his jacket, filling the hole, covering me completely, caking my eyes and clogging my mouth with cemetery dirt, and all I could think to do was scream. I didn't care about goddamn answers or goddamn memories, but I couldn't focus on the one thing that I needed: goddamn air.

Try as I might, nothing came out but that choked, ineffectual *whuffling* sound. My hands wouldn't move. Only my eyes would work, and the last thing I saw was him placing a section of floorboard across the hole above me, leaving me in a warm, forbidding darkness.

* * *

28

I snapped awake, sensing the darkness crumpling in on me, crowding me like bullies in a schoolyard. Never did loneliness plague me more than the early evenings I awoke hungover on my couch, staring down the possibility of yet another sleepless night.

I sat up and breathed in a deep whiff of a bizarre smell, something I recognized but couldn't put in context. *The Boogie House. The dead body.* Could have been. It went away before I could put it together, but I was beyond feeling shock, so I just nodded and processed the possibility that I was breathing in the air from miles away.

Nights had never been easy, but I was growing accustomed to them. With Vanessa gone, I spent more of them awake than not, though the perpetual ache of her absence was growing fainter each day. The possibility of her return had diminished so that it only occasionally flickered in my mind, like the sudden realization of something you've already done.

In the first months of our "separation" (her words), the house possessed a lived-in quality, as if it, too, entertained the thought of her coming back. The feeling that Vanessa might walk through the front door persisted long after the reality that she wouldn't had set in. All of that had disappeared, too, leaving a simple and desperate isolation in its place.

I rolled over on the couch and checked the clock on my cell. 9:30 on the dot. Too early in the day for morose dreams. I had to get out of the house.

With the vision of the dead man horrifyingly fresh on my mind, I dressed soundlessly in the dark of my bedroom and drove my junker of a second vehicle into downtown Lumber Junction. The rain had called it quits, but everything you could touch, bump into, or walk on was wet.

* * *

Lumber Junction is a town bedecked in a blue collar, a town of truck drivers and iron workers, of men who work on cars and race cars and make meth in their cars. People who live in the Junction commute and yet never really leave. They never really think to leave. They just stay because that's how it is. In that way, it was a thousand other towns in the nation and also no other town in the nation. Distinctly generic, maybe.

The town could have gone in another direction and prospered so that its people did not struggle to make ends meet, but it did not, and the result is a picked-over hull of a place. It used to be that the timber coming through gave people jobs, and the Junction was, for a short time, a hub of activity. It was situated just far enough away from Dublin and Vidalia to be pleasant and yet close enough to enjoy the comforts of slightly larger towns.

In addition, the people have mellowed to the point that they seem somewhat zombified by life here, or at least lulled into a faux-drugged existence. Bootleggers and cattle thieves and outlaws used to occupy the city, but those types, holdovers from a specific era in American history, have gone away, leaving behind desperate, working-class folks. Since there is no income flooding in, the remaining businesses are closing. The Junction's downtown could exist in any number of desolate American cities, places where the world has gotten up and moved on. It is the starter wife that never quite managed to find a suitable follow-up partner.

The pickup I drove belonged to an old buddy of mine who said if I could get it running, I could have it. That was two years ago. I'd put some plugs and wires in it, replaced the battery, and rebuilt the transmission. Three hours here or there on weekends. I kept it in order to haul things off to the landfill or help people move. Insurance was cheap, though I imagined it was about to spike. The good side was I wouldn't be driving it - or anything else - much longer. The other car was totaled, so the pickup would have to do for now.

I parked the F150 in back at Virgil's and rounded the parking lot, looking for the truck I had seen last night. A moment of clarity saw the particulars of the taillights flashing in my mind, and I thought I might be able to recognize them. No luck. I went inside, where the mood was at least artificial enough to make me forget about how fucked up the last twenty-four hours had been.

Virgil's Bar was a small, reputationless place. There weren't many fights, no one sold meth out of the bathrooms, and women going home with someone generally did so for the company and not in exchange for money.

But there were exceptions to every rule.

The haze of smoke and long-soured beer hung as thick as humidity in the air, and the reddish glow of neon gave me an unpleasant feeling. Reminded me of the Boogie House somehow.

The people who didn't stare made a point of not staring. I knew what I was doing by showing up here. At a bar. If the Junction were bigger, there'd be more for struggling alcoholics to do. More distractions. More things to keep me out of trouble. People "in the program" say that excuses only get you so far into the recovery process. What those people don't realize is that an excuse only needs to get you to the bar, get that first beer open. Then the excuses go right out the fucking window.

My best friend was nowhere to be found. Deuce was usually propped up here in the evening for a couple of beers before heading home, but his usual spot at the bar was occupied by a woman whose face was turned down and displeased.

Deuce would be pissed to know he was the last one to find out about my troubles. He liked to gossip.

I ordered a High Life and a shot of Beam and was halfway done with my beer and wholly done with the excuse that had gotten me here when two old timers came down to say hey.

"This ain't official business, I take it," the bearded, cockeyed one said, drawing his lips back into a half-teasing smile.

"Unless I was secretly hired by Miller-Coors," I replied, taking a long tug on my High Life. "How are the two of you doing this evening?"

Lyle Kearns and Red Tyson. Two old pulpwooders claiming to be retired but really just too worn down to do the back-breaking work anymore. What made them best friends was they liked to drink up their social security checks every month.

"I shouldn't be able to complain, but I still do," Lyle said. Red nodded in agreement.

Lyle was burly but withering, broad-faced and sporting a white sea captain's beard. Red, on the other hand, had no distinguishing features, except that he looked like a baseball knocked way out of shape. He was big and blunt and dumb, and you could probably pick him up and beat someone to death with him and he wouldn't register it had happened.

But even though they were like two old Chevys left on blocks in the yard, they weren't useless. A little worse for wear, but not one foot in the grave.

"I hope it's nothing serious," I said.

"I just don't feel good," he replied quickly. "It ain't anything of the mortal sort, but goddamnit, I just don't have it all together. Makes me think I'm dragging some kinda sickness along with me."

"I get like that sometimes," I replied.

"Least it ain't cancer," Red said quietly from beside him. "You see Buddy Freemantle wither up like an old sack of collards?"

Lyle nodded this time. "It gets to be most of the way through the day, and I just start feeling feverish, run down. Can't get my mojo rising, you know? It ain't cancer, but it might as well be. That's what's in my head whenever I get a sickness I can't shake."

"I think that's the way it goes after a certain age," I said. "You just start to think about the thing that's going to knock you out of your shoes. No matter how you anticipate it, it's never the thing you imagine."

"Oh, it's gonna be cancer, probably throat or stomach. Got my old man. All the drinking and smoking-"

"And the womanizing."

"And I reckon that, too. All of it has got to be grinding me down."

"I see what you mean. But you've held it off this far."

"And there might be a tumor the size of a mango floating around somewhere in me. The fact that it hasn't put me in bed yet doesn't mean it won't soon. Doesn't mean it's not working its way through me now."

We sat in silence - I guess to push aside the dangling thread of mortality just above us - and then the more vocal of the two, Lyle, shook it away. "But I guess as long as I'm upright, I should count myself lucky. Which is more than they can say about that old boy they scooped up from that old juke in them pines, I reckon."

Red said, "The Lord's Grace keep us from something so bad."

I was surprised the story had gotten to them so quickly but no surprised that it had gotten to them at all. The two old-timers were fluent in gossip but weren't idle about it. Red had spent seven years in Telfair State Prison for beating his sister's abusive husband to ground beef with a piece of angle iron, just for hearing the rumor that it was happening. After that, he just sort of found himself in the middle of other local situations. Probably shouldn't have kept it up, but round here, the cops wouldn't let the letter of the law get in the way of their sense of justice.

Word was, Arnie Hester paid them five hundred bucks to kick the shit out of her brother-in-law, Carter, for drunkenly breaking his wife's jaw. Carter fled to North Carolina but unsuccessfully evaded Lyle and Red, who brought back a lopsided version of the man. A warrant was issued for them, but it was never carried out, which had only given them cause to continue their particular form of backwoods vigilantism.

I tried to sound casual, but my voice betrayed me. It seemed a little too eager in my mouth. "You heard anything out of the Leland Brickmeyer camp recently?"

In my dreams, I am a man without biases, prejudices. I am a man who can see the truth clearly. In reality, however, I'm just someone reaching for roots on the side of a mountain.

"Neighbor trouble?" Lyle remarked, elbowing Red in what he - no doubt - thought was a sly move. The two of them chuckled and twisted onto the seats next to me. "He's richer'n hell, but that ain't news."

Lyle was lopsided with drunkenness but showed no sign of slowing down. There was not one but two shot glasses resting on the bottom of his beer mug. He was fond of busting his beers up with whiskey, and the double he was drinking now would probably put most people at a tilt, if not on their asses.

He thought for a moment and then snapped his fingers, as if he had stumbled onto something. "He's thinkin' about *national* government work. Might try his hand at a senate run. They keep their private lives tighter than a duck's asshole, so you won't find shit or shinola on him."

I nodded, pretending to mull over the information. Anyone with half a heartbeat in this town knew that Leland Brickmeyer's ultimate ambition was to spend most of his year in Washington. He'd done all he could to tip over this town in his favor. Like any kind of narcissist, he was always on the lookout for a new group to court.

"I don't think it's the political run I'm looking for," I said.

"Then what are you aimin' at? You think we can just read your mind, old boy, or are you hidin' something from the likes of two broke-down old pokes like us?"

"No, no," I said, lifting a cigarette from the pack and slipping it into one corner of my mouth. "I'm not sure of what kind of wind is blowing around on the man."

"Same as it always is. Man's looking to get his name tattooed on a building, no different from anybody who's ever thought about the forever nap."

"You think he's involved in any shady business?"

With that, Lyle eyed his buddy, who jolted like a man snatched from a nap. "What? I don't know. Whatever you say, Lyle."

Lyle leaned in. "Guy doesn't get where he is without selling off a part of himself to the darkness."

"But who and what has hooks in him?"

He leaned back, contemplating the question, and Red went on staring blankly. "His daddy cast a long shadow, and I reckon he's spent most of his life trying to one-up the man."

"He's not his father," I replied. "But that doesn't mean he's palming cards or anything."

"You used to work for the police department-"

"There's still a chance I could be reinstated."

The old man smirked. "Anyway, so you used to work for the police department. You know he's got that place wrapped up like a sailor on shore leave."

"Meaning that - what - he gets favors from them for being a 'friend' to the LJPD?"

"Ask your father-in-law about it."

"Ex. He's not my in-law anymore."

35

"Still, ask him. Fucking money. Fucking power. Think on what he's able to get away with because he can get the station a new cruiser. Or whatever."

"Small-town politics usually don't run that deep, or that corrupt."

"Few years ago, there was a town got embarrassed because the sheriff was skimming money to pay the woman he was having an affair with. Nobody would've found out, except that she fucked up and got pulled over up in Atlanta. Driving to a concert, just as drunk as a goddamn fish. Couldn't say her name if somebody was working her like a doll."

"A ventriloquist."

"Whatever. Paperwork was out of order, in the man's name. Ended up all over the papers. Anyway, if the hard rain ever started to fall on Brickmeyer, I bet he'd have a hard time getting it to stop."

He paused for a moment and then kept talking. "And that's what he's worried about. He's had too many cloudless days. Thinks they should last forever. He'll do anything to keep the sun shining."

"So you're saying he might not have anything to do with what I'm asking about?"

The old man smiled cannily. "Well, don't really know what it is you're talking about yet." The way he was looking at me made me think otherwise, somehow. "But that' the long and the short of it. He's got too much riding on his life to let some piss ant like you fuck it up, especially if he thinks it's just for spite's sake. Is it?"

"I'm just asking questions, for now," I said. Something ineffable had stirred in me, but I couldn't quite put a name to it, not yet. It'd have to have some time to mix up and roll over before I could lay it out on a plate and call it just what it was.

"And them questions have to end up with answers, or don't they?"

"They do."

"Well, then, let's get down to the business of layin' out the pieces and seeing what's in the box. Then, maybe, you can start thinking about the questions. There might be something you're missing and don't know yet. Give it all here."

I gave them the leanest version of the story, leaving out the fat - namely, any and all hallucinations on my end. They listened and nodded, occasionally grinning at inopportune times, but they did not joke. It was apparent they were trying to find an angle, an in. There wasn't always a way for them to make a buck, but if there was, they wouldn't let it pass them by. Also, I suspected they had it out for Leland Brickmeyer, too. Men like them always do.

Once I was done, the break in conversation was filled by the last minute or so of *Bell-bottom Blues*, and I listened wistfully, drinking and watching the two pulpwooders think over what I had told them. Even though Vanessa had me listening to Clapton before I figured out who Son House was, there was something about the ghost of a memory associated with that song that I never could dislodge.

Still, the tone he got out of that black Stratocaster made fine background music for heavy boozing.

In the meantime, Lyle wrung his cracked hands, eyes squinting. "Goddamn," he said, turning. "Red, you got any figures on this?"

"None," Red replied. He rarely did have any figures on things. He basically had to be shot directly at a problem for him to realize how to fix it.

Lyle turned back to me. "You think the Brickmeyers are involved?"

"Man's got too much to lose to have dead bodies turning up on his land. But - and this is a big but - if he didn't do it, he might know why somebody else did."

Lyle twirled an unlit cigarette in his fingers. His laugh approached incredulity. "That shit ain't gonna get far in this town, 'less you catch him underneath the tree yanking on the rope, if you know what I mean."

"It's the rich man's burden," I said. "The world goes to hell, and it's the rich guys' houses we'll be storming with our pitchforks and torches."

"If that ain't the gospel, I don't know what is. We was so poor when I was a boy, we had cornbread with every meal, sometimes as the meal. Had two of my pet labs one winter."

"Shut up."

"Hand to God. It's not something I wish was true. Still can't have anything too gamey these days. If you'd have given me the idea to kick down the Brickmeyers' door back then, I'd have put them on a spit."

"Let's hope it don't come to that. I don't think me pointing a finger in the wind's gonna do much, but that won't stop me from driving up and talking to him."

Red and Lyle passed a lighter between them to get the cigarettes going. The smell was dankly pleasant, something about smoke and beer mingling in a bar. "And he'd have no reason to admit boo to you. Like I said, he's looking to take up running for a U.S. senate seat in oh-ten. He'd probably offer you the whole Brickmeyer estate in hush money before he let something like this come to light."

I finished off the beer and paid for two more for the pulpwooders. "Keep an ear out," I told them, and then I left. "Oh, and if you see any suspicious trucks around here, let me know."

Lyle said, "In my eyes, buddy, everybody's suspicious."

* * *

I put Screamin' Jay Hawkins on as I drove home, turning the volume as loud as I could stand. He was a dude I listened to whenever I was out at night, riding the lightless backroads in search of something I might never find. For him, becoming a blues guy meant giving up on the dream of becoming an opera singer, putting his classical piano training aside. A guy who idolized Paul Robeson ended up performing "I Put a Spell on You" on television with a bone through his nose.

Expectations and dreams don't always match up with reality. But he seemed happy. I wonder if he was ultimately satisfied with the path his life took, or if he was just game for following it along until it ended. Kind of like the Frost poem where the guy thinks his choices made any sort of difference in how his life turned out.

It wasn't my intention to turn my inquiries into a reflection of my disdain for the Brickmeyers, but I had to start somewhere. Man had something to hide, if you asked me, and nobody had, but that was no matter. He'd have answers, or he wouldn't, and then I could move on from there.

Headlights appeared in my rearview a couple miles down the road. I had rolled down the windows to let in the smell of wet grass and honeysuckle. Once I saw I was being followed, I tapped the gas to give myself a few car lengths' lead. If I couldn't avoid the situation, my .45 lay under the seat.

I turned up "Whistlin' Past the Graveyard" and straightened in my seat. This was threatening to become something, and I was anticipating nothing for the rest of the night.

The truck stormed up, so close I thought it might ram me, and I tightened my knuckles over the steering wheel so I wouldn't be tempted to do something drastic.

Sometimes I have problems with impulse control. Or so I'm told.

In that moment, I *hoped* for him - or them - to find a way to get me out of the truck. I damn near gave in. My foot twitched on the gas pedal, and I thought about letting go.

I became acutely aware of what would happen if I just popped out of the driver's side door, holding my pistol. I wouldn't fire on them, not unless they wanted to get real nasty, but it wasn't a stretch of the imagination that I might put a few in the dirt with a good, hard smack upside the head, with or without the butt of my .45.

It would seal some kind of door for me forever, but the fire bubbling beneath the surface told me to go ahead and do it. Going over the cliff may be a bad fucking idea, but the view on the way down can be beautiful.

It's not worth it, I kept telling myself. I was trying to recall whatever cobbled together twelve-step language people had recited to me whenever I was at my worst. Make a fearless moral inventory and give your powerless self over to a misunderstood God and all of that.

However.

Just as I was about to lay out a case for letting this go, the truck reared up and nudged my back bumper, just enough to make me fishtail. It didn't send me off the side of the road, but it pissed me off. That was it for me.

Sometimes I can't help but drop the whole jug of gasoline into the fire to see what happens. It's not an attractive quality, and it's something I wish I didn't take a perverse pride in, but maybe it's just the long genetics of my southernness coming out, something that wasn't bred out of my ancestors in the last two hundred or so years. It just tends to appear to fuck everything up, and I can't help but see what it does to me.

I waited for the perfect opportunity. When the high-beams reached into my cab and whited out the rearview, I clenched my teeth, feeling the temple muscles lock up, and then I let the brake pedal have it with both feet.

I stamped so hard I thought the pedal might punch a hole in the floorboard. My tires squealed on the wet asphalt like wounded dogs, and the rear end veered drastically to one side. I waited for the inevitable, crushing impact, my whole body clenched like a fist.

But nothing happened. Once my truck stopped, absolute silence was all that rushed up to meet me. The truck had somehow swerved and missed me, and it was now speeding off into the distance. It was the same truck, all right, and I caught sight of those hellishly red taillights disappearing yet again.

I know what I should have done. In my head, it was an entirely simple decision. Watch the taillights disappear. Just give the dude time to disappear and then call the cops. That's all you've got to do, son.

Sad thing was, I wasn't even in the mood for piling onto my misery. I just wanted to get the hell on with my life and forget about this shit, but there was something that wouldn't quite untether me from the situation. Bullish stupidity is my cross to bear, I suppose.

I'd suffered enough, or should have, even if I'd brought most of it onto myself. The temptation to be a fuck-up should have been easy to deny. *No, no, I've had my fill of that for a while, but thanks.* I'd peeked behind the curtain of my unquestionably grim future, so I should have been able to swear off risk, but I guess Hephaestus is a distant relative of mine. I've dutifully created the tools of my destruction.

Sitting there, truck idling, watching the taillights become smaller, I had a choice. One voice was sound and calm, telling me to let it go. Chasing dangerous rednecks down a curvy patch of highway would only result in trouble, I knew that. And yet, somehow, there was a second, equally convincing voice, speaking in whispers about the discarded body I had found.

Then a phrase came to me, one that was both beautiful and dangerous, one that had gotten me halfway to this point.

"Aww, fuck it," I said.

I stomped the gas pedal on my aging Ford. What the other guy probably didn't know was, I'd put a low enough gear in the transmission that, completely wound out, it could top off at a hundred and fifteen, easy. Most modern vehicles have a switch that cuts the engine off at a flat hundred, and you have to get a chip override to disable that feature. Most people don't go that far, and I hoped this guy was no different.

Once I got up to speed, trees and road reflectors passed in a near-psychedelic blur. With no guiding moon and me outrunning the headlights, it was tantamount to driving with my eyes closed. I focused on the electric red rectangles, hoping I hadn't forgotten about some hairpin curve ahead of me.

As a police officer, I'd been involved in innocuous chases with people who found jail much more terrifying than running - or going through a windshield - but drunks and other common criminals will often have a moment of clarity and pull over. This fool had no intention of slowing down. The car veered dangerously on the country roads. One bad yank on the wheel, and the truck would go rolling across the landscape like a skier missing a jump.

However, the diesel on that lead truck, a V8 GMC behemoth, could get up and go a sight better than I thought. In fact, the thing could flat-out *scoot*, but I managed to keep up. It topped a steep hill, and I accelerated through the next curve to make up ground.

Over another hill, a reflection caught my eye, and for a moment I thought I saw a deer's eyes. They weren't out this time of year, not like in the fall, but they could be found here and there, and so it still got a reaction out of me. Hitting an animal that size at this speed would be catastrophic. I'd seen men tossed through windows or impaled on horns.

I backed off, let the truck take a sizable lead. It dawned on me how crazy I was acting. I had the tag number memorized; all it would take was a single phone call.

When I passed the reflection, I saw it wasn't eyes at all but the text on the door of a Lumber Junction police cruiser, and I blew right past it.

The lights went on immediately, and he pulled out behind me. Apart from the fact that I was speeding, I had been drinking, as well. Good a lawyer as Jarrell was, there was no way he could get me out of this. Topping a hundred in the truck after a shot and a couple of beers meant at least - at least - a few months in lock-up.

You know: to think things over.

The tail of something sinister was winding around me, and I somehow knew that struggling against it would only secure misfortune more tightly to me.

But still, I knew I would struggle, hoping to find the way free.

I punched the gas and was quickly up over a hundred again. That cop had set up shop out here because it was a great place to catch speeders, but he didn't realize that I knew the very routes he didn't expect me to take.

If it had only taken me a second to memorize the truck's tag, then the officer behind me would only need moments to do the same. Rather than swerve, however, I tried to get as much distance between myself and his car as I could, as quickly as possible.

A little sharp edge was working its way through my brain - about the whole situation, really - but I had no time to contemplate it. Not until I was out of the situation and back to safety.

Getting taken in meant the end of my little investigation, which would go cold and shrink to a near-invisible size without my help.

Then a solution presented itself. If, that was, I didn't kill myself trying to make it happen.

I rounded a sharp corner, the weight of the truck threatening to spin it out, but I kept the tires on the asphalt and made a hard turn down a dirt road.

The backside tires slid, and though the front end managed to hold, I couldn't keep the goddamn thing from fishtailing. Both sides of the road were surrounded by trees, and I slid into one pretty good with my rear quarter panel. I sort of bounced off and righted the truck before I went headlong into the row of trees on the other side.

I killed the headlights and coasted to a stop as the cruiser sped past on the main highway, its own lights creating a symphony in the gaps between trees. I listened intently. If he saw me, I was a goner. No way I'd be able to get past him on this dirt road.

But he didn't. He went on by, and both the lights and the sirens disappeared down the highway. I hoped he hadn't gotten *my* tag number. I guess I would know the next time I went into town, because they'd be looking for a reason to bring me in.

I spent the drive home wondering about the chase. No way the cruiser hadn't seen the truck, too, so why flip on the lights just for me? In whose pocket was the PD? They couldn't necessarily know the junker I was driving, but what really mattered was that, on sight, the cop had ignored that truck. Something to look into later.

The questions plagued me well into the night, until consciousness melted away and my waking life could not be distinguished from my dreams. Several times I was arrested and taken away, charged with murder, and several times I awakened in a cold sweat. Shadowy figures slipped in and out of the bedroom. The floorboards creaked and I reached blindly for my .45. Bad habit to start.

At one point, I dreamed of a girl with an electrified hand, from which giant bolts of blue light emerged and burned her surroundings. She was a pretty stranger, but a stranger nonetheless. She was clad in a bright red get-up - red jacket, boots, and belt - and wore an eyepatch that appeared and disappeared in the dream, depending on what my mind was projecting.

It wasn't my ex-wife, but I had a feeling of kinship with the woman, of knowing her in some fundamental way, even if I had never seen her before. Strange.

It wasn't until a light rain began to rattle on the roof that I finally managed to get some real sleep. I dreamed about Kaiju-sized trucks trying to run me over.

Fourth Chapter

Most nights, I toss and turn and blink awake in the dark with the wispy remnants of absurd events playing out in my head, tormenting me until I've had my coffee. It leveled off a bit when I quit driving a rig several years ago, but I still don't think I've slept through a night without snapping awake since I was a little boy, and probably not even then.

I guess I've seen some fucked-up things, but most everybody has that one vision that keeps them up when they're feeling vulnerable. Or maybe not, and that's just another fucked-up thing about me.

Maybe I never got over my shit the way other people do, all of the adolescent anger and frustration of a middling trajectory. It's probably why I also still let my mouth get the best of me.

Still, sleeping was easier when Vanessa and I were together. Her presence seemed to ward off whatever malaise plagued me. Sometimes I called her my talisman, and though she stopped smiling at that joke, I was never able to stop using it.

Anyway, so I can't sleep well. People leave. I see weird shit sometimes. A great scholar once said "get busy living or get busy dying," and I'm under the impression that just means exist. Get up. Go do your thing. Don't let the snares keep you from moving forward.

Might just turn your clothes to tatters and your skin to shredded pork, but don't slow down.

That's when whatever's behind you catches up.

*　*　*

There were enough grounds in the can to make a single, big cup of coffee, and I drank it slowly during SportsCenter. The Braves looked good out of the gate, but how long the pitching would hold up was a mystery. We didn't have a Maddux or a Smoltz on this year's roster, but maybe we had a couple of half-Smoltzes, so I imagined we'd end up losing to somebody in the playoffs in the fall.

I called the police station, and pleaded to speak with D.L. again. Dara popped her gum in my ear but did what I'd asked. I gave him the plate number of the truck that had followed me, and he received it without too much prodding. "I hope you're not doing anything underhanded," he said, before hanging up.

I heard the beginnings of concern in his voice, and I couldn't tell where he was placing it.

D.L. had made police work a career, but he knew he was just as much a politician as anybody else, and if there's one thing politicians know, it's staying in politics.

But I also knew that he liked me enough to let me out on a long leash, so that would give me the cover I wanted for awhile, so long as I didn't embarrass the old man in public. That would be one step too far, and even being the martyr in a doomed relationship with his troubled daughter wouldn't spare me a boot in the ass then.

Still, it gave me enough leeway to continue on with this mad compulsion of mine.

Whenever I was done contemplating what I might be doing to D.L. by deceiving him, I read this week's paper. The article in the *Junction Examiner* spared the case's more grisly details, but not out of respect for the family or anything. It had been penned by a troglodyte on the staff, one zombie-walking from check to check on a sparse path toward retirement.

And why worry? It was only a local paper in a dying industry with a weekly circulation of hundreds.

Maybe hundreds.

The publisher, Wilson Talmadge. could find a backbone whenever the paper needed a pulse but was utterly willing to compromise on just about every other aspect of the business, in every other moment of his life.

But hell, the paper was still in business. That was at least something.

The byline for this piece of "journalism" wasn't attributed to Doris Allworth, the only person who seemed to possess any sense of integrity at the *Examiner*, which was perhaps why the article didn't even mention the name Brickmeyer.

It managed to mention calling me a fall-down drunk, but I imagined that took some amount of restraint to do that. "Former police officer Rolson McKane" said all it needed to say, however. I filed it all away for later and then went about my day.

A detective named Ed Hunter arrived at ten, and when I first saw him, my heart dropped into my bowels. He didn't seem to know anything about last night. I had never met him and found him about as likable as a toothache. He stood six-four and kept his arms perpetually intertwined across his chest. His blue eyes flickered with what I could only interpret as contempt, for what reason I wasn't able to say. I joked that I could share a half-sized cup of coffee with him but that I didn't have enough for two people, especially one as big as him. He seemed okay with that joke. We made small talk, about the Braves and weather, but after ten minutes I realized he wasn't leaving until he had something to work with.

"What were you doing out at that old shack, Mr. McKane?" he asked. He didn't have a pen or paper handy, but he didn't needed it. He had these knife blades for eyes, and he stared holes right into me. Truth be told, it made me uncomfortable to look at the man.

But I did. I'm too goddamn stubborn to quail from anybody.

I stared right back at him, steepling my fingers in my lap and cracking the knuckles. I wasn't going to tell the honest truth - the *truth* truth - but I also hesitated to lie outright. What was it Mark Twain once said, "Always tell the truth and you never have to remember anything?"

"I like to go for walks, Mr. Hunter," I said. "If you looked it up, you'd see I got a citation for driving under the influence a couple weeks back. Big mess. Hit somebody with my car and everything. So instead of driving, which is frowned on with me awaiting a court date, I like to walk. I ended up over on the Brickmeyer land because I was bored and tired of trekking up and down the same stretch of pavement."

"Rain for the last two days, making a damn fine mess of the earth round here, and you decide to go for a walk. Uh-huh," he said. He pretended to scratch his chin. "Mile-and-a-half into the woods, no less. What's it like to go through all that straw and mud? You do that for fun?"

"If the occasion calls for it. Listen," I said. "I have absolutely no problem answering questions. Shit, you want, you can prop your feet up and we can get cozy. But I will not have you patronizing me in my own house. I'm the guy who found the body, that's all. That is it."

His ragged smile was meant, I'm sure, to be conciliatory, but it gave off an entirely different vibe. He was enjoying this. "Didn't mean anything by it. Just getting a picture of the situation and the circumstances surrounding your 'discovery'. If I come off as abrasive, it's only because I thought you would understand. It's the routine, you know. Cop stuff."

48

At that, I did see his expression soften somewhat. Maybe he saw the truth somewhere in what I was saying. Maybe, but if not, he was good at putting on a show.

"Oh yeah," I said. "Well, I'm no longer with the force, so."

"I understand, I really do. Man's always got to find his way, and sometimes it takes him through the briars before it lands him on the highway, if it ever does."

"You been through the briars much in your life, detective?"

A twitch of the eye, slight upturn of the mouth. He'd winced. "I reckon you could say that. Youth can be a troubled time. I've outgrown most of what I presume you're still working through."

"I'll be working off whatever debt I've got for the rest of my life. Somebody up there likes keeping me chained to the grindstone."

"I see," he replied.

The coffee tasted like cold mud, but I drank it with a measured calm while I contemplated my next series of answers. Hunter played it even cooler. What freaked me out was, during the whole conversation, his eyes never left me, not once. You can get used to people staring at you, you have enough of them doing it, but for those long periods of time like that, it's just unsettling.

At the end of a bitter gulp of coffee, I said, "What has Leland contributed to the investigation? He must be perturbed at a body being discovered on his land."

Hunter sighed. "As could be expected, he has been courteous to us so far. Inviting, even. He's a politician, after all."

"That's good." I kept my tone even, like a criminal trying to outwit a lie detector test.

"But I can tell you from our preliminary information that he's not a suspect. Having a body found on your land doesn't necessarily make you guilty of anything but being able to afford that much property, a crime I wished I was guilty of sometimes."

"Ain't that the truth."

"Ain't it? Anyway, he's been answering questions, all that. He's a friend of law enforcement." I couldn't tell if he was serious. Sure, Brickmeyer paid lip service, threw a banquet every now and then, but didn't this dude realize it was for show?

"The same way Mother Teresa was a friend to poverty."

Hunter gave me a quizzical smile but didn't respond. "And, we got a fabric sample off the body. Didn't come from the decedent, so we're taking a look at it."

"That all the evidence you get?"

"The crime scene was compromised," he replied. "Small town law enforcement got a little too excited, I suppose. Trying to play the CSI guys on television. Plus, the rain..."

"Gonna be a wet spring," I said. "Tends to wash everything away. Has he given you any trouble? Said anything strange? Brickmeyer, I mean?"

He said, "It would be contradictory for him to do anything but walk the line, and he knows that. He's an astute public figure."

"You could say that again."

"Do you have a hard-on for this guy or something?"

I realized I might have been pushing a little hard. "Getting a sense of all the angles, is all."

"Well, he knows a slip-up right now might cost him down the line. If he plays ball and the right man gets apprehended, he'll come out smelling like a rose. And if he doesn't, if he decides to flex his muscle a little too much, if he tries to be impetuous--"

"Instead of a rose, he'll be a turd blossom."

"Exactly."

"May I ask why a more-than-local interest has been taken in this case? Doesn't seem like something the bigger fish would want to bite on."

Hunter wiped at his mouth with one hand like he had mayo or something on it. "There has been a concerted effort on the part of many state governments to, I don't know, right the wrongs of the past."

I was momentarily surprised. "Something like reparations?"

"Nothing like that. Wouldn't fly with a Republican voter base. No, what has happened is that task forces have been created to investigate hate crimes committed during the fifties and sixties."

"Wow."

"It's a workload, but real progress has been made. If an unsolved homicide involved race, then we're taking a look at it."

"What does that have to do with this situation?"

"Well, it's a sensitive time, what with the political climate and all. This case falls into that very same area. If it turns out that there was some racial motivation for the murder and we're able to solve it, then that will bring positive attention to the cause. It's a win-win, politically."

"You don't seem like the kind of man who would do something for its political implications."

"Depending on how high you get, there's always a game to be played. Politically, of course."

"And practically?"

"We're finding out that many crimes once thought to be racially motivated were actually committed by other people, family members and disgruntled lovers and such. Still, though that doesn't lessen the grief, at least it proves beyond a doubt, in some cases, that simple racism played no part in them."

"Comforting."

"Now see," Hunter said, perhaps taking offense for the first time, "it can't be looked at like that. A crime is not a crime is not a crime. One murder is not just like any other murder."

"Absolutely."

"That is why it's important that the actual cause be determined. Motivation may affect how we look at them from a historical standpoint. It's not a waste of money if it brings closure. The truth is important in these matters. Wouldn't you want the right person to be fingered if you had been killed?"

"That's something I agree with. If the truth really comes out."

Hunter shrugged. "That's always the variable. We can never be sure if the truth will ever come out, let alone when."

"Good luck," I said. "Hope you find the truth."

He stood and headed for the door. His eyes never left me, and the sight of them made me want to shudder. "Well, I reckon we'll see, won't we? Take care, Mr. McKane. I'll definitely be in touch."

"Oh, one last thing," he said, stopping at the door. I had stood and was going to close it behind him. "We got an I.D. on that body. Mother came by and identified him late last night. Name is Emmitt Laveau."

I tried not to let on that my blood had gone cold.

"His mother is Janita Laveau."

At this, the detective finally smiled; it looked like a man trying to get into a suit he doesn't wear very often. "You got it, sport. The son of the woman you hit with your car is on a slab right now. Keep that in mind next time you talk to me."

Without another word, he stalked purposefully to his unmarked car and drove away. I watched through the screen door and then closed myself off from the world for a little while.

Something raw and electric swelled in me, and I succumbed to the urge to douse the exposed wires by opening a beer, downing it in mere gulps right there in the kitchen. The damned thing barely made it from the fridge to the trash can before it was empty.

I burped and closed my eyes. The rush was immediate, both relaxing and panic-inducing. Drinking, after hearing that news, should have made me ashamed. It didn't. It just made me want a cigarette. Nothing better for shaky nerves and irresponsible fears.

Fear, it should be said, is an emotion devoid of rationality, and sometimes the groundswell, the sheer force of it, can wash away anything that's not bolted down. It's what drives people to drink, to use drugs, to walk out on marriages, hide out and wallow in pity. It's what caused me to open that second beer, and then a third, all before noon. Drinking wasn't going to help solve any problems, but it sure did a good job of turning down the volume for a while.

* * *

Later, I fetched my tennis shoes from the bedroom and laced them up tight for a walk across the road. I had begun to believe that erasing my name completely off the suspect list meant ensuring the real killer didn't just slip away. Detective Hunter might have been an asshole trying to scare me, but musical chairs is musical chairs. Last one left standing when the song ends is out. Worse miscarriages of justice have occurred, and it seemed to fit with my recent fall from, well, not grace, really, but fall from *something*.

Even though bruised clouds lurched across the sky, there was no rain and no wind. Walking into the pines felt like stomping in a graveyard. I tucked the .45 into my jeans as I crossed the boundary between mine and Brickmeyer's land, ducking behind a diseased long-leaf pine just before a vehicle went by. I had lost the capacity to trust passing cars.

I approached the Boogie House with some caution. Something strange fluttered in my guts whenever I saw the faded, darkening boards of that place.

Caution tape surrounded the building, strung through the trees like bright yellow spider web. I ducked under it and gave a good hard look inside. The smell of death lingered in the air. I held my breath and stared for a long time, waiting for I don't know what. A sign. Something.

The piano began to play itself an old, familiar tune. What keys remained on the thing bounced up and down to the rhythm, and the song went through a verse and a chorus before dying out. Slowly, you see, as if the pianist were on his last breath and playing the song out as he died.

"Goddamn greatest hits melody," I said, raising my voice. "What good is fucking with me going to do here? I'm on *your* side."

It was a ludicrous thing to say, but it worked.

The song stopped, and moments later a rat the size of a pro athlete's shoe scampered out of a hole in the piano and moved across the keys. I guess the rats, they all play Fats Domino these days.

In the daylight, there was nothing supernatural about the Boogie House. Just an old, forgotten building, full of secrets that wanted out in the open.

I looked at the rat and sighed. "I wonder if that kid's life was the price that had to be paid to uncover the story behind this place," I said. The rat turned and fled back into the piano without responding. I considered myself grateful for not receiving an answer.

A crow perched on a sagging beam cawed before flitting away. I hoped it was an augur of Laveau's ghost - I wanted to meet the fucking spirit or whatever when I was awake - but it was apparently only visible in my dreams. I'd have to wait for the sun to go down, I guessed.

I went over and looked at the corner where the big guy had popped up and shot at me. There wasn't a sign anybody had been here at all. Not a scrap of paper, or an old McDonald's wrapper. Nothing. Whoever had been out here had no intention of staying, and he probably wasn't a squatter.

Or maybe he was a squatter, and I was building a case out of the strands of my own sanity. It wasn't completely out of the equation.

If not, if he had been out here with a purpose, what was his connection to the dead body? He put him out here? Was he on his way to retrieve him? Had the juke joint - and I had to keep this point buried so that I would not be committed in Milledgeville - but had the juke joint *called out to me for help?*

It was a ridiculous thought, but not necessarily untrue. If that man had come out there to take the body off for burial - or whatever he had planned on doing with it - then it was the last chance for anybody to discover that the kid was dead at all, and I had happened upon the scene at the last possible minute.

Supernatural forces didn't bother me. Didn't scare me, either. I'd had unsettling experiences in my life. I was no stranger to the other side. I sometimes feel like my mother has been trying to reach me from wherever she is since I was a little boy. Sometimes I think it's what sent me to drinking, but sometimes it probably functions as my salvation, so I take it to mean whatever is most expedient in the moment.

Dissatisfied, I retraced my steps through the woods, staring down at my feet as I walked, trying to find the diesel's tracks. I stopped. Ahead of me was a patch of rutted, near-dried mud. Bingo. Not enough to get a tire profile, but enough for me to noodle around with.

Seeing the tracks filled me with measurable hope, but all I ended up finding was a blue key chain with big block lettering: BRICKMEYER AG & TIMBER. Holding it by the edges to avoid pressing fingerprints onto it, I looked for something out of the ordinary. But no, it was just a key chain. Could have been anybody's. Taking it would be tampering. Leaving it might mean it would be lost in a shoddy comb-through of the land.

I slipped it into my pocket and went back home, breathing in deep the smell of dying trees.

* * *

When I got back to the house, as I passed through the last row of pines, I saw an unfamiliar sedan parked askew in my driveway. I dropped to my knees, scanning my surroundings. With the sun high above me, everything took on a washed-out look. I crept forward into the ditch and kept watch until a tall black woman emerged from the vehicle and leaned against the driver's side door.

I arched up out of the hole and approached slowly. "'Lo, Mrs. Laveau," I called, as I crossed the road. I could barely speak, my heart was beating so fast.

"Hey, there, Rolson McKane," she said. "What you doing jumping in and out of ditches? Playing army? I could see you clean across the road."

"It's a long story," I managed. "Being careful these days, that's all."

"Least you're on foot."

I searched for something conciliatory to say. "It's terrible what happened. I know it doesn't mean much, but I'll do what I can."

Her eyes had focused not on me, but on the copse of trees just behind my right shoulder. Thinking of what she might be looking for gave me an uneasy feeling She said, "Come on, now. Invite me inside. This damn leg of mine is just about to drive me crazy."

* * *

The sound two cars make when they collide can keep you up nights. From the inside, it sounds like the world is ending, and there's nothing you can do to convince yourself it isn't. When you dream, you can hear the sound of metal on metal, of front bumpers crumbling under sheer force, of radiators spewing steamy fluid like severed jugulars in a blizzard, of tires screaming, drowning everything else out, and all you can think is, *I will never get in a car if I get out of this.*

I hit Janita Laveau going forty-one miles per hour in a thirty five zone. It wasn't quite a head-on collision and I didn't quite T-bone her, either. The impact could be heard for four blocks, and one man said, on the record, that it sounded like Hell being unleashed on Main Street.

From what I have been told, the accident bordered on miraculous. I ran a stop sign I'd used hundreds or maybe thousands of times. Just went right through it, slowing down only when a champagne blur passed in front of me. The impact put Janita's car on two wheels, but luckily it came back down instead of careening into the IGA across the street.

The tires held, according to witnesses, and, while momentum carried my Buick across the road and into the empty grocery store lot, Janita's Caddy lingered magically on the two wheels for a few seconds, balancing between disaster and safety, before deciding to come down on the side of safety.

I wouldn't know. I was blacked out entirely, couldn't have passed a sobriety test if mere consciousness were the only requirement. They say drunks survive wrecks because they're drunk. Sober people tense up and break bones. I guess that's true. I don't want to put the theory to a test again, but I escaped with a bloodied nose and some odd little cuts on my arms and face.

Oh, and one hell of a hangover. So sore the next morning I could barely move when Deuce came and got me. From jail. But I survived. Janita survived. I got arrested, but that seemed all right somehow.

Bits and pieces come back to me occasionally. I'll hear something, and my head will tilt at an angle, the way a guitarist's will if he thinks a string is out of tune. At best I'll get a few seconds of uninterrupted carnage, succeeded by a skip in the record of memory. It only happened a couple of weeks ago, and I think that, eventually, it will come back to me without interruption. The basic story, though, works just as well: I went out, got drunk, and then drove. End of story.

Janita Laveau sat for a good while on my dusty couch, hands pressed on her lap, lips clenched, staring at the empty bottles littering my coffee table like oversized chess pieces. I sat across from her, in the exact spot the detective had occupied earlier that morning. I scratched my head and waited, wondering what she would think of the detective's oblique insinuation that I was involved in her son's death.

She spent the first half-hour painting a portrait of her son in broad, genial strokes. I had seen Emmitt around town, once or twice when he was much younger, and several times more recently. Always alone. Always unsmiling. He had spent a few years elsewhere and had returned to work "a real job," as Janita put it. He'd been an artsy-type, like the hipster kids down at Savannah College of Art and Design. He never quite lived up to his potential. He went right to hanging drywall until he could get a teaching certificate.

"He seemed like a wonderful person," I said, when she was done.

"It's a custom for people to give glory to the dead," she said, wincing at her own words, "but in this case, everything I could say about my Emmitt is true. He was an angel of this world, wouldn't hurt another person even if it was deserved. He was a quiet, gentle boy. He grew into a quiet, gentle man. Nobody who knew him would want him hurt, not for any reason. He'd never gotten into so much as a fistfight in school."

"I hope they find out who did this," I said. Acknowledging that I had begun a surface investigation into the matter seemed unnecessary and potentially insulting in the moment.

She gave me a penetrating look and continued. "The image I still have of him is one where he's just learning how to play the guitar. Just ten or eleven years old, balancing that big acoustic on his knees. The way his legs dangled from the chair he sat in made him look like a ventriloquist's dummy. But he learned quick, and he loved to play, could sit down and strum for hours without looking up. If he hadn't been so interested in everything, he might have become a famous guitar player, something like that. I guess. I don't know. My mind feels so cloudy right now."

"I hate to ask this, Mrs. Laveau, but why didn't you go to the authorities yourself? In your own words, he'd been gone for some time."

She dabbed at her eyes with a handkerchief pulled from her purse. "My son was a rambling soul, never could get tied down too long. This was the longest he'd spent in the Junction. He'd been saving money, like always, so he could travel around, do something else for awhile."

"I see."

"He didn't come home for a few days, and I didn't worry at first, because I knew how he could be, so I just washed his clothes and put them in his room. Folded them up and smelled them, smelling him, and then put them away. You just don't ever know sometimes, Mr. McKane, the last time you're going to see someone you love. I had a brief flash of that myself recently, you understand."

I did. "I'm sorry," I said impotently. "For everything, especially what I could have controlled. Never thought being careless would hurt anybody but myself, ma'am. I was wrong, and I'll be reminded of that night for the rest of my life."

"Wasn't *my* time to go," she said, finally, confidently. "I got no other way to explain it. Wasn't my time to go, and it definitely wasn't your time to go to jail. I don't bear no grudge against you, because now it seems so petty. And I used to be one to do things I might advise against now. Hmm. Do you believe in fate, Rolson McKane?"

"I don't know that I do. I heard you've been lobbying for them to take it easy on me. I hope that's why you're out here this afternoon, to shed some light on a topic that's got me worried and confused. No offense."

Janita peered over my shoulder, focusing maybe on the yard through the blinds and maybe nothing at all. There was always the woods. They loomed over everything now, literally and metaphorically, and I was continuously thinking of them. I suspect that Janita Laveau thought of them now quite a bit herself.

I knew how frantic the mind becomes when somebody dies, how it scrambles through mental archives, pulling and storing the most important ones for later and immediately dumping those without any real meaning. There wasn't a memory of my mother's life that I hadn't compromised. Time and drink and just life in general had ravaged the old file system, made my mother into a representation of the real thing instead of the real thing itself.

"The way he died," she said, "that was no accident."

"No, it wasn't. His life was taken from him." Offering her solace was all I could do. Parroting her words back to her was more helpful to the situation than risking upsetting her.

But she saw through it. She hadn't come here for an easy conversation.

"That's not what I mean. Of *course* he had no control over that. What is obvious is that somebody had it out for him, and they took it out on him. What I'd like to find out - what I *must* find out - is what in the world somebody would want in doing that to him."

"I understand that," I said.

"It'd be different if it was some kind of accident, if he got sick or fell off a roof or tried to break up a robbery. Even if he took his own life, it would be *different* from the way it happened. Better or worse, I don't know. I keep thinking about that, would that change my opinion on how it ended up, would I be more at peace, but I can't. It's just one of those things that your mind works up to keep you from going slap damn crazy."

This time, I held her gaze firmly. "Won't change a thing, I can promise."

"But it *was* no accident. And it wasn't no coincidence that you found him, either. You realize what that would mean, if it was just a coincidence?" I shook my head, but she kept on talking. "It'd mean the universe was random, that nothing means anything, and I don't want to live in a world like that. I'm a believer in fate."

60

"Uh-huh," I said.

"What I'm getting at is, maybe you were pulled into my orbit for a reason, like a planet from some other place in the solar system. I don't *like* you much, but if you was meant to help me and you get carted off to jail, then you can't help me find my son's killer, now can you?"

"What if that was fate, too?" I asked.

She stared at me, reaching one hand up and smoothing down loose strands of hair. "I can't take my chances on that idea."

"I can't in good conscience take this on if you haven't contemplated all the possibilities."

"Not for nothing, Mr. McKane, but what do you think I've been *contemplating* since the accident, since my son disappeared and didn't come home? Do you think I am taking this lightly?"

"It's something I had to say."

She rolled her eyes. "You are one stubborn-ass man."

We sat in silence. I picked my cell phone off the table and fidgeted with it, flicking it open and closing it and twirling it absentmindedly. Nervous habit.

Finally, Janita said, "I hope you're not expecting I pay you."

I laughed, and it sounded more like a bark than human emotion. "I ain't exactly rolling in the dough, Mrs. Laveau," I said.

"Neither am I," Janita said patiently. "And I won't be any richer two days or two weeks or two months from now, when you call in the dogs."

"Call in the dogs. Huh."

"And you won't be any richer, either, Rolson McKane, because you are going to do this for free."

"Wait a second," I said. "You come here, asking me to help you-"

"Uh-unh. I am not *asking* you to help me. I am *telling* you, *requiring* you, to help me."

"Really?" I wasn't actually angry, but I wanted to see where this conversation was headed, and also to push a little bit to see if she would let anything out during this conversation that I could hang onto for a while.

"I need your help, no doubt about that. But I can't ask for it."

"And I get what in return for this?"

She leaned back. "You get your life back. Maybe. Maybe this fate thing is true, and you'll get some, I don't know, spiritual reward. And you should be hoping for that most of all. Piece of mind, or something close to it."

"I don't mean to squabble, Mrs. Laveau, but-"

"Something's broken in you, son, and I believe you know that. You're off-balance. Maybe not mentally, maybe not even that much. But there is something wrong with you, and this may fix it."

Her eyes returned to the window over my shoulder. She continued, "I don't have any faith in the rednecks they got up there at the police station. They don't care a bit for my boy, especially that grizzly bear-lookin' one."

"Bullen."

"Mmm-hmm. Some of them talk about you like they'd like to see you end up the same way."

"They resent me marrying Vanessa, Chief's daughter. Thought I was kissing ass somehow. We dated a long time before I thought I wanted to be a cop. But you know how rumors are: doesn't matter when or where they start."

She sighed. "I just don't trust them to do what's best for me, for my baby's memory. There's something to it."

"I can believe that," I said.

There was another long pause, and she said, "I've been having bad dreams, McKane. Unsettling dreams. How about you? How are you sleeping these days?"

"Fine," I squeaked.

"Coroner tells me my son's been dead for five days. Five days ago, I dreamed about white horses grazing in a field. I was always told dreaming about white horses means somebody close to you was going to die. I knew even in that dream who it was supposed to be for. And it wasn't a *dream* dream, the way most dreams are."

"What do you mean?" I asked.

"Walking through the field, I saw somebody standing off with the horses, petting them, keeping them company. When it came time for the person to turn around, show me her face, she did, but I woke up."

"Who was it?"

"Me, Rolson McKane. Me in the flesh. Well, maybe, future me. Wearing the very clothes I am going to be wearing to my son's funeral."

"Wow," I said. It was all I could manage. My mouth had gone dry, and the words got lodged in my throat. I coughed and said, "That's a vivid dream."

"It was and it wasn't. That's what I'm trying to tell you. Now, the clothes I was going to wear, I haven't put them on in years, haven't even really thought about them since buying them, but I know for a fact I am going to press them and wear them for the funeral."

"So your dream helped you decide what to wear?"

"I don't know. That's why dreams do matter. You understand? I'll never know whether I chose to wear those clothes, or if I was bound to wear them anyway, if the whole thing was out of my hands. All because of a dream."

I nodded. "I've been thinking about dreams lately myself."

She smiled knowingly. "Dreams are powerful things."

"But they aren't reality, Mrs. Laveau." I sounded like I was trying to convince myself.

The woman shook her head, disappointed in me. "Just because you're not awake doesn't mean it isn't real."

"I don't know, Janita. I've gotta think about this."

"What's there to think about?" She glanced at the empty liquor bottles. "What else is burning up your schedule? You need to look for a probation officer? There a highway needs garbage picked up?"

"I'm trying to clear everything out. I'm no longer a cop. This is my opportunity to have a clean break from the force."

"Well, you are just about there. After you help me, you can have that clean break. You can pack up and get the hell out of this town and never see me again. But for the time being, you need to be a cop again."

"Seems to me I wasn't ever meant to be a police officer in the first place."

"What you were meant to be isn't up to you. Haven't you listened to a word I've said?"

"Cops don't take up personal causes. I'd be a vigilante, an unlicensed PI. Working for free, no less."

She got to her feet and shrugged. "And some things are worth more than money," she said. "Think about it. But I think the choice has already been made for you."

Fifth Chapter

I spent the rest of the afternoon cleaning my filthy house, thinking about the ways I've failed at being a good man. I've always tried, but I think everybody tries, and I can't always see the line well enough to stay on it.

But cleaning helped me think. Beyond feeling embarrassed at Janita Laveau seeing my house, with bottles and cans propped like family heirlooms everywhere, I was melancholy in a way that sitting still was only going to make worse. I broomed down spiderwebs in the corners of rooms, and because I couldn't remember what my bedroom floor looked like, I did two loads of laundry.

But mostly I thought. Why did she need my help? Why did she *need* my help? *My* help? She was a strong woman, and who was I? I could barely take care of myself, and I was no one's savior. In fact, I had ruined more lives than I had enhanced, and my armor, it should be known, has never been shiny.

What it made me think was, chances were, I'd end up being the fool who dragged the whole thing over the side of the cliff as I went down. Somebody else would have to save me to then save everything else.

I even squirted some WD-40 on the window latches in the kitchen and the living room. Some windows had no screens and I usually don't let them up except for when the mosquito and gnat populations are down. If good and greased up, most of the windows opened at least three-quarters of the way.

I saved the bedroom windows for later. They were nearly impossible to open anyway, and it took extra work to loosen them up. The locking latch on each caused major problems. The bedroom ones had been painted over, and when I bought the house I managed to get all the paint off, but underneath, the latches had rusted. I was too lazy to replace them, so I just let them be.

Afterward, I showered and dressed in a black t-shirt and jeans and hopped in the truck. The sun was incapable of killing off the chill, but it was a beautiful day, and the ride revealed a wide expanse of finely-manicured farmland. Once you turned off the road which ran by my house, the stands of trees sat back from the road like feral dogs, sparse and ragged-looking. In other places, expansive stretches of cotton blanketed the land, the dirty white sea stretching out until it was overtaken by trees.

The Brickmeyer house, too, was a sight to behold. I pulled into a driveway a half-mile long and coasted between rows of recently planted pecan trees, all while admiring the building's sheer immensity. It was a two-story neocolonial set off by a wide-open field. Leland had bought the land for pennies on the dollar with his daddy's money, and the estate was now in the awkward teenage years. Once the sod took root and the trees grew up around the house, it would become an even more impressive view.

For years - decades - the Brickmeyers had lived in a withered, vine-covered mansion, but that had since become a little museum of no importance, even in the town's city limits. Day travelers with a distorted sense of history visited, but otherwise it was a forgotten legend of a house. Leland wanted to make his own shadow, not live in the darkness of his father's.

A Hispanic woman in a modern-day maid's outfit opened the door when I knocked. "Leland here?" I asked. She made no reply, stared at me as if she didn't know who I was asking for. "Guy who owns the house? No?"

I saw her start to take a step back, and then she stopped. She was debating whether or not Leland would abide having me in his house. She shook her head, and just when I thought she was going to slam the door, a voice in the background said, "I got it, Mahaila."

I had met Leland Brickmeyer on a few unnotable occasions as an officer, but the light of recognition wavered in his eyes until we had shaken hands. "Rolson, right," he said, his voice managing certitude and inquiry simultaneously. His handshake was firm, and he maintained level eye contact, even as he asked, "What can I do you for?"

Leland, rather than asking me in, stepped out onto the top step of the front portico and closed the door behind him. He was a tall man, late forties, clean-shaven and crisply dressed. He was mostly svelte, though a slight paunch pushed against his aqua-colored Oxford shirt. He didn't smell like money but his cologne certainly did.

I took an appreciative glance of the house. "This is what my Aunt Birdie would have called rare air," I said.

"That's a saying I ain't ever heard." He was southern but disconnected, and it showed in the way he carried himself. Even the people who had known him for decades couldn't quite shake the feeling that he had snuck down here from some northern state.

"Probably not. Birdie had quite a few. Rare air's just a phrase for something most folks don't get to see up close. Like climbing a mountain, I suppose. The view's something else."

"Ah," Leland said, sort of feigning interest. He was a busy man.

I decided not to waste his time with trivialities. "The man who was found on your land. I'm the one found him. He looked awful. Neck broke, grisled and stinking like old hamburger meat." I watched him, watched his gestures, his facial expressions.

His lips curled back, revealing teeth straightened by God or money. You could picture him in front of a podium, flashbulbs erupting around him. "I heard about that. It's a shame, huh, and out there in that old juke joint, no less. *Real* shame, I tell you what."

"Looked like he'd been tortured something awful, a real hate crime-type situation. You seem like the kind of man who could get that situation solved in a hurry."

Leland unfolded his arms and placed them on his hips, looking away from me for the first time. The sun had begun to turn the sky into a fluorescent pink splatter, and sunset wouldn't come officially for another hour.

A hint of impatience crept into his posture, yet the smile remained. "Let's take a stroll, shall we? Awful close here on the steps, isn't it?"

The steps seemed fine to me, but I said, "Yeah, sure."

He led me around the side of the house to a gated wooden fence, eight or so feet high and painted a subtle shade of brown. Through that gate a small enclosure featured a hole being covered in concrete. "My whole life, I wanted an in-ground pool. My father was too damned cheap for one."

I wandered over to it and peered inside. "Looks deep," I said.

"Thirteen feet down by where the diving board will be. I am going all out for this thing." He paused. "I'm putting a hold on finishing it until this whole Laveau business is squared away."

"Why is that?"

He slipped his hands into the pockets of his slacks and said, "Well, it's distracting, and I can't work distracted. It's like trying to have a conversation with somebody who's got something stuck in their teeth. I can't do that. I want to oversee the mixing of every inch of concrete."

"Seems like a pain in the ass."

His face changed under the glow of the fading light, the expression turning toward some manner of self-interest. "It's interesting, especially laying the concrete. The concrete seals the pool. It is the foundation, keeps the water and earth separate. Something bout it speaks to me."

"Otherwise you've got a pond."

"Otherwise, I've got a giant, slopping mess. And it's the concrete that does it, something that transforms completely. Starts soupy and wet and ends up able to withstand hundreds of pounds of water pressure."

"Listen, I-"

"You know how many people died building the Hoover Dam? A hundred. You know how many were buried in the concrete?"

"No." Frankly, I didn't fucking care.

"Not a single one. The old rumors aren't true, not one of them. But it's still interesting to think about, men encased in concrete. Or dumped into the harbor wearing concrete shoes. Hell, I reckon I've got about enough concrete in my shed to bury ten men down in that hole I dug."

He smiled and winked. It was a gesture meant to seem completely harmless, but I got what he was saying, even if he didn't mean exactly what he was implying.

He continued: "You're not out here for official business, Mr. McKane, and though I don't know you very well, I'd have to be living in a cave to be unaware of your recent troubles."

"That you would," I replied.

"But if you think coming around here, sniffing at my ass, is going to get you back on the force - or worse, some kind of financial reward - then you're sadly mistaken."

Brickmeyer's hair was a thick black mat, a genetic wonder, and he used this opportunity to smooth it down. It was almost subconscious for him, a simple yet distinct mannerism.

I tried to reel it in a bit. I'd taken it as far as I cared to this afternoon. I said, "No need to skip that far ahead into the conversation. I promised someone I'd take a minute to speak with you, maybe poke my head around and see if I could make some progress."

He rolled his eyes.

I said, "You know who it was that was found out there, on your land?"

He sighed. Here was his dealing-with-the-political-opposition tone. "Emmitt Laveau. Twenty-six years old. African-American. Mere facts, that's all I got. Listen, just because some black kid got himself killed on my land-"

"I'm not accusing you of anything. That kid's mother has asked me to help out. Coming out here, I was undecided. Didn't know if I was up to playing Sam Spade for that poor woman."

"Uh-huh."

"Looking at you know, way you're acting, I'm convinced I need to help her. I feel I owe her something, since I almost caused her son to bury her, instead of the other way around. I'm sure you don't like me coming out here, but I figured the least I could do is ask some questions on her behalf."

"That's illegal, being as you're no longer a police officer."

"I'm not investigating. I'm just talking to you, man to man."

"Besides," he said, ignoring me, "though Mrs. Laveau is a fine citizen, has no one entertained the idea that, conceivably, the son set himself up for a fall?"

"What are you talking about?"

"Looks pretty awful, doesn't it? Sure it does. S'posed to. What if it was, I don't know, a drug deal gone bad?"

"Seems like a jump to make."

"No, no. Not saying anything hard and fast at all. Not whatsoever. Don't know the first thing about him. I am elaborating on the *possibilities* of what *could have happened.* Nobody wants the murderer found more than I do, but vigilantism is not the way to go. You were a police officer. Don't you have any trust in their abilities?"

"Ability has nothing to do with it. All it takes is a single dishonest officer, even in a small town, for a case to go unsolved."

"If you're wrong, you could make a complete fool of yourself."

I shrugged. "I don't really give a shit."

We stood there for a moment. I glanced at him and saw the muscles in his jaw working up and down. "Let's head back up front," he said, moving stiffly back toward the gate door.

When we got around to our starting place, he said, "Expect to be contacted about a restraining order, Mr. McKane. And if you want to play detective, you best go looking for the people who did this, the people who *actually* did this. Sobering up might help, as well."

"If you have nothing to hide-"

"I don't *have* to have anything to hide in order to want my privacy. I'm an elected official. If I give off the impression of being defensive here, it's only because it can seriously hurt my career. I've got aspirations beyond this town. You understand that?"

I nodded.

"See? Right, I knew you'd get that. These things tend to have a, well, a, um, snowball effect. One person gets it into his head that there's something fishy about a dead body being found on his land, pretty soon the whole town's going to whispering about me having somebody offed behind my back."

"I understand that," I said.

"Me even having to deny such a rumor is beneath my contempt. I don't want to do it. Shouldn't have to do it. The longer I entertain the people digging around for dirt, the more absurd and far-fetched the claims become. It's just the last thing I need right now."

"I get that. But if I find anything that places you in a bad light, I won't hesitate to come back out here and have this conversation again."

71

He stared at me with a hard, lawyerly air, trying with some difficulty to come up with a retort. When it became obvious he wouldn't, he stepped back inside and said, "Have a good one, Mr. McKane."

"Being cold to a member of your constituency is a rookie mistake," I said. "If you want to move up higher on the political food chain, you need to figure out how to kiss everybody's ass."

He gave me one final nod and disappeared inside. I stood on the portico for another few minutes, surveying the expanse of land stretching out around me. Through a stand of trees, the sky looked electric, as if backlit by neon lights. The first truly clear day we'd had in a week. The wind had died and it was humid outside and the air smelled of burnt dust, but at least the rain was gone.

I took my time getting back to the truck, trying hard to steal glances back at the windows. Leland seemed like a peeker, but I never once saw the curtains of a single window pulled aside.

Oh well.

It was then I noticed a nice, big obstacle in my way.

A truck the size of a freight liner blocked the driveway, in a circular alcove designed for cars to lie in wait. If there was a flaw, it was that the driveway only had enough space for one vehicle.

The windows were tinted but the windshield was not, so I saw the outline of a husky dude hunched over the wheel. I waved and he gave a few fingers in response. The truck was a diesel, white, had all the qualities of the one I was looking for. Even as I turned to leave, trying to get a better look at the truck's tag, it had pulled forward, giving me nothing but a blurry glance at the back license plate.

I kept glancing uncomfortably at the rearview mirror as I drove home, but this time, nothing followed me.

* * *

Despite my better judgment, I ended up at Virgil's Bar again. I felt a sense of accomplishment for giving Brickmeyer the what's what, so a couple of beers were in order. It was still light out, but the regulars already seemed to be tilting dangerously to one side. Most of them were in the bar to get business done. They were not fucking around. They drank real drinks. Got real drunk. Told sloppy, outrageous lies with a slight glimmer in their eyes. I felt very much at home.

I pinned a stool down at one end of the bar and felt a familiarity in the tattered leather as I leaned back. Every chair in the place had a heavily-used feel, and stuffing poked out of the holes not covered by beer labels or duct tape.

I took the bar-thinker's pose, hunched forward and staring into the senseless gold of my High Life. Unlike the other patrons, I wasn't contemplating where it had gone wrong with *me*. There would be time for that when this was all over. I was thinking about Emmitt Laveau, what reason he had entered my life, and the distraction helped keep my blood from doing the jitterbug inside of me.

In a late afternoon draining of color, the bar was a good companion, the stale beer smell and hazy smoke cloud pressing against the ceiling. The doors had been left open to let in some fresh air. It was conducive to drinking.

So that's what I did. I drank, and it felt nice. The beer gave me a pleasant buzz, even if I had to fight off the nagging feeling that maybe it wasn't making me a better dude.

A hard clap on the back jarred me out of my thoughts. I jerked and turned to face the third or fourth biggest man I'd ever seen in my life.

Luckily, he smiled. "Rol, it looked like you were staring into a crystal ball there." He pointed at the beer. "There ain't where you'll see anything worth finding."

"Deuce. *Jesus.* You scared me. Shit. Don't you know it's not a good thing to do to me these days?"

Deuce took a seat, pointed at my beer, signaling to the barkeep for a High Life. The stool seemed to grunt under his weight. "Fuck, man, you're the talk of the town. This is the last place I should expect you to be."

He paused and sighed. "Yet, here you are."

"Should I be worried?" I lit a cigarette.

"As a bail bondsman, I would offer up that you don't be seen drinking in public, especially *with* a bail bondsman. Might complicate your case. Still, man's got to make his own mistakes. Can't make them for him."

"Least this way," I said, taking a long tug on my cigarette, "you know I'm not a flight risk. Can't go very far if I'm tickling my drunk bone here."

Louis arrived with the High Life, and Deuce knocked back a third of it in a single gulp. He grimaced like a man who'd found a cigarette in his coffee mug. "I normally drink Bud. This stuff, pigs wouldn't roll around in." He shrugged and took another swig before putting it down. "It's cold, I guess."

"That it is. Cold beer and cold hearts; that's all they got in here."

Looking around, Deuce said, "Beats working for a living."

He turned and raised his beer to a few people, who grinned and waved back. He was the only black dude in the bar, and though the George Wallace mentality sometimes still pervaded the Junction, it had never applied to him.

People were probably too afraid to enforce it.

"You don't mean that. You're practically a workaholic, for Chrissakes."

He smiled. "No, no I don't. And yes. Yes, I am." He referenced a small rip in the neckline of his t-shirt with a disarming wink. Somebody had obviously gotten the worst end of that deal. "When your job's as fun as mine, you don't hit the snooze button."

"That good, huh?"

It was an answer he always had ready, whenever he got the question about his work. "Oh, it's a job. Has its slow days. Has its bad days. But for the most part, it's good work. Don't have the same day twice, that's for sure."

He took a sidelong glance down the length of the bar and turned his gaze back to me. "Fact is, I've pulled in about a quarter of the people here."

Louis lined five beers up on the bar and flicked off their tops with a practices flick of his bottle opener. Good bartender. Quiet guy, nonjudgmental. He served each man, as he always did, with a curt nod and servile grin, and the old bearded men, in chambray work shirts and dirty jeans, orange with Georgia clay or spotted black with oil stains, turned back to their conversations with a kind of desperate energy.

I went ahead and paid for Deuce's second round. He'd had a rough day, but he didn't mind that. He didn't have to work very hard to be good at his job. A couple years on the D-Line for the Saints afforded him the kind of leisure at his job most nine-to-fivers dream about, both financially and physically. He wasn't an asshole or a bully because he didn't have to be. He was bigger than most men by half, but it was also just his natural disposition.

Guys he dealt with now, though, don't fear big guys. They'd been hardened by the gutters of this world and tried to find weakness in a man's size. Didn't matter. I'd once seen Deuce drag two lifers in on their court dates, both men sweating and dazed but otherwise all right. He wasn't mean but he was hard-nosed and didn't shy away from violence.

I made friends with Deuce freshman year of high school, before he had scouts breathing down his neck. One of my only true friends in this world.

Maybe the only one.

SportsCenter was playing on the old tube set above the bar, and we watched basketball highlights for a minute before Deuce said, "The world spinnin' the opposite way? I haven't heard from you in a while."

He was avoiding the television, all of the scores. The spreads. The over-unders. Sometimes, he didn't care to look at SportsCenter at all. Sometimes, I covered his drinks. *Hey, man, I got a spending problem this week.* Not often, but those nights tended to be the ones where we stared into our glasses and didn't say much.

"Cooped up. Stomping patterns into the floors at my house. You know the deal. After the whole thing with you-know-what, I keep a low profile."

"And, what, stumbling onto dead men is the way to remake your image? Hey, can we change this," he called to Louis down at the other end of the bar. "I fucking hate SportsCenter."

This wasn't one of his weeks, apparently.

We lingered for a while, just concentrating on the way the end of a day feels. I finished my first beer and immediately anticipated the second. Drinking is only half the thrill of drinking. Having a full glass on the bar or in your hand, waiting on the next sip, is the other half.

It's comforting. You drink when there is a drink in front of you, and you spend the moments in between in anticipation. After a while, they all taste bland and you relish only in the coldness or of the comfort they provide in conversation.

Louis changed the television to a non-sports station, *Seinfeld* re-runs, and he turned to us for approval. One set of dudes turned in our direction, looking bent up about the channel change, but they quickly turned back to their conversation when they saw us. Or Deuce.

We stared at the screen, pretending to watch. Most everybody else could give a shit about the television, even if half of them were staring at it.

"What you gonna do, Rol?" he asked. "Can't be a cop anymore. Lotta things they can forget down here, but what you did's not one of them."

"Same as you when you decided not to play football anymore. I'll get along. I reckon I'll work on cars. Build some custom furniture, maybe. I got two good hands on me."

"When they're not shaking."

I held one up in my defense. "Steady as a board."

Deuce nodded at my beer. His eyes were full of friendly contempt. "And what do you think causes that?"

"The stress of life." I laughed. "Finding dead bodies. Running into ladies when you're drunk. That sort of thing."

I sat there, twirled the beer on the counter, mulled over how to say it. Finally, I just did. "Deuce," I said, "I think maybe this whole thing with this dead guy is bigger than just a bump and dump, more than just a couple of white boys torturing some guy 'cause he was black."

He raised an eyebrow. "And your proof?"

I told him, starting with waking up hungover and going over to the Boogie House, omitting, of course, the bit about the flashing lights and music. I took him right on up to this afternoon, with the diesel truck pulling up outside Brickmeyer's mansion. I tried to make sense of the offhand comments about the Hoover Dam and the concrete in his pool, but he didn't care about that.

"Any word on that license yet?"

"None whatsoever."

"Do you know of a connection between the dead kid and Brickmeyer? This guy didn't catch him going with a hooker or burning some kind of legal document, did he?"

"God, I kind of hope so. But no, nothing right now. Just speculation. Brickmeyer's acting weird."

"He doesn't like for anyone to assume he's anything but the Second Coming. It's a kind of complex rich kids have. Leland

Brickmeyer doesn't look like he's been in the deep end of the family's gene pool, but he's not stupid. The old man gave him a crash course in how to be a major league fuckwad, and now the old man's dead, so Leland doesn't have the guidance to keep him from slipping off the tracks."

"Normally," I said, "in these cases, the politician's banging a groupie of some kind, or hiding some kind of racketeering charge."

"Racketeering?"

"Something like that. It's usually something illegal and something awful, something worth covering up, and in this day and age, a scandal that can't stick doesn't ruin a politician's career. Think of Clinton and Bush. They avoided scandal after scandal, because they managed to discredit the charges being leveled against them."

"And you think that's what's happening here?"

"Of course I do. It's why I'm framming the hive with a stick. I want to see what happens when the bees come out pissed and ready to sting."

"Uh-huh," Deuce said. He tilted back his bottle and killed the last of his drink. Another one appeared moments later. Louis nodded and then went off to go fiddle with an unopened bottle of Maker's Mark. "And what if you're framming the wrong hive?"

"I'm good with hunches," I said, a half-assed defense.

"You know this town," he replied. "Know how people act here. We're not so far from the times when federal agents had to escort black kids into school. It can't be that impossible to imagine someone offing a dude because he's not white. And then you go and level that charge at a Brickmeyer? *The* Brickmeyer?"

I said, "He is not out of touch with reality, but he has enough handlers to keep him, um, sort of distanced from it. Friends and family, they kiss his ass to the point they need Chapstick just to be around him."

"So you want to rock the boat a little bit."

"I want to tip the boat over, dump the young patriarch in the water and see if he swims-"

"Or if he sinks."

"Exactly," I said. "He's never really had anybody in his face, so this is my chance, before he can have a chance to really disappear into his own little burrow. He cannot have enough plausible deniability to avoid questioning."

"This is all assuming that he has a part in this. Otherwise, you're ruining an innocent man."

"Right. Okay."

"Keep the blinders off is what I'm saying. I mean, the dude wouldn't have the body dumped on his own land."

"But it makes it easy to deny."

"Why not just get rid of the body completely?" he said.

"Unless he wanted it to seem obvious."

"Yeah, okay. I don't quite buy it, but if that's what you're working with, hey, whatever."

"He was defensive. I'm going to work under the assumption that he had *something* to do with it until I can no longer go down that road."

"I'll take my chances."

"If you do anything stupid, there's only so far out on the limb I can go, and not if I have to risk my own neck. Consider yourself warned."

I drained the last of my beer, tasting something not unlike rancid dishwater. "Sure," I said. "Don't expect a call, then."

"Hubris has ruined plenty of people, Rol," Deuce warned. "Don't let yourself be one of them. Small towns are like small oceans, full of piranhas and sharks."

"Piranhas are freshwater."

"Don't fuck with my logic, man. People like Brickmeyer, they're the sharks, and everybody else who wants to be anybody, they're the piranhas. Once the shark gets all chewed up and spit out, then one of those little piranhas starts growing. Gets bigger, and the cycle starts over."

"I see what you're saying."

"The key is, though it may seem like there's a lot going against you, there's also a lot going *for* you. People hiding around the edges, waiting for you to take down the shark. They'll help you, for sure, but don't be surprised if the same people who help you end up turning you into chum for everybody else to feed on."

I took that last statement to heart.

I got up, patted Deuce on the shoulder. "Be careful." He had his fingers steepled together and shook his head as I made my way toward the exit.

"And show up for your court date," he said, just as I closed the door behind me. "I don't wanna have to come find you."

* * *

I drove down the street to the IGA and picked up a whole, uncooked chicken, a sack of potatoes, cigarettes and beer and then went home.

I do sort of like to cook, but I'm not very good at it. I never could make food for groups of people or anything, or work in a restaurant, but I can fry up southern food so it's edible.

It's calming. There is something entrancing about the repetitive actions of preparing and cooking food - the constant cup-and-ball game of moving food and ingredients, only to have it end up on a plate - and it keeps me from thinking about all the things I'd fucked up. I can leave my mind in a suspended state. So I cook.

I do make a pretty mean country fried steak. I can say that.

The key is to drop whatever it is you're frying, from thinly sliced crookneck squash to cube steak, in the pan when the grease hits the right temperature. Cook it when the grease is too hot and you'll burn the flour; throw it in lukewarm grease you'll end up with mushy food. You've got to burn plenty of drumsticks before you get it right.

I rinsed the chicken and cut it up, dipping the sections into a mixture of egg yolks, salt, pepper, and Louisiana hot sauce before powdering them with flour and tossing them into the pan, which was almost too hot but not quite. Some people take the skin off because it's healthier. I don't. I leave the skin on. I'm old-fashioned. I reuse oil, sometimes old bacon grease. I do use vegetable oil, but not olive oil. It changes the flavor. My Aunt Birdie would curse God Himself if she saw me using it to cook.

For the sides, I cheated and cooked canned cream corn. I put it on the stove with pepper and quarter-stick of butter in it and let it simmer while I boiled and mashed the potatoes with the skins still on, stirring in spoonfuls of sour cream for flavor. Peel some potatoes and leave the skins on others, and don't mash them too vigorously, or you'll turn them soupy. Not good.

I made a great big plate and took two beers and my cigarettes outside and ate on the tailgate of the F150. I thought it'd be good to enjoy an evening unspoiled by rain.

After dinner, I scraped the leftovers off my plate out by the trees for the strays and put the rest in the fridge for later. I smoked a cigarette outside, wondering what to do next. If I wanted to get Brickmeyer hot, I had to do something public, something embarrassing to his family. I thought on it for a while but never actually came up with anything.

Later, D.L. called me while I absently channel-surfed. I muted the TV and answered. "You that desperate down there at the station, calling me on your own time?"

His laugh sounded like dried twigs in a wood chipper. "I don't have any of my own time, my boy. Didn't you ever learn that? I just have hours of theirs I don't spend at the office."

"That's why you make the big bucks."

"I reckon. Listen, Rolson, about that license plate you gave me."

My heart dipped in my chest. He sounded dour. "Find out who it belongs to?"

He sighed. "We did. Dead end, partner. It's stolen."

"Stolen?"

"Took the tag off some old abandoned wreck, hadn't been registered to anybody in years. Make and the model are immaterial, as you probably already figured. Down here, diesel trucks are as common as camo. We got fifty or sixty just like it, right down the color, from here to Dublin."

"Damnit."

"That's right. I know you're probably not going to listen to me, but whatever you do, don't piss anybody off. You made the find. They probably just wanted to make sure you weren't going to be any trouble."

"What's that supposed to mean?"

"Somebody saw Laveau out at your house today. That have to do with the one thing, or the other?"

"You got eyes everywhere, don't you, Chief? Lot of reach for such a small department."

"Somebody made a pass by your house." He laughed again briefly, a dry cackle. "And *you* won't be doing shit with this investigation, Rolson. I hear of you sticking your fingers in the pie, I'll cut 'em off. You hear me? You got bigger things, *personal* things, to be worrying about. Worry about those. This dead Laveau guy doesn't have anything to do with you."

"You're right. I'll back off," I said. I made it sound convincing.

"Damn better. No disrespect to Mrs. Laveau, but it looks to me like she's using your, uh, *situation* to call in a favor. She wants you playing vigilante because she knows you feel like you owe her."

"So."

"So if by the grace of God you're able to track down the killer before we do, what do you think she's going to have you do? Call us? Turn him into the police so he can stand trial?"

There was a pause on the line. I couldn't think of anything to say. "Don't kid yourself, Rol. She's playing you, big time, and it's not going to end well. Either she wants you to kill the punk for revenge's sake, or she wants you take some kind of fall. I've seen it happen before. Don't let yourself get sucked into something you can't get out of. I'd hate for that to happen to you, dumb-ass or not. Okay?"

D.L. hung up. I placed my phone on the edge of my knee and twirled it mindlessly, watching the way it spun around. If Janita Laveau was lying, she had a pretty convincing scam going.

"I guess we'll see, " I said to nothing and nobody in particular.

* * *

When the sound of high-performance mufflers yanked me from sleep, I had been dreaming about a river that was made of money. Cars had never been the thing to haunt me - I've never cared for the woods too much - but now it seemed like I was living in some hellish Stephen King novel.

I leaped up, grabbed the .45 from the bedside table, and went outside, aiming at nothing and everything. The truck had been nearby but was now tear-assing it down the road a ways. In the absence of a city, cars make a hell of an echoey racket, especially with glass pack mufflers on the back.

As I swept the perimeter, a single image from my dream kept coming back to me: someone floating in the midst of all that cash. Going down through a swampy entrenchment in bare feet, I looked for just the right silhouette. Just the right combination of light and dark. Maybe the moon glinting off a windshield. Or a gun glinting against pale moonlight. It was not so dark that I wouldn't have seen it.

It took fifteen minutes for me to come to my senses.

You're losing it, old buddy, I thought. Soon the fucking trees will be a threat. You cannot jump at every backfire, and there are a lot of backfires out here.

After another few minutes of searching, I straightened up and headed back toward the house. What was I going to do, find a truck in the mud of a nearby field?

I stopped in the middle of the road, glancing back and forth between my house and the Brickmeyer tract. Something pinged in my chest, sending shivers down my arms. The darkness of the woods was calling to me, and I considered a late-night walk.

It was silly, devoid of any real logic, but it was more enticing than going back to bed. So I let my intuition drive me into the woods at midnight.

I turned and walked toward the Boogie House. A slick wire tightened around my guts, and I felt my testicles draw up against me. A vaguely human shape was slinking between two rows of trees. I stopped cold. Could have been a lot of things, I tried to convince myself. A white-tailed deer, maybe. Or light playing tricks on me. But it wasn't. It was a person.

I moved quietly toward the woods, my mind filling with fantastically disturbing images. The woods, in turn, responded with silent awe. The chaotic weather of the last few days had subsided. There wasn't a breeze making branches rattle together. No cicadas or crickets. No raccoons scuttling about in the underbrush. Just me, the silence, and the Boogie House.

And it happened again.

The music started up, quietly at first. A guitar in the dark, playing a low blues chord progression. It was the sound of somebody warming up on a six string acoustic. I stopped and listened. The shadows around me grew into shapeless, watery pools. I kept going.

They always get fear wrong in the movies. You don't shit your pants and scream yourself blind when something happens. If you're smart, you don't do that. More likely, you convince yourself everything is all right until you're convinced it's not. And then, even then, you just sort of gulp it down and go on with your life. There's no running and screaming, just a kind of halfhearted acceptance that you or the world is crazy.

Word is, Robert Johnson gave over his soul to the devil to play slide guitar. Met up with a real mean fellow at the Crossroads and had him teach him the blues, and afterward the man just disappeared. Johnson came back a different man. A strange, drunken virtuoso. The rumor went that he played with his back to the audience so nobody could cop his style. He died under mysterious circumstances, and though most people believe he was poisoned by a jealous husband, some think his deal had dried up and the devil claimed his soul for Hell.

This midnight rendezvous felt no different, complete with an authentic soundtrack. What devil was I handing my soul over to, and for what price?

Once the Boogie House came into sight, with its gaping, rotted mouth of an entrance, the music swelled so that it sounded like someone running a high-speed drill right through my head.

I pressed both palms against my ears. The sound of the guitar rattled my teeth, a ululating whine that hurt so bad I tried to close down every one of my senses to push it out. Not that it helped. A single note hummed in the center of my head, creating a vibration threatening to split me in two. I pushed through, stumbling toward the building.

With each step, the drill bit inched into my brain. 'Ear-splitting' doesn't even begin to describe the sensation of having sound cut your head in two. I had been to concerts where the crowd pressed me against the monitor and the songs became a wall of distorted sound, and this easily put a late-80s Metallica show to shame. It was like someone sandblasting my eardrums.

I stared down at my feet. Focused on taking steps. Worked my way forward.

When I reached the entrance, I let go of my ears and heard only the wind blowing through the trees. Well, that and the throbbing *wha-wha-wha* sound your ears get after a concert.

"You have a funny way of showing love," I said. I sounded like an adult from Charlie Brown. "Is this how you treat everyone who's trying to help you?"

I stepped through the door. Death lingered inside. Not the smell of death, but death itself. You could taste it in the air, thick as cigarette smoke. The yellow tape was still there, but this place had already gone back to being forgotten. It had to get back to the business of rotting, breaking down so that all traces of its existence could be erased forever.

A flash of white flickered beside me and I jumped back to avoid it, stumbling over a ragged set of boards. I landed against the side of a table and cracked my head a good one. Stars danced a jig across my field of vision in time with my throbbing skull.

Everything melted into a blurry mess. A slow stream of blood trickled down my neck and into my shirt. The darkness in the old juke spread out, and no matter how much I blinked, the light wouldn't return. I was going to pass out if I didn't get some real oxygen soon. Real as in *not* the stuff I was breathing in here.

I drunkenly tried to find my feet. Then I began to hear them. Voices coming to me through the open doorway. I crab-crawled backward on my hands, behind the chair that had nearly knocked me unconscious. I pressed myself against the wall, wrapping my arms around my knees and peering under the table at the faint moonlight creeping inside. The pain on the back of my head was excruciating, but

I managed to keep still and to keep awake, no matter how alluring the other side of consciousness was just then.

Two figures stepped into view, framed by the misshapen door. "Man, they're gonna kick us outta town or worse, if we don't leave on our own," said a thickly-accented voice. Sounded like it could have come from a movie version of a Louisiana man.

The other man, fatter, in a whispery voice, said, "They just don't want black to rub off on 'em. The Boogie House is our idea, and there ain't nothing they could do to take it away from us."

"'Cept hang us. Wouldn't be the first time they gave somebody a rope lesson."

The bigger man patted an imaginary pocket. His hand disappeared into his body, which was nonexistent below the chest. He said, "I got a spell says they ain't gonna do shit to us."

I leaned forward woozily but didn't see what might have been in his pocket.

The skinnier, more frightened man said, "What if it doesn't work, yeah?"

"Hasn't failed us yet. Got us this joint. Got us everything we want."

"Overuse it, and there's gone be consequences."

"Like what?"

"Like Hell."

It's very easy for people to scoff at divine consequences these days, but whoever the man in this vision was had nothing but serious intentions by bringing it up.

"Aww, p'shaw. It's gonna keep the white folks at bay, least until we convince them there ain't nothing but music and drinking going on out here. No danger in that. There ain't no Hell in it, either way."

The bigger man reached out a hand to pat his partner on the back, but it never connected. They were gone. I waited until the throbbing subsided somewhat and then ambled home.

My legs felt like bags of water under me, so I didn't hurry. I loafed in a groggily fearful state. Suddenly the idea of getting back to the bed seemed unsettling. Ghosts were following me around. Real people probably wanted me dead. I was well on the way to public disgrace and a stint in jail.

But a beer sounded good right about now.

Halfway across the front yard, I noticed something was wrong with the truck. All the air had been let out of the tires. Not only that, but they had been slashed to pieces. I scratched my forehead with the butt of my gun and slunk inside, ready for another sleepless night.

I sat upright in the bed, staring into the darkness with a beer perched between my legs, intermittently drinking but mostly leaving it be. Even beer deserves a slow death sometimes. I kept the pistol nearby and occasionally glanced through the blinds, but my mind wasn't on my truck.

Sixth Chapter

I was six years old in nineteen eighty-two, the year my mother died in childbirth. She did so having her second child by a man who was most definitely not my father, and my mind hung onto that time period like a necessary password or something.

The funeral stands out, for some reason. The actual graveside service. It sits in a readily-accessible part of my memory, and sometimes I hate that most of my childhood wasn't drubbed out of me.

I remember being grateful to have the worst of it over. Red-eyed strangers told me at the wake that time heals all wounds, so I clung desperately to the idea.

They were wrong.

I can still recall the neat little details, packed carefully side-by-side for me to peruse whenever I need to, and though I try to keep them locked away, they still come to me sometimes.

Since I was so small, I couldn't see over the lip of the casket, so mostly I remember the plain brown casket. My father wouldn't hold me up to see her face, and though one random tried to give me a last glimpse of her, I buried my face in the crook of this woman's neck, refusing to look. I'd already been having nightmares, and I didn't want to pile on.

So I remember the way that woman smelled, but I do not

remember her face. I am only left with snatches of memory tied to her, and every day it becomes more difficult to pull an accurate vision of my mother's face. But still I remember things.

What I remember most came after the funeral, when it was just me and my father living in that house, so filled with my mom's presence that you couldn't plop onto the couch without her scent enveloping you.

Dad didn't take it too well, so I had to walk on eggshells so I wouldn't provoke him by existing. He was at times a quiet companion but also a raging, venomous drunk, stepping over into violent territory before he realized the drink had him by the collar. It was too late then, and whenever he was in that kind of state, he didn't care what he said or did. He was a circuit, an outlet, and all of the energy - the rage - came out of him in a single, voluminous outpouring.

On those nights, I sequestered myself in my room, sometimes seeking comfort under the box spring of my bed. I passed the time listening to him wreck the house, calling *her* back from the grave. Not really calling her name. Not really saying anything at all.

Sometimes he just screamed. The incantations of a possessed man. A sad and lost man, crawling to Hell on the broken glass of a thousand liquor bottles.

Me, I didn't pray for Jesus or anybody else to bring her back. I went straight to the source. "Mama," I'd whisper into my folded hands, "please come and take me away from the devil. That man in there, he ain't my daddy, and anyway, I'd rather have you come back to me. I love you, mama."

For some reason, I thought that heaven was far enough away that she'd be able to hear my prayers in the days and weeks after her death, that time was a factor and I had to pray constantly so that she'd have more of a chance of hearing it.

The distance mattered so much back then, partly because I imagined we wouldn't be separated forever. A child thinks in those terms, imagines forever isn't that far away. I thought maybe she and I would be reunited someday, but I prayed for it to be immediate.

Several times in that period, the door burst open and my father teetered in, falling headlong into my bed. Smelling of radiator moonshine, mumbling something about being alone. He would lie there, sometimes for hours, pleading until he was all but screaming. From underneath, I watched the springs in my bed bend and stretch to accommodate him, and my eyes would go from the underside of my bed to his feet, which dangled over the side.

This time, the monster was on the bed instead of under it.

One night, when he had guzzled himself into an unintelligible stupor, I sat on the living room couch, unwilling to try and turn on the television, when a knock came at the door. Several knocks, actually, each more fierce than the last. I used one of the bigger pillows to shield myself, thinking, hoping that he might be fooled into believing I really, truly wasn't there.

My father opened up, demanding to know what the hell someone would possibly want at this hour, and the man responded with three little words: "We got him."

I heard the roar of an engine moments later, and my father, standing in the doorway, turned to me. His eyes were so sunken they seemed to disappear in his cheeks. "You gone come with me, little man," he said, swaying on his feet. "We gone take a little ride."

* * *

I only had a single spare tire, so I didn't bother replacing any of the deflated ones the next morning. I would easily run the remaining ones flat off the rim before I reached a place to get them fixed. Goddamned cars, I thought, would be the death of me.

I had put myself in this position. I had walked right up to Leland Brickmeyer's house and tried to intimidate him into doing something stupid. My first mistake. Leland Brickmeyer was too slick, too greased up by money, to do something obvious. Still, I didn't give up hope that I might be on to something.

Over a quick lunch of cube steak and mashed potatoes, I called a junkyard dog named Jarvis Garvey and organized the rental of one of his cars, offering him an extra twenty bucks if he would come and pick me up. "What'n the hell you need a car that bad fuh?" he asked, half-jokingly, saying he hoped he wasn't being timed. He said, "I got to put a battery and couple gallons of gas in the junker before I bring it to you."

I told him that was fine, and we hung up. Garvey was an old cracker, but he was trustworthy.

I rinsed my dishes and locked up the house real tight, closing all the windows and doors and latching things that probably hadn't been fastened in years. I waited outside, lowering the rusty tailgate on my truck and sweeping the pollen off with one hand before sitting down. The sun beamed through sparse clouds. I noticed the weather seemed to be getting better, even as my circumstances got worse.

A police cruiser turned into my drive not thirty second later. Even through the windshield, the two men looked pissed. I continued to swing my feet noncommittally and stare off into the distance until they got right up on me. "Rolson," the man on my left said. His name was Ricky Walton, and no work on his part could hide his contempt.

I looked at the other man and said, "Hats off to Roy Harper, how you doing?"

Ricky glared at him. "Roy?"

Owen Harper said, "Led Zeppelin."

Owen stood six-three, sandy-haired and always smiling. One of the few tolerable men on the force, he always gave off a genuine vibe. There was nothing conspicuously cynical about him. He was missing two fingers on his right hand from trying to save a girl from being hacked to death by her drug-addled mother. He eventually got the meat cleaver away and cuffed her with the good hand. Everybody thought he deserved a special place in heaven for that one, and I agree.

Ricky cleared his throat but said nothing.

"What can I do for you boys?" I asked.

"We're getting some complaints, Rolson," Owen said.

I tried to hide my amusement. "I have no idea what you're talking about."

"You're trudging around in muck, and you're all by yourself. Keep on doing it, and you're going to get caught so that nobody will be around to help you out."

I looked down at my boots. "I guess they are getting a bit dirty," I said.

Ricky groaned. "I don't mean literally, Rolson. Dangit."

"Hmm. When you put it that way, it sounds threatening."

"It's just the way it is, man," Ricky said.

Owen put his hands on his hips and blew out a long breath. "Just stop bothering Leland Brickmeyer, Rol," he said. "He ain't done nothing to you, so just leave him alone."

"I asked him a few questions. Nothing illegal in that. I even went up to the door and knocked, like a good citizen. If Willa Jean Graham and the other Jehovah's Witnesses can do it, so can I."

They both looked exasperated. "You don't want him lashing out at you. It's the last thing you want, because he's got a long reach, and he can fuck you without touching you directly."

"Like now," I said, smirking.

"This is just courtesy. Leland's done plenty for this city and for the police force. You saw it with your own eyes."

"He's an asshole and a liar, and even if he has nothing to do with this, it won't do him any harm to get a stick in the ribs, now will it?"

I felt a shock wave pass over us. They kept calm, outwardly, but I didn't suspect they'd be doing me any favors down the road.

Owen said, "Why don't you just let this go. Let us do our jobs. If

93

you have anything to contribute, call me up. I'll be the first to help you out."

"You'll protect him. You've sold yourselves off, all of you."

"He's always got people gunning for him. He deserves a certain level of protection."

I spat on the ground between Ricky's feet. "Are you cops or bodyguards, fellas," I said, "because Leland's already got one of those."

"Let me tell you something, you drunk sumbitch-"

"No, don't," I said. "It ain't got to be a bribe to be a loyalty oath. The kind of backscratching that you do - that we all did, I suppose - isn't illegal, but it isn't right, either. If he even had a moment's involvement in Laveau's murder, he deserves what he gets. That's all."

I got up and went around to the front of the truck. I popped the hood latch and pretended to look at the engine until they went away. I thought they might try to arrest me, to bring me in on some half-assed charge, but they didn't. They piled into the cruiser and drove away, spinning ruts into the dirt of the driveway.

* * *

Jarvis pulled into my drive with thirty seconds to spare. He was a bent old man in overalls and a worn Stetson, and though he could barely see over the steering wheel, he drove like a man chasing somebody down. The tires on the maroon Oldsmobile kicked up clouds of dust as he slammed to a stop just feet from my truck. I saw him smile through the windshield.

"I thought I was going to have to wait a while," I said.

"Had to see for myself if you were bullshittin' me about the money," he said, laughing. "Can't turn down a bet like that. My damn pocket gets itchy."

On the drive back to town, Jarvis said, "Truck of yours sitting in the driveway looked fine to me."

94

"You've got a whole yard-full. I figured taking one wouldn't matter."

"No no. You know what I mean. That truck looked like it runs at least as good as this heap."

His eyes were smiling and yet not joking. To get them off me and back on the road, where they desperately needed to be, I said, "Busted a tire. I got a flat and need something to ride around in 'til I get it fixed."

"I have some old tires, though, and could get them on in a few minutes, no problem. That ain't no reason to be borrowing no car."

"And it would be better if I had a car that wasn't so tied to *me*. I guess."

He banked a curve, almost losing traction on a sand deposit on the road, and said, "Figures. I heard about you finding that Laveau boy."

"Word travels fast."

"Like lightning. You're not a cop anymore. You go playing Sam Spade in this car and end up wrapping it around a tree, you and me's going to have some words. You ain't Humphrey Bogart."

"And you ain't Peter Lorre, but you're twice as ratty."

He chucked. "I don't want to see the car on the news. Abandoned on the side of the road, driver missing, blood everywhere. Murder breeds murder. I tell you what: that boy's mother might be blessed to have you looking for a killer, but you don't' want somebody like Ronald Bullen looking for you."

"You know something I don't?"

"Something in that man's eyes is like looking straight into an empty coffin. Him and his brother."

"His brother?"

"H.W. I seen H.W. and Ronald riding around last week, like a couple of wolves wearing wool. H.W., he must've been run out of whatever town he was in last."

Apparently, Ron's younger brother had moved away fifteen years ago to go work construction or some other thing. Rumor was for a while that he went to go do underwater welding. Work like that fit him. And being gone so long made him a kind of ghost. People talked about him in the past tense, and it seemed like the world was better that way.

Jarvis pulled into his immense junkyard and got out. "Car's yours, 'til you return it. Take good care of it, and yourself, too."

I switched seats and worked the transmission into reverse. Jarvis squinted at me as if he had something to say. "What is it?" I asked.

He smiled, looked down, began to say something, then didn't. Finally, he glanced at me again and said, "I knew your daddy some."

All I could do was nod.

"He wasn't worth much, but he loved you and your mama. That don't excuse what he did, but people get tied to things they don't necessarily find right, and they forget about what's important. He certainly did. But he wasn't no monster."

He paused, trying to find different words. They must have been lost, because he became flustered. "Hell, I don't know. He was a jealous drunk, and that fire in him didn't mix well with the liquor, I guess."

He stood here for another minute, then finished by saying, "Well, shit."

With that, he turned and disappeared into the rows of cars, walking like a man who had given up long ago.

* * *

The Olds was dusty and loud but permitted me a fleeting sense of invisibility, for as long as Jarvis Garvey could keep his mouth shut.

I parked down the road a ways from the Brickmeyer Estate, and when I wasn't biting my fingernails, I kept an eye on the place. It was a big, nice, palatial estate, and though it was new, it was begrimed by a kind of dirt couldn't be washed off.

Even though the cotton fields had given way to green pastures, the old flags had been taken down, and the slaves quarters had been knocked over and replaced with garages, they'd never be able to shake history.

The Brickmeyers had been quite lax in distancing themselves from the plantation, because no one around Lumber Junction seemed to be put off by the information. However, it was downplayed somewhat when Leland's father, at an elderly age, thrust himself into politics. I'm sure the whitewashing will continue, and I'm no better than them, really, but since my family was always too poor to call human beings their property, I have the luxury of casting stones directly at them.

The way they carried themselves spoke to a private pride in a certain kind of white man, elbowing one another and winking about the way things used to be, before it got all mucked up. Most people round here say it ain't a thing for modern folks, but I have been privy to conversations about race relations that Strom Thurmond himself would approve of.

Privately, of course.

I looked from the house to the driveway, where the diesel was parked. If he was the guy from the Boogie House that night, he could help me figure out not only what happened to the Laveau kid but what in the hell was going on with the music.

If he had seen that at all.

The driver came out two hours later in a t-shirt, faded jeans, and work boots. He was about six-five, pot-bellied, with a shaved head and salt-and-pepper goatee. Even with the fat, he cut a mean profile. The dude wasn't unaccustomed to using his fists to solve (and probably cause) problems.

I gave the truck some distance as I followed it into town. It was mid-afternoon, and elderly people were shopping in the few businesses left on the square. Most had gone under just after Wal-Mart dropped anchor two towns over. A few managed to hang on, but only because the townspeople made a concerted effort to shop there. Otherwise, the square had become a collection of empty buildings, FOR SALE or FOR LEASE signs in the windows. A chain cell phone store had done all right in place of an old consignment shop, but that was the exception, not the rule.

The diesel and its driver, whose name I didn't know (he wasn't from the Junction), didn't stop on the square. He pulled into a spot at the Brickmeyer Headquarters on the same corner as the Junction's Annex. It was where Brickmeyer Ag & Timber's major business operations were conducted, and word was they were now amping up calls for contributions in the political campaign.

Brickmeyer's only son greeted the big man at the door. Jeffrey was holding a manila folder and seemed to be heading somewhere, but the big guy stopped him cold and convinced him to go back inside.

Jeffrey didn't look so good. He was in his thirties, and growing up, he'd been quite popular. Good-looking dude. Gregarious. Social. All of that seemed to have disappeared. He looked peaked, tired. Black circles made shadows of his eyes, a fact his glasses couldn't hide.

The two of them went back inside, and I waited, hunched down in the driver's seat. And then I waited some more, for what I couldn't be certain. Twenty minutes later, the big guy came stomping out, the manila folder Jeff had been carrying hanging from two enormous fingers. He slammed the door to the truck and sped off.

I slid down in the seat and listened for the truck to recede into the distance. I pulled out behind him, giving myself sufficient distance, and followed him until it became apparent that I had already seen the highlight of the day. I called the Brickmeyer office and asked what time they would be heading home for the day. "Five o'clock," said the secretary. "May I ask who's calling?"

I hung up and went to the library. It was cool and quiet, and its drowsy patrons were too lethargic to notice me slinking around the shelves.

I logged into the internet and tried googling the Boogie House. There were zero hits, but I did find an entry for a Canned Heat album called "The Boogie House: Vol. 3."

Next I checked the online *Junction Examiner* database. I couldn't find any mention of the Boogie House. I also combed the microfiche, eyeing each page for an article about the old juke joint. Nothing of interest came up.

After getting a crick in my neck, I went over to the main circulation desk and waited for Beatrice Something-or-Another to help me. She was a rat-faced woman, and her expression bordered on contempt. "Sorry," I said, "but do you know anything about that old bar where the Laveau man was found?"

Her stare could burn toast.

"The Boogie House," I continued. "Little juke out by where I live. First African-American owned business in the county."

"I don't think there's anything *official* around here," she said, her mouth gnawing on the words, "but I'm sure some people around town remember it a little. Maybe *they* can tell you what you want."

I tried a different tack. "Do you know anything about it, personally?"

"I don't approve of that lifestyle," she said. "Drinking. Gets people in trouble."

"I don't care if you *approve*," I said. Her eyes narrowed, but I was already halfway through getting my words out by then. "I asked you if you knew anything - any *facts* - about the place. Ownership history. Legal documents. That sort of thing."

A distinct look of pleasure at insulting me passed across her face. She gave me a curt *no*. I thanked her and went out into the afternoon heat. It was already muggy and only halfway through April. Walking around in this weather was like wearing a wet blanket.

I flipped open my phone and dialed my lawyer.

Jarrell's secretary answered on the second ring and sent me through.

"I am utterly swamped, Rol. You may hold a low opinion of me, but I do have other clients. I promise."

"This'll just take a sec," I replied. "What do you know about the Boogie House?"

There was a slight pause. "Take your nose out from where it don't belong. Might get snipped off."

"It's only a passing interest. Do you remember the owners?"

"My memory of those days is blurry. I was a much more prolific alcoholic then than I am now. The two men who started the juke up and disappeared one day. Closed up shop and headed back to Savannah, so I heard. They had debts around town."

"What else?"

"They weren't too popular with the white folks. One or two wives got caught out there, and I can tell you that Southern Georgia in the nineteen-fifties was not a time of racial reconciliation."

I crossed the street and got behind the wheel of the Olds, holding the phone to the opposite ear. "Would anybody have wanted them hurt?"

"Get the cotton out of your ears. Debts and angry white men. Plus, from what I remember, they practiced some sort of religious mumbo-jumbo."

"Voodoo. Hoodoo. Something like that?"

"Something like that. Listen, Rolson-"

I turned the key, and the Olds sprang to life. "I know, I know. You're busy."

"I wish you the best of luck, though. Keep your head down, and stay away from Leland Brickmeyer. If he happens to get a hard-on for you, he might not be satisfied with just fucking you."

"Wonderful parting image," I said, and hung up.

* * *

100

Jeffrey Brickmeyer appeared in the doorway just shy of five o'clock. Hurrying toward his slightly-used Beemer, he looked like a sickly version of his father. He was as tall and had a thinning shock of dirty blonde hair, which contrasted his stubble and perpetually-worried blue eyes.

I caught up with him on the sidewalk, and his eyes widened when he saw me. "Rolson, hey," he said, breathless. "You need something?"

I shrugged. Being coy had not worked for me before, so fuck it. "Any thoughts on Emmitt Laveau, Jeff?"

Something vile passed over his face, and he seemed to fight the urge to spit at me. "I thought you might still be in jail for what you did to his mama. How about that?"

Fair enough, I thought. "Maybe I should build up to the big question, huh? Start out small, like, why do you look like you know something about what happened? That a fair question? I saw you in tears when your dad's yes man came to see you, and that made me think you and your dad might be giving anybody who'll listen an earful of bullshit."

He shook his head. "I can't be held responsible for what my father told you, so take that and do with it what you will. He's got his reasons for acting the way he does, and with your line of questioning I can't blame him."

"You people are notorious for wearing masks in public," I replied. "You mind peeking out from behind it to give me something genuine?"

"Well, since you are no longer an officer of the law, what you're doing right now is illegal, so you should back off before something is done about it."

I had to physically fight the urge to roll my eyes. "Sounds like talking points straight from your father."

"No, no. It's not a threat." He raised one hand in warning. "If he's said the same thing, then I'm sure a legal document with your name on it is probably floating around the courthouse right now."

"Uh-huh," I said. "Restraining order, something like that?"

Jeffrey reached his car and slid behind the wheel. The car hummed to life, and he tossed a stack of documents into the passenger seat. He turned back to me, but I didn't like what I saw in his face. He said, "I'm surprised you're not the primary suspect, seeing as you hit that poor guy's mother with a car. Hasn't he suffered enough at your hands? Do you need to dance on his grave by making wild accusations?"

I had leaned against the side of his vehicle. Staring out across the rows of tattered and decaying old buildings on the square, I said, "That's old news. That mustard ain't sticking to the wall in the eyes of the investigators."

He sighed. All of a sudden, he looked tired. "People have to keep their private lives hidden in order to be public figures. If he's being obstinate, it's because he wants to preserve his public identity. My father didn't get to this position by being stupid, and he's no murderer. It wouldn't help his career, and that is the whole of his concern. Nothing else is half as important."

Jeffrey pressed a button and the window closed on me before I could think of another question. The car peeled out of the parking lot.

* * *

That night, I called Janita Laveau. "You that lonely?" she asked me, right off the bat.

"Guess so. I'm sitting here by myself, drinking a beer. I figured I needed to talk to somebody, since I don't like drinking alone." Which wasn't the truth, but it sounded fine for chit-chat.

"Can I tell you something I been thinking about lately?"

"Shoot," I said.

"People used to tell my mama she favored Hattie McDaniel. The woman from *Gone with the Wind*."

"Sure. I know who that is."

"She used to take that as a compliment, God bless her. The hell she had to go through to get respect, you'd think she'd have spit on people said that about her. White people, thinking they were complimenting her. She should have been angry. But she wasn't. She went along to get along, was just in her nature to do so."

"To white people back then, it was a compliment."

"Oh, it was. A backhanded compliment. If they had called her tarbaby, or Aunt Jemima, if she looked like them, should she have taken those as compliments?"

"I wasn't saying-"

A ragged, bitter laugh interrupted me. "Oh, I know that. Shit. I'm just being difficult. Now, what have you figured out?"

"The Brickmeyers are playing defense, but that just may be because a prospective Senate seat lay just over the horizon. I'm going to pursue it, but their distinctly pissy attitudes are the only evidence I've got."

"The Brickmeyers have never been on this side of sunny, have they?"

"Nope."

"And the man you saw the night you found my Emmitt."

I tried to speak but balked completely. I couldn't remember telling her about the guy who had shot at me, but talking about dreams wasn't a possibility, so I just let the matter slide. She seemed to bask in the satisfaction of stumping me.

I sighed. "I don't have any idea who that man was. Could work for Brickmeyer. Could be his bodyguard. The guy is about the same height and weight as the man I remember. But, then again, could be anybody."

Janita sucked her teeth. "Who are you talking about?"

"There's a guy, works for Brickmeyer, looks like an inbred, Appalachian Bond villain, but I don't have an ID on him. Don't know who he is, where he's from, or what his connection to Brickmeyer is, beyond the obvious. That'll be the next step."

"I can feel something dark closing in on us."

"You're gonna have to give me some time, Janita. Leland Brickmeyer says he wants to slap me with a TRO so I can't go near him."

"Guess you'll have to get creative, then."

"I can only bend the rules, not break them outright. I'm already a man sliding around in the mud."

"Why not? *Somebody*'s been breaking rules. That don't mean it's Brickmeyer, but my son isn't dead for no reason at all."

"It's slippery. If I go vigilante, I'm no better than the people I'm trying to catch."

"You ain't killed nobody," she said.

Not yet, anyway, I thought. "I guess you're right."

"Course I'm right. You know what else I'm right about?"

I waited.

"You think everything around you can be explained."

"Just because I'm not basing the whole investigation on weird shit doesn't mean I'm ignoring it. I can no more find Emmitt's murderer by trying to dream than I can solve an algebra equation by meditating on God's existence."

"Hmmph," she said. "When I was a girl, my grandmother - that is to say, my uncle's mother - used to sit at the foot of my bed and tell me stories before I went to bed about what happens when we dream."

This wasn't the kind of conversation I wanted to have with her. Still, I thought about the fact I had nearly killed her, so I indulged her. "What kinds of stories?"

"Oh, all kinds. Fantastical stories. Some of them revolved around the men who drove out evil spirits from this village or that one. Others were ghost stories her mother had confided to her when she was a child. She told me about the thin sheet that separates life and death. In her eyes, life on earth is a cocoon and we are just caterpillars. When we die, when the last breath is released, so are we."

"Does that give you any comfort about Emmitt's death, believing that something comes after this life?"

"Nothing gives me comfort, Rolson McKane. But my grandmother believed in the idea that stories, that knowledge of life and death, give us power over death. She told me so herself, but my mother warned me not to pay any attention. She tried to keep grandmama out of the house for that reason."

"Why?"

"Because grandmama had died giving birth to my mother thirty-plus years before."

I thought about the prayers to my mother, wishing for her to come back to me, in any form. "That sounds like too much for a child to handle."

"The stories were what kept me up at night. Some of them were *so* scary. I had to learn about headless men patrolling the streets, and of people being buried alive and spending the rest of eternity ringing bells at midnight to warn the townspeople."

I could sympathize with that aspect of her story. "My Aunt Birdie used to talk about a ghost that wandered down the railroad, carrying a lamp and spending nights looking for his missing head. She took me out there once, and I got plenty scared, but we didn't see anything. Years later, I found out it was swamp gas that created the light."

"How do you know it wasn't also a spirit?"

"Forgive me, Mrs. Laveau, but how do *you* know that Emmitt has been in contact with you and - by extension - me?"

A long pause passed between us before she talked again. "That's probably a question better suited for my uncle," she said. "Why don't you come on by tomorrow and ask him all about it? You probably won't be able to get him to shut up. That's a trend in our family, talking when we shouldn't. Goodbye, Rolson McKane."

With that, she hung up. I went into the kitchen and popped open a beer in the golden light of the fridge, and then I sat at the broken-down table by the windows and watched the trees wave at me for a couple of hours.

* * *

The next day, light pushed through trees to the east of me as I drove to the Brickmeyer compound. There, I waited. This time, I managed to catch Leland's right-hand man coming out of the house. I had parked off the road a few hundred feet and stalked up the main drive.

The man, wearing a button-down work shirt and faded Brickmeyer Ag & Timber camo hat, paused briefly before opening the truck door and getting in.

"I know who you are," he said through the open passenger window, slamming his door. His voice was low and resonant and only vaguely country, like he'd lived somewhere else before. "I won't make the same mistake as bossman."

I leaned against the truck, peeking my head into the cab, which smelled of dirt and grass and tobacco spit, and a hint of generic pine freshener thrown in for good measure. He pushed the key into the ignition - hard - turned it, and the engine rumbled to life.

My eyes drifted to the ignition, where a mass of silver and gold keys dangled from a single, big ring. "This your truck?" I asked, fighting the ruddy swell of the diesel.

"Company's," he replied, not matching my gaze.

I sucked my teeth. "Shame that key chain there doesn't have a company key fob, don't you think?"

"What?"

"Leland likes to doodle his name on anything he has a passing association with." I pointed at the hat. "Hell, he's even branded you.

106

You telling me that doesn't include the company cars' key rings?"

The man flushed. His jaw muscles tensed as he clenched his teeth. "Step away from the truck, dickwad," he said, "before I make your asshole match your big fucking mouth."

I pursed my lips. "Reckon I'll be on my way, then. Speaking of assholes, your boss around? You get your marching orders from him every morning? That what you do here?"

"I'm about two seconds from getting out of this truck and stomping your ass into a mud puddle, friend."

I didn't doubt that he could do it. He was built like a UFC fighter gone to seed, or a man who bench presses Buicks for kicks. But I already had my mouth open. No stopping now. "I got seven pistol rounds say I put you down like a tired bull from a Hemingway novel before you get your foot anywhere *near* my ass." I spat on the passenger seat of the truck. "*Friend.*"

"You shoot me, you better hope you kill me."

"That's the idea, Igor."

We stared in silence, him sitting behind the wheel, me leaning against the truck. In the mild heat of the idling engine. Breathing in the exhaust.

"What, ex-cop? You gonna *shoot* me for not talking to you? For not listening to your half-cocked fucking theories?"

I shrugged. He said, "What a chicken shit move."

"Coming from a grown man who babysits an entitled know-nothing."

"I hope they find your fingerprints all over the scene at that old nigger joint. I hope they fry your ass, because I'll get a front row seat. Bossman'll make sure of that."

"Oh, I bet he will," I said.

This time, he didn't answer. Rather, he sneered and raised the window to avoid answering me, yanking the column shift into reverse and backing away. He backed until he could throw the truck in drive, and then he pulled down the driveway. A couple of times the engine revved, the truck jerking forward like a dog trying to leash-train the master. He wanted to bark the tires on the blacktop, but I knew he wouldn't. He was fucking bought and paid for.

I walked up to the portico and knocked a couple of times, but nobody answered. Guess they saw me coming.

There was a BMW parked by the garage. Jeffrey's car. He had to be here. I stepped back and peered into the windows of the house, trying to find somebody looking down at me. I might as well have been trying to find answers at an empty house.

I pulled a small item out of my front pocket and turned it over in my fingers, suspecting I was about to do something both stupid and bullheaded. But I couldn't help myself. I felt the blood rush to my head as I dropped to one knee. I deposited the dusty Brickmeyer key fob on the portico and walked soundlessly down the driveway.

Your move, I thought.

* * *

My next stop was my lawyer's office. Jarrell told me nothing was new, but that my court date was coming up and it didn't look good for me to be driving around town. He also felt compelled to say that it definitely didn't look good for me to be seen at a bar. Having a drink, no less. I pretty much shrugged through the conversation and told him not to screen my calls.

"They're looking to serve you for a restraining order," he said, smiling, as if that might lighten the mood. On his face was an ancient scar, lightened by time and made less omnipresent by an abundance of wrinkles. He wasn't *that* old, but the years hadn't been kind. "You pissed in Leland's cream pie while he was trying to take a bite."

"What's that supposed to mean?"

A man's words are his identity, sometimes. "You've got to pick up on my lingo. Anyway, turns out, Leland was trying to sell that land when that Laveau boy's body was found on it. Having you poke around only made it worse. Now nobody's going to want that bunch of rotted pine trees."

I chewed on a hangnail, thinking it over. "So, whoever killed Emmitt Laveau probably wanted to punish the Brickmeyers."

"Had everything riding on that one?"

"Kind of," I replied. It wasn't like I even had a real theory, but I had kind of banked on finding a picture of Leland Brickmeyer standing next to Laveau's body, winking at the camera like they used to in lynching photos. Something like that.

Turns out, it wouldn't be that easy.

"You might want to lay off him, then. He's already beyond pissed that somebody had the audacity to dump a body out there. Now you're going around town, trying to make him out to be the mastermind behind it. If he's innocent - and it looks like he is - you might end up at the loony bin in Milledgeville instead of a jail cell."

"That's great news."

"I have told you and told you that digging around was a bad idea. If you get embroiled in a pissing match with Brickmeyer *or* the police force, you're going to look foolish and unstable in the eyes of the judge."

"Okay. Okay. I get it. Enough with the bathroom metaphors."

"Just keep your lunatic routine to a minimum, okay? You don't have to go around, trying to make up for what your daddy did."

"What did you say?" I felt sharp edges all over my skin.

Jarrell leaned forward in his chair, steepling his fingers in front of him. "Listen, buddy. Don't think I can't see the parallels between what your father did and what you're trying to do. They're perfect opposites."

"That's not it at all."

"Whatever. The thing is, you don't have to be ashamed. Nobody blames you for what he did. I defended the man, tried to do whatever I could to prove him innocent, but he had a lot of demons. I think you do, too, but this ain't the way to exorcise them."

I spat a corner of fingernail on the floor beside me. "This is different."

"He needed to go away. It was just his penance. He killed that man because, well, it had all to do with your mama. Not because the guy was black."

"I don't believe that for a second."

"Either way, he was guilty, and he did his time. Died doing it. He never got to tell you he was sorry, so now you're going around trying to make up for it by helping someone you hurt."

"So."

"It's a nice gesture, don't get me wrong. Whoever killed Laveau deserves a red hot poker up the ass, but don't screw yourself trying to bring him to justice."

My phone buzzed in the pocket of my jeans. I pulled it out, saw that it was D.L., and then pressed a button to send the call straight to voicemail. He'd have to wait. "Thanks, Jarrell."

"This isn't an act of charity. You're still paying me. But don't think for a second I don't care about what happens to you. Besides, you don't have enough money to keep me on retainer."

* * *

Deuce was pretending to be working when I opened the door to his office. He smiled without looking up and began clicking on his computer screen. "Damn, Rol, you almost ruined my game of solitaire."

"I figured you might be out seining the streets for bail jumpers." I had forgotten to check my voicemail for D.L.'s message, so I sent him a brief text, telling him I'd drop by the police department this afternoon. The old man hated texts, and so I hoped every one I sent was slowly dragging him into the current century.

"Word is, *you're* the one trying to snare people in nets, not me. Going around like you belong in one of Ed McBain's *87th Precinct* novels, and you are no Detective Carella."

"I kind of like getting all this attention. Maybe someone will figure out which literary detective I actually *am* like." I pressed send and closed the phone before sliding it into my pocket. The phone beeped mildly a moment later.

Deuce slid the mouse across the pad and clicked once, presumably to pause the card game, and leaned back in his chair. I took a seat across from him. "Do you just have a board full of shitty choices that you throw darts at, and whichever one you hit, that's what you go with?"

"Who do you suppose is spreading word around? You think Brickmeyer might be the one starting all this? *I* don't talk to anybody but you and Jarrell, and that poor son-of-a-bitch is my lawyer. He doesn't want to ruin his already abysmal odds of defending me in court."

"Clements knows what he's getting into. I know you don't know this, but the black folks around town do. He ain't always been the arbiter of social justice. Man's got some skeletons, but he's spent the better part of thirty years trying to exorcise them."

"So? That's got nothing to do with what I'm talking about here."

"Listen, you don't-" He paused. "Okay, I get it, man. I really do. But you're getting fixated on one thing. Leland Brickmeyer doesn't rack the pool balls the same way you or I do. He's got contacts everywhere, and his hands are calloused from the pud-pulling he does. It wouldn't be that hard for him to ruin you forever."

"I ain't got much else to ruin, Deuce. I think that's why Janita Laveau's got me running around on the end of a long leash. If I nail somebody for her son's death, hey great. If I don't, then oh well. It's just my life that's been fucked up. No big deal."

Deuce reached under his desk and pulled a can of soda from his mini-fridge. He referenced the can with his free hand and raised both eyebrows. I nodded, and he retrieved a second drink from the small machine humming at his feet. After he handed it over, I popped the tab and took a long swig, enjoying the fizzy burn of carbonation.

"That doesn't mean you've got to hold the match so close to the fuse. If he has some hand in this and you can find what, maybe you get vindication. But he keeps the shades drawn pretty tight, and he employs family, and they keep their mouths shut. How much did you get out of Jeff?"

"I know for a fact he's wound tighter than a guitar string."

"He's gonna take over the business if Leland ascends to the halls of Congress, and he knows that. Living in Savannah didn't work out for him, so he's banking on that big promotion."

I took another swallow of Coca-Cola and placed it on the stained Berber carpeting. "Any idea of what he did down there?"

"Shit, I don't know for sure, Rol. I was busting heads in New Orleans, and all I got to go on now is hearsay. You know they never turn off the lights at the rumor mill. It's always chugging along."

"What was it? Drugs?"

"They say he was into the club scene down there, got so used to being out all night that he just blew his day job. Came in drunk or hungover and they just kicked him out on his ass, politician papa or no."

"Huh."

"Interesting postscript to his time in Savannah. Not very long afterward, a criminal investigation into that law firm turned up some fraudulent activity. At one of the oldest firms in the city. The head partner professed cluelessness, but he got a dime in the can nonetheless. I'm not saying Jeffrey Brickmeyer had anything to do with that. From what I know about him, he's responsible, but-"

"Makes you wonder." I guzzled more Coke. The heat and all my sweating was making it go down smooth.

"Definitely does. That's my warning, Rol. You're sticking your butt cheeks right up to the saw blade, and you need to know what might happen if you get too caught up. Don't get into the inner workings of the Brickmeyer clan. If you're serious about following this to conclusion - and I have no doubt you do - you need to ask yourself *why*. Why would Brickmeyer do such a thing?"

I thought about that for a few moments, listening to the hum of some piece of electronic equipment or another. Then I stood, placed my soda can on the desk. "I appreciate it, Deuce."

Deuce crushed the can with one enormous hand and deposited it into the recycling bin behind his swivel chair. He said, "I'll do what I can for you, but I got my own reasons for keeping off the man's radar. If I hear anything else, you're the first person I'm calling. Just don't say my name too loudly in mixed company. That includes your lawyer. I'm trying to run an upstanding business here."

"Yeah, yeah."

"I'm serious. I'll talk to some people, people who know things, and if I come up with anything, I'll let you know."

I waved over my shoulder and ambled out into the too-bright afternoon sun. I sincerely hoped I wasn't getting him snarled in anything he wouldn't be able to get out of.

* * *

I rode to the other side of town and pulled into an empty spot cooled by shade. I threw the shifter into park. Two biddies in flower print dresses gave me the stinkeye as I went in the police station. Church ladies. Teetotalers. I could almost feel their scorn burning holes in me, but like everything else, I ignored the armchair judge routine.

113

The PD was darker but not much cooler than outside, and I kept my head down to avoid eye contact. Two men I didn't recognize were stretched out in the uncomfortable seats of the waiting area, anticipating somebody's release. Not counting me, they were the only civilians in the place, and they looked like they had gotten tangled in a razor-wire fence and used their faces to break free.

The hallways smelled like bleach and alcohol. I always hated it.

The building itself isn't very big. A block of ten cells in the back manages to accommodate the city's criminals without getting too crowded. There is a separate room for the drunk tank and yet another for violent offenders, the speed freaks, and the toothless wife beaters who wake up in the cell completely unaware of their offenses.

I nodded at Dara, who hesitated but then let me in, past the reinforced door and into the main hallway. Her perfume mixed with the chemical scent of the cleaners and solvents, producing a sickeningly sweet odor. I tried not to let it show, and I didn't slow down. "On my way to see D.L.," I said. "Not my fault he called."

Dara shook her head. "You're lucky he let me know you might drop by," she said. There was no good humor in her insults today.

"Thanks, Dara," I said, throwing her a mock salute, already halfway down the hall. Vanessa and Dara used to be friends, and even though Vanessa had left *me*, Dara blamed me for it. She also implied I was responsible for Vanessa's addiction. She never said anything outright, but she didn't have to.

I knocked and walked in at the same time and caught D.L. on the phone with his wife, so I gave an embarrassed wave-and-smile, and then I waited outside until their conversation was over.

D.L.'s office was dark, same as always. He had tacked up dark tapestries - he refused to acknowledge they were dark sheets - to curb the light coming into the room, and the overhead fluorescent bulbs hadn't been turned on in years. Strategically-placed lamps gave the room an even illumination. D.L. had always complained about his eyes, and being the police chief had finally given him the ability to indulge his peculiarities.

"How's she doing?" I asked, and he responded by raising one side of his mouth and one shoulder in an apathetic shrug. "Better'n you are, son," he replied. "You've been squatting over the soup bowl, so I hear. We're all on pins and needles, waiting to see what comes out."

He was looking older these days, well-built but going flabby in all the normal places. His gut peeked out over the belt, and gin blossoms stood out on his nose as if the veins had been injected with ink.

He gestured with one hand, offering the chair across from him, but I decided to remain standing. Resting my palms on the chair back, I leaned forward and said, "What's up, D.L.?"

"You tell me."

"I think I'm the one who got a voicemail an hour ago."

He leaned up in the chair, grimaced as he stretched his back. I heard a loose, watery pop. "I think you need to put on the brakes, Rol."

"I haven't-"

"It's why I wanted to talk to you in person." He paused and then said, "I wish you would have a seat. Standing up the way you are is making me nervous."

"Forgive me if I don't feel welcome."

"Aw, hell, you were always self-centered, but these are not the circumstances for you to take exception to everything. If you're standing up to make a point, well, you've made it."

Beneath his expansive mustache, the ghost of a smile appeared. Cautiously, I sat.

"There," he said. "That's much better. I had no choice but to let you go. In these hard economic and political times, you had to expect the consequences that were handed down to you."

"I hope this whole conversation isn't going to revolve around me and my accident."

"No, no, I suppose it won't. It is going to revolve around you, though."

"I've already gotten that impression." I paused. "Listen, I'm not going to do anything to interfere with the actual investigation. I'm doing Janita Laveau a favor. She wants someone looking out for her best interests."

"And that person is you?"

"I'll try to be impartial."

D.L. sat up, chair creaking, and pressed his hands together on his desk, as if in prayer. It was how I was accustomed to seeing him. He stared at me like the answer to a quadratic equation was suspended above my head. "Rolson," he said, "there is no such thing as a good vigilante. Let me tell you something. We had a preacher, lived in the Junction back in the sixties, hated alcohol. Thought every societal ill could be traced back to it. Round here, I reckon he was right. Wasn't wrong, anyway, not entirely. He used to load up his car, which was a souped-up Mustang, with baseball bats and shotguns and chase down the boys running moonshine into the Bottom on Friday and Saturday nights. Was real good at it, too. Got his name in the paper once for it. Anyway, he took it on himself to chase down two of the McCail brothers - oh, Finnius and the other one, second generation Irishmen, both of them - and they pulled a shotgun on him. He managed to wrench it away and shoot the one brother, not Finnius. Killed him instantly."

"Jesus."

My former boss smiled mirthlessly and squirmed in his chair. I think he might have known the man. "That got a lot of mudslinging going in this town, and it went on for a while. The preacher man, he wasn't able to prove self-defense and he went away. Quit being a preacher altogether and ended up provoking a white supremacist into stabbing him to death in the workyard. Got him right in the forehead."

"I see what you're getting at," I said.

"I'm not sure he did it by accident," he said. "Which makes me worry about you, Rol. It reminds me of that story about the preacher man for a reason. You keep saying that tracking down Laveau's killer is the right thing to do, but I'm not sure if you're trying to convince me, the town, or yourself, or - and I think this more likely - if you're using this as an excuse to self-destruct."

"Trust me, I'm not." It didn't come out the right way. I didn't say anything else, because I didn't want anything I said to remind him of his daughter.

He blew out a long, dissatisfied breath. "I have nothing to threaten you with except jail. Which I will enforce. I catch you peeking at something you have no business peeking at, and your future will be quite grim, son. I'm telling you now to just quit it, because you're only going to get hurt. Everybody's going to get hurt. Everything will change, and all that will be left in the midst of it will be pain and disappointment."

"I think I realize that."

"Well, then, I hope you listen to me."

I thought about throwing it back in his face, telling him that it was *his* investigation, but decided against it. D.L. was a good man, but he was still a small-town cop. Looking at the way he was starting to slouch forward made me sad in a way I couldn't really deal with. He'd always tried to be a good man, which made him a better cop, so I left it alone.

Maybe I'm not so unbiased, in the end.

* * *

As I made my way back outside, I caught up with Ronald Bullen. He was walking to his cruiser, and he tensed up as I approached. "I'm not in the mood, McKane," he said, shaking his head. "Shouldn't you be looking for something at the bottom of a pint of Beam?"

"Give me just a minute, Ron."

"You're a walking insult. Here we are, trying to get this case solved, and you go behind our backs, behind the back of the man who used to be your father-in-law, in order to settle some business between you and Janita Laveau. The fuck makes you think I want to talk to you?"

"Because I know your brother's back in town."

He slowed his wobbly gait just enough for me to catch up. "So," he said. He was sweating from the heat, the armpits of his shirt boasting wretched dark circles.

"So I know H.W. doesn't come back in town unless he's in some kind of trouble. Maybe a warrant out on him, maybe not. Either way, if it comes out he's hiding from something, I still have enough pull with D.L. to get him hauled in."

"He's all grown up now. He can handle the consequences for whatever he's done."

A battered pickup truck rumbled by, and the old timer behind the wheel waved. Bullen waved back. I said, "He isn't hard to find. Big as he is, I'm surprised he hasn't been found yet."

"Get to the point, McKane."

"H.W.'s awfully violent. If he's skipping out on an assault charge, or battery, he's looking at a serious stint this time around. He's your brother. All you've got to do is give me five minutes. Help me out. I know you don't like Leland Brickmeyer and his ilk half as much as you have to say you do."

He scratched at his stubble.

"I'll tell you what we know so far," he said. "Laveau was kidnapped and held in the Boogie House for a few days, maybe a week. He was tied up. Wounds on the wrists, chest, and feet corroborate that. The ropes were cut away postmortem."

"Any sign of them?"

He shook his head. "No physical evidence. Place is as dry of evidence as any I've ever seen. Whoever did this knew what he was doing. That's about it."

"I'm a little surprised you're telling me all of this."

He wiped one side of his mouth. "I'm still a cop. I want to see the fuckers who wailed on that poor black kid caught as much as you do."

"Uh-huh," I replied.

"And, personally," he said, leaning in conspiratorially, "I'm kind of on the same boat with you about Brickmeyer. I think the rich cocksucker's hiding something."

I was surprised to see a member of the Lumber Junction Leland Brickmeyer Police Department speak so candidly and openly against the man with the deep pockets. "Really?" I said. "That's not the conclusion I've drawn so far."

"He's been lying through his capped teeth. Investigators asked him if he ever met Emmitt Laveau, he says no way. Says he only found out who the kid was after the body was found. By you."

"And he met Emmitt Laveau before?"

"Damn straight, he has. Brickmeyer slipped up. Said he didn't know Emmitt Laveau from Adam, and I know for a fact he's lying. He met Laveau at a dinner the Brickmeyers threw last year. A banquet for star teachers, something like that."

"Teachers?"

"The Laveau boy taught special ed at the high school."

I was skeptical. "That's not really a big deal, though. It's not like the guy caught him banging a secretary."

Bullen squinted, staring over my shoulder. "Yeah, but with a guy so committed to sculpting his image, don't you think he would cover his ass by saying he might have met the guy? Now he's on the record for a lie. That'll come back to bite him, I guarantee."

"All right, Bullen," I said. "Thanks for the info. I'll keep you posted."

"Don't bother," he said. He watched me cross the road and get into the Oldsmobile, leaning against his cruiser until I was well down the street. I threw one hand out of the open window in an ironic wave, and he returned it in his own distinct way, with a single finger.

* * *

Unlike the Brickmeyers, the Laveaus weren't a historically well-known group around town. The few of them who lived in the Junction kept to themselves. That was pretty much true for Janita and her family until Emmitt's death. Now, each of them had become a local curiosity, and I even found myself in a state of anticipation at meeting her uncle. He didn't go out in public very much, and from what Janita had told me, he was very old and very strange. A week ago that might have meant something, but now I felt I could handle strange. As long as he didn't start appearing to me in dreams, I thought I could handle it.

I had never been to Janita's house before, but like most other residences in the Junction, it wasn't very hard to find. I live in an infinitely small town, just six thousand people in the entire county, and with a knowledgeable giver of directions, finding even a remote destination can be a cinch. We're not talking *Deliverance*, necessarily, but some homes have been plopped down in quite backwoods locations.

Janita lived in a small, ranch-style home off a dirt road I don't believe I'd ever traveled but one that seemed familiar nonetheless. I recognized her car in the driveway and pulled in just behind it.

I knocked and stepped back and stood with my fingers laced together while I waited, trying to ignore the smell of pepper in the air.

The door opened, and an impossibly old man stood in its wake. His skin was a rich brown, and though he hunched, the years - however many he had lived through - had been kind to him. He was thin and muscular and his eyes darted around sharply as he sized me up. He wore a dingy old thermal undershirt and creased black slacks. A smell of something burning wafted from within the house, but the man did not seem to notice. He reminded me of a gator waiting for a tourist to be thrown from the air boat.

"You the boy almost killed my 'Nita," he said finally. When he smiled that curious, mischievous smile, he looked a bit like John Lee Hooker.

One of his eyelids lowered. His accent, however mild, placed him as being from somewhere else. French Louisiana, maybe. I didn't know the Laveaus very well, but I knew Janita had lived here for a long time, long enough, certainly, for any trace of an accent to wear off. The proof lay with Janita herself, whose middle Georgia drawl sounded nothing like the Cajun-ish accent of her uncle.

"Is she here?"

His eyes never left mine. "Nope."

I couldn't help but glance back at the car in the drive. "She's not?"

"That car, it's a piece of junk. Enh," he said, waving an arm. "She rode with a friend to work today. She got too much to do to be out harassing people in the middle of the day."

"Neither of us has that luxury, I guess," I said.

"I don't come knocking on *your* door. First, you come on into dreams and you think, 'Oh, that is not enough for me. I must also make my presence known in the waking world.' Is that what you thought?"

We stood in the doorway for a minute. Finally, he said, "I reckon you want in. You gonna poke around in little Emmitt's room. That what you won't move for?"

"Is there anything in there that might help the investigation?"

"No. Isn't nothing but the residue of that boy's soul in there. It ain't easy to live with, I tell you that much."

I hoped for him to say something else, but he didn't. He was waiting on me again. I sighed. "Maybe I could talk to you, then. Get a sense of the dec...of Emmitt. I don't even have to come inside for that. It's a pretty day. We can stand on the porch and chat. Will that make you uncomfortable?"

"Very well. Go ahead, then."

"Did Emmitt have a girlfriend I could talk to? Somebody he dated?"

The old man's mouth widened, revealing unusually white and straight teeth. He laughed, and it was uproarious. Still laughing, he said, "No."

He barely opened his mouth, and yet his laughter uncannily filled my head.

"Do you know something that I don't, mister, uh-"

"Kweku. It's an odd name, I know, but it is a family name. 'Nita, she the only one matters, and she call me Kweku. Or Uncle K. It's an old name, like me. An old fellow. Name as old as speakin' itself. And no, I don't know nothing you all don't."

"I was under the impression that coming out here would answer a whole lot of questions. That's the way your niece made it out to be."

Mrs. Laveau had told me in no uncertain terms that this man was bordering on telepathic. Staring at him, a muscular, stoop-shouldered artifact, made me think perhaps she might be exaggerating.

"'Nita, she gets the rum in her, and she goes running off at the mouth. That is what she is good at."

"Oh."

"I know plenty. And so do you. You're just going through motions to convince yourself you're right. Or that you're not right. You think asking a bunch of white folks where they been is going to give you the answer. You already know the truth ain't with them white folks."

"But if proper legal action isn't taken, he walks. No retribution whatsoever. He goes scot-free. No one wins."

"To punish the guilty, you need no court. This man, Brickmeyer, is as guilty a person as I have ever seen. He makes my stomach turn when I see him smiling on the television or in the newspaper. He is hiding something very grave, and personally I do not care if there is evidence whatsoever."

"Even if he's not guilty?"

He beat one hand against his chest and then pointed a long finger at mine. "What do your instincts say?"

"I try to go by the evidence."

"But it is not evidence that enlightens you. The real answers rise out of your dreams. Out of your soul. A man needs nothing else to be true and right in this world, or any other."

"Dreams aren't real."

He smiled condescendingly. "What is reality, McKane? Is it everything we see around us? Is that reality, the things we see and feel?

"I think so."

"What about being drunk, young man? If a man changes the way he sees the world, then is that still reality?"

"I don't know. I can trust the world is still there, and other people can verify it. That's enough for me."

"Everything you need to solve my grandnephew's murder is not in the physical world. It is why so many crimes, so many murders, go unsolved. People lean too heavily on what is in front of them."

"What do you suggest I do?" I asked. "Go down to the station and tell them my dreams are trying to tell me who killed Emmitt Laveau?"

"Their minds are closed, also. They inhabit only one side of life, their experiences. They solve crimes based on the past, and the past, all of history, is nothing but chained-up prisoners. You need to step outside of that view. This crime, it deals not only with the past but with the present also."

I didn't know quite how to answer.

The ghost of a shrug passed across the old man's shoulders. He said, "There is an old story that is passed down in my family, of the people who first encountered white men. These white men, hundreds of years ago, they sailed into the port near my family's village, and they began to pluck the strongest men and women out of the town, like petals from a flower. They were ruthless men, and they did not accept rebellion in any form, would punish severely any person who dared to disrespect them."

"Uh-huh. Well, Uncle K, I-"

"When the men - there were never any women - when they did not get what they wanted, they would torture the people of the village. Once, they took an elderly man and dug out his eyes with the edge of a sword and made him eat them raw in front of the entire town. All they wanted was alcohol, which we did not have."

"You say 'we' like you were there."

The old man jiggled with self-contained laughter. "The same blood runs through me as run through them. I talk like I am with them all the time. Forgive me. Where was I. Ah, yes. Soon it came to be that hurting the old and infirm did nothing for their cause. The people had grown smart to their ways and would send the elderly and the strongest people out into the woods when we saw the ships trying to dock. But that did not deter them. They took to the children."

I leaned against the doorway.

"This is before they forced Jesus upon us, even. Since we lay near the ocean, they didn't mind dragging helpless, crying children to the edge of the water and holding them under. In the beginning, it was to make sure they sent people for the slave ships, to carry them across to America. Then, it was just for their amusement. Sometimes there would be as many as ten bodies floating in the water at a time, and the men on the ship would not allow us to bring them back in order to clean and bury them. They made sure the bodies floated away, or else they tied stones to the children's feet so they would sink."

"That's horrible."

"One day, a ship dropped anchor in the distance and the boats came, but this time it was different. These men, they were afraid. They landed their small boats and then immediately threatened us - my people - with death if we did not help them."

"Why?"

"They were wild-eyed, crazed. Said that we had sent some children

124

out there to terrify them, to make horrible sounds and to beat on the hull of the ship. We had done no such thing. But then we heard it ourselves, the sound of the children's voices and the cracking of wood. The men watched the ship sink before their eyes."

"What happened then?"

"The white men learned what it is like to be treated equally. Even now, the village of my ancestors celebrates this day, even if the ships did not stop coming."

"And what about the children?"

"What *about* the children?"

"What explained what happened?"

"Sometimes there *is* no explanation,." he said. "Or else it is..."

He trailed off and waved one hand, as if to say the answer was out in the air somewhere.

A breeze passed through, bringing a chill to the base of my neck. I shivered. Uncle K said, "Maybe that Brickmeyer got somebody casting spells our way. Come inside and I'll give you something." The old man chuckled and then said, "My niece, she convinced me to keep this business to myself. I told her, okay, I would. But I am not a patient man, Rolson McKane. I see things I don't intend to. *Les Invisibles*. All the spirits, they come to me, like Jesus seeing the faces of the unborn from the cross. It's a curse I shoulder, and the only way, in my mind, to rid myself is to deal with this problem. She don't want me to handle it. I'm old, she says."

"I figured you would shrink his head or something," I said. "She couldn't stop you from doing that, could she?"

He stared at me contemptuously. "That's an old myth," he said, leading me into the small, dark home. I followed him into a room full of recovered spear heads and bleached animal bones. "Those are people in South America. Not Africa. Understand?"

I nodded.

"You're not that stupid. I hope." He shuffled through some jars filled halfway with powder, moving this and that in and out of the way, looking for something in particular. I waited behind him, eyeballing the knickknacks.

Scanning the shelves, I saw something that made my heart seize up. An upside-down framed picture of Leland Brickmeyer leaning against the wall.

Laveau returned with a foul-smelling concoction and told me to drink it. I obeyed out of both curiosity and obedience. Already, he seemed to hold a strange sway over me.

I gave it a shot, but I couldn't down the whole thing. When I tried to bring the cup from my lips, he pressed two fingers under the base and raised it so I had to finish every drop.

"What was that?" I asked, fighting off the urge to gag. It tasted like the inside of a tree trunk dredged up from the bottom of a swamp.

He gave me a mock glum expression. "You are a sick man, Rolson McKane. Very sick. I see it all over you, inside you. This, this is a cure-all. Lord knows you could use it."

I thought he was having one over on me.

"Is that what the powders and herbs tell you?"

"It don't take a medicine man to see what's wrong with you. It just takes a pair of eyes worth lookin' through, and I can tell there's something wrong with you."

"Well, thanks for that."

"Welcome. It ain't a secret. The troubles you're having, they work like evidence. But seeing you, my word, if that don't beat all I've seen."

"I think that's enough."

"Indeed. Just know that the sickness, you carry it with you everywhere. If you don't get it under control, it will infect everyone you know, everyone you love. Your problem is that everyone else you know is blind enough that they can't see how fouled up with a curse you are."

My stomach turned as though full of cider vinegar, and my mouth twisted sideways, but Kweku Laveau shook his head. "Keep it down," he said. "It's good for you. Make you live as long as me. And I been living a long time."

I nodded and swallowed hard, clenching my throat shut to prevent something embarrassing from happening. "I think I'm gonna go now," I choked. "But this has been...educational."

Me leaving seemed to please him very much. Mister Laveau was able to turn everything I said into something he wanted me to hear. "You don't think you learned anything," he said, "but it isn't all about the clues you need to find. There are some more important things you need to discover. Trust me."

With the way he was looking at me, I couldn't help but trust him, so I nodded credulously. He patted me on the shoulder. I bid him farewell, left him staring at me from the door stoop.

I began my trek across the yard. The breeze kicked up again, highlighting the sweat on my neck and under my armpits. "It'll all work out, if I can help it," I said.

"Ainsi soit-il," he said. I had no idea what it meant, so I waved absently over on shoulder as I reached the car door.

"You, too," I said, turning to face him one last time. Thing was, he was already gone, and the door was shut.

* * *

Voodoo exists as a real practice, as much as any religion outside of Christianity can exist in the South, but it carries plenty of half-assed misconceptions. People consider it a television religion, just contrived theatrical production, nonsense superstition, and elaborate rituals. Nothing could be further from the truth.

Unfortunately, that misconception is almost true in Georgia. Money-hungry practitioners - not true followers but hacks and pretenders - had turned the sacred Caribbean practice into a profitable holistic gobbledygook.

Screamin' Jay Hawkins had once sung about Hoodoo in *I Put a Spell on You*, as did Bo Diddley in *Who Do You Love*, the song itself a play on the word *hoodoo*. That's where most people get a conception of the religion itself, so that's what they have come to expect from it, and that's what those still involved have come to give them.

But Hoodoo and Voodoo are vastly different enterprises. Voodoo is a religion, Hoodoo a set of magical practices, often called rootwork. Voodoo was brought over with the slaves and was thought to be a way of protecting themselves from the white men who brutalized them. It settled in the Caribbean and expanded somewhat in Louisiana but did not pick up much anywhere else. Georgia had rootworkers, Hoodoo magicians, but the lot of them were con-artists, snake-oil salesmen of an ancient and disturbing variety, and they didn't move far outside of Savannah.

Part of the growth of voodoo in America had to do with the relationship between what people believed it to be and what it actually was, and one fed off the other. What we think of when we think of voodoo today has a lot to do with the changes made to accommodate those beliefs. It no doubt makes sense that it has a strong foothold in New Orleans, itself a place of magic of all sorts, and that it never really picked up in rural parts of Georgia. And it didn't, for the most part. But some people made their way to middle Georgia, just as they made their way from the French Quarter to southern Mississippi and the west coast of Florida, near the religious fanatics.

I had never seen the practice at work in Lumber Junction, but people talk. Janita's uncle was a superstitious man, but not the kind of person I figured for true, real Voodoo. Most people round here would take to calling it witchcraft or devil's work real quick, so I imagine it stays underground so that people won't be run out of town on rails.

Myself, I'm not a believer, but I had to give it to Janita's uncle: I did feel a hell of a lot better after drinking that horrible cocktail of his.

Even though I probably shouldn't have, when I got home I opened a High Life and drank half of it standing in the kitchen. Some of the catch-all drink's bitterness was washed away, and after the first gulps, I stood very still and waited to see how the two drinks would react with one another, half expecting my mouth to foam over.

But the two didn't react whatsoever. Like normal, my stomach gurgled once and took to processing the alcohol. I shrugged and finished the rest of the bottle.

Outside, a slowly gathering patch of gray sky moved in toward my side of the Junction. The grass wasn't quite tall enough to be blown around, but the Devil's Walkingstick branches and creek maples swayed desultorily with the breeze's push and pull. A storm was coming. The rain had allowed a few days' respite, but now it was on the rise again, and I couldn't help but feel uneasy. Weather like this made it easy for people to hide in plain sight.

I popped the cap on another beer and picked broken chips out of a Doritos bag, all while trying not to feel the lengthening investigation pressing down on me.

"I'm not a detective," I said to nobody in particular. "I'm playing pretend, that's all."

Then, just below the whoosh of the wind, I heard a car come to a full stop in the driveway. An engine being cut off. A door being slammed. An imperceptible, imagined set of footsteps in the grass. I closed my eyes, listening, trying to hear those footsteps draw closer. But I couldn't.

The knock at the door was so loud it was startling. I waited. My mind reeled, flipping through faces like they were photos in a dated album. Who could it be? I placed the beer on the counter and knelt down, reaching around and patting the backside of my jeans. Nothing there. My .45 was in the bedroom.

Another series of knocks echoed through the house. This time, though, the guest didn't bother to wait for an answer. I listened to the click of the latch as the door was swung open. Next, two tentative footsteps on the hardwood floor. I wanted that gun right then more than I had ever wanted anything. I held my breath and waited, opening my eyes but also preparing my feet for swift action, if necessary.

The footsteps continued down the hall and were subsequently muted when they disappeared into the bedroom. From my line of sight, getting a bead on the intruder was impossible.

Shit, I thought. The .45 was in the bedroom in plain sight, right on top of the nightstand. How stupid of me.

I heard commotion in the bedroom, of the nightstand drawer being opened and clothes being thrown about, and then nothing. Silence. I waited, moving closer to the edge of the kitchen, so that I could see all the way to the bedroom.

While moving myself into position to rush down the hall, a voice resonated through the house, as reminiscent of my past as the smell of summer or the sight of the baseball fields. "Rolson? You home?"

My heart seemed to turn over in my chest. It took me two tries for my knees to lock so I could stand. Couldn't be.

"Vanessa?" I said.

Seventh Chapter

Vanessa wasn't high, but not much time had passed since she had last used. She had the frail, spent look of someone searching at midnight for something she should be looking for in daylight. The part of her I had fallen in love with had been washed away, and all that remained was a husk of a woman transparently seeking out self-destruction.

I made her a cup of coffee and had one myself while we sat on the couch and made quiet, desperate attempts at conversation, commenting on the house and the weather and how very little Lumber Junction has changed. When every other pleasantry was out of the way, I said, "Your dad has been asking about you."

Her eyes flickered. They weren't so dead, after all. "He's gonna shit when he finds out I'm back." She smiled, but it was a sad affair.

"He's been worried."

She laughed without pleasure and made a ridiculous *pffffing* sound. "Oh, fuck him. He just don't want me out ruining his reputation. He thinks I need to be chained up, 'til I can get my act under control. To him I'm some, some goddamned sideshow freak."

I swallowed. She did *look* quite abnormal. In addition to being heart-achingly gaunt, a few yellowish scabs dotted her face. She could have passed for a zombie.

"You can't go on like this forever, Van," I said.

She glared at me. "I know that."

Like every junkie, she knew exactly what she was doing. She just couldn't help herself. The addiction, the self-destruction, was part of her now.

Feeling the walls go up, I changed the subject. "How long are you in town?"

"I don't know. Couple days, maybe. I need to come down, get ahold of things. I was so scared, Rolson."

Like a man who watches himself slam a hand in his car door, I couldn't help but ask: "Why?"

"You're the only person'll have me," she said, and I didn't have the heart to respond: *Well, how do* you *know I'll have you?*

* * *

Eventually, like most desperate-to-be-validated addicts, she launched into a story about her circumstances, embellished with sometimes ludicrous but for the most part mild exaggerations. It was an effort to elicit sympathy, though she was so drugged out she didn't realize it wouldn't really work on me. I wasn't a mark for her to turn over for some favor.

She had taken up with a former bank manager named Jerry, who started with an all-consuming fondness for cocaine but quickly moved to freebasing meth, accounting for his obvious lack of employment. The real intense drug use started about the same time as Jerry's dad's death. He had pulled a Hemingway. The second wife had found him wearing a single boot, the trigger guard of the shotgun wrapped around one toe.

If Jerry's drug use had been recreational before, it certainly was not now. Coke gave him a clean high, one where he could go out and party all night and then make it to work on time, but the meth treated him

132

like a partner in a dysfunctional relationship. He claimed to have blown through thirty thousand dollars in six months' time, and when the bank finally had enough evidence to fire him, Jerry didn't realize he didn't have so much as a couch to sleep on when he got home. He'd pawned everything but his car, and the car was the next thing to go.

Vanessa didn't seem to mind. The two of them spent all of their time either high or fucking, or both. When the place in the suburbs dried up, they bounced from couch to couch in increasingly desperate situations, circling the drain, heading for that final darkness. Once - and Vanessa could not confirm if it were a hallucination or reality - she thought she had caught him in the bathroom with another man, *inflagrante delicto*.

Jerry's biggest problem, turns out, was not his addiction, but the money he used to fuel it. He owed nearly a hundred large to a group of unforgiving people taking the razor to the underbelly of America, and he could not, even in the best of circumstances, have ever paid them back. They controlled a drug ring focused in inner-city Atlanta, and even in the worst economic times, their business thrived.

One day, Vanessa came home to find the lock jimmied open and Jerry's head all over the kitchen floor. She didn't even bother to call the cops, or to close the door. She just walked away.

"Kind of a sick twist, huh," Vanessa said, finally, humorlessly. And that's about the time she broke down.

"I'm sorry," I told her, but that only made her more hysterical. I suppose she wanted me to chide her, to hate her for telling me about her boyfriend, but I couldn't.

After she stopped crying, she began to nod off. She looked at me, or at least vaguely in my direction, but her eyes were full of a strange kind of distance. So I let her drift off. Probably the first time she had slept in a day or two, maybe more. The house was drafty, and so I covered her with a blanket and left her alone for a while, going out into the backyard, walking along the treeline with my cell phone in my right hand. As much as it weirded me out to have my meth-addicted ex nodding off in my house, I figured it wouldn't hurt anything to let her sleep off her sickness on the couch.

I called Detective Hunter and told him Ronald Bullen's brother had slithered back into town, and he didn't seem impressed. Mostly, he just mmm-hmmmed me, and though I strained to listen in on the background for any sign that he might be writing something down, I didn't hear anything but contempt.

"What I'm learning, Mr. McKane, is that there are a whole lot of snakes in the garden down here, and they're all balled up in a single mass, so I'll have to go on picking through them and avoiding fangs until I find something useful besides venom."

"H.W. has a violent past," I said. "He's dumber'n a box of penny nails, but he's sort of like a Lennie to Ronald's George."

"Have you got anything on him? On Ronald?"

"I think he might be willing to give up information on Brickmeyer, if he gets it. Dude might also think the rich guy is involved. I might not be so crazy, after all."

"But doesn't he also hate you a great deal?"

"Like you said, 'ball of snakes.'"

He said he'd "look into it" and then hung up.

"Hey, no skin off my back," I said to the empty receiver. "Just tryin' to help." Really what I was thinking was, *Just tryin' to get the crosshair off my forehead.*

That evening, I cooked a pot of rice and tomatoes and poured a generous amount of Louisiana hot sauce and pepper in it, stirring the mixture absently until it was done, and then I slurped down a bowl of it right there by the stove. Being incapable of getting out of the kitchen with either food or beer turned out to be a common thread in my life these days.

It was too early to eat supper, but I had nothing else to do at the house but wait for Vanessa to wake up, so I ended up eating two bowls by myself. The refrigerator loomed in the corner of the room, and after a while I did end up grabbing a beer.

Van was still in the process of sleeping off whatever she was on, and she didn't so much as flinch when I kicked back in my recliner and flipped on the television.

There was a small report about Laveau's death on the evening news. Two hapless anchors introduced the story, and the field reporter in the Junction only did a small voiceover with B-roll of the Boogie House before turning over the entire clip to Leland Brickmeyer.

The press conference could have been a parody of small-town politics, or maybe mistaken for a cable access show. Brickmeyer looked comfortable but serious on-screen as he rested his hands on the podium. I watched in rapt disgust. How could they have fucked up *this* badly, to give this grease ball the camera in lieu of the kid's death?

"The purpose of my statement today is to offer condolences to the family of Emmitt Laveau. I've already expressed my feelings in private, but since the victim of this horrific, horrendous act was found on my land, I feel it is my obligation, my duty, to offer any culpability in the matter, if possible."

Brickmeyer clasped his hands together and stared into the camera, eyes twisted into a look of profound consternation. "The building that used to be the Boogie House will be torn down at the first possible convenience, once the investigating officers have collected all the necessary evidence. I cannot erase any of the pain levied on the Laveau family, but I can prevent such a thing from happening on my land in the future."

He paused for a beat. For effect, one might be able to say. All of it, down to the pause, was theater. Generic political theater.

He continued: "Furthermore, my family and I *fully* support the efforts of our local and state law enforcement agencies to bring the murderer to justice. I will cooperate in any way necessary to apprehend the person who committed this callous crime, even if that means using

135

my own, *limited*, political influence. No one deserves to go through what the Laveaus have endured, and I hope, through a combined effort, we can bring this monster to justice. Thank you."

People will buy that hook, line, and sinker, I thought.

Janita Laveau called before the commercial break had even started. "You believe that shit, Rolson McKane?" she asked.

"Not at all."

"The reporters didn't even contact *me* for this godforsaken story. And I haven't heard word one from *anybody* in the Brickmeyer family."

"It's a service to his public image and nothing else," I said. "He probably contacted *them* for the story angle, and since they're local, they just went with it. What the hell do they know?"

We talked for a few minutes more, about what I couldn't later recall, and then said goodbye.

I covered the pot of rice and tomatoes and finished my beer. Something had begun to wiggle in my stomach, and it didn't feel pleasant. The need to lie down was urgent. I slipped past Vanessa, snoring with wild abandon, and shuffled to my bedroom.

The bed was soft and warm and messy, and I fell into it like I had never slept a wink in my life. I didn't even bother to undress. I just fell face-first into my pillow and willed myself to feel better.

I burped, and the taste of my stomach made me nauseous. The room tilted to one side, and I pressed my palms flat against the bed to keep my equilibrium. Normally two or three beers didn't give me the spins. I dragged the small trash I kept under the nightstand next to me, just in case.

Thinking of the drink Uncle K had given me induced another round of convulsions, and I couldn't hold onto my food any longer. Thrusting my head over the side of the bed, I lost the bowl of tomatoes and rice, as well as the beer, in one violent heave. The harsh, acidic taste remained until wakefulness grayed and then disappeared

136

into darkness.

* * *

Sometime later, familiarity washed over me as I realized I was standing, once again, in the Boogie House. Intrigued, I glimpsed the area around me, reached out and fingered the door frame - which was tilted to one side and cold to the touch - and concluded this was no dream. A bit blurry around the edges, maybe, perhaps connected to my temporary sickness. But it was real. I even thought I tasted vomit.

Darkness made it appear as though whole sections of the juke had been erased. I stepped inside and saw the body of Emmitt Laveau silhouetted like a headstone against the far wall.

I went on inside, ignoring my awkward gait and watching the human-shaped patch of darkness in the corner. For some reason, he wasn't acknowledging me. Then, the shadow moved. I blinked, half-expecting it to be a hallucination. Either the shadow of something inanimate was behaving like a person, or a person was rising out of the darkness.

As I approached, the room became awash in a hellishly orange light, casting every inch of my surroundings in a sinister glow. I stumbled. In my stupor, I couldn't focus, save for putting one heavy foot in front of the other, so the room became a soupy mess underfoot.

Momentum dragged me forward. I could tell now that I was dreaming, but it made the physics of my world no more manageable. I overshot my target, as people in dreams often do, so I had to backtrack to meet Emmitt Laveau, who stepped forward, dressed in a suit and brandishing a tattered old acoustic guitar, plucking a boogie-woogie rhythm with his thumb and two first fingers. He was smiling, but the way it looked wasn't right. There was something sinister in the way his lips had peeled away, revealing broken, rotting teeth.

137

In that moment, I saw the reflection of his uncle in him. They had identical smiles, and even the facade of death couldn't mask their facial similarities. In fingerpicking that jumping, bouncy, up-and-down riff, he had that look, that certain slyness, and it shone through with stark clarity.

I didn't recognize the song, but Emmitt was looking at me like I should have known it, and the longer he played it, the more it seemed as though I did know it. It built to a blurry mess of fingers and notes, and just when I thought I had the name of the song, when it was on the tip of my tongue, he slowed to a stop.

Finishing up the last bar, he placed the guitar at his side and leaned on it. The final notes echoed solemnly through the Boogie House, but the illumination surrounding everything remained. It flickered like a dying flame and deepened to an angry orange, almost red, as Emmitt opened his mouth. His face was pallid and sunken and somewhat distorted, but yet he smiled. *"I lost some weight,"* he said. *"Embalmed me. Cut me up. Couldn't find nothing but the fact that I was dead."*

I looked down, regarded his stomach. The gassy spare tire had disappeared, cutting a more distinctly human figure, less ghastly and still horrifying all the same. The suit didn't help his appearance, either, because it hung loosely over his newly gaunt frame. Similarly, his face revealed some rot, but make-up concealed the gory bits, mostly. "I see," I said, struggling to say anything at all. The dream world was taking some getting used to.

His smile became a frown, and the shape and texture of his face shriveled into something grotesque. *"The marvel of modern make-up. Still gonna be a closed casket deal, though, I'm afraid. They couldn't quite put me back together again."*

Laveau leaned back against empty air, bringing the guitar up to a playing position and flicking the strings in a slow, dinky drone, a *bow-den-dow-den-dow-down* sort of fashion. It was the sound of a hundred years of accumulated blues, and in that moment each note coursed through me like electricity.

"*I can't speak his name, you know. One of the curses of my situation,*" he said, shaking his head somberly.

"Your killer? The name of your killer?" I asked, stupidly. He nodded, humming a troubling, dissonant melody. I stood there, dumbly enraptured, even if the notes seemed to be emanating, not from the sound hole in the guitar itself, but from my head. "Why not?"

"*Would you be able to prove the truth in court anyway? Without evidence, would this stand? 'Hey, man, I know y'all didn't find any fingerprints or physical evidence down there at the Boogie Place - whatever - but I got this cat coming to visit me in my sleep. That enough to convict somebody on?' See what I mean?*"

"Who said it would go that far?"

"*Your cloak is made of ink and not of blood. You'll stick to the shadows until this plays out, and you'll not force your breath if you don't have to.*"

"I don't know what that means," I said.

"*I wish we could go on a trip,*" he said. "*Right on down the road.*"

"To the Brickmeyer house?"

"*Maybe. Yeah. Shit, maybe not. Every time I see you, there's a goddamn chunk missing from my brain. I figure that's a literal and a figurative thing, too. Somebody did this to me, and hell, even I'm forgetting who's to blame.*"

"How come it's me, Emmitt? It can't just be that I plowed into your mom's car, can it? I'm at a goddamn loss as to what I'm supposed to be learning from you."

Emmitt smirked and returned to his guitar playing. The tempo sped up, and his fingers went from plucking the strings to strumming them, his hand a blur against the guitar's body. He sang a blues song I had heard a hundred times before and yet not a single time, and I was entranced by it.

In the orange-ish glow, his performance took on an intense, sinister quality. He bobbed his head and strummed the guitar, and every aspect was unnatural. No one could move that quickly, could produce so many melodies on a single guitar. Similarly, his voice had become orchestral, the sound of a dozen men and women singing simultaneously, a choir of such melancholic scope that I struggled to listen to it. And yet, it was hauntingly beautiful.

When he finished, he said, "*Some blues songs are full of love, even if they appear to be about heartache.*"

"Are you in love?"

He smiled. "*I got to be on down the road now. Not in the direction I s'pose you'd like me to go, but I can go. I gotta go. There's an audience waiting for me, and I am the main attraction.*"

Emmitt lowered the guitar and turned away, holding his instrument the way a child might carry an unwanted doll. He reached the wall on the opposite side of the building and disappeared on impact.

Lights flickered on, and the dilapidated jukebox in the corner fired to life, its mechanical arm exchanging one vinyl record for another. The song that erupted either from the speakers or inside my head was "Death Letter Blues."

* * *

I awoke, and though the Boogie House faded, the orange glow did not. I stared at it while my mind caught up with reality. The dreams of the Boogie House were becoming more real with each iteration, and the equilibrium of the real world was being turned upside down, so that it made as little sense as the dream world.

It took a minute to realize that the light in my room was not just the overlap between my waking and dreaming lives. It was coming from outside, and it turned out to be brake lights from a vehicle parked in my yard.

I leaped out of bed, ignoring my sickness, and grabbed the .45 from the nightstand. I stumbled down the hallway, trying to keep my balance, and through the walls I heard the vehicle pulling away. The front door was open, and Vanessa was leaning against the frame, staring out through the half-open screen door. The vehicle, so far as I could tell, was completely out of sight.

"Who was that?" I asked.

Startled, Vanessa turned back toward me. She looked haggard and sleepy. "Don't know," she said.

I stared at her.

"I don't," she said. "I have no idea. I heard a muffler, and then I got up to see who it was. When I opened the door, whoever it was peeled out. I think I startled them."

"What kind of vehicle was it?"

"I'm not sure. Truck, maybe. I just saw the taillights."

"You didn't see if it was a truck or not?"

"It could have been. It was loud. I don't know, Rolson. I'm coming down, and I can't trust anything around me."

"Okay," I said, though I wasn't satisfied.

I called the station and waited for somebody to pick up. Once I got an answer, I said, "This is Rolson McKane. Somebody's trying to intimidate me, and I'd like for an officer to drive out here to check things out."

"Who?" said the voice on the other line. I didn't quite recognize it.

"Don't know. But they trespassed on my land. Drove almost right up to my bedroom window and then drove off."

"What do you want us to do?"

"Make a note of it. Come out here. I'm sure the vehicle left tire tracks in the yard. Perhaps those could be analyzed or something, to tie them to the person who killed Emmitt Laveau."

The smoky voice on the other end of the line sighed. "We'll get somebody out there."

"Thanks," I said, my teeth clenched, and hung up. I went outside and waited for an hour for someone to show up, trying to ignore what I thought was a flicker of light in the woods.

When I was convinced that I'd still be waiting in the morning, I

141

went in the bedroom and did not sleep for the rest of the night.

Eighth Chapter

The next morning, the shower head spurting to life dragged me from sleep. I was exhausted, so rather than get out of bed, I listened to the spatter of water in the next room and stared contemplatively at the stain on the ceiling.

My mind wandered into the shower with Vanessa, if only briefly, compelled by the cloyingly fragrant shower gel, and I attempted to connect the sound of the water with Vanessa's own movements, thinking of what she must look like right now.

I had been alone for too long.

Once I snapped out of it, a sneaking sense of shame spread through me. Vanessa was sick, depressed, and no longer my consideration, sexually speaking. Still, an empty house decays quickly, more than on a simple, literal level.

Once the water stopped hissing, I shambled stiff-legged into the kitchen and started a pot of coffee, dumping spoonfuls of cheap, bitter grounds in the filter and pouring water in the boiler before flipping the switch. It burbled pleasantly while I watched.

I heard shuffling feet behind me and turned to see Vanessa standing in the kitchen's entrance, drying her hair with a towel and wearing some old clothes I had kept after the divorce.

"Showered," she said. Her lips were bloodless and tight. She looked like a broken porcelain doll. "Hope I'm not imposing."

"There's enough coffee here for you, too. You still like it black?"

"Thanks," she said.

She poured herself a cup and sat in one of the chairs by the kitchen table, the ceramic mug resting on her knees. I leaned against the door frame and anticipated something. An apology, a note of gratitude, maybe some sort of clear-headed explanation of how she'd acted before. But she gave me nothing. We drank in silence, her looking blankly across the kitchen to the living room, and me staring down at her. It was reminiscent of the end of our relationship, before she slipped out under cover of night with a suitcase and her car keys.

"I know I look like hell," she said. "God, when I peeked in the mirror this mornin', I thought it was somebody else's face in there, no shit. For a minute, I was worried a curse had been put on me."

My stomach gurgled. I still felt the unpleasantness of whatever had come over me the night before. "You look fine," I said. She did look slightly better, but she was a far sight from the person she had been.

"No I don't, Rolson." She checked her face in a nearby hanging mirror. "My face is all splotchy, and I've got pimples for the first time in I can't remember how long, and I'm pale. Oh my *God*, am I pale. I look like a freaking haint."

"Taking care of yourself will help heal all of that. Coming back here, getting away from all that...stuff, is the first step in getting better."

She rolled her eyes. "Let's hope so. I can't go out in public like this."

"How did you handle it before?"

"I stayed inside most of the time. Had no reason to go out."

I did a half-groan, half-grunt, and, changing the subject, said, "There's somewhere I got to be today. I reckon you can stay here, long as you don't go off and pawn everything I own."

She took a sip of coffee. "I ain't going to do that, Rolson. Yesterday. Well. I mean, yesterday I wasn't in my head. Yeah, I was looking through your stuff, but that was a different story. I was coming down. It's like having ants in your bloodstream. Nothing like being drunk and needing whiskey. I was absolutely dying for a fix."

"That being said, this isn't your house anymore. You forfeited that when you let that shit claw its way into your life and drag you out of town."

"I just need somewhere to mellow out for the time being. I'm tiptoeing on the ledge, and I feel like I have no choice but to jump off. Oh, Jesus."

She began to break down, but when I didn't comfort her, she swallowed the tears and ran her fingers through her hair gently, the way she used to. Vanessa had good hands, expressive, smooth, dainty hands, and she normally talked with them, using big gestures and movements to convey her ideas. But that aspect of her was gone, at least for now. She kept her hands close, like she was guarding something.

I watched her recompose herself, and I said, "If anybody comes knocking at the door, you make yourself as invisible as possible. There's a bad element sneaking around the property, and they might want to make trouble. If they start to try and get in, then call me on my cell."

She smiled, confused, but I shook my head. "It's not a joke. These people mean business, no fucking around. You get any sort of strange vibe, don't hesitate to call."

"Where are you going?"

I finished the bitterest part of my coffee and placed the mug on the kitchen counter. "A funeral."

* * *

The parking lot out behind the Tan-Shoat Funeral Home was packed with washed and waxed vehicles. People had begun to fight

145

back against the tyranny of the pollen. During the spring months, Georgia is worse than Egypt during the plagues. I parked in the farthest corner of the lot and sat drumming the steering wheel until the accumulation of heat was too much for me to bear.

The funeral home was small and quaint and neat, the parking lot freshly paved and awnings recently painted. The brick building housed one of the most successful and long-standing businesses in the county. Dealing in death is a lucrative profession, and the Tan-Shoats (they riot if you do not include both names) demonstrated an uncanny proficiency at it.

Walter Tan-Shoat himself was a younger man, too young to be handling death, but he had taken over for his father and grandfather, both killed in a fire at the family cabin. He was perpetually outfitted in a black suit and was so pale his skin practically glowed white.

Perhaps because of his youth, people didn't seem to get along with him quite the way they did with his forebears. Customers got the impression he didn't much care for people, dead or alive, so ultimately it was the name that pushed the business along. (His father and grandfather, it was secretly known, had belonged to the Klan, burning crosses in people's yards and getting blacks convicted of crimes they would not, let alone could not, have committed.)

The car door creaked open, and I got out and put on a pair of old aviators, watching grieving people exit their vehicles and move with purpose toward the funeral home.

My back itched. Goddamned suit. I only have one; it is neither comfortable nor black. It is a deep navy, too small, and smells slightly off, but it is appropriate enough for these occasions.

In fact, though, I felt underdressed. Some funeral-goers wore black, of course, while others sauntered down the sidewalk in bright yellow and green and pink dresses. Women accessorized with floppy black hats and decadent three-inch heels. Men were decked out in equally impressive suits, elaborately and fastidiously coordinated with shoes and socks and pocket squares.

I went into the cool main funeral parlor and signed the guest book before finding a seat with some non-family attendees, who took this event as a sign to chitchat about everyone in the building. The woman at my right was a shriveled old prune whose name I thought was Lucretia Davenport, and to her right was Betty Raines. The pair of them couldn't have been worse gossips, and so I spent the majority of the service alternating between ignoring them and cringing when I could not.

A hush fell over the room, and I turned in my seat to see Janita Laveau enter through the main doors, flanked by her uncle, who winked and nodded at me. Everyone in the place stood reverently as she was escorted down the main aisle.

Grief hung palpably in the air wherever she was. Janita pushed forward with dignity. She was not crying, though it was not for lack of trying. When she turned to acknowledge others in the crowd, some of *them* broke down, as if Janita was performing a reverse miracle, cursing people with grief rather than taking it away, even as she herself maintained a semblance of composure.

I leaned sideways and studied the modest casket, whose lid was shut and covered in various floral arrangements. Mrs. Laveau collapsed into a seat on the front pew, her head bent forward. Uncle K placed one arm on her shoulders and leaned in, as if to tell her something. When he was finished, she nodded and raised her head, not upward toward the heavens but straight ahead, a heartbreakingly solitary gaze.

My attention was then drawn to the casket. A basic and yet elegant brown box of a thing, it shined under the glare of the parlor's house lights, and throughout the various prayers, my eyes flicked in its direction. I had become acutely aware of the fact that a version of that body visited me in my dreams, and it cast the whole event in another light.

Halfway through the service, with Preacher Weatherhead going on and on about joy, sorrow, and its opposites, I submitted to an urge to look behind me.

Leland Brickmeyer, henchman in tow, stood against the parlor's back wall, his hands pressed together below his chin in what seemed to be mock prayer. His eyes caught mine, and he betrayed himself with the slightest smile. Ever the attention-seeking politician.

Up front, Weatherhead ended his portion of the service. Reverend Gladys Kicklighter hobbled to the podium and patted his brow with a white lace handkerchief. As if in response, the parlor air grew hotter. The suit was suffocating me. I broke out in beer sweats, and people all around me fanned themselves with the hymnals in the pews ahead of them.

I heard a minute guitar melody emerge from the front of the room, tinny as the sound of a blues-themed music box. It was the sort of scratchy tune only a slide guitarist can muster, and I glanced around. People download the strangest ringtones, I thought. I expected an embarrassed mourner to quietly end the disruption. I glanced from the pews to the podium. Reverend Kicklighter didn't seem to notice it, even though the sound continued. Did he not want to ruin the funeral by acknowledging it? Kicklighter, it should be noted, wasn't known for his even temper. However, the song kept on ringing out in the small room, tinkling along just under Kicklighter's labored breathing.

"You hear that?" I whispered, asking one of the old ladies to my right.

She grimaced. "Shhh, ain't nobody talking," she said. Her eyes flicked once at me, but she was otherwise ignoring me, perhaps understandably.

"Oh, right," I replied, straightening up like I realized how silly I was being. Strangely, the sound had temporarily disappeared, but for how long I couldn't say.

The reverend paused for a moment, his eyes resting contemptuously on Brickmeyer, but Kicklighter was smart and capable for a religious man, so he didn't allow his gaze to linger. He fixed his attention on his Bible and searched for relevant passages of scripture.

"Ladies and gentleman," he said, "it is never easy to visit this place. Generations of grief rest uncomfortably in the walls, and I suspect we will only add to the collective anguish people have experienced here. Unintentionally, of course. We should not forget that it is the function of the living to grieve for the dead, to selfishly wish them back with us, and we cannot be blamed for it. We, I'm afraid, are quite human, and humans are fearful of what they don't understand. And *Lord*, oh Mighty God, we do not understand death. But we abide it, like the flock of sheep that abide the fox stealing away with one of its own every so often. It's the way of the world, and we are tied helplessly to it. All we can do is hope to someday be freed, to hope there is no fox lying in wait for us."

A round of thoughtlessly emphatic nods and *mmm-hmm*s circled the crowd. Kicklighter took this moment to pause and daub his forehead.

I leaned forward, listening. I thought I heard a whispery voice just beneath the hum of the PA system. It easily could have been someone's quiet sobs, but it wasn't someone crying. I was certain of that. It was a voice, accompanied by guitar.

Baby I can't sleep
I tell you why for
There's a somebody
Knockin' at my back door

Over and over. The same verse, repeated until I couldn't stand it. I tried to focus on the reverend, but it was like having a conversation in a crowded room. The song drowned it out.

The murder might get solved, I thought. *It might even be the local PD to do it. But unless someone else is going through the same thing, a personal blues show in his head, I will continue to think I'm going insane.*

It was then that Kweku Laveau turned and looked at me. It was gradual but purposeful. He nodded once, as though he could hear my thoughts.

Laveau turned back to the service, and the reverend continued: "As prepared as we are to come and grieve an elderly relative, or friend, today we are not. It is unexpected why we're gathered here this morning, and many of you may be in shock. Many of you may be defiant. Many of you may be questioning why in the world God has chosen to bring young Brother Laveau home."

He paused, a calculated though effective move.

Baby I can't sleep / I'll tell you why for

He said, "And that is all right. One day, and God be blessed, let it be soon, we will *all* be shocked when we hear that eternal trumpet sounded, and we will get up and walk into that promised land, and we will be reunited even with those we lost too soon, like young Brother Laveau here. Second Peter says that no prophecy was ever produced by the will of man, but ONLY BY THE WILL OF GOD."

There's somebody / Knockin' at my back door-

And so it went. People cried. Some didn't. Others basked in the benevolence of the one and only Lord Jesus Christ, while a few seemed to be on hiatus from faith. I, myself, had taken up the call of the blues singer. My savior was a sacrificed man. I had been baptized in unsettling paranoia, and unlike the God of my youth, this one at least visited me in my dreams.

I waited for the service to end before confronting Brickmeyer, slipping out into the parking lot just after the casket was loaded into the hearse. Six men I barely recognized were pallbearers, and each eyed me conspiratorially as I dodged past them. I turned as the procession of men passed by and saw no one standing at the rear of the building.

I managed to catch up with Brickmeyer and his henchman before they reached their car. "Leland," I said, as evenly as humanly possible, "Hey, wait up for a second."

They stopped, perhaps expectantly, and turned to face me.

Brickmeyer's suit would have made a televangelist blush, and his hair was held in place by a gallon of gel. He kneaded his hands and then held one out for me to shake. I demurred. The smugness of his expression was replaced by impatience. "How is it," Brickmeyer said, "That someone who seems to turn up everywhere I do can somehow evade being served with a restraining order?"

"You two are the last people the Laveaus want to see. This funeral is about them, not you. And if I'm being honest, I think your political aspirations have eroded your sense of shame."

The big man at his side stepped forward, but Brickmeyer held him back with one gentle hand. I stared up into the giant's face until he backed down.

"Wait a minute there, hoss. I have done nothing but defend the Laveau family. I'm doing everything I can to help."

"That doesn't change the fact that they think you're responsible for their son's death. Where could they be getting that from?"

His smile became sanguine. "When you're falling out of a tree, you grab for the biggest branch on the way down," he said. "These people, they got nobody else to grab at, so they're reaching for me, since I'm just sticking out there. That boy was found on my land, and some people would think it curious if I didn't come and see the family on the day of the funeral. I can't have it both ways."

"You don't honestly expect me to believe that, do you? A press conference and some cooperation with the police won't vindicate you, if you're guilty."

Brickmeyer licked his lips. The behemoth at his side shifted his weight. "Even if I did have something to do with this nonsense, do you think I'd admit anything to *you*? You, of all people, should be commiserating with me. The same person that's after you is after me, trying to get the murder pinned on me."

I turned to the big man. "Have you been to the Boogie House?"

"The fuck kind of question is that? Course I haven't."

151

"Not even once? Not even in the middle of the night, for whatever business?"

His eyes flickered, though I couldn't tell if it was confusion or hatred in them. He took a step forward, and I planted my weight on my back foot, ready to throw a punch.

Brickmeyer said, "Bodean, don't do anything rash here, now."

I said, "You don't have enough charm to bullshit your way out of this. That fucking smug expression will only get you so far, and then people will demand real answers."

"I don't have anything to hide. Ask the detectives. Ask the police chief. Oh, wait. They won't talk to you, will they?"

"No, but Ronald Bullen seems to want you dragged through town by your balls."

I saw a moment's hesitation, of humanity, but then the act returned. "Good cop. What would he want to question me for?"

"Let me tell you something. You've got the whole town clinging to your wallet, but I'm not nearly as gullible. I'm not going to give up digging into this until I hit something solid."

Brickmeyer looked over my shoulder at an elderly couple on the opposite side of the street. "The people in this town are like saplings in serious need of cultivation. Of guiding care. It just takes the right hand. Once they're ready, they can be harvested for what makes them valuable."

Whatever he was doing was working. He was getting under my skin. "How do you know what's valuable about anything in this town?"

"It isn't their inherent value I'm interested in. With a little watering, a little care, a few dollars thrown here and there, I can cultivate the people of Lumber Junction sometime in the future."

I could hear the blood thumping in my ears. Brickmeyer tilted his head back just far enough to entice me to crush his Adam's apple with my fist. I might have, if a crowd of people leaving the funeral hadn't rounded the corner at that moment.

Instead, I leaned in and said, "Your luck's about to change. You might seem untouchable to the people in this town, but once you're laid bare, they'll see you for what you really are, and they'll pity you."

This time, I offered my hand for shaking, and Brickmeyer, perhaps thinking it an opportunity to humiliate me, took it. I squeezed, feeling the satisfying crunch of bones. As much as it stung my pride to shake the man's hand, it felt right to see that he could be hurt.

He glowered at me. "I ought to have you run out of this town, you know. The fucking termites that live here have feasted on this like it's some goddamn conspiracy, and if it ruins my chances for a Senate bid, you can bet your sorry ass there will be consequences."

Brickmeyer yanked his hand free and made his way across the road to where he was parked. I sat in the car and waited for them to drive out of sight before cranking the old car and lining up for the procession to the graveyard.

* * *

At the graveside service, I stood patiently in the background, away from the bystanders. I felt like an interloper, but still I stayed through the prayers and the traditional hymns and the lowering of the coffin. Leadbelly's "Where Did You Sleep Last Night" was stuck in my head, and I spent the whole time trying to pick it out, like a piece of meat lodged in my teeth.

It didn't work, so I hummed the melody over and over, but at least it drowned out the guitar lick emanating from the coffin.

My expectation for something supernatural was extremely high. I spent much of the service pressing my toes against the soles of my shoes in anticipation, eyeing family members and gravestones alike. I kept my ears pricked for the song's return, and I watched intently for a figure to appear in Laveau's grave, perhaps Laveau himself.

Expectations are poor indicators of reality. Nothing happened, save for one out-of-place detail. In the distance, someone hunched over a grave in the run-down section of the cemetery, appearing to pay respects but at the same time stealing glances over his shoulder. He wore a fashionable black coat and gray slacks and peculiar hat.

I moved in toward a small group of mourners to blend in a little better, but I don't think that helped. The jacketed figure crept away from a faded, tilting stone and headed for the rows of parked cars.

Disrupting the service for a chase along the grave-strewn lot was not an option. I watched the figure circle the funeral party, following his progression through the graveyard, until at last the funeral was completely over. He managed to keep his face hidden from me. Something about his gait was familiar, but I couldn't place it.

I took up a brisk walk in that very same direction, watching until the figure disappeared among the cars. Then I launched into an uneven jog, listening for the sound of an engine. A few people turned and stared, but by that point everything had been set into action, so I couldn't be bothered with funerary etiquette.

A vehicle peeked out from the others, edging along a tight row of cars, and I peered in through the windshield. The driver was turned the other way, one arm draped over the passenger headrest, and he was looking behind him. It wasn't until he'd thrown the shifter into drive that I saw his face. He did not try to hide, but a look of surprised horror seemed to grip him when he saw me, and he spun the wheel around and gouged the engine, causing dirt and grass to kick up and the rear end to fishtail. His vehicle nearly sideswiped a poorly-parked Chrysler in the process.

At the last possible moment, I managed to put myself between the driver's car and the road, and he slammed on the brakes. The car stopped mere inches from me. When he rolled down the window, I said, "What are you doing here, Jeffrey?"

Brickmeyer's son shook his head as he peered over the steering wheel. "No entry fee for a funeral."

Some older ladies walked by cautiously, their mouths agape. "Oddly enough, I just saw your father at the funeral home. Brickmeyers seem to have a real affinity for a young man they claim to have never met."

"My father's an asshole," he said. "I wanted to come and patch things over, make amends. For the press conference, or whatever that was."

"Is that what you were doing?"

"I chickened out. Couldn't stand looking at these people. They think my father had him butchered. I thought of it on the way out here. I'd gotten out of the car by the time I decided to head back, and by then it was too late."

"So you decided to take a stroll through the mossy section of the cemetery."

His eyes flicked from me to the old ladies and back again. "It was all I could think to do. At least I tried."

"I'm sure the Laveau family would be comforted by that."

"I want the Laveaus to know that we had nothing to do with it. Cut me some slack."

I measured his glance, and there was some amount of sincerity to it, so I backed off. He was trapped by the old man. I understood why he resisted, but if a man's in a burning building, does he have to have options about what to do next?

I said, "Cut yourself some slack. Get rid of your dad. He's a cancer on your life."

"He just doesn't know how to handle this kind of situation. He's not a bad guy."

"Take my words to heart, Jeffrey. Even though he's your father, the man would throw you to the wolves to get another foot's head start into the wild."

He was no longer paying attention to me, though. Some family members had drawn close to the two of us, and I turned to match

155

Jeff's gaze, only to see Kweku Laveau standing under a mossy oak tree.

Unlike normal, he wasn't smiling. His eyes could have bent steel. There was something in his hand, and he was rubbing it between his thumb and forefinger, whispering some words to himself as he did so. I thought I could see something rising from it, but that could have been part of the mass delusion I'd been suffering from lately.

I was about to say something to Jeffrey, something else about coming clean, feeling this might be the right moment, but - perhaps spooked by the old man - he pulled away, slowly at first but then picking up speed when he hit the pavement.

The car sounded like a wounded giant as it disappeared into the wooded two-lane highway. I turned back to the tree, meaning to go and speak to K about the funeral, but he was gone. All I saw was a stray dog padding off in the distance, between two rows of old bent headstones.

* * *

I left the funeral without talking to Janita, and I drove back toward town. I should have been thinking about what Jeffrey Brickmeyer was really up to, but my mind kept drifting to Vanessa. Made me miss the old her. You can't make people be who they were, because change is a constant in people's lives, but I didn't quite trust the new version. Her twenty-two year old self would have been able to parse this situation so I could see it clearly, but she seemed like she was looking through clouds herself these days, so I didn't think she would be much help.

The air in the car was on the fritz, so I seemed to bake from the inside out, and even though I had tossed my jacket and button-down shirt into the passenger seat, my white undershirt was soaked through.

Deuce called and had me meet him at his office, and then we hopped in his car for a ride out to the country. He kept a quiet demeanor, as usual, so I talked about my own problems and eyed the interior of his car. It was mostly pristine, save for two slips of paper that appeared to be IOUs of some sort. Deuce would never cop to it, but he was going through some existential crisis of his own.

We ventured out past my house and turned down a dirt road beset on all sides by junk. Used tires stacked into ominous pieces of abstract art. Rusted cars with bags of garbage spilling out onto the ground. Dozens of broken toys flipped over and faded by the sun. Signs full of buckshot reading, "No Trespassing." As if the buckshot didn't say it clearly enough.

"Almost there," Deuce said.

"And what exactly are we doing?"

"Got to pick up one of the Castellaws and make sure he gets to his court date. Minor charge of possession of crystal meth, but you know how it is with them. Be ready for anything."

Fringe rednecks, Castellaws were the kind of stereotypes you read about on the internet. Moonshine-drinking hillbillies born of incest who had moved from Appalachia at the turn of the twentieth century. Prone to suicide and abuse of all sorts, they rarely went into town. All but one or two of them lived within a hundred yards of one another, and their spats often involved shotguns.

Deuce brought me up to speed on the Laveau case as we headed toward the Castellaw compound. "Department's dragging its feet," he said, "but it could also be they don't know how to deal with this case. Vested interests and all that."

"Does that mean somebody in the department's changing the rules?" I asked.

"I don't mean to be a prick," he said, "but have there ever been rules?"

"I guess not."

"This ain't New York. The Powers That Be don't have a truce with the police force. A hit goes down in a big city, and suddenly gangsters and wannabe mafia members start turning up dead or in jail. We don't have that here."

"Because we don't have the mafia here, Deuce."

"Don't matter, don't matter. You, for example. People got you pegged for town-drunk-in-waiting. Somebody could shut your file cabinet for you and make it look like it was the booze that had you march right over the cliff. Maybe spread some empty bottles of Beam around your corpse."

"Murder-for-hire is not something that happens all too often down here. People just out and shoot somebody, if they don't like 'em."

"Doesn't take much to sink the boat. Shark down in New Orleans got his hooks in a partner of mine - real nice guy and all - and bled him for six figures. When my buddy couldn't pay up any more, he got put on notice. He thought he could ride it out, being a high profile wide receiver and all. Month later a 'carjacker' put four in his brain pan."

"I think I know who you're talking about."

We hit a rough patch of dirt. "They had to use a mini-vac to get all of him off the sidewalk. Real fucked-up situation. He coasted on the delusion until it dissolved right in front of him."

"Sounds like it."

"It's easy to exploit a man's weakness, twist it to make something intentional appear accidental. Anybody under the sun knew homeboy was fond of expensive cars, so of course he got jacked driving his Escalade. Made it easier to believe it could actually go down that way."

"And you know it went down another way?"

"Man, the shit I could reveal to you, partner, would make you lock up shop forever. Problem is, I should know better than to convince you. You've got a bug in your ass about the Laveau case, and building it up is only going to make you want it even more."

"Then why are you telling me all this?"

"I don't know, brother." He paused, blew out a dissatisfied breath. "I reckon I just want you to be safe, that's all. You got a good heart."

"Thanks."

"The problem is your head is usually jammed so far up your ass you can't listen to it beating to know better."

"But you said yourself the LJPD was tripping over its own shoelaces."

"Rumors in this town float like turds in lemonade, but I ain't heard the slightest peep about a dirty cop. Brickmeyer treats that place like a preacher's daughter who gets naked after a couple beers, so it could be anybody."

"Bullen."

"He's got a poker face like a Halloween mask, Rol. It don't ever change. He was blessed at birth with the ability to look unhappy about everything. I wouldn't take that too far."

"But he has access. He's been on the force long enough that people don't even think twice about him. And that's the big thing. He could be the inside guy for Brickmeyer."

Deuce laughed out loud. "Impossible."

"How's that?"

"The happy juice is pickling your brain, old friend," Deuce said. "Bullen can't stand Leland Brickmeyer. Can't stand the whole Brickmeyer clan."

It was my turn to sigh. "Yeah."

"Leland's daddy took what little land the Bullens owned a few decades ago."

I stared out of the window and tried to come up with an alternate explanation. Deuce kept on talking while I contemplated.

"I did a bond for a dude a couple years back who told me everything. Said Leland's pops, William - they also called him Big Bill, on account of his fat ass - had a real hard-on for the Bullen land. It wasn't much, but it's practically overflowing with trees. Good ones."

"Oh yeah, it's over by the old abandoned intersection, where they were thinking about building a new school way back when."

"Right. The haunted one. That place used to be owned by the

159

Bullens. Their daddy whore-hopped and gambled around town, couldn't hold a job, even when his wife was still alive. When it got to be too bad for a peckerwood like him, and he couldn't siphon off another dollar for himself or his family, Big Bill promised in secret to give him a loan and use the land as collateral. That's what I was told happened in private, but what happened in public was that Brickmeyer said he bought the land fair and square. Since Bill had some pull around town and Josiah Bullen wasn't nothing but a drunk, the Brickmeyers ended up with the land."

"I just figured Ron was plainly spiteful. I didn't know he actually had a reason."

"To complicate things, word is that town officials worked in collusion to back up the Brickmeyers. After all, they had their fingers in each other's pies."

"So this town was basically carved up by a small group of people and has been kept that way ever since."

"You got it. Local politics at their finest. Bunch of damned shady people in Lumber Junction, but truth be told, the Bullens ain't any better."

"You think they're involved in the murder?"

He seemed to contemplate this for a time. "Hard to say. But they got something the other, more respectable folks don't have."

"What's that?"

"A grudge. Combine that with the fact that Ronald and his brother are sick little puppies, and then you've got no way of predicting what they're capable of."

"But you can't decide if they're involved or not. Seems like a battle between the two of them. The only unknown is how or why the Laveau kid got sucked in the middle of it all."

"Never can tell. There are problems between families that go back a hundred years. You can go and ask your old father-in-law all about this town. His people go way back here, too. Not quite like the

Brickmeyers or the Stokers, but they have a history. Pop in on old Al sometime and see if you can't wriggle out his family's involvement in all this."

Deuce chuckled. I said, "Well, I'm glad you think it's funny, because I surely damned don't."

"The problem is that the system ain't broke for those who ain't broke. Unless you've got some trick up your sleeve that I don't know about it, the money's always going to win. It's just the way things go down here. Same as everywhere else, I reckon."

"It doesn't have to be that way."

Duece considered it. He said, "And if this was your problem, then you would have a clear moral obligation to fight it. But you are choosing to be a part of this, fella."

"It's a kind of injustice. If I don't fight it, on some level, I feel like I'm siding with whoever did it."

"You need to be asking yourself, 'To what extent should I be involved?' It ain't all that clear. Just because you want to help doesn't necessarily mean you have a right to."

"You're starting to sound like D.L."

"No, I'm not," he continued. "D.L. represents *the law*. He's telling you what you ought to do legally. He's acting on behalf of your best legal interests. And of the law's interests as well."

"And what do you represent?"

"I'm helping you decide where you practically fit in, and even though you don't listen to me, I got to keep chipping away at you."

"I'm just trying to make things right."

"No, you're not. There's something running just underneath it, something you're not telling anybody. And it's making you irrational. I don't want you getting yourself killed because some decayed thing is wriggling around in your brain."

"Yeah. Well."

We crossed through an open gate and rounded the corner to find a ragged set of trailers put up on cinder blocks. In the front yard, a skinny, unwashed kid in overalls had something dangling from one hand. On getting out of the car, I saw it was a snake.

"What the world you doing playing with a snake," Deuce said to the boy.

The kid, startled, waited for a moment and then held it up and shook it. "It's dead," he said, and smiled. His teeth were the color of rich caramel. He wasn't older than four or five.

"Where's your daddy?" Deuce asked. "He inside?"

The boy nodded. "Be careful. He's on them drugs, and he's cleaning his gun. I heard it go off a while back. He might turn it on you the way he did mama."

Deuce glanced back at me and then turned back to the boy. "We're going to go inside, maybe talk some sense into him. If we can't, you don't go in until he's sobered up some, okay?"

"All righty," the boy said, and he turned and went running off down the hill, holding the dead snake above his head like some kind of monstrous streamer.

"You carrying?"

"Nope," I said. "I talked to you right after I left the funeral."

"You want to wait out here?"

I shrugged. "Whatever you want."

Deuce stared at the house for a minute, then said, "Follow in behind me. I might need your help. Marcus Castellaw's a big 'un. And if he's cleaning his gun, it's the first time he's cleaned anything in his life. I don't want him turning that damn rifle or whatever on me."

We took a few steps toward the house, and Deuce added, "He's unemotional, as well. Real stoic. You won't know he's going to strike until he actually does it."

The clay yard was decorated with broken secondhand things, lawn mowers and toys and chairs. Plastic Coke bottles and candy wrappers littered the ground. I wondered if these people had ever owned anything brand new in their lives.

The irony was that these people used to live off the land by hunting and fishing. Being dragged into modern life had reduced them to unwashed vagabonds. They had lost sight of even the few things they did right and did well, even if most of it was wrong.

At the top of the broken cinder block steps, a purely rotten smell wafted through the open door. It reeked of spoiled food and stale body odor. Something just underneath that smelled raw and meaty, like blood but more metallic.

Not again, I thought.

"Jesus God," Deuce said, pulling the neck of his shirt above his nose.

The single-wide's interior was as junk-filled as the yard. I stepped in cautiously behind Deuce and covered my mouth and nose with my tie. How anyone could survive in this was beyond me.

There was a small bedroom at the end of the hallway to our left, and part of Marcus Castellaw was visible, laid up in the bed. Deuce raised his pistol and went down the hall in a slow and measured way.

"Mister Castellaw, we're coming back there. If you're holding a firearm, I'd like for you to drop it right now."

There was no answer. It scared me shitless in a way that was becoming customary, of late. I waited for a response in the form of a pistol shot.

Deuce basically blocked the entire hall and had to turn sideways to get through the doorway. Nevertheless, a sound I will never forget emerged from the bedroom. It was a watery, bubbly, dejected gurgle, something out of a Stephen King short story. "Help me," he said.

A moment passed where nothing happened, and then Deuce turned to me, his eyes more panicked than I had ever seen them. He dropped the gun to his side, and he said, with surprisingly calm, "Call 911."

I backed away, working entirely on instinct, and hurried outside. I barely had a signal but managed to get through to a tinny-sounding man on the other line. I was only able to describe our position as being "out where the Castellaws live," and he seemed to understand that, so I finished the conversation and walked back inside on gelatinous legs.

Deuce met me in the living room area. "He's hallucinating," he said. "Says he can see the line between life and death and is thinking about taking a step in one direction. There's probably enough meth in him to kill two horses."

"What happened?"

The big man grimaced. "Go see, if you want to know."

So I did. I walked back there to see Castellaw. On the crate next to the bed lay an open baggie of meth and a recently used pipe. The chemical smell of it still lingered in the air.

Castellaw himself lay unmoving on the bed. He'd shot himself in the head but had missed enough of the brain to finish the job. He was a big, shirtless mound, almost as big as the bed itself. An abstract spray of blood covered the pillow behind him. His eyes moved from side to side, without a trace of life in them.

As I entered, his lips curled into an ironic smile. "I missed," he said.

"Don't talk, Mister Castellaw," Deuce said.

He ignored the advice. His voice was low and whispery but entirely audible. "Death ain't nothin' but a doorway, and on the other side of it I can see my wife."

"I see," I said, making idle chatter. I could feel Deuce glaring at me from behind. "Is she in heaven?"

"No such thing," he said. "She's been here the whole time. I just couldn't see her for all the other shit in the way. But now I can. She's here right now, matter fact."

I felt my throat tighten up. "Is she... the only person you can see?"

Deuce placed one hand on my shoulder. "Rol, that's enough."

"Ayuh. There's others," Castellaw said, and his smile broadened. A trickle of blood slid down the side of his face. "Somebody special you

164

lookin' for?"

The pressure on my shoulder increased. I tried to put it in the back of my mind. "Is anybody talking about me? Can you see anyone else?"

"Rolson?" he said. He cringed, and his eyes went distant. "Can't you tell?" He tried to laugh, but the gesture only seemed to happen inside of his mind.

"Stay with me," I said. "Tell me if there's anybody in there named Emmitt. Emmitt Laveau. Has he tried to talk to you? Have you dreamed about him?"

Before he could respond, Deuce looped one arm around my stomach and dragged me backward. My hands reached for anything to grasp, but the molding only tore away as I was flung to the floor of the dirty single-wide.

"The hell's wrong with you, Rolson? Have you completely lost it?"

I tried to get something intelligible out, but "uh" was all that occurred to me.

"He's *hallucinating*. He's on the verge of death. He's not psychic. Every answer he gives you saps a little more energy from him."

"But what if he's not hallucinating."

The look in Deuce's eyes was hateful. "You've lost your mind, man. Go wait out in the car. I'll be out there in a goddamn minute."

* * *

I waited in the passenger seat until the ambulance took Castellaw away. Deuce followed them out and got into the car. "He might live," he said, turning the key and slipping the transmission into reverse. We didn't talk on the way back to town. I wasn't going to bother trying to explain myself to him. Not that he'd be obliged to listen to me at this point.

While involved in my own thoughts, I must have drifted off to some other place, because I didn't even see the little boy scamper up and knock on the window.

"I was about to come looking for you," I lied, smiling.

"I bet y'all done forgot 'bout me," he replied. Smiling draped his father's face over the boy's features. It was a mask of ignorance, one he'd be wearing the rest of his life, even without his messy heap of a father.

I started to lie to the boy, but I said, "I've had things on my mind, and lots of important stuff has been slipping by me. Like keeping you safe and sound."

"I'm safe," he said, holding up the snake. "Look at this. I ain't even got to fear what crawls with no legs. God punished snakes by makin' 'em slide on their bellies, and I ain't a-feared of them."

Well, it's dead.

That's what I wanted to say but didn't. I glanced from the house and then back at the kid. "I see that. What's your name?"

"Nod," he said. "Ain't my real name but nobody's called me by anything but Nod since I can remember. Teachers don't even say my real name anymore. Didn't take 'em long to figure out I don't like it."

"Where's that come from, the nickname?"

He had been looking at his snake, kind of staring down at his feet and the other things surrounding them, so when he looked up at me, he had to squint. I kind of half leaned out of the car to give him the impression that I wasn't hiding in the squad car.

"Daddy. One time he said something 'bout me being the one to make him live out here, like a bunch of nobodies."

"Uh-huh."

"But I also used to shake my head when I was a baby. Didn't never stop moving my head, even when I slept, so I been called Nod ever since."

He shrugged, and it seemed like an automatic gesture, one he ended up giving every time he had to explain himself and the origin of his name, so it didn't appear to bother him all that much.

Before I could tell him he was a smart kid, he said, "My daddy ain't havin' a spell, is he? I can't take him when he gets to grinding his teeth, clickin' 'em together and rubbin' 'em so they make that sound. It ain't a sound even a crazy man could abide."

"I didn't see him grinding his teeth."

The kid looked worried.

"You know," I said, "my daddy died a long time ago, and so I haven't had him around in a long time."

"That's sad." He said it perfunctorily, the way people are supposed to say something whenever they hear bad news. There was no emotion behind it. The kid was starting to stare at his daddy's trailer.

"Even though he's gone, he's taught me an important lesson."

The boy just stared.

"See, he was a hard man to get to know. Stony. Harsh. Kind of like your old man. Did what he wanted to, and he didn't care much for people telling him how to live. He lived his own way, and he never really took anybody's advice on what to do, no matter who it hurt."

"What'd he teach you?"

"He taught me that you don't have to end up like your daddy. And he taught me that you can't worry for him the way he worries for you. He should be worried about *you*, not the other way around.

"I'd just as soon live in the woods by myself than live without my daddy," he replied. The idea of loss was the only thing he'd taken from that whole bit. Oh well. He'd learn, I supposed, and he'd probably have to learn the hard way.

I was about to invite him to play in the yard until Deuce came out, but that was about the time some DFCS people showed up and tried to explain to that boy they'd be taking him somewhere else. Far away from here, probably.

* * *

167

When Deuce dropped me off at my car, I couldn't abide the thought of going home yet, so I ended up stopping by a place called Nana's Kitchen.

Other than a Dairy Queen and two gas stations serving food from behind the counter, Nana's was one of the only restaurants in town. It served comfort food, cooked mostly by the owner herself. Truth be told, I wasn't even that hungry, but something about being out among people (and not at a bar) was enticing. I still hadn't recovered from the bout of sickness I had suffered the last time I'd drank.

As usual, the place was overly crowded but there was no line so I was able to order immediately. I felt eyes all over me, but eventually I got over it. I settled for the fried pork chops with a side of mashed potatoes and creamed corn. I waited by the counter as the food was scooped onto a plate and handed to me by one of the black women who worked with Nana.

A handful of seats were available, and not a single one seemed inviting.

The only smiling face to meet my own belonged to an older lady in a flower print dress and thick glasses. "Mrs. Sidley, how are you?" I said.

She put down her Dean Koontz paperback and raised a wrinkled, arthritic hand for me to shake. "Have a seat, Rolson. I'm about getting tired of sitting by myself anyway."

"I appreciate it. How have you been?"

"A whole sight better than you, I suppose. Didn't I teach you better than to go out and drive when you were drunk?"

I stabbed one pork chop with my fork and knifed into it. It was tender and juicy and fried to perfection. I chewed with relish, trying not to think of my run-in with the Castellaws. "Of course you did, but adversity's a sweet milk."

She smiled. "You should have studied English. Instead, you became a truck driver or a wannabe soldier or some such thing."

168

"Don't forget cop."

I poured a touch of A1 on my plated and sopped it up with a fatty bite of pork. The batter mixed well with the tang of the steak sauce.

"And yet you had potential to be the first college graduate in your family. Your mother should have gone to college. I taught her too, you know."

"Really?" It wasn't surprise I was actually experiencing - Mrs. Sidley had taught nearly every LJHS graduate in the last several decades - but rather I felt like she wanted to tell me something so I pretended not to know it.

Mrs. Sidley drank from her sweet tea and took care to place the base of the glass back on the water ring on the table. She said, "Real smart girl. Loved to read. And articulate as all get out. Back in those days, it was like pulling teeth to get my girls to talk about books in class. They would always preface what they were saying by implying they were probably wrong. But not your mother. She would come right out and say what she thought. She was an absolute delight, and you were just like her. Not afraid to speak your mind. Very brave for a boy in an English class."

"Thank you. I only wish I could have seen that side of her."

She smiled wistfully. "I know you do. My mother died when I was young, too, and every day the picture of her in my mind grows fuzzier. Only a few pictures remain, and with time her features have grown indistinct. It's like somebody is deliberately distorting them in my memory."

"I think that's a shame."

"Well, yes, I suppose so. But it isn't the memory of the way she looks that sticks with me. Something binds a mother to her children, and all these years, I have never lost my link with her. I think about her all the time, and it's never anything specific. I just think about her, and that speaks to a part of my, well, soul, that nothing else can satisfy. That's what you should try to take with you, Rolson."

169

I mixed a spoonful of potatoes and corn and lifted them to my mouth. I chewed and swallowed and said, "I've been looking for that feeling my whole life, ever since she died, but it's not there."

"Maybe there's something interfering with it."

"Maybe," I said. I imagined the kind of static that might keep someone's life force - or soul or whatever - from communicating with someone in the living world.

She sat there for a moment. "Well, reckon I better be heading on. This novel won't finish itself."

As she packed up her book, something occurred to me. "When did you retire, Mrs. Sidley?"

"Last year," she said, smiling. "They had to drag me, kicking and screaming, out of that school building. I suppose it was the right thing, though I still have a mind like a sharp weapon."

"Do you ever remember going to a dinner at the Brickmeyer place?"

"Several. Couldn't quite stand them myself, but they *do* know how to throw a party."

"How about one-"

"Where Emmitt Laveau went? Yeah, there was a banquet for teachers that year, but Emmitt probably shouldn't have been invited."

"Why not?" I asked. I started cutting into my second pork chop.

Mrs. Sidley paused, choosing her words carefully. "Don't get me wrong, I don't want to speak ill of the dead, but Emmitt wasn't exactly the best teacher. He loved the kids, and he tried very hard, but I think he was a drug user. Sometimes I could smell it on him."

"Are you sure?"

"Honey, I was a teacher for nearly forty-five years. I can smell marijuana when the kids even *think* about smoking it. Besides, he was an artisty type. Teaching was his fall-back profession. He didn't see himself doing it for the rest of his life. He didn't think the kids could tell the difference, but they could. They always can."

"What else do you remember about that night?"

"I remember Mr. Laveau and someone else talking quite a bit. In fact, they stood around and chatted the whole night away."

"Do you remember who it was?"

"Gosh, no. Not for the life of me. There was white wine there that night, and I only drink once or twice a year. When I do let it rip, however, I can never remember much the next day. Is that all, Rolson?"

"I think so, but if you can remember anything else from that night, please don't hesitate to call me. It seems as though I'm trying to recapture some of the courage you saw in me in high school."

She leaned forward, sliding the strap of her purse over her shoulder, and said in a low tone, "Other people around this town may look down on you for what you're doing, but I'm personally thrilled. Your mother would be proud of you. Please continue to do what you think is right."

"Thank you, Mrs. Sidley."

She was beaming. "And be careful about that lawyer of yours. Clements. I never did care for him. He's done a lot of good for the black community here recently, but something tells me it's to make up for being such a horse's ass about race relations years ago."

"I will."

"He defended your daddy. Do you remember that?"

"I do."

"Something about the way he operated in that case struck me the wrong way. The man deserved his conviction, no doubt about that, but I don't think he got a fair defense from that old snake. Clements, I think, made some major mistakes in the courtroom. Anyway, nice to see you, Rolson."

"Yes, ma'am."

With that, she got up, patted me on the shoulder, and walked out. You couldn't tell that she was a day over fifty-five, even if she was

171

pushing seventy. I returned to my food and ate in silence.

By the time I got to the end of the meal, the steak sauce, corn, and what remained of the mashed potatoes had bled into one another, and I ate it as if it were a single dish. It was starchy, sweet, and tangy, and I couldn't believe how full I was afterward. All that remained on the plate were the pork chop bones. I asked for a to-go cup of sweet tea and drank it on the way home.

* * *

Quarter past nine, a car pulled up in the driveway, and I was at the door with my pistol before the lights went off. It was about goddamn time somebody came to do me in; I almost thought the monsters in the world had forgotten about me.

Vanessa was lying on the couch, and though the TV was on, she wasn't watching it. Her eyes were glazed over and she was shivering, so I knew she was probably going through one hell of a withdrawal episode.

She didn't even sit up.

I peeked through the blinds and sighed.

Turns out, it was just Deuce, and as he got out and approached the house, I went out in the front yard, sliding my piece in the back of my pants. I still couldn't meet his eyes. I'd made a clear error this afternoon.

"Get in," he said tonelessly.

I hesitated, looking for the right kind of question to ask him, but he had nary a single ounce of care for that kind of nonsense in him, at that particular moment. "Get in before I put you in," he said, "and you don't want that."

I turned back to the house and saw the ghostly expression on Vanessa's face. She looked curious but simultaneously disinterested. She'd told me that meth addicts often get a bad case of the downs when they're coming off the stuff, that they can't be happy for much of anything, and it was evident the way she was looking at me from the doorway.

I hadn't said goodbye, and a part of me felt that absence. But, like everything else, I just squeezed it into something manageable and pushed it to a place marked "later." I'd get whatever was happening with her sorted out as soon as this was over with.

She'd understand. She'd have to. Fuck, who knew what she was even thinking. Or if she was thinking about anything but her own recover.

That's why I had to put those thoughts away.

On the road, Deuce didn't talk much. We got to where we were going, and I started to understand. All this time, I had been looking in the wrong places for answers.

He drove down a winding dirt road, the kind over which old, mangled trees had grown, giving the appearance of hands plunging down toward the car. It looked as though they might snatch us off the road and into darkness, never to be seen again.

As we drew closer, a light expanded in the distance, and when we passed through an old gate, I saw it was a fire. We stopped and got out, and the reason for this excursion became clearer.

It was a drum circle, of sorts, but with guitars instead of bongos. People of all ages were there. A man just to the right of the fire played his Dobro like it was an extension of his hand, and clearly he was the one the crowd was watching.

Of course, he played the guitar the way you'd imagine he would, and all of the things that could be said about a guitar player could be said about this man. It wasn't that he was good; it was that he was flawless. Everything he did, from chord changes to phrases, was flawless, and he never so much as glanced at the fretboard as he played.

No, his eyes were fixed on me.

We wandered over, and I watched the old man slide his way

through some decades-old tragedy. He didn't play for a long time, but he also didn't stop immediately, but when he did, it felt like exactly the right moment. It was something that could have been seen as a parlor trick if it weren't such a genuine gesture.

Deuce flicked his eyes at me, and I searched for something to say. "When did you pick up the guitar?" I blurted at the man, a question one step shy of *Can you play Crossroad Blues?*

"The blues ain't just something you pick up," he said. He smiled, knowing perhaps that what he was saying about the blues was the sort of thing anyone who ever talked about the blues said. "Won my first guitar in a poker match when I was sixteen years old, ain't let go of it since. This thing done seen two wives and a child buried, not counting all the friends come and gone in that time."

I knew what needed to be asked but couldn't quite find the way of getting the words out. They hung in the part of the mind that controls pride. In front of these people, all of the odd, personal experiences seemed like melodramatic extensions of a distressed mind.

The ones who had stopped playing had not resumed their previous conversations but were instead staring at me, at us, perhaps waiting for me to stop talking so they could recommence playing.

It was difficult to ignore them, but I tried. I closed my eyes to give myself the right amount of courage, but all I saw was the face of a dead man.

"My dreams, they've been giving me fits lately, and I want to know why," I said. I opened my eyes, and what I saw was a man who knew - really knew - what I was talking about. Whatever I was experiencing, he had seen in some form or another.

"Dreams, they put a frame on reality," said the old man, "but they ain't reality. Just like a picture ain't reality. It's a moment from reality, but it's just a little thing, just an itty-bitty fragment of the whole thing. And you, I suppose, been looking for answers in your dreams."

He smiled a toothless grin. His eyes were old and dim, but he saw my distress. I glanced over at Deuce. "I didn't tell him anything," he said. "This is his thing, man. He's been freaking out black people with it for years."

"I've been doing some seeking, yeah," I said. "But it has been for a purpose. And I was told it was the way for me to find what I'm looking for."

"So long as you remember," he said, "and you can't always remember your dreams. Who knows how long you've been looking for something you haven't found."

"Just ask him the question, man," Deuce said. "You nearly flipped out today, and I didn't bring you here to learn how to play slide guitar, so just out with it."

I gulped. "How did I come to see things the way that I do?" There was a too-long pause for my comfort, and I felt the eyes of all the musicians surrounding me, so I kept talking. "I mean, it can't just be hallucinations. It can't be I'm haunted? Or is that it? Is it something in between?"

Other members of the group smiled, but it didn't feel as though they were judging me. They seemed to be smiling out of a shared knowledge. Seeing all these people, I felt something I couldn't quite explain to people. It was the way I felt three beers into a night that led to me walking around The Boogie House, and I was experiencing it while stone sober.

"Well, now," the old man said, smacking his lips, "It ain't like turning on a light switch and seeing what was hiding in the dark. You remind me of an old feller I used to know, used to come up here and play guitar on occasion. Fella from Statesboro. Or was it Savannah?"

I thought maybe I knew the answer but considered it too much of a coincidence to believe. He was talking about a little-known blues musician, whose talents had been best exemplified in the works of those he influenced, leaving his voice a kind of ghost in the walls of the industry.

"Can I assume you played that guitar in the Boogie House?"

Even saying the name of the place in that man's presence sent chills through me. Here was a man who had experienced all of the worst the South had to hand out, and for some reason the Boogie House itself seemed to embody all of the evil of southern racism.

But he didn't let it shake him. He smiled, and though it was etched with lines deeper than I am old, he still managed to keep the corners of his mouth turned up.

"Whoa, that place, it hasn't been on most people's lips in decades, and in the last week you make it a household name again. You know what the people, what they're saying about you?"

"That I'm crazy as a shithouse rat. That I'm stirring up problems to get a paycheck from Leland Brickmeyer. They think I want hush money to pay off my lawyer and get a light sentence on my DUI charge."

"And you do *not* want these things?"

Everyone's eyes shifted from him to me. I felt my blood tingling in my veins, the hair standing up on my neck.

"I just want to solve that young man's murder."

"You care about that boy?"

I thought about that question. "I want justice done, yeah."

"That's not what I asked you."

Again with the eyes. I tried not to feel them on me, and I turned to Deuce, maybe to give him a bit of what I was feeling, but he, too, was staring at me and so I flinched.

So I answered the question truthfully. "I want the dreams to stop. I want to stop seeing things that aren't there. I want people to leave me alone."

"But   that   is   not   all   of   it,   either."

"No, I want to know how I came to see these damned visions in

176

the first place."

"That's what I thought," he said.

"I've always had weird dreams," I replied. Up to now, I had not really thought about *why*. The only good reason, I'd sort of told myself, was that I was involved in a strange coincidence. But I guess that wasn't good enough, nor was it the truth. "But...not like these. Not ones that felt so real."

"There ain't no Indians buried round here. Ain't nothing in the soil or the air that made you start talking to the dead in your dreams, either. No, what you got you got *honest*."

Even before I'd met Uncle K or slammed into Janita Laveau, my mother came to visit me. Those dreams, too, gave off a sense of connection with the waking world, but I had shrugged them off for years. Maybe it was her.

Or maybe it was someone else. Denial is a strong state-of-being.

"The man I met recently-"

"The old coot who plays with dirt and spices, yes," the old man said. His smile had turned somewhat vicious. "He has laid on thick with the rootwork and the potions and whatnot, eh? Sounds just like the charlatan bastard."

"It seemed to have worked on me," I said.

"He never stepped one foot inside the Boogie House. What do you think he knows about what's out there?"

"I don't know," I said.

"That place does have a power, young man," he replied, "but it doesn't have to do with magic. All the power in that place comes from the people who struggled to keep the boards from falling over. If there's something haunted about that place, it has to do with the way it just up and died. We're all to blame, all of us who let it go to hell like that."

"Maybe the, um, magic left it, and it has only returned because of...what happened."

"That may be the truth, and it'd be a sad thing for a white man to breathe life into an old black juke joint." He appeared genuinely pained by this admission, and I nodded in agreement. "But, then again, race ain't never been simple down here, now has it?"

"No," I said.

"I hate to tell you that sometimes people get a dose of something they didn't want, and it stays with them until it's run its course. You see, my guitar, I carry it around, but I'd bet it's brought me as much torment as it has fortune, but I can't let it go, no more than you can let go of the thoughts in your head. You just accept things are the way they are, and you don't worry about what's on the other side of the line. You'll know when it comes your time to know. For now, you focus on what's on *this* side of the line. If it wasn't important to pay attention to what you've been seeing, you wouldn't have seen it."

With that, he began plucking a familiar blues rhythm, and the others joined in. Deuce tapped me on the elbow, like he thought we should get out of there, but I ripped free of him. All of the old man's acolytes stopped playing, and the old man himself jangled out a few more notes, but he couldn't keep the charade up for long.

"I did not come here for some mystical cold reading," I said. "I am here because I can see ghosts - actual ghosts - dancing in the Boogie House, can feel the disappointment they felt when it closed down. Something in me gives me that power, and I want to know where it comes from, who gave it to me."

His eyes pushed me back a few steps. He never lost his calm, but now there was a coldness in his eyes. "And if it was that easy, son, I'd've told you right off. You don't listen, do you? You talk. Okay, I'm telling you to listen now."

It seemed like even the wind had stopped to pay attention to him.

"You got a little bit of it honest, I bet," he said. "You say your mama, she comes to you in dreams?"

"I don't think I did," I said.

178

"But I bet she does. She come from somewhere else, somewhere they practice with the dead?"

"Some of her family comes from Savannah," I said, "but she never mentioned-"

"To a little boy? She didn't mention ghosts to a five year old? You not any smarter than that?" He did smile again, finally. "And the old man, no? He never gives you the midnight blues?"

"No," I said. "I don't think of him much."

"Or think much of him," the old man said, chuckling.

"Can you help me? Can you - can you help me do it on command? I want to *choose* to go to that world, to see all of those things when *I* want to."

"Take it easy," Deuce whispered, but I ignored him.

"You claim to know so much about the other side-"

"I don't know nothing about any of that," the old man said. "But I do know it's not something you can choose. You done went to the old fool out in the country, and he filled you with ideas about black magic and-"

"And he was right."

The old man nodded. "I see," he said. "You came out here looking for answers."

"Of goddamn course I did."

"You being able to look through a crack in the window doesn't mean it makes any sense. It may never make sense. And if you can accept that, maybe you can make sense of it."

I gaped at him.

"Listen," he said. "Let me tell you a little bit more about the Boogie House."

"Okay," I said. "Great."

"The men who ran that place thought they was charmed. One of them had a gun pulled on him down in Savannah, just for being black and in the wrong place, and when the white boy wanted to kill him

179

pulled that trigger, it didn't do nothing but click."

"It just clicked."

"Misfire. Now, it happens that young black man had a charm he got from an old folk healer down there, not even minutes before."

"Sounds like magic to me," I said sarcastically.

The old man waggled a finger at me. "They say that old woman still strolls herself around town, even today. It's been seventy-five, eighty years since this happened."

"Could be a weird coincidence."

"Right. Baby born covered in hair don't make werewolves real," he replied. "Some people got a little something extra when the cards was dealt. Others got a little bit over the span of a lifetime. But ain't just anybody can pick up a doll and start sticking pins in it."

"I see," I said.

"Anyway, that old boy - but of course he was young back then - thought he'd hit something big. He'd always been a believer in all that but never took up fate on it. That night, with the white boy and the gun, convinced him."

"How'd he end up in the Junction?"

"The other'n was a whorehopper, and he knocked up a white woman - daughter of a major politician down that way - so they fled up here. Had cousins selling radiator booze by the five-gallon bucket. Those didn't get poisoned were coming back for a second bucket every once in awhile."

"My daddy's family was a bunch of bootleggers," I said.

"Ah, so he might not be all bad," the old man said. "Either way, them two boys, they used his money to put up four walls, and they charged a nickel per head that first year, back when it was just a shack with a plywood stage."

"My mama said Blind Willie McTell played there." This was how I'd gotten around to asking him about the blues man from before.

180

He shrugged. "Might be so. Might be one of them things just got passed around because it could. He spent some time up in Milledgeville, I reckon, but I ain't never heard a him coming down this way. On his way back down to Savannah, or Statesboro. Could be. You believe it?"

"I'll believe just about anything these days," I replied.

I had actually grown interested in this story, even if it was bringing me no closer to Emmitt Laveau's killer. If the owners of the Boogie House practiced any kind of hoodoo, maybe that's what was giving off the mystical vibes.

And my mother; well, I had no way of knowing that was true or not. I had something wrong with me. Might as well have been some gift from her.

It'd be one of the only things I got from her.

"Well, you'd be best to keep a skeptical heart, my boy, because you don't want to become one of them fools believes everything, from flying saucers to whatever. So, the two best friends filling the black folks with liquor. They made a good living that first year, but that was because they was too afraid to expand. It was a bad time, you know, to be black."

"Has been for a long time," Deuce said.

"It's gettin' better," the old man replied.

"How come the whites didn't try to shut it down that first year?" I asked.

"Didn't know about it. People kept a general hush going. You give some people who ain't never had nothing a little something, and they're liable to crush it, but these people didn't."

"Were you one of them?" The old man was old enough, it seemed.

"Not that first year," he said. "I didn't come in until later. When things got worse. Secrets get out. Most white girls, they were too afraid to come on out that way. Some of them wanted to, and they had secret boyfriends, but none of them dared step a foot out there, at first."

"But inevitably someone does." It made me think of my mother, who had made a less significant but nevertheless controversial choice to run around with a black man behind my father's back.

"And that girl didn't keep her midnight liaisons to herself. Which, you can imagine, ended up drawing white men with shotguns out to the Boogie House. Became a cycle. People figured they'd best reach out and appease them white fellas, and so they'd end up paying in various ways. Sometimes it was money, and other times, it was...other things."

"Did anybody ever get killed out there?"

The question seemed to sting him, because he reacted physically. It could have been a fly or a gnat getting to close to his face, but I don't think it was. He had been looking at the neck of his guitar, but he turned to look at me head on, just then.

"There were a few incidents." His mouth flipped, and he frowned bitterly. "Difference between an accident and an incident is that one ain't planned, and the other is an accident. There were beatings, and some died, but nobody was going to listen to people selling liquor and playing music the white folks didn't approve of."

"Why didn't they just shut the place down outright? I'm sure they didn't have proper permits, or a liquor license."

More than a few eyes turned in my direction on that one, Deuce's included.

"I mean, if they had all that power, and they hated what you were doing, why didn't they just force them to shutter the place?"

"That question got asked, but I'll put it to you like this: A bully doesn't want the kid with glasses to take them off. He wants that kid to keep wearing them to school. Maybe the bully hits him on this particular day, and maybe he doesn't, but he always wants the option of having somebody to bloody up."

"I see," I said. I could have brought up something about the kid with glasses standing up to the bully, but this was 1940s or 1950s Georgia. *South* Georgia. No such thing was going to happen. Them even having a place to go to like the Boogie House was a rebellion, of sorts.

"I reckon maybe it had a charm to it, too," he said, continuing. "Some men tried to set a fiery cocktail to it back in '65, must have been early in March, after that pretty white girl was shot in the head down in Selma. Emboldened the Klan types. Some fools showed up - drunk as Cooter Brown - trying to light their bottle of moonshine on fire so they could throw it. One fella, the most backwards peckerwood you've ever laid your eyes on, waved a pistol around like it wasn't load, which of course meant it was."

I turned to Deuce. "Do you know any of these men?" He shook his head. They'd be old, but there was a chance they'd still be alive. And if a man was alive and living in Lumber Junction, Deuce knew him. It was just the man he was. He knew people. That was his thing.

"The old boy got his jar of hooch lit, and he threw it, but it didn't quite go the way he thought. People were screaming already, because they thought they were going to be shot or set on fire, but that's not what happened. The bottle busted on the sidewall, and some of it burnt, but the flame trailed back through the vapors - or something - and put a hurting on that boy. He didn't hardly have time to blink before he was up in flames. He and the others."

I could picture this happening, and something told me it wasn't just my brain calculating how people of this era would look. There was something quite real about the vision.

"They burned real slow, but nobody let them go up completely. They tossed jackets and whatever else they had lying around to put them poor bastards out." He chuckled. "Most of 'em would have said they wouldn't piss on them white boys to put out a fire no more'n an hour beforehand, but here they were, ruining their going-out clothes on some peckerwood Klan members. Matter of fact, one of them said, as he was dusting the soot off his jacket, that he couldn't get the white off of it. Everybody busted out laughing, but I reckon there was some truth in that as well."

"How did it catch the whole lot of them?" I asked.

"People disagree about what they saw," he said. "Some said they were too caught up in the moment to be able to tell what really happened, so they figured the fire jumped from one person to another, but I can tell you it didn't. It attacked that one boy, the one holding the gun. He was the one ended up getting it worse, even if he wasn't intending on hurting anybody."

"And what did the police have to say about it?"

The old man just peered curiously at me. I wasn't surprised. In my mind, I saw them dragging bodies into the woods, digging holes deep enough for them to never be found again. Then I saw them - all of them - arguing about how to keep everyone quiet.

Guess there needn't be a disagreement about it, if them boys were never found.

"So that's why I wouldn't know any of them," I said. I caught flickers of old, tattered images in that moment, memories from other people's minds, like pictures tossed in a fireplace.

"They didn't make it through the night," the old man said. "I bet they're still buried out in the woods near that juke joint, if I had to guess."

"I don't believe it."

"You ain't got to. Truth don't mind skepticism."

"But aren't there rules?" I asked. "I feel like I'm seeing things right now. I even think I see a younger version of you."

"Tell you what," said the old man, "you find the logic of your situation, you go out and do some math and figure out what in the hell ties everything together in a little bow, you come back and give it to me, okay?"

"Okay."

"The world is messy, and everything in it is messy. Life is a damned broken mirror, the shards scattered all over the floor. You might be able to paste some of them together, but there's always going to be little bitty pieces sliding under the furniture, or too small to see, and then you'll never be able to pull it all together. What you got to say about that?"

I was stumped. "I agree. Life can't be tied up like that. And memories, well."

"The only way you find answers is to keep looking. You expected to come out here and have me hand everything to you. I've told you more than once, it don't work that way. You will get one little clue here and one little clue there, but you will never jump on the one answer."

"So you're not going to try to preach some message to me now?" I asked.

"The time of the preacher man is long gone, and only the echo of anything meaningful he said can even be heard anymore."

"Grandpa, you shouldn't be talking like that," a beautiful, curly-headed girl said.

"I'm just telling the truth, and it must hurt you because you'd tell a lie if you were in my place." He smiled wickedly, but that seemed to shut his granddaughter up - if that was, in fact, his granddaughter. He turned to me, and he said, "You don't care none about some dead white boys, though, do you? It's the owners you want to know about."

"That's right," I said. I wasn't entirely sure if that was the truth, but I thought it might lead me somewhere true. "I want to know what happened to them, why they disappeared. How they disappeared."

"Word is, they was going to get a southern send-off, and I think you know what that means for black men, so they kicked on out of town before they could receive it."

"But that isn't what happened," I said. "If it's that easy to make a few white boys disappear, then for a couple of mystic strangers, it's got to be even easier."

He nodded and pushed his lips out and hummed. "I reckon everybody was surprised to go out there and find all the lights out and the doors closed."

"Did no one look for them?"

"They didn't have no family up this way - none that wasn't in jail, I don't think - so it was just the people going out there and drinking that cared about them two men, so it wasn't long before they were forgotten."

I shook my head. "That's a shame."

"Oh, people tried to reopen the place a few times. Kicked the doors open and tried to get the lights and sound going, but it was different."

"There was a pall hanging over it, knowing they had disappeared?"

"Hell no. The equipment wouldn't work right. The lights flickered, and there was some strange things that we didn't want to think about happening out there."

"Like supernatural things."

"It felt like dancing on the dirt of a freshly-dug grave," he said, "and couldn't nobody stomach that. Plus, the charm seemed like it had been taken off that place, because that's when the white folks started trying to shut it down, started making a big mess of a little old bar for blacks."

"And do you ever think of those men?"

"Don't have to. I hear them in my head all the time. It's the way regret goes, son. You live long enough, and all the things you wish you had done - or had done differently - start to whisper to you in ways you find hard to deal with."

There was a good, long, awkward pause after that. Finally, he said, "I think it's time you go. They get restless when they can't play for however long they want."

I think Deuce forgave me, after that. He didn't say much on the drive home, but he did talk about how it was some kind of weird gift I had and that he hoped I didn't erase it with Beam.

Truth be told, I felt the weirdness of these visions was stronger when I drank. The idea of tying one on made me actually afraid. Not that it would stop me, probably.

* * *

That night, sipping beer in the dark by myself on the couch - I had given Vanessa the bed to sleep on - I started to see it all a bit more clearly. I had been missing the point of these sleepwalks into the woods. In my mind, I had conceived them as keys to unlocking doors, but they weren't keys at all. That was my fault.

They were flashlights, peering into the dark corners of the history of that building, of the people who went to the Boogie House and sweated away their pain and suffering.

I had foolishly underestimated their intent. Little details began to surface to me again as I slept, as if I had somehow been given a highlighter for the energy in that room.

If it were going to help me solve the case involving Emmitt Laveau, I had to quit trying to squeeze answers out. I had to see them for what they were, as artifacts.

As I started to get buzzed, I felt the familiar swimming quality associated with going to another world, and this time I eased up on the beer, because I didn't want to miss it. I felt like I had been missing out on something by not embracing this all along.

It was a gift, and I was throwing the box away with the present still inside.

At first I thought I felt the presence of someone else in the room with me, and then I saw him. Or her. Or it. But eventually the feeling itself went away. I downed the lukewarm drink in my hand and tried to sleep, but Emmitt Laveau didn't visit me in my sleep that night.

Instead, I went searching for my mother in a darkened land, in a world lit by a black hole of a sun. It covered everything in its path like a blanket of absolute nothingness. It wasn't real, but it was like one of those dreams that yanks you awake halfway through, that leaves you wondering if any line at all exists between waking life and all the rest of existence. Dreams and death and comas and fantasies. They all sort of meld together in the wake of particular types of otherworldly experiences.

My hands were gone, replaced by stumps, though one appendage ended in a rudimentary claw dangling near to the ground, and even though I "came to" halfway into whatever was happening, I immediately understood the whole situation.

I was dying. It wasn't dark because the sun itself was black but because my own lights were going out. I was ambling along the edge of a trail in the woods, and in the distance someone was vaguely visible among the trees and the pine needles and the darkness.

This time, I wasn't anywhere near the woods by my house. These were mountainous woods, the kinds of woods that exist only in a wilderness rarely touched by humanity.

But the edges of my vision were closing in, and I seemed to be making no progress toward the figure ahead of me. It was apparent, though, that it was a woman, and I assumed it was my mother, though I could only discern that she was a white patch against the darkness of the canvas in front of me.

I stumbled and fell, but each time I slipped, I got up and was closer to my target. I looked down and saw that the reason I couldn't make progress was that one of my legs was broken in half, the bone showing, insect-like, through the meat of my shin. It was the sort of injury that wouldn't heal, and the me in that moment - the dream me - didn't care.

The only thing that mattered was making it to that one person to catch up with her and tell her the thing stuck in my head. It was more than just a few words; it was a feeling that I had to get out of me. It was so intense, it felt like it was burning its way out of my throat.

I wasn't crying, but tears moistened my cheeks, electric against my skin.

I fell again, and this time I was twisted around so that I was completely lost in this wood. I got up and saw what was knocking me down. It wasn't the leg, after all.

A beast straight out of Dante's visions of Hell was pursuing me. It was a giant, multi-legged beast, a lumpy mound of evil with hundreds of eyes. It was ugly, and it was vile, and it wanted me dead.

There was no escape.

It approached, and I felt something deep in my chest. When I looked down, I saw that I had a fist-sized hole in me. My shirt caught fire and the flames spread up to my neck. I scrambled to my feet in time to feel another blast rip its way through my upper torso. The beast was no longer a beast but a set of men, and they were hunting me.

I turned and ran, but I didn't have the energy. My field of vision had been dimming, covered by thick, dark branches collapsing in on one another and making it impossible for me to see the road ahead.

But still, I desperately ran forward, knowing that this was my last chance. The figure ahead of me was a series of white lines, or dots, like pixels, but I thought maybe that I was closer than before.

Each time my pursuers knocked me down, I got back up, a bit slower each time. I could hear their voices, but they came out like a high-pitched buzzing, a colony of bees in my ears.

All of a sudden, I came to a clearing and stumbled forward into the tall grass. My vision was a pinprick in front of me, and I headed toward it, desperately trying to convey one last thought, whatever it was. The words roiled inside of me, and though I could tell they were there, it was as though I had inhabited some other person.

Another volley of gunfire knocked me horizontal, and this time I couldn't get up. I crawled ahead, dragging myself on elbows roaring with pain. I looked down again and saw that the one hand was not gone but holding a sawed off shotgun. That's why it seemed to dangle loosely beneath me.

I struggled to my knees and then fell sideways. If only I could stay upright, maybe I could fire the damned shotgun. Balancing the barrel on one mangled forearm, I fired blindly. Three henchmen dropped unceremoniously, action figures toppled by an indignant child. The others marched ahead, firing in a sort of horrific, synchronized attack.

More of me was flung into the air in a fine red spray, but I didn't stop. I racked the shotgun with the crook of my arm and fired a second time. All but one of the men dropped to the ground as I readied yet another round. Click. Click. Click. Empty gun. Empty brain. My one remaining thought slithered off to another remote corner of my head, where the lights had been knocked out. I tapped the trigger again. Click. Not enough rounds left. Never enough rounds left.

In the absence of gunfire, I heard a tiny buzz, like the sound of bees on television. It sounded artificial but was real enough to make me snap my head sideways. The buzzing transformed into a bizarre whirring sound, and I turned and crawled forward, trying to separate myself from the last of the men. If only I could make it to the edge of the field, maybe I could be lost among the trees.

My eyes locked on the figure ahead of me. She had stopped to watch me, but she didn't hurry back to help. She was a pale, willowy statue, concerned but held aloft by something ethereal, something I myself probably couldn't see. Truth be told, she was all I could see. Everything else had gone dark, and I was quickly fading.

So I crawled on.

I felt the killer, his footsteps shaking the ground beneath me. He was no man but something else, and I thought that if I didn't look back, if I only kept facing forward, maybe he couldn't affect me.

The woman was my focus now, though. I made my way toward

her, and when I got close enough, I saw that she wasn't anyone I knew at all. It wasn't Vanessa, and it wasn't my mother. When she saw the blood and the tears, she turned and ran. The last I saw of her was her back as she ran into a thick covering of bushes on the other side of the field.

I couldn't hang onto the words any longer, so I blurted them out in a single, dying breath. I had been hanging onto them for no reason, because in my haste to get them out, I slurred them together so that they made no sense.

The muscles in my neck gave out, and I came to rest right there, face down in the grass. The last moment consisted of me feeling the hot metal of a gun barrel pressing against the back of my neck. I smiled because I knew I'd be dead before he could kill me.

When I awoke, I went straight for the fridge and guzzled down two beers while standing in its dim, sickly light. My stomach turned, and I knew I'd be sick. Only a matter of time.

It was then I began to believe in what both the old man at the fire tonight and Uncle K had been telling me. I believed in the idea of a wavy, unsure truth and also in the power of the magic that was "curing" me of drinking. I needed it for now, but I was thinking about taking it easy so that I didn't ruin my chances of solving this murder.

I'd just have to be sick when I had to be sick, I guessed.

As I tossed the second beer into the trash, I saw the flash of a man in the kitchen, a tall, lanky figure in a hat and old suit, and the feeling of Emmitt Laveau's presence washed over me.

I broke down, kneeling and weeping until Vanessa appeared in the doorway. She put her hand on the back of my neck, and I wrapped my arm around her knees, breathing in deep the smell of her until she pulled away.

"I'm thinking 'bout going to a meeting," she said, "if you want to go with me."

I shook my head and grunted under my own weight, as I found a seat at the kitchen table. "This isn't about my drinking."

"Not for nothing, but everything is about your drinking. That's why we was so perfect for one another. Back to back, we held each other up."

I nodded, because a part of me knew that, but it was a part of me that was in severe denial.

Instead of talking about it, we sat on the back stoop and smoked cigarettes in silence, watching the wind blow rain clouds in our direction. At one point, she reached over and slipped her hand into mine, and I felt such an electric charge that I nearly let go out of instinct.

"I wish the world hadn't fucked the two of us up," she said.

"I know."

"We could have been happy, if there were worlds other than this one."

I stubbed my cigarette and flicked the butt into the distance. "Maybe there is another world out there," I responded. I let that settle and then said, "We could be happy there."

"I'm so lost, Rolson, I don't know if I'd be able to find you." She sighed. "But hopefully that's the point. If we spend our whole lives lost and searching for something, maybe we use up all the hurt and the pain, and we can be happy after it's all said and done. I just wish it didn't have to hurt so much right now, especially if we don't know what comes after."

"Or maybe it doesn't mean anything, and we have to find meaning in this world," I said. "You and I have been dragging one another down into the darkness for two decades now. All the hurt that's been heaped on you isn't just applied to you. It applies to me, as well."

Her eyes were wet with tears, but she wasn't sobbing and heaving the way she normally did. Maybe she was too tired for that, or she didn't have any of that left in her.

"I'm just sorry, so sorry, and I don't know how to make things right. It'd be easy if it was a little bit, but I spent the last few years going through life like I was being controlled by somebody else. I don't know that I could even count all of the bad shit I did. I mean, even to *you*. The list is so goddamn long-"

"Don't worry just yet about apologizing to me," I replied, cutting her off. "There'll be plenty of time for that, but don't make anything up to me. I'm fine."

She nodded.

"Matter of fact," I continued, "don't worry about making anything up to anybody for a very long time. You've been walking through a field full of burs, and there's so many of them you can barely move. You try to pick them off, one by one, you'll be doing that for the rest of your life."

"Well, what do I do instead?"

"You tear off the clothes that are so sullied with those things, then people will notice that. They'll forgive you by the sheer change you've undergone."

"That doesn't mean they'll trust me again. You'll never trust me again."

I patted her on the leg. "Trust is a whole different beast, and yeah, you've got your work cut out for you there, but for every day you spend fixing yourself, you'll be one step closer to regaining trust from all the people who want to trust you. All the people that don't want to trust you, who want to hang on to the past, well, fuck them."

"And where do you stand?"

"I want to be in the first group, but I don't know if I am," I said, and then I got up. "Let me know if you want me to take you to the meeting."

"Will you think about going with me?"

"I'll think about it," I said, and then I went inside.

* * *

193

The next day, I dropped in to try and see Jeffrey Brickmeyer, but the frumpish secretary told me he wasn't in. Something about her tone made me think differently.

I tried to play it cool. "Where's he run off to? I had an appointment with him right about now."

"His father's called him off to get some documents signed and notarized and" - she glanced at her watch - "he might not be back before two or three."

"Huh," I said, propping an elbow on the counter. I started talking real loud. It felt like my Fletch moment. "Did he hitch a ride?"

"I don't-"

"Because his car's parked out back in the alley, and it's not like him to hide that car of his. You know it registers a hundred and sixty miles per hour?"

"Mr. Brickmeyer, he just-"

"Well, I tell you," and at this point, other people in the office began to stare, so I raised my voice, "he said something very interesting to me yesterday *at the graveside service for Emmitt Laveau-*"

"Hold on a moment, Mr. McKane," the blond secretary said. She was from out of town, and I had never met her before. Her name was Debbie, and she looked like a child who has messed her pants and cannot find the courage to ask the teacher for a bathroom pass.

However, she was saved from her lies, because the man himself appeared hastily in the doorway, sweating somewhat and bearing a wild-eyed countenance.

"Rolson," he said, smiling, using his father's kiss-assy, phony political posturing. The man was politically illiterate. Or completely literate. I couldn't tell. "Don't pester Debbie just because I told her I didn't want visitors."

"Covering for liars is not something that should go on her resume."

194

"It's not her fault a wolf walked into the building. Come on back."

I followed him to a neat and sparsely-decorated office. Almost totally unexpected from the bedraggled man to whom the office belonged. It was a space entirely without style or personality, with only a lone portrait of his father hanging on the wall behind the desk. The eyes solemnly watched us from on high. I couldn't imagine working eight hours a day with that hanging over me, but I guess Jeffrey really looked up to his old man.

I seated myself across the table and waited for him to start. He scratched at his stubble, which was quickly turning into an unkempt beard. He watched me for a long time before he spoke.

He said, "My father would castrate me with a rusted spoon if he caught me talking with you. In one of his offices, no less." He pulled a hand from under his chin and began to chew madly on a fingernail. "I feel like I'm being set up for something."

"Aw, he's so busy, he doesn't have the slightest idea what you and I might talk about."

"And what is that?" He sighed, but it rang hollow. "I'm so bored with the Emmitt Laveau thing. I've already said all I've got to say on the subject. Being the go-between is driving me crazy."

"No, no," I said, shaking my head, feigning casualness. "That is the farthest thing from my mind at the moment. Like your dad, I'm a busy man. I've got a lot of interests."

"Like what?" he asked, in a mocking tone.

"Land."

His eyes grew steely and opaque under the artificial light. "What kind of land?"

"Stolen land."

He made a skeptical huffing sound. "Give me a break, McKane."

"What? Am I being too dramatic? Should I have brought a sad 40s orchestra with me?"

He dropped his hands on the desk in exasperation. "You have

195

done everything under the sun but call my family a bunch of slavers. Murder, land theft, political corruption. What are we not capable of?"

"The more that is leveled at you, the farther you and your family recede into secrecy."

His eyes gleamed. "And let you turn it into a witch hunt? If we begin to answer these ridiculous charges, they won't stop until we've been caught in some tiny, insubstantial lie. If we don't drown, we will be put to death. If we drown, we are not witches. It is a no-win situation."

I smiled. "Covering up for the old man is a bad idea, given the history you have with the Bullen family. He's a cop, and he's not going to worship at the Brickmeyer altar if he thinks he's been wronged. Just keep that in mind."

"His father was a drunk who regretted giving away the one thing in his life that had value."

"Giving?"

"Selling. Whatever. Don't get caught up in semantics, McKane. You're not smart enough."

"And yet, I'm the person who pointed out someone who might have enough of a vendetta against you to act on it. Most people, they lie down and take it because you're local royalty. Not Ronald Bullen. He'd do something about it."

"So?"

"So, you don't seem too concerned about it."

He pulled a small trash can from underneath the desk and flicked a piece of nail into it. Then he started chewing on another one. He talked from behind his hand. "I trust the authorities. They've got the public's best interests in mind. You should know that."

"And your daddy has got his political future in mind. I know that, too."

Jeffrey leaned up. He wasn't being insincere before, but he put on his best sincere face for my benefit. "A lot of people want to see him fail. It isn't a secret that envy shows pretty green on the townspeople's faces sometimes, even though my family has brought plenty to Lumber Junction over the years."

"So then it must be that *they* don't see what it is. If you can't sell a product to the public, ultimately it's not the public's fault. It's the salesman's."

"You know how it is maintaining a public persona."

"Do I?"

"Your name has been all over the local vent page, the web site where all the gossips go to air out their grievances."

"Oh," I said. "Luckily, I don't give a shit about the internet."

"Either way, they've got a lot to say about you, and I have to admit I've not been an advocate on your behalf. But I want you to understand something: people have got my family all wrong, especially my father. He's not a bad man. He's worked hard to overcome his upbringing."

"That big house must have gotten lonely."

Brickmeyer the younger glared at me. "My grandaddy was an old school southern kind of man-"

"A racist."

"Well, yeah. He was better than his own grandparents, but each age is a progression. He wasn't a monster, but he was no better than the men of his generation."

"So, your daddy had to shrug off all the black hatred indoctrination he suffered at the hands of your grandfather? That it? Is that your family's big struggle? Trying to accept all human beings as human beings?"

"That's the *South*'s struggle, McKane. It isn't out in public as much anymore, but it's still there, and my father, as much as any man I've known, has agonized over how he was raised, and he made a vow years ago to change. Not out loud, maybe, but he's a different man, changed in all the ways most people only wished they could be different. And he put that into me, so I've gone even farther than he has."

"Every man has his prejudices, Jeff. It's not just your family that struggles with identity and race and all that, even in a small town."

"Brickmeyer Ag & Timber employs more minorities than any company in five surrounding counties. My father is polling at over half of the black vote, which isn't bad for a man with an R next to his name."

"Let me change subjects. I hear that, in addition to giving back to the police force, the Brickmeyer family is committed to showing educators how charitable you are."

"If you're referring to the teacher's dinner, yes, we try to have one every year, but with the way the economy's going we may have to skip it this spring. It's a shame, but that's the reality of things these days."

"Who handles the hosting and invitation duties?"

He leaned back in the chair and interlaced his fingers. He debated a moment before saying, "It's a communal effort. Mama does some of it. I do some of it. Daddy handles other things. We have a party planner, too, so that's not a real easy question to answer."

"But you are in charge of some aspects of the party, right?"

His jaws began to work from side to side. "Right."

"Are you the one who invited Emmitt Laveau a couple of years ago, or was it your father?"

"So we knew him a little bit."

"It's the cover-up and not the crime-"

"He was one of a few dozen people there. You think any one of those people died in the last few years, and people would be tying our names to the death?"

"How well did you know him? Was he your dealer?"

His eyes flashed. I'd hit bone. "Out," he said.

"Or did the two of you just get high together?"

"Out," he said, through clenched teeth.

"I bet that fact hasn't seen the light of day, has it?"

"Get out, or I'm calling the police," he said. "And you'll see how loyal the LJPD is."

I stood up and nodded. "Have a nice day, Jeffrey."

* * *

The cruiser caught up with me ten minutes later and threw on the flashers immediately. I made a U-turn and drove downtown to a public spot before pulling over.

I rolled down my window and smiled past Ricky, whose stomach blocked my view, to Owen Harper, who was glancing around nervously. "My old friend," I said. "Owen, how are you?"

"Out of the car, alkie," Ricky said. He was furiously chewing a piece of gum and staring somewhere off in the distance. Behind him, Owen fidgeted with his shirt front, pulling it away from him like it was sticking to his flesh.

"I'd like to know what it is I've done wrong."

"Come with us, Rolson," he said, adjusting his sunglasses, smiling in a way that suggested he'd like to see me buried next to Emmitt Laveau, "or I'll make sure you're on the front page of the paper as the lead suspect in our town's little homicide."

"You don't have that kind of authority," I said. Behind Ricky, Owen did a sort of nervous dance, moving from foot to foot, hands resting on his hips. I caught sight of his mangled hand and then looked away. "And if we're being honest, if I'm the best you got, y'all sure are doing a shitty job down here."

Ricky spat his gum on the cement next to me. Spittle misted my face. "I can make it my business, and I can make it stick long enough to make you go away."

"If you had influence, you would have done it already." I tried to maintain a steady voice, even though I was on the verge of slamming

199

the door into Ricky's gut. "Leland Brickmeyer would have you put me in jail without hesitation."

I looked into the dark lenses of Ricky's glasses. I saw the outline of his eyes behind them. Then I said, "Give me whatever bogus traffic ticket you've dreamed up and let me get the hell on my way."

Ricky paused, thinking. He pretended to run one hand along to the top of the car. He gave it a once over with his eyes, tilting his head to get a look at the front and back ends. The corners of his mouth turned up, and he glanced back at Owen once before returning his gaze to me. "I don't remember you getting a new vehicle, Rolson."

My hands tightened on the wheel. I could see where this was going, so I kept quiet. Ricky could drum up any sort of reason to arrest me, but I figured that, as long as I stayed in the car, I'd be all right. Lord help me, if they got me in the backseat of that cruiser. The last place they would take me was the police station.

"Why don't we take a look at your license and registration, please, sir," he continued, smiling wider. "Once we make sure your paperwork's all in order, you'll be free to go. If not, we might have to bring you with us until it gets, you know, *sorted out*."

"Something tells me that if I go with you, I'm the only the thing that will get sorted out."

Ricky actually laughed at that. "I tell you what, McKane. You hop out the car and take a ride with us, and I promise to return you in one piece. You don't, and you will end up regretting ever taking a stroll into that old nigger joint."

"Owen," I said, talking past Ricky. "You don't agree with this, do you?" I was appealing to his sense of decency.

"My wife just had a kid, Rolson. I've got to keep above water," he said. His eyes wouldn't meet mine.

What choice do I have now? I thought.

Just as I was about to get out of the car, though, a second cruiser pulled up, and out stepped Ronald Bullen. He adjusted the belt on his enormous waist and lumbered over. His eyes were restricted to small, angry slits. "What's the holdup here?"

Ricky shriveled noticeably. "McKane's driving a car isn't his. He flat-out refuses to show his identification."

Bullen regarded me with irritation, no different from normal. "McKane?"

I rapped the steering wheel with the heels of my hands, trying to push down my frustration. "It's a rental. Jarvis Garvey lent it to me. Somebody slashed my tires, and, well, you know what the case is with my other car."

"It's a wonder anybody would let you touch a vehicle." Bullen wasn't pleased with anybody here.

"Touche," I said.

"He's been causing trouble all over town," Ricky said.

Bullen ignored him. He was focused entirely on me. "You give Ricky cause to pull you over?"

Ricky raised his hands in frustration. "Aw, Christ, Bullen."

"Ricky, please," Owen said.

"Shut up, Ricky," Bullen cut in. "I'm talking. If you had any gumption, you'd have gotten him out of the car by now. Rolson, these men bothering you?"

I balked. I didn't quite know how to answer the question. Ron was not prone to anything but insults. A couple of answers floated in my head, but I couldn't reach out and grab a single one. I just stared at my hands, watched the way my fingers drummed the steering wheel.

"I might've stepped on Jeffrey Brickmeyer's toes a little bit," I said, finally.

Bullen snorted. When he next spoke, he stared directly at the two forlorn cops. "His old man can afford harder shoes than that. If he can't handle getting them stomped every once in awhile, he's got no business riding the man's coattails into politics."

I kept still while Bullen and Ricky stared one another down.

201

Owen's eyes burned holes in the side of my face, but I kept my eyes fixed in the distance.

Finally, Ricky said, "Owen, let's ride out. Let this sack of shit deal with the alcoholic. If he plows into another helpless woman, it's gonna be his ass in the wood chipper."

"I doubt it," Bullen said under his breath.

Once they had pulled away, he turned back to me. "Get on out of here, Rolson. I don't think they'll bother you, for now."

"What do you have against them?"

"They're shills for Leland, and I don't care for either one of them much."

"And how are you managing to stay out of the fire? I heard heads are on the chopping block about this," I said.

"They wouldn't dare shitcan me," he said. "I've got the keys to all the secret rooms. They let me go, and the beans I spill would haunt this town for years."

"I see. But that still doesn't explain what you're doing helping me."

He crossed his arms and leaned against the car. Across the street, a little girl was riding a bicycle on the sidewalk, weaving between pedestrians. Bullen watched her disappear around the corner on her Dora the Explorer ride and then said, "I used to think you had a stick up your ass for no reason. A real sad sack, and I can't stand that self-pitying shit. This was all based on what happened when you was a kid."

"Folks generally have sympathy for people who lose their parents at a young age."

Something in his face twinged. "See, that's part of the problem. It's coming back to me. You have a sense of entitled sympathy. Nobody's exempt from a painful upbringing."

"Well, you're telling me now, so-"

"Rolson, listen. Damnit. What I've come to realize is, you've shown yourself to be more than just a self-destructive asshole. And I'll tell you another thing."

"Nothing's stopping you now. You're on a roll."

He smiled, seeming to reflect on something other than me. "The other thing is, you're giving Leland Brickmeyer one hell of a guided tour through his personal nightmare."

"What's that mean?"

"That man's not had to work for anything his whole life. He's been able to buy off the opinions of the town. Been happening in the Junction since the railroad tracks were laid. You're the first person to call bullshit on him, and he don't know how to respond."

"I'm not doing it to frustrate him. I think he's hiding something."

Bullen pushed off from the side of the car. One hand reached up to scratch the back of his head. "Either way, even if he's not guilty of covering up that boy's murder, he's being exposed for a phony. If that's all you can accomplish, I'll be satisfied."

As he walked away, I experienced a moment's pang of regret at not asking him about his father's land. I had been grilling everyone else, but I guess Bullen had done me a solid, so he was off the hook. For now.

He reached the rear of the car and stopped, seeming to contemplate a minor point, and then he came back to the driver's side door. He said, "Oh, and here's a picture that showed up at the office this morning."

It was me and Leland Brickmeyer shaking hands outside Emmitt Laveau's funeral. It had been shot in such a way that obscured our mutual hatred. From that angle, the handshake appeared sincere. I was mortified.

As I surveyed it he said, "I managed to snag it before anybody saw it."

I looked for the photographer's viewpoint. I said, "Not that anybody at the police station would see anything wrong with that picture, save for the fact that I'm in it."

"Touche," he said. The word tumbled out awkwardly. "Isn't that what you said earlier?"

"Yep."

"There's one of two implications here. Either the photographer wants people to believe that you and Leland are hiding something together-"

"In which case, the blackmailer's completely off the mark, because nobody has enough of a beef to implicate Leland Brickmeyer." I wanted to finish by saying *except you,* but my mind choked on the phrase.

He said, "This story's getting pretty big. If a party interested in running against Leland wants to cause static, this would be the easiest way to do it."

"But that implies I'm the suspect. That's the only way this works."

Bullen shrugged. "The other thing I was going to say is that whoever took the photograph wants to throw *the both* of you under the bus. If you keep showing up around the Brickmeyers, that might be exactly what happens."

"This is the only one, though."

"Who's to say there aren't others?" He nodded at me and sort of half-smiled. "You can keep that one."

"I'm still going to track down your brother," I said.

"Good luck," he replied.

With that, he turned and strolled back to his cruiser. The way I used to look at him, I thought his walk was something of an arrogant saunter, but it wasn't until then I saw that it was a slight limp that made him walk that way. He was hurting, and it wasn't a recent thing. He might have been carrying one of his legs with him his whole life, hurting the whole time.

I drove away with my mind full of burs. Along the side of the road, someone had placed little political road signs, as if there were an election, and the text on them read "We Stand Behind Brickmeyer."

Another one read "The Brickmeyers are the foundation of this town."

Jesus. No one group was credited with the sentiment, and it might have been fine if there weren't just so many of them. One seemed to appear every fifty feet for the whole of my drive home, as if the message were meant specifically for me.

Well, isn't it, I wondered.

* * *

A man who doesn't want to be found in a town as small as Lumber Junction can become damn near invisible. If H.W. was going to answer any questions about his recent whereabouts and why he was in town, I'd have to flash a light on him, make him scurry out of the pantry.

It takes a special kind of person to draw him out in the open, and it just so happened I had two people in mind for such a task.

I went to Virgil's and seated myself next to the old pulpwooders, telling them what I needed. They responded, in turn, with nearly toothless grins. Lyle said, "Boy, there something wrong with you? For the longest time, I thought your right hand *was* a Miller High Life. Now that you don't have one, it seems maybe you're not disfigured."

Red elbowed him. "I can see the reds of your eyes have turned white. That makes you suspect, partner. Can't be trusted, no sir."

Giggling at their own jokes, they flicked dirty peanuts into their mouths and washed them down with beer.

"Laugh it up," I said, hoping the change the subject, "but I'm here strictly on business."

They regarded each other with pat skepticism. I waited, my eyes bouncing from one to the other. I said, "I can wait. Take your time."

I went down to my end of the bar and ordered a Coke, no ice, and sipped it without looking in the pulpwooders' direction. I didn't want to spook them. They thought me being sober meant I was up to something, no different than when an old drinking buddy finds Jesus.

It took them two songs to reach a decision. They approached me, keeping their distance as they spoke. "You need somebody to be smoked out of the woodwork, so to speak?" Red asked. He looked sort of like Popeye, if Popeye had done forty years of knuckle-grinding work.

"It needs to be kept secret. As if you can't tell, people are skeptical of me. I show my face, and folks get edgy. Can I trust you?"

"Ain't that what it's all about? Ain't that why you called on us?"

I sipped my soda. It was somewhat flavorless here, like chewing raw lettuce at an all-you-can-eat buffet, but it kept my hands moving, and at a bar, having a distraction was the main point. I said, "This man, the one you're scouting, he might be dangerous, but-"

"You just give us a name and a fitting down payment, and we'll make sure daylight touches his ass by tomorrow. Then we'll contact you when we know the *for sure* location."

"I just want you to *find* him. That understood? He finds out anybody's looking for him, he's gone. He'll leave town. I do not want that."

The old man cackled and elbowed his partner again. "Ain't no problem at all. I heard about your troubles, and I don't blame you for wanting somebody else to take some heat off of you. Shit, I'm a hunnert percent stunned that you would step foot back into a bar, what with the potential for jail brushing up against you at every turn."

"Everyone insists on reminding me of that."

"Cause ever body thinks you're as crazy as a goddamn *loon*, that's why," he said. "I ain't no different. It's like watching a snake fight a mongoose. You can never tell which one's gonna end up laying belly up in the grass. No offense, Rolson, but right now my money's not on you."

"That's all right, I suppose, so long as you don't do anything to tilt the odds."

Red raised his hands defensively, smiling in a way that made me sick to my stomach. He rubbed his hands together, popping his knuckles, and a glimmer of life flickered in his bloodshot eyes. "Hey, you're the paying customer, bud. That's the only thing's gonna influence *me*."

"Let me ask you something else," I said. "You guys have been living in this town your whole lives."

"Didn't even leave the county for the first fifteen years of my life," Red said.

"Same here," Lyle added. "Had a friend take a photograph of me at the county line one time, right before I crossed it the first time, and that ain't no joke."

"That when you was drafted?" Red asked.

"Yessir. Got shipped off to Khe Sanh in late '67, just in time to see the U.S. Air Force bombed Central Vietnam to the Dark Ages."

I said, "That must have been a hell of a time to see the world. Listen, in addition to all of this other business, I've been thinking a lot about my lawyer-"

Red smiled and sucked air through one of the gaps in his teeth. "You just now figuring out he's an old, limp prick?"

"Sort of," I said. "He's always been kind to my family, but people have let slip some things he might be keeping chained up in the shadows of his younger days."

"Anybody old enough to remember him don't know of no shadows," Red replied, and Lyle nodded in agreement. "Man's got the benefit of time behind him."

"In what way?"

"Distance always makes the past look softer than it probably was at the time. Makes things forgivable, but - man alive - he was a snake and a scorpion when he was a young feller."

Lyle added, "Even called Big Bill Brickmeyer a 'nigger lover' in a town meeting one time, full in view of all the black folks starting to take Dr. King's lead on that race stuff."

"What?"

"Mean as a goddamn rattlesnake," Red said. "He damn sure was."

"What changed in the man?"

Red raised his eyebrows and blew out a long breath. "Mid-eighties, a black kid in his twenties turned up dead, but nothing came of it. Things was different back then. This kid was sort of a troublemaker, had no mama and daddy. Wasn't nobody concerned with catching whoever threw him in a ditch."

Lyle took a swig of his beer. "We all have something to be ashamed of from back in them days," he said. "Nothing like that, but we didn't help matters none."

"Anyway, after that story sort of went away, Jarrell seemed to have a change of heart. Started fighting against all the shit he'd been fighting for all them years. It looked sorta funny on him at first, but he started to wear it well, and - hell - that's the man I reckon he is today."

It wasn't something I wanted to hear right now, but it was filling in some of the pieces of my own life. If he was this staunch a racist when I was a kid, it would explain why he had defended my father in court.

Red raised a hand and waggled one wrinkled finger at me. "And that dead young man ain't the half of what Jarrell Clements has done in his life."

I thought of the bumbling, slightly pudgy old man he had become, and I had trouble imagining his more vicious side. But I had to trust these two, because I don't know if they knew what guile was, let alone how to put it in action.

Lyle cleared his throat. "There was the time he said he was going to gut that old preacher man."

"The one that was out at Ridge Bluff all them years? That's right. Said all their jumping around and screaming wouldn't do no good, that they was still on a quick ride to Hell."

"Do you think he's a different man, or just pretending to be that way?"

Red took some time to stare into his glass. "Hard to say," he said, finally. "Man's heart is damn near impossible to know. But he's made a damn fine living these last twenty some-odd years doing the right thing."

"That gives me some thinking to do," I said. "Keep in touch."

I downed the Coke, paid, and left, glancing once over my shoulder on my way out the door to see the two men scheming already.

* * *

I called Detective Hunter that evening. He answered the phone on the first ring. I ran through my encounter with Jeffrey and the traffic stop and told him about the picture.

"Leland Brickmeyer isn't even on our radar," he said. "You don't have much to worry about in that regard, but I can't deny people aren't looking into you."

"That's fine," I replied. "They won't find anything but me trespassing on his land. I just went over there to ask him some questions earlier."

"What did you and Jeffrey talk about?" The clack of computer keys rattled off in the background like popping knuckles.

"Do what now?" I stalled, debating my answer. If I told him about the teacher banquet that an Emmitt Laveau had attended, the detective's sixth sense would be aroused. If too much pressure was placed on Leland and Jeffrey, they would put up a perpetual stonewall.

"You glossed over your discussion with Jeffrey Brickmeyer. What did the two of you talk about that angered him?"

In the end I decided to tell the truth. Something told me I might need Hunter's assistance in the future. "He knew Laveau."

"Knew him? How?"

"He lied about meeting him. I had a conversation with an old

209

teacher who confirmed Laveau attended an event at their house, one where all involved parties were present."

To his credit, the detective refrained from any sort of response. No sigh. No *Goddamnit*. No nothing. Just the machine gun fire of keys. "I'll look into it," he said.

"I know it doesn't amount to much, but it's proof that some lies are being floated to the public. They might have never talked to him, but damnit he was at their house. We know that for a *fact*."

"Mmm-hmm. Okay, it's not a big fuck-up, but it fits. Secrecy is a Brickmeyer thing. Leland is no different than his old man, who was apparently as paranoid as a mob boss. Leland's reticence is probably related to how his father raised him."

I moved the cell phone to my other ear. "Thankfully, the youngest scion isn't quite so tight-lipped."

"He would be smart to distance himself from his father. He'll get dragged in by association, and something tells me the old man wouldn't hesitate to stick junior in his place, if need be."

I didn't tell him that I felt the exact same way. "It won't get through to him. I told him the same thing, but he's got daddy issues. Wants to prove to the old man that he's capable of shouldering the legacy. He's even got a life-size portrait hanging on the wall above his head."

"Well, that's all you can do," Hunter said. "You know what's funny?"

I could almost hear him smiling. "What?" I asked.

"In the grand scheme of things, who is Leland Brickmeyer? Nobody, really, right? A local politician. A state senator with no sense that he's bumping up against the ceiling. And yet, here you are, implicating him in a murder, and he's lying to protect his career."

"Some people have no shame," I said.

"I guess you're right, McKane. Take it easy, and keep your ass safe."

* * *

Driving home made me anxious. I wasn't satisfied with anything right now. There was so much to consider, from the revelation about Jarrell Clements's history to the pictures and the cops tightening down on me. I imagined things would get sticky from here on out.

Also, I wasn't convinced about Ronald Bullen. His turnaround could be a ploy, and yet he had given me solid information, so I wouldn't betray him. Not yet. Besides, if he was beginning to trust *me*, there was a possibility I could get some inside information from the department.

Checking the time on my phone, I saw a missed call from Jarrell. A coldness spread through my chest and not just because of what the old pulpwooders had told me. Tracking down Emmitt Laveau's killer had distracted me from my looming court date, scheduled two days from now. Too many loose ends needed to be tied together before I entered that courthouse, for two reasons. Number one: the longer the murder investigation lingered, the more distant a possibility an arrest would become. Number two: there was a chance *I* was going to jail for some indeterminate amount of time.

In the state of Georgia, pleading guilty to a DUI makes you subject to several penalties: a stiff fine, in upwards of two thousand bucks; probation; loss of driving privileges for at least six months and more likely a year; and, what I feared most, jail time. The minimum sentence is one day, and the maximum is an entire year, if there aren't other, extenuating circumstances. Like a car accident. Injury. That sort of thing.

Jarrell didn't answer when I called back. Part of me was thankful. I didn't have time to worry about the future until it was the present.

* * *

Vanessa spending this time with me felt strange, but I had no real way of dealing with it, other than to let it happen. I felt ineffectual. She had left me, run off with another guy, leapfrogged from bed to bed, nearly killed herself with drugs, and she had come back, acknowledging what she had done.

And, coldly or not, I had welcomed her back, let her just come back into my life. I couldn't just tell her to leave. I still felt like there was something we hadn't dealt with, and I wanted to come to terms with it before we parted ways. If we parted ways. That thought, too, circled in the back of my mind.

I can still recall the good times. They're packed up and hidden in the attic of my memory, but they still exist. If remembrance were painted in broader strokes, there's a great portion of my life I wouldn't want to experience, even in thought.

But Vanessa and I had been happy enough. Even the worst marriages aren't completely empty.

Everything started well. We dated throughout high school, and I can remember our first date, which could also double as our finest hour. In a gesture that in retrospect seems simultaneously nice and corny, I invited her for a picnic near a lake north of the Junction. She wore a floral print sun dress and little leather sandals, and I can't for the life of me remember what I wore, but it was too hot for the weather and I was nervous, a sixteen year old boy on his first real date. I ended up sweating through my shirt on the drive and kept wondering if Vanessa thought me strange.

I forgot the blanket and, despite that, Vanessa enthusiastically volunteered to kneel in the grass by the lake in order to eat our sandwiches and salads and pieces of fruit: grapes and slices of watermelon and whatnot. When we were done, she backed up and reclined against an old oak tree, and all that comes to me now are the indentations of the ground on her knees and the blades of grass that remained. That one detail is as fresh and clear as the moment it happened. Everything else has blurred, like shadows on a wall, but that one moment remains unsullied by time.

I went over to her and brushed the stray blades away, gently, trembling all over, and she grabbed my hand and guided it up her thigh beyond the edge of the dress, pressing my fingers down so they experienced the smooth warmth of her skin. The shiver that passed through me then still hits me today, triggered by the distinct smell of a certain kind of spring air.

But memory is unreliable.

The house was alive with light when I pulled into the driveway, so I knew for at least another day that she hadn't slunk away to find some new and desperate way to hit bottom.

Vanessa was sitting on the couch, watching some reality show, her chin propped up on her knuckles, and she smiled at me as I came through the door. "You okay?" she asked, and I nodded, a complete lie.

"Just tired," I said.

I went into the kitchen and grabbed a beer. I twisted the cap off and set the bottle on the counter, staring at the condensation. The idea of drinking made my stomach turn. I thought about the time before, of throwing up, which in turn made me think of the rancid cure-all Kweku Laveau had given me. Maybe it had taken a few days to get its claws into me, but now that it had, the damn thing wouldn't let go. It wasn't that I didn't want to drink; it was that I almost physically couldn't.

When I brought the High Life up to take a swig, the smell of it sent a sickening pulse through me, and I ended up pouring it down the sink, watching it fizz and bubble going down the drain. Instead, I poured myself a glass of sweet tea from a fresh pitcher Vanessa had made - she couldn't live without the stuff - and went in the living room.

"Court date's the day after tomorrow," she said, muting the television.

"I know."

She had that same disaffected look about her, but there was something else to it, too. She seemed to be missing something that would make her complete, and I searched for what it might be.

"That what you're thinking about?" she asked.

"I haven't really thought about it much over the last few days." And I definitely couldn't tell her what I was actually thinking about. My eyes darted once to her thighs, covered by jeans, and it brought me back to the day by the lake.

"That old coot Clements going to be able to get you the minimum on the DUI?"

"I hope so," I said. "Janita Laveau's going to make a statement on my behalf. What have you done all day?"

"Cleaned up this pig sty for you." She paused. "As a way of saying thank you, I guess."

"Thanks," I said, looking around. She'd even managed to mop the hardwood, which I absolutely never did. I returned her smile and joined her, sitting on the opposite end of the couch.

"I know it's weird having me here," she said, leaning back against the headrest and staring at the ceiling. "It should make you feel good that I trust you enough to come back like this."

Not exactly, I wanted to say.

"It's confusing, Van," I said, turning my attention to the muted television. "And I'm not in the mood to talk about it."

"Well, fine." In my periphery, I saw her make a face. Just a slight tweak of her features, but enough to know that she was displeased.

And this is how the past is dredged up, not in the pleasant memories but the half-forgotten anger of a thousand petty arguments.

I sighed. "Stay as long as you need, and we'll talk about the awkwardness later. I've got a lot on my mind, from the DUI to everything else. Just stay clean and we'll be all right until then."

She ran her fingers through her long, dark hair. "I thought we might have an opportunity to talk. About. Um, us?"

"Is that what you cleaned up for?"

"No, I just thought it'd be nice."

"There isn't any *us* right now. You're staying here because you need help getting that shit out of your system."

"But it's been nice being here," she replied. "It's like you said. I can't be concerned with who I was but only try to be a new me."

"That's not what I meant." What I'd meant was, I didn't mean for that to apply to *me*.

"I guess I'm just trying to make up for things."

I saw her eyes growing wet, but I couldn't soften. I had grown calloused in the time she'd been gone. Hell, I reckon I'd always been calloused, just not toward her.

"Listen. Okay. Yes, it has been good having you here. Fuck, Van, I never asked you to leave. You did that all on your own."

"And I'm-"

"Don't. *Don't.*" I tried to pick my way through all of the things I wanted to say, like choosing a blade for a good, old-fashioned knife fight, but looking at her made that hard to do.

"I am, though," she said. "Sorry."

It was impossible not to clench my fists and my jaw. "And if you get the jones again? If I wake up at midnight to the sound of tires on the road?"

Everything about what I felt was ugly and mean, but that didn't keep me from wanting her. All the time she had spent away had locked away desire, but even starved it hadn't died in those chains.

She was crying openly now, and I leaned in and put my face between her neck and shoulder, and I smelled her, the way she used to be. I was shaking, and some of it was from sobriety and the other was from being pissed off and lonely.

Her hands were on me, on my back and on my neck and then in my lap. I kissed her just below the lobes of her ears and ran one of my hands down her side, down below the hip. We were both desperate and unhappy, but at least right then we had each other.

She unbuttoned my jeans and slipped a hand inside, and I found the latch of her bra with one hand and tried to unhook it. It was going to happen like this, and it was going to be a mistake, but it was going to be made.

But then something happened. My head became disoriented, and I felt the edge of my mind becoming blurry with one of those visions. It was faint, but it was there for me to experience.

Not now, I thought. Not now, not now, goddamnit.

Had I been drunk, I might have seen everything, smelled the stink of their indiscretions, but I caught enough to make me pull back. I didn't know if it were my imagination or a true vision, but it was enough to push me back.

Her eyes widened when she saw the look on my face. In that instant, I saw her face not as it had been on that day by the lake but cracked with drug use, sliding down a man's chest beyond his gut, kissing him every few inches, and then disappearing so that the top of her head was all that was visible.

I flinched. "What?" she said, reaching back to where she had been holding me.

I pushed her hand away. The image in my head was gone, but the silhouette of it remained with me, and I felt sick. "I can't," I said.

She leaned back, her face a question mark.

I got up, and I went into the bedroom and picked up an old Stephen King paperback, lying on the bed and letting my eyes go over the words, even if I had no idea what it was I was reading. Several minutes later, I heard a sob as loud as a dog's bark and then the opening and slamming of the front door. The junker Van was driving groaned to life, and she went squealing off into the night.

Fine. Just fine. That was her MO. I just hoped she wasn't going out to get high, and I spent the rest of the night wondering where she was.

It wasn't until I went into the bathroom to start a shower that I found a silver coin lying face up on the sink. On one side was a prayer for serenity - *God grant me the serenity to accept the things I cannot change -* and on the other the words "one day." I found another one on the nightstand on the side of the bed where I normally slept when we were together. She'd meant for me to see them, to give me a hint, I think I might have reacted differently had I seen them first.

* * *

"You believe in voodoo, Deuce?" I asked him outright. We were leaning against the bar, under the faint, orange glow of the neon signs. The smell of beer was so strong it was like it was being pumped in through the vents.

But that didn't mean it was unpleasant, either. A bar's smell is often agreeable if you have spent enough time in them, particularly in the afternoon. I don't know if that's sad or not, but it probably is.

"Not any more than a normal man, I suppose, old buddy," he replied. Then his face changed. "Wait a minute. I thought you were supposed to be the one to disregard all that spiritual nonsense."

It was early evening - too early, even, for the street lights to flicker on - and yet the bar was half-full. If I didn't know any better, I'd have thought there was something heavy in the air. People seemed restless. That, and the pulpwooders were noticeably absent, their normal places now manned by a couple of strangers in dingy work shirts.

"You say that," I said, "but I'm sitting on a stool in a bar and I don't even have the *urge* order a beer. Have you ever known me to do that?"

Deuce took a drink and placed his frosted mug back in its spot, rested his arms on the rail. "It doesn't have anything to do with your scheduled appearance in court tomorrow, does it?"

There was a hint of disapproval in his voice, but only a hint. I mean, he *was* sitting here with me, after all.

"No," I said, though I hadn't thought of it in quite that way. It sort of shocked me. "At least I don't think so. I think it has to do with something out of the ordinary."

"Would you get the cotton out of your mouth, Rol? You're talking nonsense."

"Janita Laveau's uncle."

"The old voodoo man."

"Yeah." I saw two kids, maybe not even twenty-one, necking in the corner. My heart did a weird two step and then went back to normal. "He gave me some godawful drink the other day, and, well, I don't know. Something happened."

"He gave you anti-drinking juice?" Deuce smiled wryly. "The people at Budweiser would shit themselves if they knew that existed."

"Don't be patronizing. What he gave me tasted like it had been scraped from the bottom of the Okefenokee. Called it a cure-all."

Deuce shook his head and groaned absently. He wasn't focused on me. He had become infatuated with a sliver of frost, using a fingernail to push it around the surface of the glass. "And you drank it? That old man handed you a cup full of chum, and you went and you drank it?"

"I was trying to get in his good graces. I wanted some information out of him, and, I don't know, I guess I thought drinking that mess might help me. Goddamn folk magic."

"Magic doesn't even begin to describe voodoo."

"How would you know?"

"I was in the NFL, buddy," he said. "Nobody in this world is more superstitious than a professional athlete, *especially* a football player."

"Really? Even in the pros?"

"Think about it. Football is regimented like no other sport. It follows very specific rules repetitively. As a football player, you get caught up in the repetition. You practice the same game plan, the same plays, the same *movements*, until there's not much more you can perfect.

It's easy to become fixated on the little things."

"I guess that makes sense," I said.

"That's how players get caught up in believing superstition. Coaches tell them from a very young age, 'It's about the little things. Do the little things right, and you *will* win football games.' Now, that mentality transfers over. The player begins to think the way he brushes his teeth or what he keeps in his locker will have an impact on the game. As long as you're winning, people don't say anything. People, all people, begin to believe these superstitions themselves."

"That's insane. They can't all believe that."

"This coming from the very same person who thought it completely understandable to elicit information about the afterlife from a suicidal hillbilly high on meth-amphetamines."

I scratched my chin, wondering if I should relate my bad dreams to Deuce. "I have my reasons."

But he had already moved back to thinking about his days in the NFL. I could see him thinking about something, hesitating. Finally, he said, "One teammate of mine - and no matter whether you believe me or not, this is no shit - but one of them, a perpetual Pro Bowler, had his own personal mojo man."

"I would have thought that crazy a month ago. Hell, weeks ago. It doesn't sound so bad now."

Deuce finished off his beer. The amber liquid drained into his mouth, leaving only suds, and he placed the mug on the bar and burped. It was dainty and constrained for such a big man, and I nearly smiled. Meanwhile, I sipped on my Coca-Cola.

"Consulted with him before every. Single. Game."

"And what exactly is a 'mojo man?'"

"Think of that old Muddy Waters song, 'Got My Mojo Working.' Not much different than it sounds. Dude keeps little charms and things in a bag called a mojo. He don't do everything the voodoo men do, but he does some things. Kept a criminal's hand with him at all times."

"A *human* hand?"

Deuce nodded in a way that made me wonder if he was having me over. "Lopped off at the wrist. It was all shriveled and desiccated. Saw it for myself before a game against Carolina."

"What possible use could it serve?"

"Said it kept him outta jail. Said, and I'm just saying, but he said he ain't been locked up since he got that hand. What he *didn't* say was he'd given up bum wine, too, but I'm sure he didn't take that into account."

"You'd think he'd of just put himself under a spell, if he was so powerful."

Deuce motioned to the barkeep for another beer. "Logic and spirituality don't mix much. You should know that. Look at your situation. It isn't logical that dirt and grass mixed with water would make you stop drinking."

"I suspected he might have been up to something when he gave it to me, but I just figured that he'd be doing...different things."

"Well, voodoo ain't got nothing to do with sticking pins into dolls and chanting at midnight, either. That's where they get it wrong in the movies."

"The movies always seem to do that."

"Christianity influenced the voodoo practiced in the U.S., but what they believe doesn't have much to do with a man dying on a cross two thousand years ago. That's what the Pro Bowler's main guy told me, that voodoo, on its ear, just means 'contemplating the unknown.' and damned if there ain't a lot of that going on."

"I never knew you had a grasp on all of this."

The bartender dropped a bottle of Bud in front of him, a napkin underneath, and Deuce took his time transferring the beer to the stein, tilting the glass and the bottle simultaneously. My mouth soured watching the bottle empty.

"What people don't realize is that voodoo is powerful because

220

people believe it, like how believing in God makes people think they can pick up live snakes or drive planes into skyscrapers. There's power in that, good or bad, and you can't deny it."

"True."

He said, " This is no different. Just because people in movies who doin' voodoo look crazy as shithouse rats shouldn't shake the fact that a lot people do think it's very real. When that belief is there, nothing can displace it. Half the power of voodoo is believing in it yourself, and if you believe it as a priest, so will the people subjected to it."

The door opened and light flooded in, stomping out all the shadows. The spell of the bar was momentarily broken, and, as if the voodoo talk was somehow itself a trance, Deuce changed the subject.

"So, big day tomorrow."

"What is going to happen will happen," I said distractedly. On top of everything else, I was worried about Vanessa now, too.

"You don't seem worried."

"I've got other things on my mind."

A loud racket emerged from the other side of the room. Buford McKibben, an old and not-quite-retired small engine repairman, slapped the video poker machine and let loose a series of curses only vaguely resembling English. His voice cut like a saw blade through the jangle of Willie Nelson's guitar.

When Buford finished his rant, Deuce's attention returned to me. His face was bathed in that orange light. He said, "Well, at the very least, you've got one day in county lock-up. That's just the rule. Don't you think the people who did this know that? If you take too long a nap, something's going to disappear, I can tell you that. Then you'll have the rest of your life for this to be on your mind, and I can guarantee you don't want that."

"I know. I reckon I'll have to make a big move in the next day or so."

"Big meaning stupid."

"Pretty much."

"What is driving you to do this?"

"'The sins of the father are visited upon the son,' and, God help me, I was witness to something as a kid I was never meant to see, and I've been paying for it my entire life. Some part of me thinks helping the Laveau family will get some of the muck off my hands."

"All right," he said, trying to sound bewildered, though the look in his eyes told me different. "It's your dog you're putting in this fight. Just don't be surprised if you have to put him down afterwards."

* * *

Deuce left shortly thereafter, and I remained glued to my barstool, ordering Coke and staring blankly at the television. I thought about Emmitt Laveau the rest of the evening.

I still didn't have a sense of who he was, really. All I had to go on were the memories of friends and loved ones and a few supernatural dreams.

I knew a few things, though. He had given no one reason to harm him. He had attended Georgia Southern down in Statesboro for a couple of semesters before dropping out to wait tables in Savannah. After bumming around that city for a couple of years, he returned to Lumber Junction with a temporary teaching certificate in hand. Wanted to work with special needs children at the high school.

Two women I had spoken to broke down in tears talking about him. Lorreta Barnes had said, "I had never, until this whole situation, thought racism a problem in this city anymore. God help us all."

Was it, though? I wondered. Could I be certain racism was to blame, or were people hiding something about him and the Brickmeyer family? Jeffrey, especially, seemed weirded out when I mentioned Laveau around him.

Several possibilities emerged, but the most obvious to me was that he had moved back to the Junction to run away from something in Savannah. It made sense that he would come back home if he had run into some trouble down there. However, no mysterious strangers had been noticed snooping around town, and in Lumber Junction folks tend to notice unfamiliar people.

He and Jeffrey Brickmeyer both had had troubles down in Savannah, but they'd lived down there at slightly different times, so there was no real connection between them. Strike that from the investigation.

"Another soda," I said to the bartender, and when he brought it and I reached for my wallet, he shook his head. "This one ain't on you."

"Thanks," I replied.

"Oh, I didn't do it," Louis cackled, nodding over my shoulder. "He's been paying for them since Deuce left."

Leaned back in a chair was Leland Brickmeyer's right hand man. Somehow, in here, he looked more ragged than the last time I'd seen him. He raised his beer, held it there for a second, and then tilted his head back like he wanted me to come sit with him.

I checked the length of the bar. Could be some kind of set-up. But I didn't see anything. Nobody even seemed to notice I was there, except the one guy, Brickmeyer's heavy hand, whose name was Bodean Driscoll, Deuce had told me.

I couldn't say now what made me do it, but I did go and sit with him. I felt a little woozy, but I attributed that as much to being in a bar as anything else.

He said, "Drinking cokes, huh? Better watch it. Makes it hard for people to be charitable and buy you a beer."

"What do you want?"

"Grab a seat, big guy," he replied. "I got no beef with you."

"What the fuck are you doing motioning me over here?"

He smiled. "Hey. Whoa. I just bought you a drink, man. Doesn't

223

that entitle me to a few sentences? Just give me something to work with."

My muscles were so tight I thought I could feel my bones clenching. The way he smiled just begged for me to deck him; I don't know why. I guess I was tired, ill, grasping for anger. And something was spinning in my head. "Did Brickmeyer send you here?"

"Which one, the boss or the fairy?"

I stared.

"All right," he said, laughing about his little joke. "Yeah, the big man sent me out here. Figured I'd be able to calm the tide a little bit, seeing as every time the two of you were in each other's presence, you tend to go goddamn nuclear."

"Were you the one chasing me that night, after I left the bar?"

He didn't react. I expected something. Jesus, even if it was ridiculous, I expected him to laugh at me, but all he did was give me that smile, that all-knowing grin. He reminded me of a crocodile.

Finally, he said, "Boy, you sure don't disappoint, do you? Leland said you'd bring the crazy, and I had seen it some myself, but he didn't tell me you were this fucking nutso. Je. Sus. No, I ain't had a part in people fucking with you. I come here to make amends."

I stared at him. He said, "I ain't shitting you, man. I'm an honest guy. Got to work for Mr. Brickmeyer because I've got a security background. I just happen to have a head for numbers, too, so I fit in real well with his model for running business. That not make much sense to you? Probably shouldn't. But with guys like you sniffing the air around him, especially with the way you're staring at me, Leland has no choice but to have people like me around."

"What was Jeffrey doing at Laveau's funeral?"

However tough his facade, this last comment elicited a reaction. His flesh-colored eyebrows twitched. "I didn't see him. Didn't know he would be there, actually."

Something in the man's eyes betrayed him, like a light flickering after an electrical surge. I looked away, careful not to let on that I knew he was lying.

"No, no. He came out to the graveside and pretended not to look interested. Know anything about that?"

"I done told you I didn't know shit. You think I'm just an errand boy. Why go and ask all these questions?"

"Somebody's got to answer them. Why not you? Plus, and I think this is the more related point, you strolled in here and started buying me *drinks*." I gestured at the Coke.

"I am like the, uh, *intermediary* between you and my boss."

"So you're giving me the polite shine-on. Buying me flat Coca-Cola and showing off your personality. Forgive me for being skeptical."

He leaned forward, resting one elbow on the table between us. "No offense taken. Brickmeyer wants to see to it that you give up this personal mission to ruin his name."

"A bribe? That what you here for?"

"It won't help to use that language." He paused, perhaps to think of the exact way of easing himself back into his former point. "You're looking at some jail. Not a lot, mind you-"

"Bare minimum's a day in county. I can swing that."

"One word from the big man himself, and your problems could be washed away. He's got some influence with the DA."

I thought it over. "And all I'd have to do is give up on my investigation?"

"That's it, chief. Just head back out to the country and don't make a peep for a while."

I thought of Emmitt Laveau and Janita. I thought of my dreams. I thought of my mother. "Forget it. I'm sticking with it, but don't let that get between our newfound friendship," I said. "I'm liking these free drinks."

"Personally, I don't give a damn what you do. You're an alcoholic in complete denial. I suspect you'll probably end up tripping over your disease."

"Sounds like a broken record, that idea. Let's get on something fresh, like Jeffrey Brickmeyer."

"Go ahead."

"What gives with his attendance at the funeral?"

He looked around, peeking at some older couple in the corner, and then turned back to me. "Jeffrey's a private man. Got that from his daddy. And they aren't keen on the hive getting throttled around like this."

"I've never seen a more thin-skinned politician in my life."

His smile widened, but he shook his head. He took another swig of his Bud, finishing it off, and jangled it in front of him. "You want that soda topped off? I'm getting another brew." He shrugged noncommittally. "Long as it's on the boss, you know."

I told him no, but he insisted. I shrugged, and he went to the bar with my cup in hand. No skin off my back; it wasn't like I was going to drink it, either way. He was basically wasting his time and his hospitality.

As he stood there at the bar, I felt a wave of groggy nausea wash over me. I leaned forward and placed my face on my knuckles. Something was making me woozy, like a Nyquil hangover. Being caught up in conversation with Driscoll had distracted me, I guess, and I hadn't realized how sick I was.

At one point that evening, before I'd realized there were eyes on me, the bartender had taken a call, turning his back to the bar and stuffing one finger in his ear to hear the person on the other line. My mind was hazy, but I couldn't recall if I'd had a drink in front of me at the moment, or if someone Bodean's size had sauntered up to the bar, maybe to sprinkle something into my soda.

Or was this another manifestation of Uncle K's punishment? It certainly reeked of his involvement, but I no longer cared, one way or the other. I felt punch-drunk, and everything around me was growing dimmer.

"Hey, you all right?" Bodean said, and I nodded unconvincingly. The spins hit me like the blunt end of a claw hammer, and I tried to stand, thinking maybe getting myself upright, getting some good ground underneath me, might help.

It didn't. I lurched forward, knocking the table sideways, sending both it and Bodean's glass to the floor.

"Hey, come on," cried someone in the bar. "The hell you doing serving somebody this hammered?"

"Shut up," replied Louis. He sounded like he was talking through water. "I haven't ever seen Coca-Cola do *that* to a man before."

I closed my eyes and expected the floor to rush up and meet me, but two hands caught me and propped me up instead.

"Easy now," Bodean said. He hefted me up, placing my arm across his impossibly broad shoulders, and carried me over to the bar. "Cup of water for my friend here."

I don't remember much after that. The water stands out as familiar, and Bodean patting me on the back, but after that, only moments are available to memory. A soothing voice. Vomiting. Bright lights. Angry voices. Then, darkness. Just. Darkness. I did not dream of dead men, and I suppose for that, at least once, I was thankful.

Ninth Chapter

I remember some parts of that night, the night my father took his revenge on my mother's lover, but most of it as a narrative breaks up into indistinct parts.

I do remember seeing my father choking him, beating him, kicking him. I remember the sound of bones breaking like pieces of crackling over a fire. I remember how the hangman's rope glistened under the glow of headlights.

And I remember blood, spilling from a man both guilty and innocent, and I remember the way his eyes widened with knowledge of his own looming death. Those eyes...I'll never forget. The memories from that night are like a backlit manuscript, one I will be forced to carry inside me for the rest of my life.

It doesn't always come back to me as a single, continuous event, like a movie running from beginning to end. Sometimes I catch only a snippet, but I am always beholden to it when it appears.

Often, I will be transported back to that night doing ordinary things. Once, while standing in line at the hardware store, someone stepped in beside me with a length of rope, and I had such a violent reaction to it that some people thought I was having a seizure. Instead of rope, I saw blood-stained twine being wrapped around a man's hands and feet to keep him from struggling, even then as he fought for breath, for his very life.

But, of those things, what I do not remember is what my father's accomplices looked like, not for the life of me. The single biggest shame of my life. I am only thankful that no one else knows that I saw what I saw, not even Vanessa. Just me and the shadows of the men who were there.

Whenever I am pulled back into that night, I am a child again, literally and figuratively, bound to the torture I witnessed. The men laugh and mock their captive, their faces obscured by gray smudges of the sort found in poorly-developed film. Only my father's face stands out, and it is such a grotesque, misshapen scowl, a devil's mask of scars and wrinkles, that I can't help but be drawn toward it, afraid that breaking my gaze will somehow cause him to see me. And so I remain among the high grass and trees that hide me, dozens of feet away, and I watch a man die.

I never stepped forward. Never said a word, and so though I can't carry the weight of his death - that would be co-opting his pain - I can't unburden myself of it, and I guess maybe it's why I had become obsessed with the Emmitt Laveau case.

Sometimes I see his face in a crowd, or in the corner of a dark mirror, and until this past week, I thought I was a little crazy. Maybe I still am. Maybe my dreams are not proof that I am sane but that I am even crazier than I thought. Or maybe he's always been there, and I never realized it.

Even joining the Lumber Junction Police Department at twenty-five, on my birthday, ten days after September 11, 2001, and after seven years of aimlessly working jobs I didn't care for, the roots dragging me downward had not loosened. I felt trapped in a limbo caused not by me but by a dangerous and humorless man, and if fate played any role in my life, it was playing one now.

* * *

230

I woke when daylight broke through the sterile white blinds. Squinting, I prodded my body with trembling fingers. My veins felt like someone had injected them with radiator fluid. I was shaking. It was as bad as any hangover I had experienced. As bad as one anybody in any lifetime had suffered, I was willing to bet.

I tried to turn over. Something tugged at my arm. I found myself neither shocked nor surprised to be in a hospital room.

When my eyes could bear it, I looked up. Sitting across from me, under the wall-mounted television, was D.L. Vanessa's dad. My old boss. A shadow lay spread across him, his eyes staring unblinkingly at me. I said, "I didn't do this."

"God*damnit*, Rol, what the hell is wrong with you? You are missing *court*. The judge is likely to have you stoned to death - on a DUI charge, no less - for being caught drinking and driving."

I didn't even want to think about court. "Listen. Ugh. Hear me out."

"Have at it. Knock it dead." The wide-brim hat he'd worn every day since I had met him lay on his knees, and he spun it nervously as he waited.

Not only did attempting to talk hurt, it made me look guilty, so I settled for awkward silence. Thankfully, the doctor saved me from having to explain myself. What was I going to say? *Hey, boss, I got witnesses can say I was definitely just drinking soda...down at the bar.*

The doctor gently opened the door and smiled, padding right over to the edge of my bed. He smiled but didn't mince words. He said, "It was a mixture of Antabuse and Rohypnol. Whoever did this wanted to make sure you looked quite stupid last night."

Behind him, D.L., fiddling with his hat, said, "Thank God." As if that actually helped anything.

The doctor ignored him. He said, "Now, your liver activity is way up. Has anyone prescribed Antabuse to you?"

231

I maintained steady eye contact. It seemed necessary, somehow. "I don't even know what that shit is."

"I'll take that as an absolute no, then. Let me explain. Antabuse is prescribed to people with extreme alcohol dependence. It's medical name is disulfiram, and it basically causes you to get very, very sick when you drink alcohol. When the beer, wine, liquor, whatever, is metabolized, the disulfiram blocks the body from converting the acetaldehyde - which usually gives you hangover symptoms - into acetic acid - which prevents them - so the effect of the hangover is magnified. Somebody really got you good, too. That's why you feel like you've been thrown out of a building."

I listened to D.L.'s boots click on the hospital room floor as I considered this new information. I said, "Seems a bit harsh, doesn't it?"

The clicking stopped. I looked up. Both the doctor and D.L. were giving me awfully discouraging stares.

"The Antabuse," I said, "it seems a bit harsh on alcoholics, right?"

"Truth be told, Rolson, you shouldn't be drinking in the first place."

"I wasn't."

"In a bar."

Exactly what I was expecting. "I didn't have a drop. I drank Coke the entire time. It can be verified, I swear. I was just meeting Deuce there."

I couldn't help but notice his eyebrows bunch up and his mouth droop. He sighed.

"They also found alcohol in your system. Point one-oh. Enough to get you put in the tank. Officer Walton said he brought you here because you were acting like the Bogeyman had got after you. We ran some tests, sedated you, and now here you are."

I couldn't remember much after the Coke Bodean Driscoll brought me. A connection was forming, though, if Ricky Walton brought me in. He and Driscoll could have gotten me sauced after they roofied me. I

232

said, "If they talk to the bartender from last night, he can vouch for me. I don't remember much but that shouldn't matter, should it? Hell, talk to Deuce. He can vouch for me."

D.L. sucked his teeth. "Well, I think this is damn good evidence that you're pissing *somebody* off. I hope you know this means it ends here."

"Mmm-hmm," I replied. The doctor was pretending to find something interesting on his clipboard.

"I'm serious, Rol. This is about as deep as the shit can get before I put you in jail just to keep yourself safe." He pulled a chair to the hospital bed and clasped his hands between his knees. "Listen, I'm right there with you. You feel like you've got something to prove, and I can't blame you for trying to make up for what you did to Janita Laveau. It was a shitty thing, and even if you've got some enemies over at the force, they know you're a pretty good man. The problem is, I cannot go up to Leland Brickmeyer and make these kinds of accusations. It just cannot happen."

"Looking after your ass will only mean you'll run face-first into something."

"That's inevitable, no matter which end you try to protect. I just ain't got the right amount of kindling to get this fire started. No offense, buddy, but you're unreliable. You hang out in bars, after what you did, and now you've got some crazy scheme to upend this town."

"There is no balance in this town."

He ignored me. "If all you got is conjecture, then I can't listen to it. In fact, I won't listen to it. If you can't produce any solid evidence to connect the Brickmeyers to that young man's murder, I'm afraid I'll have to turn a deaf ear. I've been patient to the point of parody with you. But this is it. Consider yourself warned."

I looked away from him, rather abruptly, and stared down at my feet, which stuck up underneath the white sheets of the bed like small, nameless headstones. I said nothing. What was there to say to that?

233

"What are we going to do about court?" he asked. He was in the process of standing up. He obviously understood I had no intention of talking to him today. I needed to think, and the longer he browbeat me, the longer it would take for me to get over it and move on.

"I'm not going to do anything about it today." I kept my attention focused on my feet.

"Okay, listen. I'll talk to Jarrell and Judge Monroe about all of this. Given the fact that somebody drugged you, perhaps he'll listen to me and move your court date." He pointed at me. "But I can't guarantee that, you know. I'll do what I can."

"Thank you, D.L." It was almost physically painful to say.

He walked over to the door and said, a bit weakly, "I might not be here, if you hadn't talked Vanessa into coming to see me. So, I guess, thank *you*."

I could have sworn I saw his lip tremble just before he walked out of the room. I tried to roll over but couldn't, so I just spent the next couple of hours staring at the ceiling, thinking of what to do next.

* * *

At lunchtime, as I tried my best to fork down a block of ground meat drowning in a thin brown substance, Jarrell Clements thundered in, briefcase in hand.

"Woo boy, it's a hot one out there today," he said, smiling. My predicament could not have bothered him less. "You're lucky you ain't out in it."

"And even luckier to see you in person, I suppose." I pushed away the plate of slop and instead sipped the Mello Yello I had bribed out of a rebellious nurse.

"Boy, they sure can't get you down, can they? Even when they're trying to put you under the jail, you're still holding strong. Shit, I tell you, I might've lost every bit of nerve if what has happened to you had happened to me."

"D.L. came by to see me this morning. He was here when I, well, when I woke up. I told him all about what happened, and he sort of believed the doctor, who more or less corroborated my story."

"I've heard."

"How?" I tried to see the evil of that man's youth, but I couldn't quite see it on his face. He really had changed in his old age, it seemed.

"Lawyers are priests who use black magic. If they revealed their secrets, they would fail to enchant the audience. Speaking of enchanting audiences, how much of this story is the truth?"

I considered it. "Of what I told him? Everything. I'm not that into trusting reality at the moment, however, so don't quote me. I've been told I left the bar with the bad guy."

His smile was humorless. "Which makes you sound like a whore."

He watched me impatiently, his fingers tapping on the briefcase. I imagined several defenses for myself but ended up listening to an unidentified machine hum somewhere in the room.

"I called up the good Judge, and he'd already had a conversation with the chief. We might have to make a formal appearance, just so you can show yourself to be sober and upright in public for once, but I don't think it will be a huge problem."

"It doesn't look good, though, does it?"

"Could be better, but, hell, you're making it interesting. With somebody trying to dispatch you, it will be impossible to convict you on this second charge of drinking and driving. I'll make sure of that. The prosecution will be more than willing to let you cop a plea on a single charge than risk dragging through a trial. Being a victim only gives you sympathy, which they would obviously want to avoid."

"D.L. doesn't seem to think that's the case."

"Aw, D.L.'s just pissed at you. He treats you like a son. That second charge wouldn't stick to my latest issue of Playboy." Jarrell squinted and did one of those half-smile things, tilting his right hand back and forth, like a DJ having a seizure. His age-old scar glistened under the light. "The first charge, not so easy. It's an uphill battle."

He winked, and his open eye glimmered with a strange mixture of emotions. "But you have me on your side, and if that don't make you confident, then I don't know what will."

* * *

They let me out later that day. Jarrell, going well beyond his capacity as lawyer, chauffeured me to the impound lot. He even put up the money to get my half-assed rental out. "Something your daddy would have done for my boy, if I had one," he said, assuring me. "I won't even roll that into what you owe me."

Before he drove away, he stopped me and decided to tell me the thing that had obviously been cutting at his insides.

"You should know that your favorite local royal family is making the rounds on this," he said. "D.L. called me and said *an associate* of the middle age fucker's called and suggested you be put away for your own well-being."

I cocked an eyebrow. "D.L. going to bite on it?"

"You're here and not in jail, right?"

"Uh-huh."

"You got to wonder how long he'll be able to go without caving though, Rol. That man is a saint, but there's only so much he can do to keep your pecker out of the food processor."

"Brickmeyer ain't the law," I replied coarsely.

"But he and Judge Stanton play a smokey card game every once in awhile, and if you think he don't have some influence, you're dumber'n that asshole thinks you are."

"He stepped over the line," I said. "He comes any closer, and I'll put him down myself. He won't have to worry about a reputation."

"Listen," he said. "You and I both know that D.L. is a good man, but he's a company man. He's been in the system so long that he's become the system."

"He still knows what the right thing is."

"And that's why no arrest has been made." He smiled. "D.L. will do whatever is best for D.L., and though he's taken a shine to you, it doesn't mean he's gonna put up with you poking the beast forever. Brickmeyer may not be doodley-shit on the national scale, but around here, he moves mountains. Don't you forget that."

I got out, thinking about the issues Jarrell had brought up. It hurt to think of D.L. as anything but a centered, well-meaning man, but it wasn't the only spur in my boxer briefs at the moment.

Paying the impound fee was painful, even if Jarrell had lent me some money. This had to clear up quickly or else I was going to have to forget about playing detective. I thought about disclosing my financial situation to Jarrell but thought better of it. Instead, I told him goodbye and watched him leave. He threw one hand out the window as he sped away.

I hopped in the ride and rolled the windows down. The world was full of pollen, and a breeze swept the hairs back on my arm as I passed the city limits headed into the country. The sweet-bitter smell of blossoming flowers and the way the sun glinted off the windshield sparked small brush fires of memory, which I stamped out in hopes of keeping myself in the present. I had found out that no good comes of being so wistful.

I arrived at my destination and pulled to a stop, noticing the squeal of ever-deteriorating brakes. Leland Brickmeyer's pseudo-palatial estate loomed in the distance, and as I peered up at it, every window seemed to hide a differently menacing shadow. It now appeared more like an insane asylum than the home of the local well-to-do.

Off to one side of the house, a van labeled Middle Georgia Pools & Spa was parked. One door was open, and a tube seven or eight inches around snaked around the side of the van and disappeared behind the door to the fence closing off the backyard area.

Unlike before, I didn't have to go up to the door and beat on it until I was sent away. Someone was rushing down the driveway to meet me.

I stepped in front of my parked car and leaned against the hood, crossing my feet at the ankles and my arms at the wrist, staring straight into the diesel's cab. Bodean glared red-faced at me through its dusty windshield.

He didn't result to pleasantries this time. The way he got out of the truck told me he was ready for violence. "Don't you have any fucking better sense than this?"

"Guess not," I said. "I tend not to watch my feet in a pasture. Might get some cow shit on my sneakers, but I always find a way to make it through. Judging by the last few days, I figured I'd be safer here than in a bar."

He brought one hand up to his nose and snorted defensively.

"That ain't entirely true," he said, and then he spat. It landed on the blacktop right at my feet. The smell of tobacco filled my nostrils, dirty and harsh, like rotted mint. I felt a fine spray against my face, but I did not wipe it away. I wasn't going to give him the satisfaction.

I laughed. It felt as though something inside me was unraveling, something that had been coming loose for years. The consequences of my actions seemed far away, like a silhouette in the distance of a fading sun.

"I don't know what in the hell you think happened, but I can tell you for certain I didn't do it."

"So I laced my own Coke? Yeah, that's how I take it. No ice, no bourbon, but a dash of Rohypnol."

He shrugged. "We talked for a minute. You had a conniption on the floor. By the time you came back around, you were ready for a beer. I suggested you have one, and you did. Then you had another. And another. Free and clear, on your own will. I had nothing to do with that."

"You're a liar."

Bodean cut his eyes away from me. He said, "Listen, just get the fuck off the driveway and leave the man alone. He's done everything he's been asked to do. I don't think he's got anything else to prove to the townsfolk, and especially not to you. It's all done."

"What do you think the Laveau family would say to that? That it's all done?"

"I could give a fuck. Boy got himself in something he couldn't get out of. Not my fault. Not *his* either," he said, pointing a long, meaty finger in the direction of the house.

I glanced up, thinking maybe I'd see someone staring guiltily through a parted blind. Wrong move. I should have kept my focus on the behemoth. I felt the impact of the fist before I had a chance to react. He had brought the pointing hand down like a hammer against my jaw.

The ground jumped and caught me. Pain flared up the backside to my neck. Flat on my back, I looked up at him, with the sun glaring down, obscuring his face. But I knew he was smiling.

Heat from the blacktop scalded my back through my shirt. I was dazed, and my jaw felt a couple sizes too big, but I wasn't hurt. Not *hurt* hurt.

Bodean reared back, as if to kick, but I rolled sideways in time for the blow to miss. He looked like a big kid practicing field goals, and with one leg hiked up in the air, the other was left vulnerable. I kicked out, used both feet to try and break his fucking kneecap.

I connected, and he seemed surprised by the force. Something underneath his pants sounded off, a pop that could have just as easily been the cork on a cheap bottle of champagne. Bodean dropped, clawing sideways to pull himself away from me.

"Ah, my knee. Shit!" he screamed. "My fucking knee!"

His leg was askew, though I didn't think I'd kicked hard enough to break anything. He grunted and snarled, spitting into the dirt and blowing up little clouds into his face. I stood and rubbed my face. Blood made a bright smear on the back of my hand.

I glanced up to see three men in white work jumpers holding pool equipment. They stared, wide-eyed, but did nothing to intervene.

Driscoll pushed himself up and lunged forward, away from me, favoring the bad leg. I followed a couple of paces behind, watching him. As soon as he'd gotten some semblance of balance, I charged. He made for a big target. I lowered my shoulder and caught him below the shoulders, sending him sprawling once again into the dirt.

Bodean screamed in unintelligible syllables, raising one hand, presumably in surrender. He was trying to roll over. I knelt and punched him square in the back of the head. His face bounced off the ground and then rested there. He moaned and spat into the dirt.

I knelt so that he could turn his head to see me. Not that he did.

"Come near me again, and I'll kill you," I said. "I don't have much of anything to lose, and bud, I bet I don't care half as much about that as you do. You can tell your boss the same damned thing."

Tenth Chapter

I drove home with my legs shaking so badly I could barely press the gas pedal. Coasting into the driveway, I saw Vanessa's junker. She'd come back.

I walked in the front door and pretended like nothing was wrong, but Vanessa waw right through that. "Something happened," I said. "But maybe that's not what you want to talk about."

"Don't," she said. "Let's just forget that last thing. It was. Well. I reckon, shit, maybe there's something wrong with the both of us."

It wasn't difficult for me to agree to that. I'd spent my whole life pushing bad memories into the dark corners of my head.

So I told her what happened. When I'd finished, she told me to calm down, but I couldn't.

"The Brickmeyers are bat-shit crazy, and I can't get a single break on them. They might not be conspirators, but then what are they doing? Fucking with me for the fun of it?"

"That's your problem," she said knowingly. "Trying to figure out the Brickmeyers. Those people are no good."

"I'm beginning to see that."

"All they do is hook people in with their bullshit and then they use them until they don't need them anymore. Then they discard them."

"How would you know?"

"I've lived here all my life, too, you know. Well, almost all of it." She pressed her lips together and searched for something to say. "Look at anybody in this fucking town. They've all been strung along, thinking the man in the big house is the savior. You need something. One of them can offer it. Look at what Leland's daddy did to his first girlfriend."

"What are you talking about?"

She took a deep breath. "When Leland's daddy graduated from college and moved back down here, he started dating this girl - whose family has since moved away - and they had a fast courtship. Her religious beliefs were dead-on with the time, and she refused to bed him, despite his advances. They got engaged, but he grew disinterested and distanced himself from her. It came out that she was pregnant, and when she wouldn't leave him, he started dating other women, throwing it in her face. He'd even take them home to their house."

"Jesus, that's awful."

"She showed up uninvited to a party one night, and when he introduced her to the woman he was at the party with - the one he would eventually marry - this poor, pregnant girl went home and hanged herself. She was six months along. They'd set up a joint account together, and the parents tried to access in order to help pay for funeral expense, but they found it only had a penny in it."

"Brickmeyer had drained the entire thing."

Vanessa nodded.

"How did this not follow him around like a bad smell?"

"They smeared that poor girl and her family. It's why they moved. Those people, the Brickmeyers, they won't stop until every single person in this town is under their thumb. That's why they're so frustrated with you. If you don't stop, you'll end up like that discarded fiancee."

"I can't stop now. You know that."

"Guilt cannot be your only motivator."

"Someone else will die."

"You don't know that," she said.

"Yes, I do. But I don't believe I'll be making any more trips out to the Brickmeyer place. My welcome has been officially worn out."

"It's about time."

"That doesn't mean the family's entirely off the radar, though. Leland's put some distance between the murder and himself, but Jeffrey's still a wild card. If only I had some dirt to use against him, I might get him to turn on his father and give me some leverage."

Van smirked. "Well, there's one thing you can use against him."

"What?"

Her smile widened. "You honestly don't know?"

"No, I don't."

"Why do you think he moved down to Savannah?"

"To be a lawyer?"

She laughed outright. "Maybe that was part of it. But what he actually did was follow a man down there. He got fucked up on drugs and then scrambled back to the Junction."

My heart did somersaults in my chest. I couldn't believe my ears, but I tried to keep my voice under control. "What?"

"Uh-huh," she said. Her face was the sight of someone having it over on somebody else, but I knew she was telling the truth. "Jeff Brickmeyer is the last of the Brickmeyer name, an only child, and their name ends with him."

I had to take a minute to let it sink in. "How do you know that?"

"One of the joys of drug addiction, my dear. You end up in the company of people who know *everything* about everybody. When I was down in Savannah, everybody I told about my hometown told me about Jeff and his lover."

"That still doesn't answer my question."

"Touchy. My God. Well, some dealers I knew down in Savannah,

243

they told me. The gay scene and drug culture sometimes overlap, so it was only a matter of time before the big Brickmeyer secret reached me. It's not even a coincidence, really."

"How does that fit into the investigation?" I was grasping at straws.

She shrugged. "No idea. Thing about Jeffrey is, his father either doesn't know or lives in denial. Jeffrey'd rather die than give up that information. Maybe Emmitt Laveau wanted to upend Leland's boat. If it got out just as the political campaign was firing up, Leland would have a hell of a lot of explaining to do. Georgia is a conservative state."

"Uh-huh," I said. I mulled it over. I leaned back on the couch. Something that Bodean Driscoll said came back to me. He had called Jeffrey Brickmeyer a *fairy* but it wasn't just a sidelong slur. He'd meant it literally.

I sank into the couch next to Vanessa, wanting to place my hand on her knee, or else to reach up and slip my fingers through her hair just over the ear, the way I used to.

But I couldn't. Most often, people attribute an inability to forgive on pride, but pride is just a byproduct of emotional scar tissue. No matter how sober, how sweet, and how responsible Vanessa became, the mental image of her fucking another man for drugs would never leave me.

"Vanessa," I said, finally, clasping my hands so they would stay in my lap, "what *is* this?"

"A moment between friends," she replied, her voice the very definition of innocence. "You were right the other night. Don't complicate things. You aren't doing anything wrong, so far as I can tell. We're just, you know, sitting on the couch."

I stared at her for a while in the quiet pleasure of the afternoon. Strange as it sounded, being with her in those slowly passing moments, like sitting on a rudderless ship, felt more ghostly than any dream.

Then she said, "I don't know why you're questioning this anyway. You finally got what you wanted. You were always afraid of me running away. Now I'm tied to this couch, and I'm afraid what I'll do to myself if I leave."

"I know," I said, looking away. And I left it at that. I couldn't quite meet her gaze.

* * *

"I gotcha all fixed up, Rolson," the voice in my ear said. There was a profane outburst in the background, and then the voice said, "Scuse me. *We* got you covered. We do, me and Red. My bad. Jesus."

"What's the information?" I asked.

On the phone was Lyle Kearns, and he sounded somewhere on the other end of blitzed. It was just after dusk, and Vanessa had gone to spend the night at her father's. They were attempting a fragile reconciliation and had agreed to meet with one another to talk through her situation. It seems as though the closeness of this afternoon had made her somewhat claustrophobic.

Lyle said, "H.W. is staying with some used-up old skank. Part-time hooker. Y'all still call it that? Turns tricks sometimes. She used to have a real bad man for a beau and a pimp, but we didn't see him. It's just her and Bullen."

He talked some more, and I wrote the details on a stray piece of paper. "Laina Donaldson, probably. Fried hair, sort of bleached blonde-looking, with the roots showing. Scar across her cheek?"

"That's her," he said.

"Yeah. Busted her for possession once. Maybe she's trading sex for protection, that sort of thing. She's not got a strong instinct when it comes to men."

"Maybe. Shit, I don't know. She's all dried out. Pot-smoking alcoholic. Does blow and crack sometimes, if she can afford it."

"And how do you know all this?"

"You don't worry about that. Just know I found him." Some more screaming in the background. "*We* found him. He's got her buying him groceries and drugs, goes out in the evening and brings 'em home with her. Whatever she can get her hands on. This is all coming from the guy owns the place, Kevin Weeks. Says he has to keep an eye on her so she doesn't burn the fucking place down. Plus, the men she's let home in the past tend to beat the shit out of her, so he's had to call the police more than once."

"I see."

Lyle cleared his throat. "Both of them spend the day getting lit up on whatever's lying around. As long as you don't ambush them, you might have a shot at talking to H.W. I got to tell you, though, the man's keeping an especially low profile, not just for the sake of being a homebody. Snakes that crawl into holes generally don't like to be dragged out by the tail."

"I'll be all right."

"I'm just telling you to be careful, that's all. He has a violent past."

I said goodbye and hung up, lying awake in bed most of the night, watching phantasms dancing and lurching on the ceiling. It was the first time I'd felt hopeful in days.

* * *

Calling D.L. would do no good. Even if I were on the list of people he would listen to at this point - and I was not - Vanessa curried even less trust from her father. I called Deuce and asked him to meet me at the bar, and even though he acted distant, eventually I convinced him.

"Damn, that's something I didn't even know," he said, when I told him the story. We were sitting at the bar but hadn't ordered. He was taking his sweet time to digest the story.

Deuce was a thoughtful guy, and he wasn't quick to siphon off new information so that it was forgotten. Watching the dude take in someone else's story was like watching a scientist keep up with records. For every detail he was given, he seemed to catalog it and place it in its own file for later use.

"What do you make of it, though, Deuce?" I asked. It was one hellacious revelation, and yet I didn't quite know what to do with it. Kind of like walking around a playground with lit dynamite.

Louis came over and took our orders - I just got a Coke - and then went away. Deuce continued to slowly shake his head, in time with some internal rhythm that did not match up with the jukebox.

"I don't know," he said, at last. "I've got mind to believe Van on this one, Rol, but she might have moths up there when it comes to her memory of Savannah."

"She swears up and down it's the truth," I responded. "I believe her. I don't know. Part of me thinks she might have dreamed up the whole thing, but part of me is like, 'why the hell not?' Why not believe her?"

"Either way, doesn't mean it has any connection to the corpse," he said. "Not every thread is tied off at both ends."

I sort of clicked my teeth together while I draped myself in that information. Could be true, I suppose. But he and I knew that wasn't the truth.

"Of course," he continued. "Could mean he'd have motivation to have someone shut up."

"If he went to that party a few years back, maybe he caught Jeff in the bathroom with an illicit party guest. That's reason enough."

"Yeah, but years ago? Political scandals, sure, but that piece of information isn't a 'dump the body' kind of discovery, is it? Maybe twenty years ago."

"Maybe ten."

"Maybe," he said. "Listen, but even the event was a couple of years back. Why would he wait that long to get his revenge? Or to shut his file completely?"

247

"Seems like it would be a case of the cover-up being worse than the crime, yeah," I said. It made a certain amount of sense, if somehow Laveau had reason to blow up the Brickmeyer political machine. Wait until a crucial moment, and then light the fuse.

"If the Brickmeyers are wound as tight as you say, then perhaps what happened was a sad, violent overreaction."

I sighed. "Seems like a shame that someone's life could come down to that."

The bartender brought Deuce his beer but only gave me a dour look. "I ordered a Coke," I said, not unkindly.

"Can't serve you no more," Louis said, though, and he turned on his heel and went the other way.

"I'm not even drinking," I said to his back.

"Damn," Deuce said, "Things is fucked up when a white dude gets refused service right in front of a black man holding a beer."

"The progress of society," I replied. Thinking about having a beer still made my stomach do gymnastics, but somehow my misery was stronger than my instincts and my will to do good.

"Circling back to the Brickmeyers. 'Overreaction' is a strange word to use."

"Why's that?"

"You know they didn't do their own work," he said. "If somebody had tied Emmitt Laveau up, had beaten him within an inch of his life to keep him quiet, it wasn't the Brickmeyers-"

"But who the Brickmeyers hired."

"Right. And so it would be someone with a temper. Someone with an edge toward being irrational."

"Well, the hulk they hired to be Leland's bodyguard fits that description. He's big, and he's got eyes like a viper. I can imagine he'd roid out if he didn't get something he wanted."

"Like a promise to keep his mouth shut."

"Right. Bodean Driscoll. Word is, he retired from MMA after

injuring his back, so he took to being hired muscle for assholes and rich paranoid types."

The Brickmeyers certainly fit that description. "He ain't so tough," I said.

"Until you get him frothing," Deuce replied. "He probably's just waiting for the opportunity to tune you up. I bet he's got all kinds of ways to do that."

"He and I have come to an understanding," I replied.

I wished for a beer to materialize in front of me, and when that didn't happen, I started watching the bartender real close.

Louis waited a few minutes before he slipped up, but nevertheless he slipped up. The bar phone was in his hand, and he was talking to someone when we made eye contact, and he hung up. "You see that?" I asked.

"I ain't seen anything but the Hawks give up thirty in the fourth quarter. Any luck tracking down H.W.? I'd have helped you, but my dance card is full right now. Bunch of weed peddlers growing plants in their fields decided not to show up for their court dates. That's getting really interesting."

A woman sauntered up on the far end of the bar, opposite of where the bartender had been standing, and was drunkenly trying to flag him down.

"H.W. is a non-starter right now. I've got a bead on him, so I'm going to stop by where he's squatting after I leave here. Give him some time to work off a hangover I'm sure he's got."

"And you think he's involved?" Deuce asked.

"He's got the benefit of being out of sight, which means I'm not fucking with him."

"I bet he'd appreciate that."

"But he's also a variable. I feel like he might fit in this thing somewhere. If he doesn't, no skin and all that, but if he can find something interesting to say, I might be able to use him later."

"He's a big one," Deuce said. "He could probably lay the pipe to some poor soul. Has done it, I know for a fact."

"But I circle back to that idea of him being Ron's brother. What reason would he have helping out the Brickmeyers? Old feuds don't just clear up."

"Unless he's two-timing his brother. Ron's playing a dead hand right now. Could be because he wants to keep the old boy from getting in trouble-"

"Or it could be because he genuinely doesn't know what H.W.'s up to," I replied. "They're pretty tight, so I don't think that, but who knows?"

Deuce finished his drink and signaled for another.

When he finally made his way down, I said, "Bossman making you do this?"

He ignored it, so I kept at him. "Or is it someone else? You guys worried about your liquor license, or maybe some competition springing up? That it? All to stay on the right side of a grudge."

He placed a Bud Light in front of the woman, ignoring her pleas for a shot of Jager, and then said, under his breath, "I'd get up and go - *now* - if I were you. Five minutes, and you'll wish you weren't here."

When his eyes met mine, his countenance was earnest. He wasn't a bad guy, and though it was obvious he was caught in a fight he didn't want to be in, he was still taking sides.

Man's got to keep eggs in the fridge and bread on the table, I reckon.

"You go ahead and go," Deuce said. "I'll cover for you here. They can't be desperate enough to try to go through me to get to you."

I couldn't just leave him here. He was a respectable guy, and getting caught up with me was only going to get him hurt. "I can't let you do that," I said.

I thought about how well he was liked around town. How people still asked for his autograph. How he still signed every one of them as though they were his first.

"No. Uh-uh partner. You're already up to your ass in the swamp. You get any more stink on you, and it'll never come off. I know how to deal with lowlifes."

I stood up. "I owe you one."

Before I left, Deuce caught me by the elbow. "You mind loaning me twenty?" he asked. "To pay for my tab?"

His eyes were full of trouble, so I nodded and handed him what cash I had. He must have been having a down week with his bookie.

Seems like I wasn't the only one getting my roots hacked up. There was something he was hiding, too, but since he didn't want to tell me, I didn't pry. He'd get into it when he was good and damn ready, when it was too late to help him.

I slipped out the back door and came face-to-face with a dude I'd never seen before. He had one hand held out, and for a moment I thought he was holding a pistol. I recognized the car behind him, and I suppose I'd noticed it following me around town.

"Rolson McKane?" he asked.

"Yes," I kind of stammered. My instinct was to put my hands up.

He smiled and pulled one hand from his pocket. He was holding an envelope. "This is a restraining order. You've been served."

He placed it in my hand and walked back to his car. A moment later he was gone. "Doesn't matter," I said to the empty parking lot.

A slip of paper wasn't going to keep me away now.

* * *

A couple of cars pulled up as I made my way around the side of the building, and two or three big dudes wearing Brickmeyer Ag & Timber overalls sauntered into the bar.

I pressed myself against the side of the building and waited until they were safely inside before I crept over to my car and drove away.

It was not my intention to get Deuce dragged into all of this, but the longer I involved myself in the Laveau case, the more convinced I became that I was a black hole, destined to drag everyone I knew into the void with me.

* * *

Trailer parks are not as prevalent in small towns as people think, though a disproportionate amount of violence, drug abuse, and poverty occur in them. The people rarely form any lasting bonds, and the parks themselves come together almost out of a blind sort of coincidence. They are featureless, the general rectangular shape notwithstanding, and The Wagon Circle was no different. Tenants sold or binged on drugs, and those who didn't were in recovery and bound to relapse.

Laina Donaldson's piss-yellow single wide occupied a stamp-sized area in the back corner, on the other side of two particularly depressing excuses for housing, which had rusted and abandoned tricycles overturned in the yard. Laina's was not quite as repulsive, but only when speaking in relative terms.

I had modest intentions: I just wanted to test the waters with H.W., see what I could draw out of him without spooking him. For that reason, I parked way back by the road and walked in.

The impossibility of my mission became evident once I saw him. He appeared in the doorway for just a moment and then vanished into the darkness of the trailer. Moments later, Laina stumbled through the front door and walked barefoot to meet me.

"Hey there," she said, forcing a smile. "Something I can do you for?"

Years of drug- and physical-abuse had left her scarred and withered. Misshapen, in a way. She still had the leanish look of a younger woman, but the proportions were out of whack, as if gravity was pulling her in all directions at once. She might have been pretty in an alternate universe, one where she wasn't locked in closets during childhood or raped in adolescence. Her deep blue eyes showed signs of having glittered once, but now they only seemed dull and speculative, distrustful.

"I need a word with H.W.," I said. "I saw him inside. Just send him on out so we can talk. I'm not in the mood for a routine."

She showed mock bewilderment. "Don't know who you're talkin' 'bout. Just me here. I would invite you in, but the house ain't decent for company. You understand. I've been trying to kick, and I just ain't been in the mood."

Her smile returned, revealing cigarette-stained teeth. Remnants of makeup cracked on her face, leftover from the night before.

"All right," I said. "Guess I was mistaken. If you see him, will you relay a message?"

"Sure," she said, adding, "if I see him and all."

"Great," I said, raising my voice so that everyone at the park could hear me. "Tell him I'm going to personally look into whether or not he has any outstanding warrants. If he does, then, well, he knows what happens from there."

Her face grew flush, and she reached out with both hands in an attempt to push me away, trying to yell me down by saying, "Stop it! Stop it!," but in her stupor she telegraphed her intentions, and I only had to step aside to keep her from assaulting me.

I kept talking, this time to Laina. "And you don't want the authorities digging around out here, do you? Last time I took you in, it was for drugs, wasn't it? That's an awfully small living space in there. Not many hiding places, I suspect. The longer you go without an arrest, the longer you can say you've been clean. Am I wrong?"

"Stop it," she slurred, her face tight with anger and frustration. "Get out of here, you dickhead. He don't want to see you."

I gave it another moment, dodging a swipe from her bony hand, before backing away. "All right," I said. "Just know I'll be back."

I turned to leave, just as the screen door rattled uncomfortably against its hinges. I turned to see H.W. standing on the top of the makeshift staircase. "Let's go on and get this over with," he said.

His skin was the color of breakfast ham in light syrup, brought on by years of working in the sun. He wasn't so much barrel-chested as he was just plain enormous. He had country bulk and was nearly two of me. His eyes remained perpetually narrowed, and his hands constantly searched for purpose during conversation, scratching and picking and rubbing to keep from being completely still.

He waited for his lady friend to go inside, and for a time he gave only half-answers to my questions. I tired quickly with his routine. He sounded like he'd been coached to avoid answers, so I said, in a voice halfway between whisper and growl, "Since you're doing your damnedest to avoid saying anything, I'll go ahead and speculate for you. I think you and your brother are involved in Emmitt Laveau's murder, and I know I don't have evidence, but my hunches have proven pretty accurate lately."

H.W. seemed unfazed. "Hmm. Yeah, I don't know what in the hell you're talking about. Maybe Ron's involved, but I don't have the slightest idea."

"What else you got going on in the Junction?" I nodded in the direction of the house. "Other'n her, what's got you coming down here?"

The big man turned toward the house, placed his hands on his hips. When he turned back, his lips were oddly parted, and I sensed he was on the verge of saying something. Dark, wet circles had formed under his armpits, and he picked at the front of his shirt, trying to fan himself off.

"It ain't got nothing to do with Ron," he said, finally. "I ain't even talked to him."

I nodded as though I understood. "Random question: what

happened to your brother's foot?"

He gave me a curious look but didn't seem angry. "What do you mean?"

I tapped one leg. "Right leg. Never noticed it before, but it seems like he carries it a little bit. Doesn't look like a limp, but I'd bet that's exactly what it is."

"Oh, that? He's had that his whole life." All of a sudden, his face brightened a little, like he had been let off the hook. He laughed mockingly. "You ain't never noticed that, McKane? And you a cop, Jesus."

"How'd he get it?"

At that question, his eyes darkened somewhat. "Accident when we was kids. Never healed up right, and he just never thought to try and get it fixed once he got grown."

"You do it? You give him a bum foot?"

He stared but didn't answer. That wasn't why I had come out here anyway, so I didn't pursue it any further.

"If you're not plotting something with your brother, then what in the hell *are* you doing in the Junction? I thought you were off setting fires underwater."

He scratched the back of his neck. "I, well, I'm down here cooling off."

"Going south? Not your best idea."

"I tried to stomp a fella's guts into the dirt at a bar up in Oregon. I'd have turned his lights out for good if some of my buddies hadn't pulled me off him. He lived, from what I heard, but his plumbing's all frigged up now. It ain't exactly attempted murder, but it ain't far from it, either."

"And you think I won't turn you over?"

"You won't, McKane. You're not a cop anymore. You don't have a reason to be flipping over rocks and taking the magnifying glass to the cockroaches, do you?"

I didn't want to tell him, but it was exactly what I was doing.

"I'm not interested in your bar fights, H.W. It's completely off the radar, so your secret's safe with me. If, and I sincerely mean it, you can help me out."

H.W. ran his fingers through a greasy patch of hair, staring right into me. "Why don't you go and talk to him about all of this?"

I said, "You know Ron isn't going to admit anything."

"And you think I will, you hittin' the bottle like a demon's on your back? Why would I help?"

I gave the question a minute to sink in. "Because it wasn't your brother out there in the Boogie House, was it? It was you, and you saw the same thing I did. That's why."

H.W. wasn't as hard as his older brother. He was a big guy, sure, but not nearly the poker player he pretended to be. He stiffened, and he stood across from me, his eyes searching me. He didn't answer.

"I don't know what I saw out there, either, H.W.," I said. "I really don't. And nobody knows that was me out there. Just you and me."

A flash in his eyes. H.W. sniffed and ran one forearm under his nose. He thrust his tongue between his gums and his lower lip. He laughed and said, "I'm the one with the problem? Are you even listening to yourself?"

"Do the right thing," I said. "Give up what you know. Your brother will be in hell before the devil knows he's dead; there is no doubt about that. If there is a line between order and chaos, he can't find it. He's real messed up."

He produced a look of mock confusion. I didn't care. I stared him right in his cavernous eyes. "But you still have an opportunity. You just have to make that decision."

"I think you ought to leave, partner. Yeah, I don't like any of the things you're saying. My brother deserves better than what you're giving him." Even though the words were harsh, there was no conviction in them.

"No he doesn't, and you know that. You both have reason to punish Brickmeyer. Had he taken my family's land from me, the only thing of worth ever attached to the Bullen name, I'd want to mess him and his family up, maybe create a scandal."

"You best get on out of here."

"Did it take murdering a young man and dumping him on that land to teach him that lesson?" I asked, watching H.W.'s expression tighten. It might as well have been a stone carving.

"You don't have the authority to come here and fuck with me like this. I ought to whoop your ass just because."

"All right," I said. "All right. You win. I shouldn't have come out here and harassed you. I'm out of line. You can go on back in there with her, if you like. I just hope you have a prescription for penicillin."

"Come on, man. You're coming up here, accusing me of all kinds of heinous shit. I'm a victim."

"No offense, H.W., but Emmitt Laveau is the victim. I hope you don't have trouble seeing that."

H.W. hit the side of a junker Thunderbird with a wad of phlegm. He used bodily fluids like projectiles. Each conveyed a different emotion. Without a doubt, this one was hatred. "Jesus, McKane. How in the hell do you think I'm gonna answer these questions?"

"Truthfully."

"You got me on the defensive. I can already feel my hackles rising, man. I ain't even on the stand yet, I can hear the rope swinging in the wind."

"Okay, H.W. One more question and I'm out of here."

"This better be good, McKane. I'm gettin' real tired of the road we're treading on."

I leaned against the Thunderbird, freshly minted with H.W.'s spit, and crossed my arms, one hand holding each elbow. "Does he visit you in your dreams, too, or was it just the one time at the Boogie House?"

I made sure not to blink. It wasn't his answer that mattered, but his response. Guys like him have pat answers for everything. The lie wasn't what mattered. What mattered was how he reacted. If I was going to get anything on the big heifer, I'd have to outsmart him.

But he must have seen it coming, because he gave me nothing. His eyes shifted ever-so-slightly, almost imperceptibly, and they didn't blink. He stuck his tongue between his teeth and smiled. "Goddamn, man, it's a wonder you ain't a lawyer, asking all these crazy-ass questions. It must be true what they say, that the bottle's starting to pull you under the water with it. No wonder Vanessa split on you, son."

I smiled because I didn't want to let him think he'd won. But he sort of had. While I stood here, something *real* could be happening to my ex-wife, and H.W. had an alibi if he needed one, but not me.

He seemed to notice that, too, because he winked. "Yeah, that girl's a little too trusting for her own good. Why she's so fucked-up in the first place, don't you think? She just, you know, lets anybody walk into her life with something to offer her, no matter what it is. She keeps on like that, somebody's gonna take *real* advantage of her."

I flinched, swallowing the urge to punch him. "Don't think your brother's going to be loyal once things go downhill. He'll burn down your world around you, leaving you no choice but to dive in the fire. I promise you that. If I figure it out before you get the sense to speak up, you might not even have the luxury to save your own ass."

And with that, I walked away, hands shoved into my pockets. It took every shred of composure to keep from looking behind me. I listened for the sound of approaching footsteps, but all I ended up hearing was Molly Hatchet threatening to break an adjacent trailer's windows.

* * *

On my way out, I saw the rear bumper of a truck poking out from

258

the side of the half-assed garage. When H.W. disappeared inside, I doubled around behind the trailer park, winding through a small field dotted with trees and covered in brier bushes.

Once Laina's place became visible from the field, I ducked behind a tree on the other side of a rusted barbed wire fence, and that's when I saw it. There it was. The truck. The goddamned truck I had been looking for. White. Diesel. Gently-used. Same stolen license number as the one in my memory.

A thought struck me then, one related to the night the cop chased me. He had tried to pull *me* over, not the truck. It didn't prove that the force was in Brickmeyer's pocket - or the opposite, that it was in Bullen's debt - but it showed me definitively that trusting the LJPD was out of the question.

It had to be a solo effort from here on in, even if it meant dismantling the entire police department, cop by cop, to do it.

* * *

I called the pulpers to thank them, but no one answered. I let the phone ring enough times for my ear to sweat from pressing the receiver to it, but I got nothing.

Odd.

Next, I tried the bar, but the guy who answered told me he hadn't seen them. That *definitely* was out of character.

Maybe they're hiding out, I thought.

When my mind shifted toward other, darker thoughts, I slipped my phone into my pocket and tried to think of it no more. They had done a serviceable job, and I'd hear from them soon enough.

At least I tried to convince myself of that.

* * *

I made an unannounced trip out to the Laveau residence directly after that, my head cloudy with the implications of what I'd found.

Janita appeared in the door in a sleeveless sundress. Her mouth opened, somewhere between a smile and a question, but she let me into the house without actually speaking a word.

The door slammed behind us, and I circled a small recliner before resting my hands on its back. I groaned quietly to myself. The anxiety of returning here was instantaneous. My stomach burned, my mouth filling almost instantly with the taste of the cure-all her uncle had given me.

If the exterior of the house conveyed darkness, the interior magnified it, a dank, bitter, sorrowful place. The air was heavy with death, smelled strongly of it, simultaneously sweet and tart and flowery.

"I 'pologize about the smell," she said, adding, as she walked toward the kitchen, "I don't know what's happened. Something must've crawled under the house and passed on."

"It's all right," I managed, despite the pain in my gut. "I can barely tell it's there."

"Rolson McKane, I know that's a lie."

"Maybe it's your uncle's cooking."

"Ha! Maybe. You get used to it, after a spell. You want something to drink? I just made a pitcher of sweet tea."

"I thought I'd make this a quick visit. I don't want to impose."

She went into the kitchen. "Nonsense. Have some tea. There's something I want to show you. And you don't have to hurry. It ain't going nowhere. 'Sides, I'm bored out my mind out here. Attention's been heaped on me to the point that I'm going through withdrawals."

The sound of cabinet doors opening and closing and glasses clinking on the counter echoed through the house.

She said, "As a matter of fact, I'm so lonely I damn near miss having that crazy uncle of mine around."

"Where's he gone?"

"What's that?" she asked. She was busily stirring something.

"I asked where your uncle had run off to," I replied.

"Oh, who knows. Sometimes he just up and splits for a few days. Full moon makes him jittery, I reckon."

I stole a glance at her uncle's collection of assorted voodoo knickknacks, which did not look sinister and disgusting anymore. It now looked pedestrian, like the herbs and spices a hippie practicing alternative medicine might keep in the pantry.

Perhaps because I had paid so much attention to the abnormal trinkets and potions on my last visit, I had not noticed the abundance of photos of Emmitt smiling roguishly at the camera. Emmitt leaning against a wall, wearing shades entirely too big for his face. Emmitt sitting in the middle of this very living room, holding matchbox cars toward the camera like treasure. Emmitt staring straight ahead, unsmiling and seemingly looking at something in the distance beyond the camera.

In the kitchen I heard the tinkle of spoon tapping glass. "Don't worry. K's not going to do anything drastic. Yet. I think I got him reeled in pretty good for now. That's not an easy thing, you know."

"I bet," I said absently, staring at the battered cup the old man had forced me to drink from. "He's got quite a collection of...antiques."

"None of that is worth bunk to anybody but him. Had it all his life. Made half of it."

Her footsteps were surprisingly light for a robust woman, and she appeared in the doorway with two pint glasses and handed me one. The limp seemed to be leaving her, and though I was pleased to see it, I said nothing.

I tilted it back and savored the rush of sweet and cold. The tea was delicious, maybe too sweet, but just right for the circumstances. It almost seemed to wash away the oppressive heat of the afternoon, and I was incapable of not drinking it. My stomach needed something on it, because the rumbling was making me sick.

"Delicious," I said, placing the glass on a table stacked with gossip magazines.

"K taught me to make tea that way, or rather he trained me. He cooks spicy food, and nothing calms the heat from his jerk chicken better than tea. But it has to be so sweet that the sugar dang near won't dissolve. First time I made it, he complained. 'It's too bitter,' he said. 'Needs more sugar.' I kept adding a little bit more every time, and of course he kept on complaining. Finally, I dumped a whole mess of sugar in there, thinking I'd show him, but he drank down a whole glass, gulped it like he'd spent a week in the desert, and he smiled at me and said, 'Now it's just right.' That man, I swear."

"It's sweet," I said. "But I've lived here my whole life so it's nothing I can't handle."

She looked down, as if a fly might have landed on an ice cube, and then said, "That drink my uncle gave you, it was a cure-all."

"Uh-huh. I think that's what he called it."

"It doesn't have much power if you don't believe."

"Meaning what, exactly?"

"That it was probably a test, seeing how his piddling affected you."

"Voodoo."

She made a sour face. "He don't use that word. Makes him seem so much like a joke. He's already got it bad enough. People cross the street when they see him."

"Who?"

"Everybody," she said, smirking. "Somebody hears voodoo, they think about the devil. It's nothing like that. My uncle's a superstitious man, but he's no different than any other uneducated person his age. It's just that the superstitions have taken place of the other stuff, the stuff that has real power."

"Like the drink."

"Like the drink. The stuff people don't understand. There ain't no need to fear what isn't mysterious. Do you know what I'm saying?"

262

"Yes," I said.

"The fact is, that it is mysterious *is* powerful. People say they're skeptical of anything that ain't got a direct explanation. But you look. Most folks still make a point to walk around ladders or build skyscrapers without floor thirteen. They still say 'God bless you' when you sneeze. Superstition is powerful, 'specially in a place full of spirits as the South."

She took a long drink from her tea and set it back on the table, matching up the bottom of the glass with the wet ring on the table. She saw me watching and said, "Old habit. My uncle's got some little things, some peccadillos, that he's caused me to take up. This is one of 'em. No idea why I do it, but I do."

"I know somebody else who does the exact same thing." I lifted my own glass from the table and finished the drink. "Let me change course, Janita. Your son, did he practice, um, the same habits as your uncle?"

"Emmitt had enough to set him apart. He was always trying to make himself the most normal person alive, had no stomach for his great uncle's...beliefs. Hated to go out in public with him. Made Emmitt crazy when the old man's superstitions popped up in public, like some kind of mania. So, no, I couldn't see him doing it. God, I could only imagine."

"Did you ever see your uncle put, I don't know, some kind of spell or something - God, I don't have the vocabulary to talk about this - or some other kind of whatever on him?"

She said she had never thought he would. It seemed off-limits to her. At this point, I was just trying to figure out how he was visiting me in my dreams.

"How did Emmitt spend time trying to fit in?"

"That's not what I'm talking about. He didn't change to fit in, to be popular. He just didn't want to be harassed."

"What are you talking about? I don't believe I understand."

263

Janita stood, taking both of our glasses from the table. They clinked together as she headed for the kitchen. She sighed. "Let's go back to his room," she said forlornly, "and we'll see what we can dig up."

In the kitchen, she poured the ice into the sink, placed both glasses on an adjacent counter.

"We don't have to go in there," I offered.

She turned and stared. "Yes, we do. Come on. Follow me down the hall."

Dozens of framed photos lined the walls, and I caught fragments of them as I walked, trying to avoid being too intrusive.

In one picture, a boy I assumed to be Emmitt smiled precociously from atop a step stool, his face alight. He couldn't have been older than six or seven. In another, he sat in his mother's lap, his hands folded respectfully in his lap, and in that photograph he looked to be about two or three.

"Lot of beautiful pictures," I said.

"I need to take care of them. They're all I have left."

"You have memories."

"Memory is unfaithful," she said. "You remember so well the night you got arrested?"

I got the point.

Emmitt's room was small and spare and neat, and the only mess - a pile of clothes at the room's center - seemed to have accumulated after he died.

"Still can't touch 'em," Janita said, referencing the clothes. "They got his smell on 'em, though, and that's nice."

I surveyed the place, taking in mental sips of the scenery.

"You're the first person to come in here since. Well. Anyway, I get people keep offering to come and help me clean up his room, and I keep telling 'em, 'He was just about one of the cleanest children I ever met. No need to come help me.' They don't understand. It's like a painting. The second I change something, it's like I painted over it."

We stood in awkward silence for a few moments. I almost thought I could feel the grief wafting off of her.

Finally, she turned and walked past me. "Might do you some good to be in here. I can't stand it for more than a minute."

I circled the room once, unable to focus on any single detail. After that, I stood in the middle and began to take a mental inventory. The furniture was old but well cared-for, clean and sturdy. Unlike the hall, the bedroom had very few pictures. None with his uncle and only a few with his mother. The rest were random school photographs.

In the corner stood a bookshelf, sparsely filled with classic works of no particular period, among them a dog-eared copy of Homer's *Odyssey*, Whitman's *Leaves of Grass*, and Oscar Wilde's *The Importance of Being Earnest*, among others. Stacked on the shelf below that was a small collection of more modern books: *The Mysteries of Pittsburgh*, *Running with Scissors*, *Naked Lunch*.

I walked to the corner and retrieved the guitar case, placing it on the bed and snapping each latch before opening the lid. The guitar inside wasn't extravagant, but it was nice. A beginner's guitar. The action on the strings might have been a bit high and the wood somewhat thin, but otherwise it was a good instrument. I looked around, checking behind me for some reason, as if somebody might oppose, and then called out, "May I take it out of the case?"

"What?" Janita yelled, clanging something around in another room.

"The guitar, can I take it out and look at it? Just a hunch."

"I reckon so," she said, a bit timidly.

"I don't have to."

"No, no. Go ahead."

I gently retrieved the guitar, pushing the case aside before taking a seat on the bed. The instrument felt nice in my hands, comfortable, and I finger-picked an old blues lick, expecting a wild sensation to overtake me, something from my dreams. I got nothing. Just the satisfaction of playing guitar again. I'd sold my own years ago. It hurt to press down on the strings, but I fingered a C and then strummed a generic rhythm.

Something didn't fit. Emmitt Laveau was no blues man, like the dreams I'd had. He was educated, happy, seemingly soft-spoken, not the sullen, wild-eyed man I had met in my subconscious. "Was Emmitt into the blues much, Janita?" I called.

"No. uh-unh. Not whatsoever, that I can recall."

Hmm, I said under my breath. It made no sense, in relation to the Boogie House. Old building had nothing to do with either the life or the death of that young man, and yet, it was the reference point for everything.

Frustrated, I flipped the guitar over and checked the back, looking up and down the neck and body. It had been recently cleaned but not played.

When I turned it back over, I noticed a white triangle in the sound hole. Some companies will glue a logo inside the guitar, but this wasn't part of the original construction. I flipped the guitar back over, with the sound hole facing the ground, and shook it, hoping for the object to fall out. Same tactic I had used to retrieve lost guitar picks.

I turned it back over. Peering inside the sound hole, I saw that the white edge was in fact the corner of a picture, and the picture had been taped inside. It wasn't impossible to accomplish, if you had small hands and did it while the strings were off.

If I used one hand to push the strings out of my way, I could get the other almost completely inside. With my middle finger, I scratched at the small rectangle of scotch tape.

Finally managing to scrape the adhesive from two corners, I pulled evenly on the picture and brought it out.

It was a Polaroid, only a couple of years old. Emmitt stood on the left, wearing a long sleeve rugby shirt and baggy jeans. He was leaning against another young man, arm wrapped around his shoulders. Both men smiled carelessly at the camera, mutual body language suggesting they knew each other quite well. Intimately, even. In the background, an old, quaint river roiled past, and I recognized some of the landmarks. They were in Savannah, posing next to River Street.

The other person in the picture, smiling in a way I had never seen before, confident and careless and happy in a childlike way, was none other than Jeffrey Brickmeyer.

* * *

I held the photograph inches away, glaring as if I didn't quite believe what I was seeing. It wasn't easy to accept. I replaced the guitar in the case and sat on the bed, dumbfounded, staring at Jeffrey and Emmitt.

Janita reappeared in the doorway, wiping her hands on an old dish towel, and I folded the picture with one hand so that it couldn't be seen. "Whatcha doing?" she said, her brow creased.

In that moment I had to make a decision. Either I could hide the picture, or I could be honest with a dead man's mother. Something about the sadness in the woman's eyes made my decision for me.

"This came out of the guitar," I said, standing up. The picture felt electric when I let go of it, and I watched her eyes grow wide with comprehension.

"Oh, Lord," she said. A tear slid from her eye and bounced off her dress before landing somewhere on the floor. "Oh, Lord, Lord. Uh-unh."

I shoved one hand into a pocket and clasped my chin with the other, searching the carpet. "I'm sorry," I said. I was speaking entirely on instinct. "I wish I hadn't found it."

"No, no. The truth is the truth. And this," she said, brandishing the picture, "is one hell of a truth, I tell you what."

She placed one hand on my forearm, nodding, and pulled my hand out, into which she placed the photograph. "I always suspected. No. No, that's not right. I knew. A mother knows her son. But I never, not in a million years, knew this." Flicking her eyes up, staring into mine, she said, "I promise that. I would have told you. Lord, have mercy."

I felt pressure on my forearm, and I realized that she was gently pushing me away. I stepped back and watched her. She, in turn, ran one palm down the length of the bed, straightening the wrinkled sheets, and then collapsed.

My hand shot out to grab her, but she landed wholly on the bed, face-down. She rolled over and sobbed openly, arms outstretched as if in embrace. She looked like a woman touched by God in a Pentecostal church, quivering on the ground and speaking in tongues, made dumb by the spirit of the Lord.

Except, of course, she wasn't praising God. "Leave me," she said, between great, heaving cries, and that's exactly what I did, nodding and sliding the picture in a pocket before sneaking out the front door.

Backing out of the driveway, I took one last look at the house. A trick of the mind caused the house to quiver like it labored underneath an unseen weight. I turned to look at the main highway, and I didn't glance back at the Laveau house.

* * *

I went directly to the newspaper office and spoke to an old friend. Doris Allworth had worked at the paper since people started putting ink on paper, and I knew her because she had played bridge with my Aunt Birdie for years back when I was a kid.

She smiled and stopped typing when she saw me. Even though she was older, Doris had maintained mental sharpness through a seeming inability to quit writing.

"You haven't come to give me the scoop of a lifetime, have you?" she asked.

268

I walked on in and sat across from her impossibly messy desk. Books, Diet Coke cans, and old newspapers - of course - covered every square inch.

The picture of Emmitt and Jeffrey was in my front shirt pocket, and I wanted to slide it out and throw it on the desk, but I didn't want to show my hand before the ante.

"I need you to work with me on something," I said. "It is big news, but I want to manage the way it is released, and I've got to know I can trust you before I hand any of it over."

"Young man, it is not my policy to make deals for information. Even though this paper is a weekly, and we often have more pictures than words, I will not compromise my journalistic reputation because your aunt and I used to deal cards every so often."

The picture almost felt hot in my pocket. "I have uncovered something that could change the Emmitt Laveau case instantly."

For some reason, I snapped my fingers for emphasis. Doris only stared at me.

Apparently unimpressed, she said, "To be a reliable source, you have to be *reliable*, Rolson."

"Yeah, I read the article about my accident in the paper a few weeks ago. It's not something I'm proud of, but I'm making amends, and this may help."

And yet, I didn't want to show her. My fear was that releasing the picture would not only ruin the Brickmeyers - the intended purpose - but it would heap unnecessary anguish on the Laveaus.

She leaned back and clasped her hands on her lap. "Just show me what you got, Rolson. I'll take care of the rest. No promises, if it gets away from me, but if this thing is as juicy as you say it is, I'd rather have it and not get everything my way than to get none of it."

I balanced the two possibilities. What would Janita Laveau think of me outing her son to the entire community? More importantly, what would her uncle think? Or what would he do?

In the end, I suppose there hadn't even been a choice. I'd come straight to the paper, holding the picture like a hot potato. Any attempt in me to be coy about my intentions was mere self-preservation.

I showed Doris the picture of Jeffrey and Emmitt. A cynical twinkle emerged in the news reporter's elfin face.

"What am I looking at?" she asked.

I pointed to Jeffrey Brickmeyer. "Leland Brickmeyer claims to have never met Emmitt Laveau. This picture is pretty clear evidence-"

"It's not that clear," she said, cutting me off.

"But it's clear enough evidence that either what he is saying is a lie, or else that at least one of the Brickmeyers has - had - a close relationship with the deceased."

"I see where you're going with this, but we don't run a gossip mag. This is just a picture. It is uncorroborated by anything factual. One picture a scandal does not make."

"Leland Brickmeyer is a liar, and he is hiding something about his involvement with this case. If there is any one entity that should have a vested interest in making sure the truth comes to light, it is this newspaper."

"And it is your vested interest to bring down that man, I assume."

That one almost stung me. "I don't care about Brickmeyer, in the broader sense. He might not be part of the plot to cover up the kid's murder, but he's got some questions to answer."

"Or at least need to be asked," she added.

The air conditioner blasted a wave of cold on me as I sat there, watching her, trying to figure out in what direction her wheels were turning. "Interesting," she said. "Bet they didn't figure this sort of thing would emerge."

The Examiner had done little more than glorify Brickmeyer's PR offensive, and I hoped this might help to turn the tide somewhat. "I can't run the story without the picture."

My heart sank. "I know," I said.

"I also need to have it scanned."

I nodded, adding, "Long as it ends up in my hands by the time I hit the door."

She smiled in a way that both comforted me and sent my heart into my throat. "Leland Brickmeyer is going to shit a brick when he sees this. I've got to be honest. We can run an article tomorrow."

"Do you have enough time to put something together before the issue hits print?"

She exhaled. "Won't be much in there. Speculation, mostly. I'll reach out for a comment, but who knows how that will go."

"You've heard all the rumors, though. You know most of the information is solid, even if it's not totally confirmed. And it's not like you have to say anything is definite. You're just going to ask questions that need answers."

"All right, all right," she said. "Stop selling. Rest assured that I'm not going overboard with this story, though. It's going to be a grounded question mark, not an exclamation point."

"I understand that."

"Good," she said.

"This'll be a 'crucible' moment for him. He's got to decide how well he can hide in plain sight."

"Let's get to work. I need you to sit down and tell me everything you know. The police department has been stonewalling us, of course."

"I could have come to you sooner," I said.

"They're still going to know I've talked to you. You're the only person who would get within sniffing distance of Brickmeyer and the Laveau kid's death."

"It just needs to be out there in the world. Leland Brickmeyer cannot just win because people are afraid of unsettling him."

She made a raspy, phlegmatic sound, the smoker's giggle. "We can put it on the site as well as in print. People will have the weekend to talk about this, and if the simmering anger grows to a boil, Leland will have some tough questions to answer on Monday. And I'll be the one to ask them."

* * *

After I left the newspaper office - picture in tow - I flipped open my cell and stared at Janita Laveau's number as I walked to my car.

She needed to know about the picture, needed to know that it was probably going to be splashed all over the newspaper tomorrow, but I sort of hoped that Doris would take care of that. If there was anyone she needed to speak to about the story, it was Janita.

Still, thinking about what was going to happen made my stomach turn. It was a necessary evil, but it felt evil nonetheless. I closed the cell.

Maybe later, I thought.

Instead, I gave Deuce a call. Something had occurred to me. "Get ready. I need your help with the Brickmeyers," I said, getting behind the wheel of the Olds.

"No can do, hoss," he replied. "Meet me at my office. Big things are going down, and they involve you, my friend."

"What things?"

"You're not in public are you?"

"About to ride down the road."

"Get your ass here, and come to the back door. Don't let anybody see you." He hung up. I sat there for a few minutes and then did exactly what he said.

I parked across the street and snuck down the alley to Deuce's office. He was waiting with the door cracked. "Come on in," he said.

Deuce locked the front door and flipped the hanging sign to CLOSED. I fished in my pocket for the picture of Emmitt and Jeffrey. "I've got proof that Jeffrey knew Emmitt Laveau. I think they might have been lovers."

"You've got bigger shit to worry about now," Deuce replied, not even glancing at the photograph.

We sat down and Deuce explained. When he was finished, I tried to put the pieces together. I was incensed. "I don't understand why an APB would be put out for H.W. and me. I went to find him to convince him to disclose what he knew."

"Or to tell *you* what he knew, right?"

"Right."

"Nevertheless," Deuce said, "a picture of you two chatting it up outside Laina Donaldson's trailer surfaced with the police. He's wanted on a pretty heinous assault beef - and they're definitely going to question him about the murder, if they catch up with him - so you're getting dragged into the quicksand with him."

"That's ridiculous."

"You've created a stir. The men you've pissed off are in positions to put you away."

"I'd put money on the fact-"

"Hey, watch it with the gambling stuff."

"Sorry. But Ricky Walton is under Leland's thumb, so I wouldn't be surprised if he's the one orchestrating this. He's got more than one reason to. All he'd need to do is produce some physical evidence of H.W. from Laina's place and *find* it at the Boogie House. Then Leland could stand up and call for retribution-"

"And swift justice wins out," Deuce said. "A kick in the ass for the both of you."

"Yep. Damn. All in the name of protecting his son. I should have never confronted Jeff. That's what put this line of defense into action."

"But you can't pin Jeffrey's nuts to a wall based on this. A picture of them together isn't any sort of evidence of guilt. It's what, evidence that he lied? If you show him that, all he has to do is make up an elaborate story."

"It's going to be published in the paper."

"If it doesn't get censored somehow. Did you even ask Janita if that would be okay? I think she'd have a problem with you dragging her dead son out of the closet."

I thought about that for a minute. "I hope to have this all zipped up pretty soon."

"That doesn't change the fact that her son would be outed on the cover of the local newspaper."

"I have to take the chance that she'll understand. If the Brickmeyers aren't shaken up, they won't ever become accountable to their lies and hypocrisy."

"Well, good luck with that, Rol," he said. "I can't be a part of what you're doing."

"Why not?"

He sat forward, moving his keyboard aside and placing his elbows on the desk. "You're risking alienating everyone around you to catch Leland Brickmeyer or his son in something illegal. It has become your white whale, and you're going to end up hurting more than just yourself if you don't slow down and take a look at the motivations for your actions. Jesus, you're starting to get obsessed."

"Okay," I said. "I can respect that. You can't go down the rabbit hole with me. But tell me one thing: How did you find all of this out?"

"Ron Bullen called and told me to warn you. He's looking for his brother, but the guy's probably already blown town. Good luck getting anything else out of him. He's probably in the Midwest somewhere by now."

* * *

Leaving Deuce's office, I kept my head down. I flicked the phone open and made an emergency call. For the first time, the detective picked up on the first ring. "Hunter," I said, "someone besides the ref is calling the game."

He grunted. "Something strange is going on. Don't know why you're an interesting party to the locals, but you are. Lord knows it's all getting mucked up."

"Can you keep them off my back?" I reached the car, unlocking the door. It was a long shot, but I was working entirely in long shots right now.

"Not much I can do directly, but it looks like they just want to make sure you stop pestering everybody. If they bring you in, they can make you look like a suspect and discredit you so that anything you say will look laughable."

I got in, slipped on my seatbelt, and stuck the key in the ignition. "You have got to believe I had nothing to do with any of this."

"I'm beginning to," he said. "I had my doubts at first, but-"

"Bag full of snakes."

"Bag full of snakes," he repeated.

I turned the key and put car into drive, easing out of the spot and riding away, all while checking my mirrors for police cruisers. I didn't see any. "Janita Laveau gave me a picture of her son and Jeffrey Brickmeyer in a more or less loving embrace. I think this is all a defensive maneuver, but I'm afraid if I contact him, they're going to lock me away and forget about me as long as possible, and the picture will most certainly disappear."

"I want to see that picture," he said. "ASAP."

"Doris Allworth over at the paper has one. If you want the original, you'll have to come find me. I'm not going to stick my head too far out of the ground, if I can help it."

"All right," he said. "I'm going to make sure Jeffrey Brickmeyer is brought in for questioning. Until then, keep yourself out of trouble."

"I'll try," I said, and when I hung up, I punched the gas pedal to the floor.

* * *

When I got home, the house was all lit up. Again. I threw the car into park and went inside, finding Vanessa bundled up on the couch, knees to her chest, chin on her knees.

She looked up at me with wide eyes. She'd been crying recently. "Sorry about the lights. Thought I heard something outside a little while ago," she said. "And I think I heard gunshots some time ago."

I didn't want to entertain the idea that somebody who was looking for me might have shown up when only Vanessa was around. That thought shook me in a way I wasn't prepared for.

She smiled and added, "I guess this couch has become my security blanket. I don't think I've left it all day."

"It's all right now," I said. "I'll go flip them off."

"Can't we leave them on? I'm still shaking."

I went into the kitchen. Somehow, looking through the window made me shiver, even with the curtain drawn. I felt eyes all over me. It was an abject lesson. I couldn't make the mistake of assuming that my territory was off-limits. Attacking a member of Brickmeyer's crew had obviously opened up the playing field.

I made Vanessa's favorite meal for the second time since she'd arrived. I boiled some rice and then tossed in two cans of stewed tomatoes and a couple spoonfuls of pickled jalapenos. Without some pork to throw in the pot it would be somewhat flavorless, but I let it slide. I had more on my mind than comfort food.

"Did the cops show up today?" I asked.

"No. They supposed to?"

"Maybe."

"Well, today *nobody* did. I got nothing out here but that creepy noise a while back."

"What did it sound like?"

"A guitar," she said. "Well, it was more like two cats mating, but I'm pretty sure it was *supposed* to be somebody playing guitar."

"Huh," I said, trying to gloss it over. "That is weird."

"You think you gonna catch the people doin' all this?" Vanessa said from the living room, as I sneaked a glance outside at the dark outline of trees.

"Hope so." But I wasn't feeling too optimistic.

"I mean, really. This past week's paper was real negative, Rolson, saying it'd be a long investigation."

"Right," I said. "It might drag on, but I doubt it'll be an investigation at all from here on out. I just have to find a way to nail Brickmeyer."

"He doesn't have his head completely up his ass, though you think so."

"He's an abomination. I just haven't found the right thing yet."

"He's been a politician for long enough now, and even if you're right, even if you found him standing over the body, before it was all over, you'd be the one with all the suspicion, not him. He'll find a way to slither out from under the tin roof, and it'll ruin you."

I actually managed a smile at that. "Not much left to do there."

On the stove, the frothing red mixture gurgled and popped, sending a spray of red droplets across the counter. I pulled it from heat and slid the pan over to a cold eye. I went over to the cabinet and found the two least dirty bowls.

One slipped from my grasp and clattered on the stove, sending flecks of red all over the counter. I cursed, and Vanessa said, "Without bad luck..."

* * *

When she noticed me watching her, she said, "You want one?"

I shook my head. I was locking up the house. "Haven't had the desire the past few days."

She seemed to question it but only took a long drag on her

277

cigarette in response.

She wore a modest skirt, red chemise, and her hair was pulled half-up and half-down, the way I liked it. She was finally healing, and the weight she'd put back on looked good on her. Before, she had been hauntingly thin, and it was like looking into a coffin, but now the future was brightening somewhat.

She finished the cigarette and returned to her former place on the couch, feet tucked underneath her, one elbow on her knee, the other on the couch's headrest. The air around her was pungent with smoke and yet was sweet with her natural scent and fruity body wash.

"You should probably stay with your folks for a few days," I said. "Until I've got everything sorted out."

"Where are you going to go?"

I shrugged.

"Rolson, you can't just disappear. What're you going to do, sleep in the Boogie House?"

It wasn't an easy question to answer, mostly because I didn't have one. I'd thought about where I might hide out, and I'd find somewhere, but the exact location was a mere question mark.

I had packed up a suitcase for her, tossed some clothes and toiletries into a duffel bag for myself. I felt the clock tightening on me, but for some reason I couldn't tear myself away. Here I was, locking the doors and tightening up a place that might be worth burning down more than breaking into.

I was sitting on the couch, trying to think of some final words to say before we departed, when she did something shocking. The hand on her knee reached across and clasped my own. She slid her fingers between my thumb and forefinger, and I tightened my grip. A high-speed sledgehammer thrummed against my chest.

In a time in my life when nothing was clear or easy, when every day presented itself as an even more torturous digression from the previous one, somehow the warm, soft feel of her skin on mine made sense. Even as an addict, she had soft skin.

I allowed myself to give in to momentary weakness, recognizing nothing was under my control. The jurisdiction I had over my own life had grown smaller each day, and lingering just outside the circle were the old feelings I harbored against her.

She slid closer to me, shifting her weight so she could drape her legs over my knees, and I felt the swell of her breasts against me as her head drooped and then rested on my shoulder. I let go of her hand and placed one arm behind her, pulling her closer.

I leaned in and nestled my lips between her jaw and shoulder. Her hair covered her face, and I placed a gentle, timid kiss on the spot above her collarbone. She tensed, her neck and shoulder going rigid, but eventually she loosened so that I might kiss her again.

She was quivering, too, but what I had taken to be sexual excitement turned out to be quiet sobs working their way through her. She lost her breath and sucked in a harsh, tortured breath.

"I thought this is what you wanted," I said, still unsure of how to proceed. I was confused, paranoid. I wanted her but didn't know if it was something I'd regret later or not.

She didn't answer, so I whispered to her, "Isn't this what is supposed to happen now?"

She shrugged, but there was little uncertainty in the gesture. I sensed her pulling away from me, pulling away from this. Even if I didn't know how much regret I felt, she was becoming more certain of hers.

She stopped crying but pulled her fingers loose from mine. I wanted to hold on, at least until I figured out what *should* happen next, whether I should make *the speech* now or not, but everything was moving too fast for me, now, so I just let it happen.

"Are you thinking about someone else?" I said, sort of blurting it out before my mind could deal with the jealousy.

Again, her shoulders raised in that most indifferent of gestures. She wouldn't meet my eyes. Her head was tilted so that her hair hid her face. She was staring down in the direction of the source of my confused embarrassment.

"Choice is all we really have in this world," I said. "The guy you were with, he set in motion his own trap, and there's nothing you could have done to stop it - just sort of holding him down - and you weren't in the shape to do that."

She started to shiver again, and though she ignored me, I kept going. "Plus, that isn't any way to live life, forcing people to do what's right for them. If they can't see that their shortcomings might be causing some pain, then you can't make 'em see it."

There was a cold, still silence in the room. I reached out and brushed her hair aside, but she caught the motion and pushed my hand away. She then used the middle to fingers of her right hand to tuck her hair behind her ear.

Since there was nothing left but embarrassing things to say, I guess I thought it was time to say them. "There's days - and this might be something you don't want to hear - but there's days I wished I'd held you down so you couldn't run off and leave me. It would have been better for you to stay and work through your problems. I'd have helped you. But I could no more force you to do that than to make you keep on loving me. I let you go, and that was stupid, but hell, choice is what gives life meaning."

Speaking into my shirt, she said, "I don't even know that this is even about *him*."

I asked the obvious question.

She shook her head, pulling away just long enough to catch my gaze before returning her face to my shoulder, where the wetness of her tears soak through my shirt.

"Do you feel like you want to get high?" I asked, once she had mostly stopped crying. She began to shake her head no, to deny herself an honest answer. Thankfully, she stopped herself, nodding balefully.

The process of crying started all over again, but she caught herself before her feelings became uncontrollable. I said, "This isn't easy for me, either. My stomach has been prickly over the subject since you got here." I nearly said *home* but was grateful I didn't.

"It comes and goes," she replied. "Honestly, I've been keeping too busy these last few days to think about it." She paused, measuring my reaction. "But I can't lie: you've got me thinking about it right now."

"Have you thought about treatment?" Even as my mouth formed the words, I wished I could have grasped them with both hands and shoved them back in.

But there they were, hanging out there, just as I'd intended them, even if they were hastily thrown together.

"I may be plenty fucked-up," she said. "That shit dug its heels in against me and led me so far off-track that I may never find my way back. But how fucking dare you tell me I'm the one with a problem."

"Listen, Vanessa."

"DUIs. Missed court dates. I may be running from something, but I know what the hell I'm running from. You don't even know that you're running right beside me, lost as you ever were."

"I'm not judging you."

"That's why we made such a good team. We were both lost, stomping around in woods so confusing we could never find the right path. But at least it made sense to us."

"I haven't had a drink in days."

"Now doesn't *that* sound like denial? Don't pretend like you have something you can hold over my head, Rol. This isn't about us. That what you were going to say? This isn't about us, this is about getting better, blah, blah, blah. How many times do you think I've heard this shit from my dad?"

"You came to me. I thought you trusted me."

"I came to you because I thought you would *understand*. I know I'm an emotional money pit, but I've come to terms with that."

I'd had enough. "Then how can you hold me hostage? You walked right into my house, cleaned yourself up, at least temporarily, and you settle into domestic life just like you had only just returned from a business trip. Then *this* happens, and you tell me you've come to terms with who you are? I don't buy that."

She glared.

I said, "I don't. I don't believe you. You're still looking for something, and people might not know what they're getting into with you, but they continue to because they see something still there. I still see something there, Vanessa."

With that, I reached out for her, but she flinched away like I had threatened to hit her.

She stood up, her fists balled, and went to yank open the door.

It was then I saw the flashing lights.

The cops had shown up, but at least they had given me time to destroy my tentative relationship with my ex-wife before doing so.

"Come on out, McKane," said a familiar voice. It sounded like Ricky Walton, but the bullhorn distorted it so that I couldn't tell.

I knelt down and scooted around to one side of the couch. "Close the door," I whispered to Vanessa, who had frozen in the doorway.

There were multiple cruisers out there. Even though I hadn't really paid attention to them pulling up, I knew they were out there. This had to be a big deal. If I was going to be tossed away and discredited, this had to be a big fucking deal.

Vanessa remained in the doorway, her back to me, despite my pleas for her to come back inside. It was a tense situation, and I didn't want her to provoke them, to do something that would cause them to hurt her, but she didn't seem to see it that way.

"Vanessa," said the amplified voice outside, "Come on out now. Step aside and let us in. We've got a right to be here, and you'd best to get away from Rolson before he hurts you too."

"Van, don't listen to them," I said desperately. "Just step back in and let's think of the next move."

When she finally did turn to face me, her eyes were filled with tears, but there was a smile on her face. She'd already made her decision.

She swung the door open wide and started yelling. "He's in here! He's got a duffel bag full of clothes and a pistol. He was planning on running from y'all. That's what he told me!"

I didn't stick around to see her run out into the front yard as though I had been holding her hostage. I couldn't stand the indignity. Instead, I bolted through a ragged kitchen window and fled into the high grass behind my house.

It wasn't the best solution, but I got a good ways away before I heard the sound of a half-dozen pair of feet in my house.

The ground was mushy from all the springtime rain, so I had to wade out a bit farther before I found solid ground again. Thankfully, I'd holstered up my pistol earlier that night, so I had it with me. I pulled it and cocked it and waited there in the darkness. I didn't want to make any noise while I knew they were actively looking for me.

Flashlight beams skirted around the grass, but none hit me directly. Some of the fellas on the force pretended to see me and call for me to come out, but I stayed put and sooner or later they gave up.

They tried to comb the area, but they must have thought I had darted on farther down the field than I had, because they overshot my position by a half-mile or so. I watched their flashlights in the distance and slowly made my way back to the house.

One of them had stayed behind, but he fell asleep in the cruiser an hour later, so I was free. I snuck in through the window and grabbed a bottle of Beam and some beers, along with my duffel bag, before disappearing into the woods across the way.

Cure-all or not, tonight I could not be sober.

* * *

It only took two beers and a shot of Jim Beam to draw the devils out of their hiding places. I was in the woods, a good distance from my place but not within earshot of the Boogie House. It scared me to know what I might do - or what I might see - were I to go there.

Sitting with my back propped against an old tree, I waited to be found as I downed what remained of the booze. My ears burned, and I thought I heard the jangle of a distant guitar riff. Feeling the alcohol course its way through me, I began to realize that the existence of the visions was not contingent upon intoxication, but the level of intensity was.

So dumb, I thought. Should have figured that out the first day.

The devils came closer, slipping out of the shadows, driven into the light by my irresponsibility. Monsters splashed around in the pit of my stomach, and yet I kept drinking, sweating through my clothes. The edges of reality became melty, like plastic in a bonfire. The air around me thrummed with an electric energy, and anyone who's ever gotten drunk sitting down knows standing up is quite an event.

To hell with Laveau's sickness, I thought. To hell with the cure-all. To hell with Vanessa. Goddamnit, to hell with Uncle K and Janita and Emmitt Laveau, too.

And to hell with me.

Being angry didn't stave of the sourness in my stomach. At some point, I lurched two rows over and puked up a great deal of what I'd drunk. That didn't deter me. I drank until my eyes were physically incapable of staying open, and then I slipped headlong into a dead slumber, the sky spinning recklessly around me.

* * *

When I came to, I was stumbling through the woods, still

experiencing the fabric of reality ripping at the seams. It was like trying to stare into darkness through running water. Once, I tried to touch it and almost fell down. My hand passed right through the wavy membrane without sticking, but a distinct shock pulsed inside me, shooting down my arm and around my heart, settling at my ribs.

So dumb, I thought. So drunk and dumb.

And that reminded me of something. I stopped and looked down. There was a beer in my right hand. I held it aloft against what little moonlight cascaded through the trees. Less than a third remained. Then, I became aware of a pressure in both front pockets, and, reaching down, realized I had a High Life in each. They were suddenly cold against my leg, and it was then I felt entirely and fully conscious.

I must have blacked out and snuck back in the house for more beers.

Without hesitation, I drained the remainder of the beer in my hand and stuck it mouth down in my back pocket. The flash of otherworldliness returned, illuminating the world around me. I saw unfamiliar shapes dancing between rows of trees. My stomach, too, then awakened, something unpleasant pressing against the lining, turning it, making me desperately want to vomit. But I didn't. I choked back the urge and felt the warmth of the alcohol coat me like an aura.

I uncapped a beer and kept walking in the same direction. That tactic seemed to work for me during my blackout, so why stop now?

A pale blue light distinguished itself from the ubiquitous darkness. It pulsed with a four-on-the-floor rock beat, and moments later the accompanying music rose to ear splitting levels.

I noticed the drums first. A snare that sounded like a neck snapping with every strike. A severe, cringe-inducing crash cymbal. A bass drum deep enough to flatten my chest.

The accompanying guitar screeched like an injured panther, and once or twice I had to cover my ears. Whoever was playing stuck doggedly to the highest frets, but nevertheless it sounded good in a chaotic, anarchistic sort of way, reveling in the destruction, in the basic biological function satisfied by feedback.

I reached the ragged clearing that used to be the Boogie House's parking lot, and a few wispy silhouettes darted along the edge of the building and stopped. They melded together into what could only have been a lover's embrace.

I stopped to mark the moment with a swig from my beer, raising the bottle in mock salute, but received no acknowledgement in return. My stomach lurched, but I forced myself to accept more alcohol. I'd be paying for it in the morning, but this seemed worth the anguish.

Reaching the doorway, I peered in at the ruckus. People danced, dripping sweat under the glow of convenient overhead lights, gyrating to the raging drumbeat, bodies nuzzling and bumping together under the auspices of uninhibited musical passion.

Black men and women were dressed in tight pants and low-cut shirts, in jewelry and leather jackets and butterfly collars and sunglasses. The amplified acoustic guitar of past visions had been replaced by a bright blue Fender Stratocaster, the high-pitched yawl of a blues singer's voice replaced by a somewhat lower and funkier version of what I had heard in the Boogie House before. The song transmitting over the speakers was not about hell or redemption but black solidarity and individual pride, and the people, whose faces occasionally rose above writhing shoulders, seemed more open and free and determined than those in past iterations. Late Sixties, maybe, was the time period. They were angry and happy and ready for something to happen, and I had the feeling something was about to do just that.

As soon as I stepped in the door, the music stopped cold, and I jerked unconsciously at the abrupt volume shift. I expected the throngs of people to turn toward me, maybe attack me like a zombie horde.

The patrons had ceased dancing and were now staring in my general direction. I'd never felt so exposed and so naked in all of my life, and I thought about running but couldn't. I couldn't move, let alone run. Their eyes held me transfixed, and I sought desperately for something to say but remained mute. I felt the hatred of a hundred sets of eyes staring right through me. The eyes of a hundred ghosts.

The spell was broken by the sensation of movement behind me. I felt a rush of air and instinctively moved aside, glad to get away from the crowd, whose eyes, thankfully, did not follow me but remained fixed.

I turned to look.

In walked a younger, healthier, sharper version of Jarrell Clements. Law school graduate Jarrell Clements. Trying-to-make-his-name-as-a-young-lawyer Jarrell Clements. He adjusted his pants and snorted defensively, taking a cursory step toward the bar. "Y'all servin' whiskey here," he said. It was odd hearing a high-pitched version of his particular drawl. It was the sound of a young man trying on his adult voice.

Something inside me perked up. That voice. There was something about it that was so familiar, and I didn't have time to contemplate it.

"Yessir," the man behind the bar said. He was old and somber and had a perpetual hangdog expression about him. "We got permission to."

Two heavy-set white men stepped into the bar behind Jarrell. They were brandishing shotguns. I turned to face the crowd, comprised of a sea of horrified faces. The smell of sweat was overpowering, and the guitar amp's feedback was nerve-racking in the juke's unsettled air.

"From who?" Jarrell asked.

The crowd parted and a man stepped out in front of them. I recognized him from an earlier hallucination as one of the owners of the Boogie House. "Hold on a minute," he said, his voice unexpectedly calm. He flicked his head back toward the stage. "Sam, could you shut off the amps for us a minute. That's awfully loud."

Very little had changed about the man. In fact, he looked to be the same exact age as the version of him from twenty years before.

Every head responded by glancing back at the stage, and the sweaty, frightened-looking guitar player nodded and then went about turning knobs and flicking buttons.

"Now," the owner said, "what is it you've come out here about? We done paid up and begged to be left alone."

"Evening, Devereaux. There have been a *plethora* of rumors surrounding this place. Wanted to come down and see the hype, firsthand."

Devereaux smiled forcefully. "Just a little bit of drinking and dancing," he said. "No different than the things white folks do on Saturday nights. Now, if you'll excuse us."

Jarrell spat on the floor. "That ain't what I'm talking about. People drinking don't concern me." He smiled, took a moment to think of his next words. "A few people in town have been gettin' sick."

The bar owner looked as though this were a question he'd answered a hundred times. "And we have something to do with that?"

"It's just odd, I reckon. It's all people critical of this place. They're the ones turning ill. Mayor's wife, who don't care too much for drinkin' *or* dancin', took to her deathbed. Doctors can't figure out *what's* happened to her."

"That's a shame," the owner replied. Behind him, a young woman murmured, "We ain't had anything to do with *that*."

"It is a shame. It is," Jarrell continued. "I guess you people'd say it's her own doing, a *coincidence* she grew sick when she started advocating this place be shut down for the benefit of decent society."

Devereaux's face grew serious for a moment. "Quite the coincidence," he said. Devereaux was the bigger of the two men who had run the Boogie House. I remembered him from the dream-slash-hallucination. I wondered where the other man was, the skinny co-owner. Winston, I believed his name was.

The white intruder sauntered over to the bar. "Jack Daniel's, please," he said. "Neat." The bartender hesitated, and Jarrell feigned surprise. "Don't want to serve a white man? Isn't that, uh, *reverse racism*? Don't I have my *rights*, just like y'all?"

Devereaux walked over to him, saying, "Please, Mister Clements, just say what you've got to say so we can get on with our night. We were in a pretty good mood, but now you've got people all riled up, and it may take us well on into the night to get over it." With that, he tried to smile, but it didn't quite work. "So I guess the people can thank you for giving us something to work out."

"Where is Winston?" somebody in the crowd asked.

It was Jarrell's turn to smile. "Oh, we had a talk with him. He's decided it's high time to get the hell out of Dodge, and he told me to tell you it would be a good idea for you to do the same."

"He did no such thing." Devereaux's voice was cold and angry but held a hint of fear. Maybe more than a hint, to be honest. His accent had also become less obvious, and I suppose it was in an attempt to gain credibility, to let some of the rumors of witchcraft to fall by the wayside.

"Well, then, why don't you wait around for him and see if he shows his face in this joint, this *town* even, ever again? I'll bet you a dollar to a dime that nigra won't do so much as telephone in the future."

Devereaux grew quiet, waiting for Jarrell to continue.

"Listen to me," Jarrell said. "The old guard in this town is theatrical. They like to ride down the streets at night, wearing hoods, burning crosses in people's yards. That's all fine with me, but it don't work practically. It's all show, and show don't do anything. it takes *action* to keep the Junction safe."

"Uh-huh," Devereaux said, tensing up. There was a tightness in his voice, as if he knew what was coming next.

"And if you think I'm gonna let some chicken blood drinking niggers take over this city-"

The sound of the owner's fist connecting with Clements's face was louder than any distorted guitar. He just hauled off and punched young Jarrell right in his jaw. Devereaux himself even seemed surprised at the action. His eyes grew wide as he backed away, hands aloft in a defensive gesture. "You deserved that," he said, half-defiantly. "Sir."

"Goddamnit!" Jarrell screamed, patting his cheek with one hand. Blood had begun to seep from an elongated gash just below the eye. The young lawyer held his hand in front of his face, shocked, and said, "Look what you done to my face."

"You can't come in my business and insult me," he said, rounding the corner of the bar, intending to go behind it. Slowly pacing. Slowly moving. Trying to defuse the situation.

Jarrell turned to the men behind him, and they stepped forward, raising their shotguns. "I'll call you whatever the hell I *want* to call you, voodoo man," he said. An evil leer broke out across his face, and although his mouth began to form itself into a shape, as if to emit sound, Jarrell didn't speak again.

An uncomfortable rumble broke out in the crowd. People turned and whispered to one another, and the temperature of the room rose by about ten degrees. Devereaux lifted one hand, and every mouth hushed in captivated awe. "Leave this place," he said. "Keep to yourself, and we'll be sure to keep to ourselves out here. Maybe that's the only answer."

Jarrell spat again, and this time it was bright red. "This won't end. Even if I leave tonight, go out that door, nothing will be forgotten."

Devereaux placed one hand in his pocket, pulled out a small charm. His lips moved in a sort of unintelligible whisper. I couldn't hear what was being said. I doubt anyone else could either. When he finished, he said, "I'm willing to take that chance."

He began to shake the item, and his hand became a blur of back-and-forth motion. Jarrell's eyes widened, but he mostly disregarded the display. He said, "All's I'm telling you is that you *will* be shut down. No amount of backwoods gibberish is going to stop that."

"And what if I pray for *you* to get sick?" Devereaux said, smiling grimly. His hand vibrated so that it looked both visible and invisible, simultaneously. "What if I do to you what you say I did to the mayor's wife, eh?"

"I don't care," Jarrell replied.

"What if I place all my focus on you? Are you prepared to accept that?"

Jarrell nodded, but it was apparent he *wasn't* quite prepared. The voice that came out of him this time was even more thin and childish than before. "Or, what if I have you killed, right here and now? Do you think there's a snowball's chance in Hell I'd get convicted? What do you think would happen to this place then?"

Devereaux's hand increased in speed, jerking back and forth so quickly that his arm seemed to disappear below the elbow. An audible whirring could be heard above the breathing of the bar's tired, drunk patrons. "If you kill me, these fine people will drag you out on the dance floor and tear you to pieces. Those guns don't have enough ammo for all of us."

The eyes of every person in the Boogie House had turned into dull, unseeing orbs. They stared straight ahead, enchanted, full of vacuous and abstract hatred. They were just waiting for a sign.

I turned my attention to Jarrell, whose face had become flush with embarrassment. He was slowly realizing this wasn't a fight he was going to win. His weight shifted backward, and he reached for the shoulder of one of his accomplices for stability. "This ain't the way it ends, jigaboo," he said.

"I'm not going to pray for you to die," said Devereaux, as the white men moved for the door. "I'm going to do the opposite. I'm going to pray for you to live, Jarrell Clements, and I'm going to focus all the rest of my life on making sure you help the people you hate. I hope you live a long time, and I hope you are haunted every day by the things   you   have   done."

291

The world began to swirl in front of me, to grow black and thick. My head was spinning. I tried to hang onto consciousness, but it was becoming difficult.

I experienced another flash, this one more brief - a mere photograph compared to what I'd just seen - and saw a lone man counting small stacks of money. He was leaning against the bar and negotiating ones, fives, tens, and twenties in a deft, efficient manner. He subconsciously rolled a toothpick from side to side in his mouth as he ticked off the numbers and tallied the night's results. The Boogie House was dark, save for the light behind the bar, casting a haunting shadow across the man's face.

"Hello, Winston," a voice called from the darkness.

Winston jumped, knocking aside one of his neatly arranged stacks of money. "Who's there?" he asked, reaching underneath the bar, presumably for a weapon.

A deafening *crack* resounded in the open room, ricocheting twice off the walls before lodging in some part of the building. "I wouldn't get any crazy ideas," the voice continued. "You might end up getting blood all over your money, and wouldn't that be a shame? What banker wants to go through with that? Money with blood all over it?"

"Wouldn't be the first time, I think," Winston said.

I recognized the voice. This, too, was Jarrell Clements. A pillar of the community. An old friend of my father's. The man charged with defending me in court.

"What do you want?" Winston asked.

At this, Jarrell laughed. It was an oddly tinny sound. "You and your mojo man partner are no longer welcome in this town. We're plum tired of your act. Folks are getting hurt - good, white, Christian people - and it's all your fault."

"I don't-"

The gun erupted again. This time, the bullet skimmed the top of the bar and lodged in the wall behind Winston. Jarrell stepped out of the darkness and into the light, brandishing a firearm, flanked on either side by two men. *Not* the two men who later accompanied Jarrell to harass Devereaux.

One of them was my father, no older than sixteen or seventeen. He had a length of rope in one hand and a sawed-off shotgun in the other. His eyes were frightened and his posture wooden, but he stood his ground. "Do we have to do this?" my father whispered. "Can't we just-"

"Gotta be done," said the third man, who then stepped in behind Jarrell's other shoulder. It was then I started to be dragged out of this drunken half-dream, but I managed to get a look at the third man, whose face, though less wrinkled and wrecked by age, was still recognizable. It was Jarvis Garvey, the old timer who had lent me a car not even a week ago.

And then there was only darkness for a while.

* * *

When the light of the morning made me open my eyes, my hand immediately went to my forehead. Elephants were doing the Buffalo Two Step on my temples. I cannot even begin to describe how my stomach felt, but if I had to wager, I'd say it was somewhere between toxic spill and volcanic eruption.

It was early and cold. I was lying not in, but near, a puddle of my own vomit, somewhere out in the woods. My clothes were covered in dew and a weird smell, something fiery and electric and sweaty, like nothing I had ever been exposed to before.

The Boogie House was nearby - I was drunk enough to still feel its presence - but I wasn't near it. I made my way to my feet, which was a longer trip than you'd expect, and then made my way home.

I stopped at the end of the treeline and knelt down, watching. No cruisers in the front yard, but I couldn't be too careful, not now.

Ten minutes later, an officer stepped into the doorway and then disappeared again. He'd flicked a cigarette into the yard and then gone back to whatever work he was doing.

Eventually, he left when a cruiser dropped by to pick him up. I staggered unevenly and checked the entire house before relaxing.

I slunk into the shower and sat down for a while, letting the warm water cascade all over me. An exaggerated sense of loss and regret intensified my hangover. I tried not to think about my dreams or Vanessa, but I failed on both accounts.

These things happen, I thought. It'll get better.

What probably wouldn't get better was my personal relationship with Jarrell Clements. The revelation of his past, well, I had to think about that, and I was in no condition to think.

As I was leaving again, I found a clear plastic bag tied off with a nice red bow sitting on the stoop. Inside was a complimentary, "special edition" of the paper. Above the fold was a very telling headline.

NEW EVIDENCE SURFACES IN MURDER INVESTIGATION

SENATOR'S SON KNEW MURDER VICTIM, PICTURE VERIFIES

I read the article, which was mostly conjecture, and then re-inserted the paper into the bag and made my way across the road and into the woods.

This time, there was no music at the Boogie House. No spirits. Just the quiet sobs of a heartbroken and lost man. I found him standing over the spot where Emmitt Laveau had died, his back to me.

"You loved him, didn't you?"

He jumped, startled, and turned to face me. He looked to be on the verge of bolting the other direction when he saw it was me. Wiping his eyes with the sleeves of his shirt, he said, "Yes. Very much."

There was an intense amount of hurt in his voice.

I put both hands in my pockets. "Why didn't you just say that from the beginning? You think I'd resort to schoolyard talk, call you names? Accuse you of murder? Something like that?"

Fresh tears made their way down his cheeks. "My father," he said simply, as if in explanation.

I nodded, staring at a bit of chipped wood at his feet.

Jeffrey said, "But now I don't care. Not about his political campaign. Not about the company. I'll help you bring them all down, my father and the Bullens. They deserve it, and it's the only thing I could do to pay them back for what they did to Emmitt."

My heart sank. "What about the Bullens?"

"You didn't figure *that* out?"

"No."

He stared down at the ground, thinking through how exactly to lay it all out for me. Then he said, "The Bullens, they, well, they kidnapped Emmitt, threatening to do all sorts of bad things to him if my father didn't drop out of politics and sell them what used to be their land."

"And your father balked at it?"

"He tried to bribe them, said he'd do anything for this to go away. He was getting ready to give them the land, make it look like a sale, and throw some money on top to sweeten the deal. He wasn't about to give up politics. Apparently Ronald and his brother got impatient. And." He snorted, choking on his tears. "They killed him. My father thought it would look like a cover-up, and in trying that, he ended up creating a cover-up."

"Would you be willing to say that to the police?"

He looked me right in the eyes. "Anything to put those monsters away."

* * *

Something about Jeffrey's sudden admission didn't make sense, but sometimes the truth doesn't. I went to Nana's Kitchen for breakfast. I figured the police force might be a little distracted this morning to be tracking me down.

After I ordered, I tried calling the pulpwooders. There had been only silence from them since they had first told me where to find H.W. Bullen. All I got was Red's answering machine.

I sat down to eat. My breakfast consisted of a platter, with two fried eggs, two slices of butter toast, thickly-cut slabs of fried ham, and grits with butter and cheddar cheese. Nana's grits are legendary around here. People three towns over stop by to have them.

And as good as the food is, I thought I'd only be able to stare at it, rather than eat it. My stomach was on the other side of fucked-up, and the smell of all that fat was off-putting for a while. Once I finally mustered the courage to start eating, though, I was able to push through. It probably wouldn't sit well with me, but I'd at least be full and on my way to recovery.

Once this was all over, I was thinking about making the no-drinking policy somewhat permanent. Until then, I'd sit on the fence while the fields burned around me.

Halfway through, as I scooped up some grits on a piece of ham, the bell on the door jingled and in walked a sorry sight. "Rolson," Bodean said, limping over and taking up a chair across from me.

I opened my mouth to protest, but he took a seat without asking. His face was bruised and slack with exhaustion. He looked like he hadn't slept in days. "I ain't here to make trouble," he said. "I want to talk to you, for real."

I turned and saw Nana slip into the back of the restaurant. She was the only person working today and had to keep up with cooking, serving, and running the register. She wouldn't have time to peek in on us.

Chewing a mouthful of eggs, I said, "Okay. Shoot. Tell me what you know."

"I know that I'm getting the fuck out of town," he said. "Bossman's losing it bad. He's on the verge of tipping the boat all the way over, and I don't want to go into the drink when he does."

"Awfully loyal of you."

"Give it a rest. I got family in Texas I'm going to stay with. I'm digging a hole, and I ain't going to look out of it until this whole thing blows over, and I certainly ain't going back out there to the Brickmeyer place. Them people's got shit for brains, and I've had enough of trying to gloss it over."

"Be more specific."

Bodean watched me scrape a spoonful of grits on top of a piece of ham. He said, "Leland's not used to pressure like this. Politics keeps him at arm's length of reality. All the arguing and insinuations and shit are not real in that arena, and now that he's caught up in something genuine, he doesn't know what to do. Like that newspaper. I suspect you had something to do with that, didn't you?"

"What is his level of involvement, Bo?" I asked.

"I ain't real clear on that," he replied. "But I do know that he's willing to give me up to the cops, throw me under the bus, if it saves his ass."

"If you didn't do anything, wouldn't they be forced to let you go?"

"I knew you listened to blind bluesmen; I didn't know you'd become one. You should've realized by now that whatever officers Brickmeyer doesn't have in his pocket Bullen's got in his. If I go in that police station, I ain't coming out. If I'm suspected, the case'll die with me. They'll make sure of that."

I considered this. "What else do you know about the murder, specifically?"

He cleared his throat but did not speak for a long time. I finished off my eggs and grits and left a corner of meat on the plate. "I know Leland's been phoning Ronald Bullen at odd hours, having frantic conversations with him. If not for Jeffrey being so calm, sumbitch might have already gone off the deep end. Man can't handle this kind of pressure."

"What were the conversations about?"

He shrugged. "Always went in another room to take 'em. I tend not t'ask questions, but I can't help but think all the calls began around the time that Laveau boy went missing."

"Nobody really knows when he went missing."

"Brickmeyer started talking to Ronald the week before Laveau showed up at that old nigger joint. At first, you could hear Leland screaming through the walls. Couldn't tell what he was saying, but you could tell he was saying it with some *force*."

I peered at him. "And you're not just playing me here? Just to give the run-around?"

"I'm protecting myself now. It ain't tough for me to roll over on the dude, but he's gotten himself into some bad shit. There's this guy, up near Atlanta, and he's not in the mafia, but he's not that far from it, either.

"Huh." It was the sort of line that a dude would give to somebody to lead him into a trap, so I didn't bite on it the way I guess he thought I should.

He sighed. "I don't know the dude's name, but his hammer is a madman. Evil as all fuck. Limber. Limmer. Something like that. You hear that guy's name, you get the hell out of the way. He's nobody to be taken lightly."

"I don't have anything to worry about," I said. "It's Brickmeyer who's up to his elbows in this guy's business. Not me."

"Yeah, but your name is not completely out of the conversation," he replied. "And your old lady, she's got a lot of shadows in the corners. Don't forget that. They might try to - I don't know - use that against you. The boss has gotten frantic, and he keeps the waters smooth as glass on the surface, but he's hurting."

"Good. I hope he keeps on hurtin'. I'm going to make sure he hurts until he gives up the truth. I'm afraid I won't get a wink of sleep until that happens."

He smiled. "I bet you don't even know why you're helping at this point."

Well, he had me there. "It's the right thing to do?" It was the answer that stood out but was not by any stretch of the imagination the truth. The entire truth.

"I don't think it's so selfless as that. You've had it pretty rough in your life, like me. We've both had dry runs of shitty luck, but the difference between you and me is that I was smart enough to work for the people who made me jealous, rather than try to drag them down into the briars with me."

"Maybe," I said. "Maybe you're right, and I've been dreaming all this up to kick Leland Brickmeyer in the nuts for having money. But maybe - and this is something I've had to think about a lot - there is no meaning to it, or else I'll never find it. Most likely I'll just stagger from this fuck-up to the next one without an inkling of how I should have gone about it."

"And I reckon that's what I'm trying to avoid by getting out now, while there's still time for me."

"All the blood that needed to be on your hands is still there. You're just trying to scrub it off so *you* don't see it. Doesn't mean nobody else won't."

He tapped one of his enormous fingers on the table, watching it. "I guess that's something I'm going to figure out how to live with."

"You could always turn over, face the right direction. Hell, you could probably do some good. There's this detective-"

"Listen, man, I got to go. I was on my way out of town when I saw you parking, and I had to stop in and tell you. You don't have to believe me, and I reckon it wouldn't make sense for you to, but you won't have a chance to follow-up with me to find out if it's all true or not."

"But why? You're the hard case. Brickmeyer paid you to be his muscle. You're not supposed to think about what's happening."

"If you can figure out which of these shadowy sumbitches killed Emmitt Laveau, then I ain't got nothing to worry about. Good luck."

Without another word, the behemoth sauntered out of the restaurant and disappeared down the street, favoring the leg I had nearly broken.

* * *

I drove down a winding road made of hard Georgia clay, listening to the shocks squeak beneath me. The sky was as silvery-gray as the side of a dull blade. Trees rushed by and disappeared at intervals, like silent, ever-present guards.

I found the man I was looking for on the screened-in porch of his impressive two-story cabin, drinking a cocktail that made the entire room smell like rum. "How you doin', sport?" he said. "Come on in and have a seat."

I drew up the chair next to him and leaned back, looking over the orange sunlight reflecting off the man-made pond just on the other side of the yard. A small dock jutted out into the water, a ten foot aluminum boat tied up tight on one side.

He was in repose in a way I had never witnessed, and if not for the warmth he exuded in those moments, I might have thought he knew why I was out there. I told him as much - at least about the calmness - and he replied, "Even clowns wash off the make-up after a show."

The rocking chair squeaked amiably as Jarrell swayed back and forth. "I need to log these hours?"

"Actually, this is a social call," I replied.

"You're lucky I used to bum around with your father. I don't normally dispense with complimentary counsel. Go ahead, I'm listening."

"You know the politics around here," I continued.

"I wish I didn't. Cocktail?"

I shook my head.

"Good boy," he said, swirling his own concoction, the ice tinkling in the glass. He was either drunk or sedated. "You need to stay away from this shit until everything passes."

I didn't answer him. Across the pond, one kind of fish or another splashed, creating a mild ripple across the water's surface. Jarrell's smile widened, and the lines in his old face deepened.

"You read the paper today?"

He grimaced. "Oh, hell, if it doesn't have anything to do with keeping you out of jail, I don't give a rat's furry ass about it. But I can tell something's working. Little Leland walks around like that stick up his behind has been jammed in a bit deeper."

"'Little' Leland?"

He stared at me for a moment, his eyes looking into me for *something*. He used one hand to rub the scar on his cheek. The other swirled the glass, causing the ice in it to tinkle amiably. "Shoot, I can remember that boy soiling his britches in the first grade. Like I said, young man, I am *ancient*. You know how old dirt is?"

"No."

"Well, I'm a day older'n that, so go figure. He ain't quite got the swagger he used to. Something's got him down."

"Good," I said.

"Leland, he ain't tough like his daddy. His daddy was a mean sumbitch, I tell you what. Leland is soft, more like his mother. It's amazing he's made it as far as he has. Jeffrey's just like him. Life doesn't always go in cycles. Neither one of them's got the nerve of a shelter dog. I remember back when Leland went to high school. Walked around like he was real hot shit. You know the type. Not much different than he does now. But he had something going against him."

I was suddenly interested in what the uncouth old man had to say.

"What's that?"

"Haven't you been listening? Gumption. Leland had no gumption. Tried out for baseball. Couldn't make it. Tried to run track. Couldn't even do that. Lord, I remember the time he actually tried to play football. Somebody broke his collarbone during practice and he passed out. No kidding."

"What has that got to do with anything?" I asked.

"Some people round here thought he was queer when he was younger. Once he got to college, though, he started whoring around, had a pretty public meltdown when he moved back. But he married a fine woman, which shut most everybody up."

My hands were sweating. I clasped them in my lap, trying to pretend that I was staring out across the pond. "Hey, bud, what's got you all juiced up?" Jarrell asked. "You look like something deadly's crawling around your boxer briefs."

"What do you know about the night my father killed...that man?" The fucking guy's name had even gone hazy in my mind, after all these years.

Both bushy eyebrows raised up in a look of surprise. He seemed to stumble over a thought before saying, "Why, just what he told me. Strung him up and beat him to death. Bout all there is to tell, Rol."

"How'd you feel about what he did?"

He stopped rocking for a moment, and the amplified silence was only cut by the wind in distant branches. He pursed his mouth as he stared but he never betrayed himself, and he started rocking again. Man had the look of a survivor, like a cockroach in the wake of an H-bomb.

His voice was strained when he talked again. He said, "It was a horrible thing. No man deserves what he got, not even for what he did to your father. Lot of people criticized me for defending him. That's old ball, man. What you want to go digging around in that for?"

"You wouldn't have had a reason to kick my dad's bucket over, would you? Let him go into the net?"

"I don't know what you're implying-"

"I didn't keep quiet to protect you," I said. I looked down. My hands were shaking. "I did it because I blocked it out. Seeing you and Jarvis Garvey there that night, being witness to all of it, that wasn't intentional. Suppressed memories and all that."

Jarrell's eyes went to his drink. He had stopped rocking back and forth, and the air was so still I was almost afraid to disturb it.

"I don't know if it's because I'm so near to this investigation, or what, but it's coming back to me, slowly but surely. I can remember, clear as day, seeing the both of you standing in the light of my father's high beams, hanging that poor man. Lynching him."

"You best watch your mouth," he said. His eyes thinned to slits. "Your freedom's on the line here, not mine. You think anybody's gonna believe you, somebody raising as much hell as you are right now, going and accusing folks of killing black people. You think anybody's going to pay attention? Shit. Gimme. A. Break."

"Not only that," I said. "I don't think it was the first murder you were involved in."

"The hell you talking about?"

I steeled myself. "The owners of the Boogie House. I think you and my dad and Jarvis Garvey had them killed and then covered it up."

The old man stared, wide-eyed.

I stood up. "What happens to me happens to me. If I get a year in jail," I shrugged, "I'll do it. I'm going to stand up and pay for what I did. You've spent the last forty years hiding from who you used to be. No matter how many people you defend around here, you'll never make up for the three - or more - you had killed. Or killed yourself, with your own goddamn hands."

Jarrell watched me amble down the steps of his porch. "If I were you, I'd be thinking about how I was going to turn myself in. Detective Hunter is involved with a task force to dredge up old business in little towns like this, and he's become fond of my insight. He's the one who'll believe me, I figure."

"You have no evidence."

"Oh, I'm sure something will turn up," I said, and walked away.

* * *

The clock ticked on. I called Hunter, left a message, and then I called the pulpers again, leaving yet another voice mail. Nobody was answering except my best friend. Even Deuce seemed preoccupied, though, and he said it probably wouldn't be a good idea for me to be seen (a) in public (b) having a beer, so he declined hanging out.

I just went home. I got the feeling that having my face and then showing it in public would be a good idea. I was treated to the mental image of pitchforks and torches. Those who weren't on the side of the Brickmeyers thought I was just a fuck-up trying to upend the balance of the town. That, or they were convinced I was having some sort of mental episode and was taking everyone down with me in the process.

When you exist in your own head, as I do, then you can't be entirely certain if you're crazy or not. Looking at it from the outside, it was hard to argue with anyone making the points my brain was currently making.

I parked down by a gate near the Boogie House and hoofed it to my place. If the cops were waiting me out, then I'd have to sneak everywhere from now on.

Or until they catch me.

"Or kill me," I mumbled aloud.

The house and everything surrounding it was as dark as the road had been, and I had to fumble for my key a couple of times to get it in the lock. The door creaked open, and I stepped inside.

No cops. No flashlights. No one screaming for me to put my fucking hands in the air.

And yet, still.

Instantly, something felt...off. I cut my eyes in either direction and moved to my left, into the corner of the room. In the bedroom, I heard the constant, monotonous *wha-wha-wha* of the fan blades. I knew for a fact I hadn't left the fan on. I never left anything on.

Cops could've done it, I supposed, but I didn't think so. It wasn't time to convince myself *out* of conspiratorial thought.

I wanted to call Vanessa's name. It wasn't entirely unreasonable to think she had come to her senses and was in the back room, doing whatever, but I didn't fully believe that. Something odd tingled inside me.

My knees began to ache, and perspiration formed at my temples. I felt unsteady on my feet. I was without my firearm. My pistol lay under the bed, in its case. I crept forward, careful to shift my weight to keep the boards from creaking. I reached the edge of the hallway and stopped, rearranging myself so I could peer around the corner.

The fan's whirring grew louder as I peeked into the hallway. The moon cast no light, so I had no shadows to work with. Only the sliver of the light in the cracked bedroom door.

It was then I heard the first click, which in most situations signified a pistol hammer being cocked. The click was followed by a coarse, assonant grinding, and I knew instantly what was happening. I rose to my feet and bounded down the hallway, yelling gibberish I thought sounded somewhat official, "Stop right there!" or "Freeze!" or something like that.

I rushed into the bedroom to find a man yanking violently at a window. If there was one thing I knew, it was that it wouldn't come up that easily, not unless he was bionic. Any other set of windows, maybe, but not these. Had he been hiding anywhere else, he might have gotten out before I could catch him.

I stopped cold, held my hands straight out, miming holding a gun. He had his back to me, so he didn't know I wasn't packing, not yet. My entire body pulsed with adrenaline.

"Stop!" I screamed. "Stay right there. I will fucking shoot you!"

He stopped.

"Put your hands up!"

He obliged.

"Turn around, slowly, keeping your hands up."

* * *

"Don't shoot me, man," he said. "I ain't got no weapon."

"I don't either, but H.W., what the hell are you doing here?"

He looked like he wanted to answer but couldn't. He stood stock-still by the window, not quite sure what to do with himself, with his body, his hands held out in front as if calming a rabid dog.

I didn't see a gun, so I scanned the bedroom. It was trashed: papers and clothes strewn about, drawers flung open, mattresses askew, and the closet door sagging on its hinges.

"You do all this?"

He lowered his hands, gauging my expression, staring at me with that dumbfounded look. I noticed the thin sheen of sweat on his face and arms. He'd been working frantically, looking for something. "People talk about you, McKane, say you're out there, maybe a closet fruit, so I figured you might have a journal or a diary or something."

"Why?"

"To see what you knew about...that night."

I took a tentative step toward him; he, in turn, took a tentative step back. "So you were there."

"My life's on the fucking line here, McKane. The Brickmeyers are already floating the idea that we killed that boy. I didn't. I know they said you was involved somehow, but I don't believe that, neither."

"Jeffrey Brickmeyer's got a completely different idea of what happened."

"He's fucking lying, man. I swear. We roughed the Laveau boy up a little bit, trying to get something useful out of him, but the way he looked the night he was killed, somebody really put the wood to him. He was unrecognizable as human."

I lowered my hands completely. "That's going to be a hard defense to manage."

"We hit him, but only with the intention that he come out and talk about being Jeffrey's bottom, get him to say that Leland knew and hid it from the public to help his own career. You know people in Georgia wouldn't take to that. It'd ruin him. Ronald knew that."

"How did Ronald find out?"

"Caught the two of them together. He was out on patrol."

"And the reason you're here."

"I had to find out what you saw. Ronald hoped the Brickmeyers would keep all of this secret, cover it all up, but then the paper came out today, and, well, shit I figured I had nothing to lose."

"I don't have a record of that night."

"It's just, well, God, such a damn *weird* thing to say in public. Out loud to somebody. Ronald don't even know I saw what I did. I was too freaked out to even tell *him*."

"He'll find out soon enough. What *did* you see?"

"What?"

"I know what I witnessed. What did you see out there? It might be different."

"Shit, I don't know. It was like dropping a television in the tub. I saw a commotion, and red lights, and people being dragged down into hell. I saw me and my brother, and I saw two black fellas get blown away and dragged outta the Boogie House by their necks. That place is cursed, man. I ain't never heard of nothing like that in all my life."

It was completely different from what I'd seen. "Did you recognize any of the men from the hallucination?"

"What?"

"Their *faces*. Did you see their faces?"

He sputtered, trying to fake an incredulous laugh. "I tried *not* to see what was happening. I thought I was losing my damn mind."

"But did you see them?"

"The people's faces? No. They was just smudged. Blurry, you know, like a picture taken at dusk where everybody's moving. It was all just a blur. Is that what you saw, McKane? You see the same thing as me, or am I going crazy?"

"I think everybody around here's gone a bit crazy," I said.

"Ain't that the truth." He placed his hands on his hips. "Ron tricked me. Told me he'd get my warrants taken off the books if I helped him."

"If you kidnapped Laveau."

"Right. But I swear on my life, McKane, we didn't do nothing but slap him around some. We ain't killed him. Somebody framed us, came in behind us and killed him off."

I stared him square in the eyes, thinking about the pictures randomly sent to the police department. "Well, I reckon that's something you'll have to explain to a lawyer," I said, intending only to mean he'd have to talk about this *sometime*.

However, his expression changed immediately. He became beet red, his whole body rigid, and his eyebrows converged to a single black line above half-opened eyes.

"No," he said. He was gearing up to whoop my ass.

I knew I didn't have a chance if he got going, so I tried to catch him before he got charged up. I didn't have time to lunge for my piece - which was under the bed - so I took two quick steps and smashed him in the face as hard as I could.

The punch just seemed to wake him up, to distract him. He rubbed his jaw with one hand, staring at me, though his expression had smoothed out somewhat.

But it hadn't. It was like the threat of a fight calmed him.

The impact of his fist sent me into another plane of existence. I had to blink to stay conscious. He had a hell of a right hand, and it knocked me to the floor, onto the pointed edge of one of my drawers, just out of reach of my weapon. I managed to stay aware enough to reach for the pistol case. I thought I was about to get the worst beating of my life.

But that didn't happen. H.W. ran from the room, and I listened to his thunderous footsteps as he disappeared down the hall.

I retrieved the .45 and followed him, swaying punch-drunkenly on my feet. No sign of him. I got to the end of the hall and flipped the light on.

The front door hung wide open, and I've got to be honest: I didn't want to go through it. Not at all. Still, I crossed the living room and edged up toward the door, watching for any sudden movement. None came. I swung around and peered outside. Nothing.

My entire body seemed like it was buzzing with a faint electricity. The yard lay empty, deathly still. I couldn't hear the big man lumbering off into the distance but still I had to make one last appeal to him. "Hey," I screamed, "I'm not gonna turn you in. Come back and talk to me."

I went off into the front yard and ran toward the road. Every few steps I glanced behind me, keeping the .45 handy. I tripped once and nearly fell but managed to keep my feet despite the darkness.

It was about the time that I reached the road that I saw the faint glow of taillights, but they were nowhere near. H.W. had stashed his vehicle down the road a ways so he could escape through the woods. His truck disappeared around the curve, and I backtracked to the house, fumbling for my keys. They weren't in my pocket.

I went back inside, thinking I might have dropped them on the table next to the door, but they weren't there, either. The bedroom yielded no keys, too.

When I went back outside, I noticed that my car - Jarvis Garvey's,

309

really - wasn't parked in the driveway. I walked over to where it had been and stared at the dirt on the ground as if I might find it there.

H.W. had an accomplice, probably his brother, who snatched the car while the two of us were talking. It had to have been an impromptu theft, because they hadn't planned on me showing up.

I sighed. It wasn't my car and wasn't worth the time it would take to find it, but I was pissed. Why take the fucking car? What purpose would that serve? What were the Bullens going to do, drive it into the Brickmeyers' kitchen?

Back in the bedroom, I dialed Deuce's number, nestling the phone between my ear and shoulder as I cleaned up some of the mess. The junk strewn about my bed needed a place to go until the morning.

When Deuce picked up, I told him about what happened, told him to keep it from the police, and then I closed my phone and lay in my messy bedroom, pressing a frozen bag of peas to my swollen and throbbing eye. I suddenly had the urge to talk to Vanessa. In sobering up, she had become so zen about this world, more objective. It was as though she could see truth for truth's sake, and I needed that stability.

But who knew where she was. My eyes fixed on an uncertain dark point on the ceiling, and I stared at it, waiting for headlights to appear, until my own lights went out.

* * *

Emmitt Laveau wasn't the only person to visit me in my dreams that night. This time I ended up in the Boogie House during an elaborate party, bumping into people long dead. I stood with my back to the bar and listened to the tinkle of shot glasses and the inexplicable roar of laughter.

A group of people parted, and I saw Vanessa in the center of the dance floor, hands clasped behind her back, smiling sweetly across at me. She seemed - like the others - to glow, and I followed the

310

illumination to her.

I leaned into her and we danced, turning slowly with the gentle back-and-forth rhythm of the piano. The song was slower but not quite bluesy. More of a traditional jazz ballad, and it lent itself to slow-dancing. "I'm going to miss you," she said. Her voice tickled my ear.

"I didn't mean to make you mad," I admitted. "Please don't go away. I still love you."

"I love you, too," she said. "But that's not all that matters. You can't repeat the past, Rol. It never works out."

I nodded, and wetness stained the shoulder of her dress. I said, "I'll be here when you're ready to come back. The house will always be there."

"The Boogie House is nothing but ashes," she replied.

I tried to tell her that wasn't the house I was thinking of, but then I saw who was playing the piano and stopped. Emmitt Laveau was stooped forward, his hands moving deftly over the keys. "Give me a moment," I said, and then I went over to where he was playing.

I turned and caught one last glimpse of Vanessa before the crowd swallowed her again. She was beautiful, unmarked by her addiction. She was the person I always imagined in my mind when I thought of her, young and pretty and elegant - innocent - and the way she smiled then would stay with me forever.

I waved and turned my attention to Emmitt.

"Hey, partner," he said, not looking up. "I'm lucky to be playing at all, or for you to be hearing it, for that matter."

"Why's that?" I asked, watching his fingers. The song was slow and sweet and sad, and the people in The Boogie House murmured with the music.

"I'm six feet under the earth. Do you even realize how loud this must be in the graveyard?"

"I'm going to find your killer," I said.

He smirked. "I know."

He added a little flourish to the melody, and I admired the way his hands moved. I almost got caught up in the music, felt the swell almost pull me away. I had to force myself back into the conversation.

"I think the Bullens did it. I think they tried to frame Leland Brickmeyer with it to get their land back. Or something like that."

"Seems about right. I'll just stay here, if you don't mind. I'm real busy right now."

"That's okay."

"The longer I keep playing, the longer they let me stay. Whenever I stop, I can feel the darkness coming in closer on me. So I don't. I don't stop playing, 'cuz I like it here, and I'd rather not leave."

"I understand that," I said.

"I won't like the alternative. I don't think anybody does, and that's why they stay here. They figure if they stop, then the party stops, too."

"Nope, I guess not. You don't have an opinion on me finding out who killed you?"

"That's my mama, I reckon. Not much I can do from here. Maybe it'll change my situation, and maybe not. It'd be better, I suppose, if you found out. Might help you, and it might help mama out, but it's no consequence. Plus, I don't know if I want to know what exactly happened to me."

"But it might keep the darkness away."

"Nope," he said, banging away on the keys a little bit harder. "The darkness always comes around, no matter what you do. You'll figure it out, I'm sure."

I hadn't considered that. "I guess you're right," I said.

"Lotta good I am. I can't even help you out. But at least you know where to find me."

"Is there something you want me to tell Jeffrey?"

But he didn't respond. He just smiled and kept on playing. I felt the others crowding in on me. Turning on me. When I glanced back, Vanessa had disappeared, and in her wake stood a group of shuffling party goers, staring unhappily in mine and Emmitt's direction.

I thought I might have a word with Vanessa before I was dragged out of my dream, but she was nowhere to be found.

I tried to rush back to the center of the dance floor, but the crowd converged, blocking me in. I tried to find her dress, or glimpse her hair, but she had gone away, and I went to my knees, trying to peer between the feet of other dancers for a sign of her light blue glow. But I didn't see anything at all.

* * *

I got the call from Vanessa's dad just before dawn. I answered without checking the number. "Deuce, hey, anything new?" I asked.

It wasn't Deuce. D.L.'s voice sounded ragged, the chain rattling on an old fence. "She overdosed. Found her this morning." He paused. "She's gone, Rol."

As if to put a finer point on it, he added, "She's dead."

By some miracle of will, I managed to hang on to the phone long enough to press the little red *end* button. The phone beeped and then died.

Outside, a dry breeze kicked through the pines, the clouds above threatening rain, and the branches clicked on the side of the house.

Eleventh Chapter

Vanessa had bottomed out. She had reached a point where pursuing normal life no longer kept the shadows away, and instead of helping her out of the grave, I had thrown the first spadeful of dirt.

When my face stopped aching enough for life to be tolerable, I got out of bed. I snatched on a pair of pants and a shirt and kicked on my sneakers on my way out the door, but instead of calling Deuce to come and pick me up, I walked toward town.

Consequences and warrants no longer concerned me.

It was just the way of things, I guessed. The beginning of a penance I would be paying off for a very long time.

Several cars passed me once I hit the highway, and not one offered me a ride, not that I was in any kind of mood to accept generosity. The silence kept me stitched together.

I found the car a half-hour into my walk.

The Olds had been abandoned two miles down the road, on the shoulder next to a pair of dumpsters. All the windows had been smashed. Ditto for the windshield. Tail lights and headlights, too. The body was in okay shape because someone had taken a bat to it instead of an axe or chainsaw.

I flipped open my phone and dialed the detective. "Hunter?" I said when he answered. "I'm out of the private tracking business. Let me

315

tell you what I know."

"What changed your mind?"

"Two decades' of momentum hitting a brick wall."

Our conversation was brief. I filled him in on what Jeffrey had told me, going into as much detail as possible, finishing up with H.W. Bullen's break-in. I didn't mention Vanessa, but she circled my mind for the conversation nonetheless. "They might deny it later, but they pretty much unloaded their consciences on me, so I think it's information you can go on with some confidence."

"Would've been nice to get this revelation sooner, McKane. You walked a thin line there for a while."

I cleared my throat. "I hope you can sort out this mess, Detective. Oh, and one more thing."

"Mmm-hmm." He sounded distracted.

"You said you're part of the task force to sort out unsolved hate crimes from way back, right?"

"Right."

"You might want to look into Jarrell Clements and Jarvis Garvey as accomplices in the murder my father was convicted of, and for the disappearances of the two men who used to own the juke joint where Laveau was found. I suspect there might be bodies buried somewhere in the vicinity."

Hunter inhaled sharply, as if to say something else, but I snapped the phone shut before he could. Then I turned it off and stuffed it into my pocket.

I thought that availing the detective of all my knowledge would somehow lift my burden, but the funk surrounding me continued to swirl. No catharsis to be found. I brushed away the broken glass and, clenching the wheel, thought about Vanessa for a while before driving off.

* * *

316

I ended up at the Laveau residence.

I got out, adjusted myself, and headed for the front door, which was already open. A pungent, unpleasant smell wafted out into the open air. It had a faintly musty odor, like skunk spray that lingers long after the little guy's been scraped off the tire tread.

Through the screen, I saw a silhouette working diligently in the kitchen, and I went right on in without knocking, expecting to see Janita. Instead, Uncle K was standing in the kitchen, fiddling with something that was ostensibly meaty but so putrid-looking I stared somewhere else.

He didn't acknowledge me at first. Then, without looking up, he said, in his naturally raspy voice, "Hey, there, crazy person. What did you come to mess and gom with today?"

"What kind of spell is that?" I asked.

He smiled, never looking up. His fingers moved deftly at skinning the small animal. "Dinner. So, the kind you eat, I s'pose."

"Uh-huh."

"I just bought this knife. You like it?"

"Sharp."

"Every time I pay for anything at the store, I can hear what people think. *'Is he gonna use that to stick in some doll?'* It don't change, not one bit." He laughed. "People are the same."

He picked up a small piece of the meat and stuck it in his mouth, chewing diligently as he finished up. Once he cleaned the knife on a nearby towel, he scooped the remainder of the meat into a bowl with onions and cilantro and lemon juice, and he he mixed them together with his fingers. "Old family recipe," he said. "Janita won't touch it. Says it taste like sushi been left out in a swamp too long. Don't reckon you want some?"

K saw my expression and waved off the offer. He said, "Ah, hell, you people. I didn't want you have any of it anyways, damnit. Didn't

317

even offer you to come in the house."

I leaned against the kitchen counter. "I'm done," I said, trying to sound noncommittal. I was thinking about Van and her parents and how fucked-up my life was, and I couldn't muster the strength to care about Emmitt Laveau right now.

"And yet the killer walks around, free as a blessed man," he said, adding, "C'est la façon dont il va. I guess I should not have expected anything less."

"It's all pretty much locked up," I said. "Do you want me to tell you what I know?"

"The men, they kidnapped him, and they tortured him, but they did not kill him. Or at least they say that is the truth."

It took all my strength to keep my mouth closed, though I shouldn't have been surprised.

His eyes flicked in my direction. "You think I don't know things, because I am old, but I know plenty. I see *everything*."

I started to lose my temper. "Then why drag me into this? Why not just go ahead and tell somebody? Or pull up some evidence of your own?"

"People, they cross the street when they see me. You think they gonna believe me when I tell them the local king had something to do with my grand-nephew's death?"

"I just said Brickmeyer didn't-"

"Here, you come into my house and you say that you have a handle on all the things about this case, and you don't even know the truth."

"One of the brothers basically just admitted to me that he had something to do with what happened to Emmitt. Do you just have a hard-on for Brickmeyer?"

I was beginning to sound like everyone who talked to me.

"I don't got a hard-on for no man," he replied. "The fact you still

318

don't see clearly tells me you know *nothing*, and you need to see the truth of the matter."

"No offense, but the only truth you've helped me see is that I drink too much."

He turned away from his food preparation, smiling. "You want me show you something *real*? Something *visionary*? I need to rub chicken blood on your forehead, start moaning and making voices for you?"

"That's not what I'm saying."

"Listen. Come here. You and me, we take a trip, okay? I'll show you something."

"I told you, I'm out. Done. I've got to go and see some people about arranging a funeral."

He waved his hands contemptuously at me. "You never cared about any of this. Your funeral will wait. This happens now, if it happens   at   all."

Something about the gleam in his eyes was alluring. "I don't-"

"Come along, come along," he replied. "That Brickmeyer man, he needs to get what he has been asking for, and if you - or I - don't give it to him, he will never get it."

I paused in the doorway, and he pushed past me.

"You know that is the truth," he said. "You worked at that police force. You think that worthless bunch would make a wave that would drown the man? I do not think so."

My heart sank. "If we make this thing quick."

"All right, then," he said. "Let me go out back and get the shovel. We are going to need it."

* * *

We rode in my battered vehicle. On the way, I stared through the windshield as Uncle K talked, neither asking for my permission to speak nor caring if I opposed it. I wasn't in the mood to participate. But then he hit upon something that interested me very much.

"The men who owned The Boogie House, they practiced the religion, like me. Didn't know them, not personally, but they had their hands in all kinds of things."

I thought about that for a minute, reaching for a connection. "Do you think that might have something to do with the supernatural aspect of your grand-nephew's death?"

He smiled, as if I had just complimented him. "The spirits that got a grip on that place do so because the men that owned the building conjured up something and never put it down."

"And the Bullens? Did they know that?"

He scoffed, making a *p-shaw* sound. "Hell no. They needed a place to keep him, and they were heartless so they took him there. That place, it might have pulled them there, pulled them in like they were holding a magnet, but them men, they didn't know any better, if I say so."

"Emmitt?"

Laveau raised an eyebrow. The old man's eyes became watery and distant with remembrance. "No, not Emmitt. He didn't know nothing. The boy was special, damn special, but he didn't know nothing about the other side of the death line."

"But you do. You know. I mean, you really *know*. Why aren't you doing anything?"

His face turned into a scowl. "You drive. You don't bother with me. I know what I'm doing."

I couldn't let it go *now*, not after I had struck him right between the ribs. "And me, how did you pull me in? Have you been slipping me drugs to make me have fucked-up dreams?"

His eyes sent my stomach twisting. "You don't need my help dreaming up sick things, no," he said. "Just you living has given you an attic full of dark places. Your dark places. Not mine, not ones I put up in your head."

320

"But I didn't start dreaming about the Boogie House-"

"And maybe you didn't have any reason to dream it up 'til you nearly put my 'Nita to rest. Rolson McKane, all you are is darkness, and you almost dragged her into it. Just dragged her in so she'd never be seen again. That she almost died had nothing to do with her or little Emmitt, but *you*. Me, I tried to help you, but I can't help you no more. Whatever's gone bad in you, it sours all the good around you. Maybe I made the blade you cut the world with sharper, but it's always been in your hand."

I was speechless.

His lip turned up in a snarl. "You pretend like you didn't know that, but you did. You can choose to forget your past, but that is one thing you must never, ever forget. Now you shut your mouth and do what you're told, lest you ruin one more chance to see the world clearly."

* * *

"Pull in the graveyard like normal and take the main path down to the woods," he said, as we approached the last stretch of country road. "Let me out by the tombstone, and drive on down there and park. Don't want nobody seeing you."

I did what he said, parking down by the copse of trees, and then I walked back up to where the old man stood, shovel slung across my shoulders. I looked at him for a moment, and then he gestured toward the ground.

We were standing by Emmitt's grave. The dirt was still fresh looking. I glanced from the headstone to him.

"This don't sound like any kind of voodoo ceremony I've ever heard of," I said. "Would you have me dig up the body?"

The old man smiled viciously. His face became a collection of wrinkles. "Who said anything 'bout digging *up* the body? I just said 'dig'. I'll tell you when you're done. Don't worry 'bout that."

I didn't move. I had stepped through some muddy patches in the last few weeks, but this was beneath even me. My heart and stomach felt as though they had switched places.

"Dig," he repeated. "You want me help you see truth, get to shoveling."

"This is too far," I said. "I'm not doing this. This is - this is just *crazy*."

I felt the same kind of rawness in my gut as when I drank. The cure-all (or the drugs I'd been given) obviously had a long tail, and even though I had been impressed with Kweku Laveau's mysticism, I wasn't about to dig up a fresh grave. No way.

"If you do not dig, then you give me no choice but to put you in my sight line, and you do not want that, no."

The intensity with which I stared at him did nothing to draw out *why* I might be doing this, and after a while, I felt myself consigned to it, pulling the shovel off my shoulder and sticking its blade into the ground. I said, "I'm sure Janita would not approve."

Looking into the old man's eyes, I felt a shift. The longer he looked at me, the more I felt compelled to do what he was asking. Whenever he blinked, a humming in my brain stopped, and whenever his eyes met mine, the humming returned. It wasn't as though I had *no* will, but I didn't feel the need to follow my own instincts for now.

Finally, the old man said, "My niece will not be aware of this. No set of eyes in this town will see you. Else, you're in trouble, boy."

"I think we'd both be," I replied, and the man only made a wet coughing sound in his throat. In the distance, thunder signaled an approaching storm. The sky was a deep, bruised purple, occasionally split by slivers of lightning.

"I'm not digging up this whole thing," I said. "If this is meant to teach me a lesson or something, just let me know when I've learned it."

But I did it. I hesitated, and yet I still shoveled, and it brought me closer to something. Maybe not the answers I was seeking out - I guess I'm a seeker - but toward something meaningful. If I could derive no truth from this exercise, I could at least manufacture it out of thin air.

At first I worked slowly, mechanically, self-consciously, listening to the harsh clink of the shovel in the earth, but then I sped up, and soon the physical aspect of shifting aside the dirt faded into the background. The work took center stage, and after a while, I didn't care about the nature of it. I fell into a sort of trance, shoveling as though exorcising some kind of demon, ridding my soul of its dirtiness. It seemed to bring out everything raw and dangerous which had plagued me emotionally. I reveled in each thrown clump of dirt. I began to think that the work itself was the meaning of this whole production, and I continued.

Once, old women drove up in pristine sedans. They pulled in and looked questionably in our direction as they walked toward their destination, but K just smiled and waved and the women departed from us without a word. I half-expected the authorities to show but none did. With Janita's uncle standing there, arms folded across his chest, I experienced a strange comfort.

Once I had slipped into a monotonous rhythm, my mind drifted, as if the thoughtlessness of the physical work afforded it the chance to contemplate more important ideas. Every thought I encountered was something I had been putting off, but it was also something that I needed to deal with, so the stinging sensation that pricked me every so often was welcomed without protest. I began to thrive on the grief, thinking not for the consequences. I felt sobs creep up from within, and I began to work with the image of Vanessa at the forefront of my mind. Crying and shoveling. Crying and shoveling. Crying and shoveling.

And as I worked, the day shifted from morning to afternoon. For a time, I thought I had become delirious.

Then I hit something hard. The tip of the shovel clanged against the surface of the coffin. In that moment, the reverberations seemed to shake more than my hands. That broke the trance, and the cloud over my brain lifted. But by then, I didn't care what came afterward. I realized he had brought me here for the work and the work alone. The ending was just the ending; the work was what mattered.

"Whup," the old man said from somewhere above me. "Them ain't roots you done got into. Open it up."

I hesitated. At least I *thought* this had been about the work. "Go on," he said, and I heard the rustling of his pants as he moved around to get a look at the coffin. "I can promise he won't jump out at you."

"That only happens in my dreams," I said, kneeling on the soupy dirt covering the casket lid. Exhaustion kept trying to convince me to lie down for a bit. My muscles ached severely, but I felt as though I had cleansed myself somehow. A baptism by dirt.

"Hurry up," Uncle K said, somewhat impatiently.

I wiped away clods of mud, revealing the newness of the casket, fully intending on opening it...at some point.

A close, murmuring thunder warned me against it, but on impulse I grabbed the shovel from behind me and began to cull the mud and dirt away from the sides of the casket, listening to the near-sickening scrape of the blade against the elm top. It was then I felt God's judgment closest to me, as though Kweku himself were an arbiter of the Big Man Himself, and I was ashamed.

A great wave of nausea filled me, and I was vaguely aware of the extremity of my tunnel vision, blackness pushing in around the edges, but I pressed on, commanding my limbs to keep moving, shoveling away the dirt and mud and rocks and bits of grass.

I pressed one hand down the side, looking for the handle, and the first raindrops pelted my back and thudded on the wood and dirt surrounding me. Uncle K remained remarkably, uncharacteristically quiet. Even the shuffle of his feet and quiet swish of his pants had receded into silence, but I dared not address him. This was almost done, and not a minute too soon: I felt like I might burst open, like a plastic bag filled with blood punctured by a needle. The edge of consciousness lay only inches away, muddled in the strained darkness of my vision, and I felt myself being dragged away from it.

Finally, there was enough debris scraped away to attempt to open it. I fingered the side latch. I ignored how bad I felt, how very near the point of collapse I had come, because I only had this one motion to complete. Reach down, pull open the casket, wait for enlightenment.

There was no flash of lightning as I opened it, but there was a flash of some kind, and something electric shot down my spine. White hot pain exploded in the back of my head, and with reality fading all around me, I peered into the final resting place of one Emmitt Laveau, seeing him for the first time in the flesh. So to speak.

My senses - or rather my imagination - sharpened by exertion, superimposed the images of Vanessa's face and my mother's face in the space next to Emmitt's already rotting corpse. A trinity of the dead. I screamed out the old voodoo man's name before slipping down, down, down into the darkness, which reached across my field of vision and closed the curtains on the fading afternoon light.

"I think you are ready," said K from behind me. I felt another sharp pain, and then my lights went out completely.

Twelfth Chapter

The night my father killed my mother's lover, Terrence Birrell - when he hung him by the neck and laughed while the man gasped for air and clawed at his throat to relieve the agony - I watched from a nearby row of holly bushes.

My daddy had told me to stay in the car, that he had some business to do, but of course I hadn't. I'd slipped out and walked along the edge of the path leading back to where he had gone. I knelt down and watched in rapt horror. I saw the maniacal, unhinged look on the old man's face when he tied the rope around the victim's neck. Two men stood there with him, laughing angrily, spitefully, helping to finish up the disgusting business. Of all the things I could not remember, his accomplices' identities were the most troubling. Finally recognizing Jarvis Garvey and Jarrell Clements locked everything into place.

Seeing my father draw a man into the air and then wrap the slack around a stake plunged into the ground was almost eclipsed by my inability to look away. The three men cracked open beers and watched, waiting for the man's dangling feet to stop twitching.

It was there, under the fragrant and prickly holly trees, that I last prayed to God. Kneeling there in the dirt, staring wide-eyed at this atrocity, straining against inevitable tears, I asked the Almighty to deliver this poor man. He received no such assistance, just more agony.

My father and the other men taunted and harassed him, spitting beer onto his clothes and hurling obscenities at him. They happily waited for him to die.

After that, I sort of lost track of the minutes. The nightmare show played out for some time, but I lay amidst the bushes and the brambles and closed my eyes, staying well after the headlights of Clements's and Garvey's cars had gone, when only the dead man and I remained.

At some point, I fell into a hard, uncomfortable sleep, in which I dreamed about nothing and still seemed aware of my surroundings. My terrified thoughts were drowned out by something else, something that reached out from the darkness and squeezed its cold fingers around my spine. It was a sound, the faintest of croaks, no louder than a grown man's whisper.

It was the sound of a rope straining against a tree limb.

Swinging. Back and forth. Back and forth. Back and forth. Desultorily with the wind, as if it were the most natural thing in the world.

When I reawakened, I ran, running because it was all I knew to do, relishing the way the tall grass whipped against my clothes, because it replaced the hellish creak of the rope.

At one point, I tripped and fell against a tree, and when my forehead struck the roots, I saw in that flash of a moment my face transposed over the face of one of those men, my own mock smile glinting in the car's headlights. That image has stayed with me all these years. I walked, bleeding, all the way home and sneaked back into my room after my father passed out. I avoided him, and he didn't mention anything about my disappearance. Two days later, he was in jail, where he would die an embittered, pathetic shell of a man.

That is one of the reasons, I suspect, I've kept my head down all these years, why I've left the past to be the past. It wasn't until I joined the police force at twenty-five, after watching two planes rip into buildings I myself had never visited, killing people I would never have known, that the distant, underwater feeling broke, and I began the process of swimming back toward the surface.

Being a police officer never completely changed it, because I continued down the same path, and getting the DUI seemed right in a lot of ways when placed against the background of my life, but even that feeling snapped the moment I saw Janita Laveau standing in my driveway, already having forgiven me on a level to which I could probably never forgive myself.

* * *

My eyes opened to the dull sensation of raindrops pelting my forehead. I stared up out of the grave of Emmitt Laveau, above the dirt, into the slate gray sky, where the clouds swirled like an omen of the worst kind. I half expected a rogue's gallery of the undead to be staring down at me, ready to drive me the short distance over into insanity.

But the sky was all there was, and I was happy to see it, happy that my dreams were just dreams. I leaned forward, sitting up, and immediately shot a hand to the back of my head. I wondered how long I had been out. I didn't bother to call out for Uncle K. Instead, I patted the wetness on the back of my skull and brought my fingers around to see. Blood. The old man had whacked me a good one with the shovel and left me here.

It was then I noticed, too, that I was covered in dirt. My legs and chest had been covered up, and I had difficulty sitting up and brushing it off. Had the old man planned on burying me? If so, what had stopped him?

I worked my way out of the grave and heaved myself onto the grass. I rolled onto my back and stared at the abundance of raindrops. Once my legs stopped shaking, I got to my feet and walked unsteadily toward the car, which was nowhere to be found. The old man had swiped it while I was taking a shovel nap.

Damnit. Wasn't even my car.

I walked three miles down a cracking, dilapidated back road, soaked head to toe in rain and mud and getting more soaked by the minute, my head throbbing. I was busy trying to invent increasingly filthy words to curse the old man with, should I see him. At least it distracted me from my head.

I trespassed on an old patch of land that ran right by my house. It, too, was owned by the Brickmeyers. Dried branches and old bushes crackled under my feet like brittle, forgotten remains as I walked.

I was exhausted. Really tired, despite sleeping in the grave. I was the kind of tired that made me question living. I tried not to think of Vanessa, tried to keep my mind on putting one foot in front of the other, but she kept popping up in my thoughts. Not the Vanessa of my dreams, the Vanessa in tight jeans with a beer in one hand, cigarette dangling from her lips, but the strung-out, junkie body double of Vanessa, unimaginably skinny with frightened eyes. In this image, she pleaded with me to help her, almost understanding that I could not.

I couldn't muster any emotion beyond misplaced regret. I was pissed at myself, but in a disconnected way, as if something had been unplugged. I wanted to hate myself, to muster up tears, but nothing came. I was just tired and bewildered. The walking wounded.

* * *

I went down a tree-lined hill, through an open gate, toward a small pond in the distance. The rain had slackened, but the abundance of gray sky told me the storm wasn't finished.

When I was nearly level with the pond, I stopped. Standing in the middle of the pathway, I was entirely vulnerable, but still I moved forward.

The pond had no bank. The grass ended abruptly where the water

330

began. An occasional tree protruded from it, but otherwise it was just muddy brown water.

Something jutted out above the surface about ten yards out. It was white and metallic and drew me in as if by hypnosis. By the time I realized, I was knee-deep in water and continuing forward.

It was a truck. A white *diesel* truck.

I slogged ahead, smelling mud rise out of disturbed water. The truck had been driven so that it was submerged well above the license plate, but I already knew what I was approaching. The driver's side window was down, and I heard a fly buzz as I looked into the cab, instinctively covering my nose and mouth with a forearm.

First thing I noticed was that he hadn't been dead for long. Couldn't have been. H.W. Bullen sat slumped on the passenger side of the truck, head lolling back with the eyes staring forward. He was a bloody mess. The passenger side window existed only in jagged shards that protruded from within the door like broken teeth. I saw two gunshot wounds - one in the neck and the other in the chest - before I backed away in disgust.

A whole cloud of flies erupted from the back, prompting me to look. In the bed of the truck lay the two pulpwooders. They had been given the same treatment as H.W.

* * *

I tried to get in touch with the authorities, but my phone had died. Completely dead. It was the graveyard nap. Even surviving all the shit I had put it through, the phone was not impervious to the steady flow of rain. When I pressed the red button, the screen flickered miserably and then blinked off. Still, I tried to turn it on every few minutes, nervously flipping open and then closing the hinged screen so I wouldn't scream.

Thirteenth Chapter

I walked home in my wet clothes. I was hoarse and tired and my head hurt. With no keys, I had to finagle my way into the house through a stubborn window. I kicked my shoes into an empty corner of the living room and went straight for the shower. H.W. and the pulpwooders weren't getting any deader.

I dressed in a dirty old shirt and jeans and started out toward town. With no phone and no vehicle, I was left with my own two dogs to get me everywhere. However, just as I topped the hill down from the house, an elderly neighbor offered me a lift. I agreed, telling him my destination, and we rode wordlessly to town. He dropped me off and waved absently as I closed the door.

I went up to the front door and knocked. A trim woman on the other end of middle age answered the door, made up and yet haggard all the same. We exchanged a moment of silence before she spoke. "D.L.'s in the study," Paula said, somewhat hoarsely. I smelled something sweet and familiar on her breath. Something brown and in a bottle with a name like Jack or Jim or Evan on the label. "Get you anything?"

"No, thank you," I replied.

"Lord, I'm hurting," she said finally, as if in explanation. She wasn't waiting for me to heap on sympathy, not that she needed to. "This ain't supposed to happen."

I leaned against the iron railing. "I know."

"Parents don't bury their children. I'm burying my only daughter." It seemed to echo a statement from Janita Laveau.

"You did the best you could, Paula."

"Lord. Lord. Lord." She pressed her lips together so that they turned white. She swallowed, catching herself. Her stare passed through me, settling nowhere in particular, and she wiped at the corners of her eyes.

"I wish I had come sooner," I said quietly. "You probably needed some help."

"Nothing you could have done. Not this morning, anyway. I reckon you tried to help her, and she, well, God, I think she was just beyond being helped." She paused, shrugging. "I never smoked dope once in my life. I hadn't even had so much as a beer since she was born. Dee, well, he did some, but not really in front of her and not to an extreme. But today, I sat down and drank a whole pint of whiskey. D.L.'s, of course, since I didn't have anything of the sort in the house. I hate the way it tastes, but I drank every last drop of it."

"Huh," I said. "Did it help?"

She rolled her eyes. "It got me drunk. Made me sick, *so* sick. But it didn't help. In a way, I wanted it to pain God to see this happening to me. To *us*. Don't He give a good goddamn we're here in this predicament?" She paused, looking down at the floor, maybe for an answer. Then she added, "I just want to know what we did to bring this on ourselves."

It isn't anything *you* did, I wanted to say, thinking maybe it was *I* who had cursed *them*. It seemed as though I was the common factor in their misery.

But I let Paula say her piece.

"When she got hooked on that dirty stuff, I blamed you. God help me, I did. I didn't think the two of you were right for each other. She was always a seeker, looking in the wrong places, and well, Rolson, you're just so blessed quiet. You're an enabler, and not without your problems."

"I'm sorry," I said. "I loved her. If I could have locked her up to keep her from doing this, I would have."

"I'm going to blame everybody for this, long as I live. I don't have reason to, but I got something lodged in my heart that's gonna keep that feeling from ever leaving me. It'll be trapped there until my dying day." She paused again, then, straightening up, said, "Come on in. It might start raining soon."

"I think it will," I said, and followed her in.

The house smelled like leftovers - Paula said people had brought over all kinds of food - and she led me down the hardwood hallway to a bare, paint-chipped door. Our feet echoed in the house, as quiet as the graveyard had been. She paused just outside and put her hands on her hips, sniffing once and then running hair behind her ear with one finger. I looked down.

"The viewing will be tomorrow night, the funeral the next morning at eleven."

I said that I would be there.

"Go on in," she said. "Nothing to be afraid of, except he's worse off than I am."

D.L. was sitting in a leather chair behind his desk, eyes half-closed, smoking the most pungent cigar I've ever encountered, clutching a half-empty bottle of J&B. Through the nebulous haze of smoke, I saw that he was both drunk and distraught, but he straightened up somewhat as I approached him.

"I should have come earlier," I said again, but D.L. waved off the idea without responding. He'd leveled his focus on the scotch glass for now.

I didn't know quite how to proceed, to push the conversation forward, so I shared in a mutual silence with him. I sat in the chair across the desk and waited, and in turn he sat quietly in the darkness of his office, feeding off the silence.

"I handed in a resignation today," he said, after a spell. "Can't do it anymore. I've got no will to protect and serve. Got no one I want to protect, save for Paula. Whole damn town could be dead, for all I care."

A knife went through me. I thought about H.W. and the pulpers but kept my mouth shut. He seemed to be eternally out of the mood to hear bad news.

I said, "It wasn't your fault."

"I'm as much to blame as anybody, no matter if we raised her to avoid drugs or we pushed the dope into her lungs. She's my daughter, and I'm responsible for her always. I should have never let her go, not even for a second."

I started to speak, but he quieted me with another wave of the hand. "I'm not interested in avoiding blame, Rol. I know I tried to help her, but it doesn't feel like I did enough right now, and I don't want to hear any different."

"Fair enough," I said. "Let me know when you're ready for it."

"Maybe never," he replied. "I don't know. Pity is the damnedest thing, and when you're wallowing in it, you don't ever imagine yourself getting out. All feels so *close*, you know?"

I nodded.

"And so for now I just want to be drunk and stay drunk and forget that there's anything outside of the walls of this house. Everything outside here should just disappear. Like it's all a dream."

As if on cue, he swilled from the bottle of scotch and then replaced the cap. He said, "Reality don't work like that. We can't just sit in here and wither away. There's plans we got to make. Calling relatives and getting ready for the funeral, that sorta thing."

"I'll help any way I can, D.L.," I said, and he nodded this time.

336

He said, "Thought I had myself ready for this moment. Lord knows I pictured it enough times. But there ain't no right way to rehearse for death. When it comes, it's sloppier and meaner than anybody can predict."

He added, "And it fucking hurts, too."

"But you couldn't have picked up every junkie, everybody she could score from. By and by, it's got to be up to her."

D.L. paused. He looked like he was trying to cobble the words together from a jumble of letters on his desk. "Vanessa didn't buy from a street dealer. She didn't self-destruct."

That hit me as curious, and I felt an ever-growing pit in my stomach. "I don't think I follow."

I did, but for some reason, I wanted D.L. to tell me, as if he weren't in enough pain himself.

"She was *killed*, Rol. I don't have any proof, and I don't know exactly how, but I've been working in law enforcement long enough to know the difference between an accident and a goddamn murder, and I can tell you that this was no accidental overdose."

"Oh," I said. It was all I could think to say. My mind began to swim away from me. D.L. wrestled with his tears and eventually got them under control.

"I've got hunches, even if they're all I've got. Now, this ain't something I could tell Vanessa's mother, but it's been rolling around in my head ever since I got the call."

I thought of the way Van had been acting the last few days, talking incessantly at some points and then clamming up without any indication why. It certainly made sense that she might have been doing something to get herself in trouble.

I said, "She was running. Maybe in looking behind her, she plowed into something she didn't see coming."

"Maybe," he said, "but I think it's even worse than that. I haven't any evidence, but man alive, I've been having these *dreams*."

337

My mind rolled over, but before I could start the process of formulating a question, he continued talking. "She mention Brickmeyer around you?"

I thought about it. "She might have mentioned him a few times" - I was thinking specifically about our conversation regarding Jeffrey - "so, yeah, I guess she did."

Something about the way he looked at me confirmed my silent suspicion, that, were this not an accident, that the Brickmeyer family had had something to do with her death.

However, I didn't want to step too far, to speculate too much. D.L. - God bless him - was not in a state to think clearly. If she'd been held down and pumped full of drugs, fine, but I wasn't about to gloss over the possibility that her demons had gotten the better of her.

"She made some curious explanations for herself when she came to stay with us those nights. Had a lot of questions about that murder, about the dead Laveau boy, and about you. Laid on the couch and chewed her fingers, asking all sorts of things that wouldn't naturally have occurred to her."

"And so you think the Brickmeyers approached her, maybe promised to hook her up, if she snooped around the case?"

"It's a cynical view, Rolson, but I just got to believe it's the case." He paused. "I know you ain't got to believe it, and you probably think I've gone loony, but every time the wheel comes around on this, something else clicks into place."

"I don't think you're crazy, D.L.," I said.

"And it doesn't make a difference to me what people think, or are going to think, because I saw the look in her eyes when she came back home. She was different, more like the little girl I remembered, rather than the monster she had become, and so I can only believe she'd changed. Whether or not it was the truth, I'll never know. She never got a chance to prove that to all of us. But I think I had it right."

D.L. wavered, eyes glossy with tears, and he pressed both hands against his face. Covering himself. Hiding from his true feelings. Trying to push them back down.

Once he'd caught himself, he continued. "How about her *boyfriend?* She ever tell you about why she left him?"

"He was killed. She didn't feel safe, so she fled back home. It seemed right."

"That ain't why she left him. Vanessa, God rest her soul, she had a lot of problems, and maybe this last thing sent her over the edge. Maybe she couldn't atone for it, but she stole that poor sumbitch's money. Well, I shouldn't say that. It wasn't *his* money at all. Was an organization's money, if you catch my drift."

I was having trouble making the connection. If Brickmeyer was going *quid pro quo* with her, then there was no need for a transfer of money. She would be given drugs for information. Push the right button and receive a pill. That sort of deal.

But if she had stolen money, then that added a whole new wrinkle for what she was trying to hide and who she was trying to hide *from*. That I hadn't noticed any strangers lingering around town didn't mean they weren't here and weren't looking for her.

Or maybe they had just only made it down to Lumber Junction now.

"Maybe this was their payback," I said. "The drug ring's. What if it wasn't Brickmeyer at all?"

He looked impressed." You might've made a good cop, someday, if you had gotten all them cobwebs out of your head."

I still didn't buy it entirely, because I figured they would have come around the house looking for her before now. I would have noticed some heavies asking around town about Vanessa, and usually the guys tracking down money aren't too subtle with the locals.

Suddenly, the memory of that truck riding away, seemingly for no reason that night, popped into my head. Explained some things.

Maybe.

And thinking about it left me with an unsavory conclusion. "So she didn't come back because she wanted to."

"I'm sure some of it was because she loved you, so don't get the impression she was using you. That's where some belief has to come in, even if it is delusional. Some of it was earnest. But she was a sick girl. She had a lot of problems."

We sat silently for a long time in shared grief. Finally, D.L. said, "I need to be alone now, son. Don't forget to say goodbye to Paula on your way out."

Over my shoulder, opening the door, I said, "I'll make sure I find out what really happened, D.L. Whatever will put you at peace."

I left without telling him about finding all those bodies in the pond back in the woods. He'd had all the death he could handle for the day.

* * *

D.L. and his wife lived in a neighborhood just outside town, so I left them and walked into the city. Walking kept my mind moving.

Walking away, the embarrassment began to sink in. What had I thought I was going to do? What had been so important that I not go see about family first? Like it or not, D.L. and Paula were family, and running off to confront my own tenuous desires only exposed how little I had grown.

Dropping by Deuce's office got me nothing. He wasn't around, and though I knocked for several minutes, he never appeared. I stood on the corner and thought about it for a time before heading on, not quite sure where to go next. The bar wasn't an option and the Laveaus lived well out of town. Also, I had no friends, so I had no choice but to walk along the edge of the road.

I found myself on the doorstep at Nana's soon after.

"You look like the walking wounded, Rolson McKane," the

340

woman behind the counter said, as I approached. The room was filled with the penetrating aroma of fried things, of chicken dipped in eggs and flour and dropped into too-hot grease, of greens simmering in a silver pot with salt-cured pork, and of hot, sweet cornbread cooking in the oven. "You hungry?"

"Not really," I said. "Right now, I don't feel like I want to eat ever again."

"Nonsense," she replied. "You ended up here for a reason, and lord knows I'm a believer in fate."

"I think I just need some company for a minute. I need to get my head together before I move on down the road."

Her eyes caught the bandage on the back of my head. "Looks like somebody tried to take your head apart for you."

"Job hazard," I said.

"For somebody's unemployed?" She cocked a smile. "Tell you what. I'll make you a plate of food, and you don't want to eat it, you don't have to."

"No, honestly. But thank you."

"Can't stop me from doing something at my own restaurant."

I shrugged, and she grabbed a plate from beside her.

Nana had bought the restaurant after Herman's death, as a way to control the way the years rolled by on her. It didn't keep her from aging, of course, but she didn't waste away like the town's other widows. And it wasn't just a time waster, either. Nana's Kitchen was popular enough to be written up in local and regional magazines, starting a few years back.

"There's a gossip rag's worth of talk going around about you, son," she said, pulling back lids and dumping gobs of food onto the plate, more than was customary for a normal serving.

"It's probably all true," I said.

"Let's hope not. People can't figure out the angle on you, or else it'd just be one rumor going around. They figure you ain't extorting money from Brickmeyer, but plenty of people still believe that, what with your recent run-ins with the authorities and all."

"I'm not trying to skim money."

"You know how the clothesline talk is in this town, though."

"People believe what they want to believe."

"Well, then, that means you actually want him pinned up for having that young black man killed. Good luck with that, because I see it sticking to him like I see my chances for winning the lottery improving."

I sniffed. "You've heard about Vanessa?"

She nodded, avoiding eye contact.

I said, "How much do I owe you?"

She slid the plate across the counter and sighed. "When I first started up the shop, little Leland's aunt had a restaurant of her own. Remember that?"

I nodded. Of course I did.

"Wasn't too good, was it? No, it wasn't. But people went over there because the woman serving the food was kin to the right people. It was more like communion than anything else, but when I opened up, people slowly started jumping ship, because the food was better. That old haint tried to get her nephew to force us out of business."

The way she was looking at me made me smile, despite myself. "You want to see the Brickmeyers punished for that?"

"You damn right I do. I don't see anything morally wrong with that. 'God, smite my enemies' is in Psalms, I think. I don't see wrong in somebody getting what's coming to him, and Leland Brickmeyer has plenty on the way."

"That so?"

"There ain't an ethical bone in his body. Every good thing he's done is for show, and everybody kisses his ass so he doesn't turn on them. Even though his aunt's place has been out of business for a few years, there's still people who won't come in here and eat because they're afraid Leland Brickmeyer might see them. Hell, he hasn't once stepped foot into my place, not even to taunt me, and I consider myself lucky for that. You go on and eat."

I smiled and nodded at the plate of food and took it over to the table over by the front window, and Nana followed me, her hands clasped in front of her ample belly. I stared at the print of her dress as she sat down across from me. The chair seemed to grunt under her.

The food was wonderful, salty and fatty and so hot it scorched my mouth. I ate voraciously, shoveling spoonfuls of creamed corn and lima beans into my mouth. I hadn't realized I was hungry at all, let alone how hungry I was. She had also given me mustard greens, and I ate them without dousing them in hot vinegar, dipping my fried pork chop in what remained on the plate.

Nana waited until I was nearly done and said, "I'm not so bitter about the world, Rolson. Not really at all. When you get as old as I do, things either run off your back or embed in you and work around until you're nearly gutted. After my husband died, I thought people'd pretty much leave me alone, let me have my own corner of the world.

"And they didn't. Leland Brickmeyer didn't want to let me have the one thing I wanted, and I came to hate him for it. I can imagine you feeling something similar. That poor dead young man didn't ask for what happened to him, and yet here's somebody covering it up. I know that's got to sting. But you've got to keep your head on straight. He's got practice at this. He's used to letting people hang themselves on their own rope. I imagine that's what he's doing to you right now, letting you tighten the knot below your Adam's apple. He's able to keep his distance from you because he can, and that's his power."

That's when I had an idea. "I know you just gave me an entire plate of food and all, and I appreciate it, but can I also use your phone to call for somebody to come pick me up?

"You aren't drunk right now, are you?"

"No, ma'am. I just don't have a vehicle to speak of. My last one was...confiscated."

"Well, I'll tell you," she said, fiddling with nonexistent lint on the cuff of her dress, "I've got Herman's old junker of a motorcycle in a shed right out back. Some of his old stuff I've been meaning to get rid of."

"I see where you're going, and I've got to say no. I can't-"

"You can't afford to say no to me right now," she said. "You're in my debt. Herman's been gone some time, and though there's some things I'd never let anybody touch, let alone take. There's some things of his I just have never got around to selling off or trashing. That motorcycle of his, he nearly killed his old self on that horror, and I can't stand the sight of the damned thing."

She waited for something, maybe some kind of refusal, but I kept quiet, so she continued talking. "I reckon if you promise not to wrap it around a light pole, you can *borrow* it. For today. Until you get your car back, that is. If it can crank, you can drive it."

"Really?"

"Some people run through women because they don't know how to handle them. That seems like you, except with cars."

"I have no idea how to repay you."

She smiled, and this wasn't the look of a sweet old lady. "Make Leland Brickmeyer sweat. Make him grovel. Make him lose something he really wanted, a business deal or something. Hell, end his political career. I'd *love* to see that."

"I'll try my best," I said.

* * *

All in all, the process took half an hour. I siphoned out the old gasoline and replaced it with a fresh half gallon from one of Nana's red cans in the shack's front corner. I fiddled with several other things not worth mentioning.

Finally, it cranked, and once I got my bearings, I dropped the keys back off with Nana. I couldn't believe she'd let me use her dead husband's junker motorcycle, but then again, I couldn't question providence.

Since my cell phone was more than useless, Nana let me make a quick phone call. I left Deuce a voicemail, telling him to meet me at my house in a few hours, and then sped towards the country.

* * *

My hope to see my borrowed Olds in the Laveau driveway was dashed the moment I rounded that last corner. The yard was empty and the door wide open, a pervading darkness inside.

I rolled to a stop and propped the bike on its kickstand before heading cautiously for the house. I had no gun and the hairs on my neck were doing handstands.

Inside, pictures and magazines and other detritus covered the floor. Somebody had dumped the place. I wanted to call out for Janita or Uncle K but my mouth couldn't make the right sounds.

A series of pronounced footsteps resounded from the back room - Emmitt's room - and my heart did a swan dive. "Hello?" the voice asked.

I breathed a sigh of relief. "Jeffrey, what in the hell are you doing here?"

He appeared at the end of the hallway, wearing a hangdog expression. "I could ask you the same thing, sport. I came here to talk to Janita."

"About what?"

There was a sheet of paper in his right hand. He gestured toward Emmitt's room. "Him. *Us.* Everything. It was time I did right by him."

"Mmm-hmm," I said, watching the way his eyes shifted.

345

"Thanks to you," he said. It should have sounded angrier than it did. "By disgracing my entire family, you inadvertently set me free."

I wanted to get the hell out of there. Something about the way he was looking at me put me on edge. "What's that in your hand?"

He jerked as if being shaken out of a dream, bringing the slip of torn paper up in front of him. "Oh my God, that's right. The note."

His hand was shaking when he handed it over. I read it twice carefully before returning my attention to Jeffrey. MEET ME AT THE NIGGER JOINT ASAP. I WILL KILL YOUR NIECE IF YOU BRING ANY COPS.

"The Bullens," he said.

"Yup," I said, pretending to scan the note. "What do you think?"

His expression didn't reveal anything more than his style of nervous energy. He looked more haggard than ever.

"What do *I* think? I think we need to go get that maniac. It's about time he stop terrorizing the city."

I folded the note and slipped it in my pocket. Jeffrey stared. "Evidence," I said. I brought my hands to my hips and surveyed the living room. It was destroyed. "I'm going to make a call."

"Not the cops, I hope. That won't do any good. My dad, he - I don't think he's taking this too well."

"I'm out of the secrets business, Jeff."

"He'll kill her. He'll kill her, and then he'll go for my father. He's crazy. Certainly you've learned that by now."

I didn't trust it, but I didn't let on with Jeffrey that I didn't trust it. Instead, I nodded to mollify him. I couldn't tell if he really thought the Bullens would go after *Janita Laveau* before his father.

"I'll check in with the detective. He'll think something's up if I don't."

It was a lie, but I maintained a placid, calm demeanor. He sighed, scratching the back of his head. "Sure, I guess, but don't tell him where we're going. Just say, I don't know, that you're not sure of what's going

346

on."

"Of course," I said, and turned away.

* * *

I prayed for my cell phone to turn on one last time. I just needed to make two phone calls. After that, I could retire the damned hunk of plastic forever. The tip of my thumb throbbed from the pressure of pressing down on the power button. But the phone's screen remained dead and blank.

Glancing back in the house, I saw Jeffrey just kind of standing there in the living room. He was obviously frazzled. He paid me no attention but occasionally walked nervously around the house.

I heard a weak beep. The phone. I flicked my eyes toward the screen just in time to see it light up. The damn thing was working! It dragged through various booting screens and made it all the way to the halfway point in my contacts before it died again. I wanted to scream.

"Phone goofing on you?"

Jeffrey had a slightly malevolent grin. He was leaning against the doorway. I felt a sudden and inconsolable rage rise up within me, but I managed to shove it back down. "Got a little rain on it."

"Phones are fragile things. That's too bad." He looked up, taking inventory of the sky. "At least it's cleared up. Riding that motorcycle would have been hell in the weather we were having earlier."

I began to panic. If the phone didn't turn back on, I couldn't call anyone. If I couldn't call anyone, no one would know my whereabouts. Just Jeffrey Brickmeyer. A fact that was *very* unsettling to me.

"Let's hope I can get it up and running, right?" I made sure to look him in the eyes. "Otherwise, I might have to use yours, eh?"

I thought I'd caught him off-guard, because he flinched, but he made a concerted effort to turn his shock into a fluid, *I-don't-know-what-you're-talking-about* kind of shrug. "Don't have it on me," he said.

"Damn thing's always dying on me anyways, so it'd probably be as worthless as yours right now. Needs a new battery, you know."

"Right, yeah. I think mine's starting to dry out. Fingers crossed," I said.

He smiled. "Fingers crossed."

The second go-round, the phone made a near-complete recovery. I managed to get the detective on the second ring. Jeffrey watched me the entire time. "Hunter," I said. "I know I said I was out, but I've got some information you might want to-"

"Save it, McKáne." He sounded like he was talking through clenched teeth. "Where are you? Are you hiding out?"

"I'm at the Laveaus' house."

"We sent a cruiser by your place. Any reason you're not home?"

"Trying to tie up some loose ends."

"Do you have a solid alibi for today?" he asked. "Any witnesses?"

My heart began thudding in my chest. "D.L., at the very least. Why?"

"I'm only telling you this because you've been honest with me. Leland Brickmeyer was just found floating in his own pool. The one he just got through building."

I tried to play it cool, shifting around so that I could smile, plainly and falsely, at Jeffrey. I even managed a half-hearted thumbs up. "Uh-huh," I said, glancing back at Jeffrey, who was giving me a strange look. Both of his hands were shaking. "What does that mean, exactly?"

Hunter sighed impatiently. "Means he's dead. Somebody killed him, tried to make it look like an accident. Damn poor job of it too. Couldn't have been a more obvious drowning, according to the M.E."

I had a momentary flash of my first conversation with Uncle K, and something about it pinged with me. Something about water and drownings. "Any ideas?" I asked.

"None yet, though I'll tell you that the car you've been putting around town in was seen out here earlier today. Kind of a bad coincidence, don't you think?"

You wouldn't be telling me this if you suspected me, I thought. At least I hoped that was the case. "Absolutely," was all I could muster. "No, you're right."

In the background, somebody was saying something. Hunter covered the mouthpiece with one hand and yelled before returning his attention to me. "Now, what is it you wanted to talk to me about?"

Jeffrey's eyes bore into the back of my head. I whispered, "You're busy with the senator's situation."

"Just tell me, Mc-"

The phone went dead. For the last time, I figured. I replaced the worthless hunk of plastic in my jeans pocket. "Guess the water was too much for it," I said.

"Happens," Jeffrey replied, a bit too gleefully for my taste. "You want to hop in the Beemer with me? In case it starts raining again?"

"Where is it?" I knew I hadn't seen it on the way in.

"Parked around back. Somebody sees what happened in there, they might start to think I was involved."

"I see." I weighed my options. "The bike's a loaner. I leave it out here and something happens to it, I might as well count myself as a missing person."

Not funny, Jeffrey's look told me. "All right, suit yourself," he said. He paused, thinking of what to say next. "So, do we try to sneak up to the Boogie House? I've got a pistol in the glove compartment."

"Let's just get out there," I said. "I'll think of something on the way. Maybe we can take Ronald Bullen together."

He said, "You think both of them are out there, Ron *and* his brother?"

I ignored him and headed for the motorcycle. Luckily, it cranked on the first try.

* * *

349

My mind raced along at the speed of the asphalt beneath me. I watched the younger Brickmeyer's car closely in the bike's handlebar mirrors. Occasionally, I goosed the throttle and stepped out way ahead of the BMW, for no other reason than it made me more comfortable. Jeffrey looked nervous, and I didn't want some unfortunate accident to befall me.

I tabulated the casualties in this mess. Leland Brickmeyer could be added to the list, probably at the hands of Kweku Laveau. Maybe the same for Red and Lyle. H.W. Bullen. Emmitt Laveau. And, of course, Vanessa. Would Janita be added to that list by the end of the day?

I took the straightest, most visible route out to the Boogie House, going right through the center of town. I drove without being noticed. I was a ghost. A phantom. As I watched the town disappear behind me and the Beemer speed up, dread rose in me and I gouged the throttle, redlining the bike all the way out to the Boogie House.

Circumstance had boxed me in. I was afraid that if I stalled, Janita Laveau might end up dead. Sure, it might be a trap, but at this point I'd rather be the one to get caught up.

I didn't know what I expected, but I was going to damn well find out. I just hoped the spirits which had helped me along to this point would see it through to the end.

* * *

I parked the motorcycle in the woods a ways from the Boogie House and approached cautiously.

"Hey, McKane, wait up," Jeffrey whispered urgently, getting out of his car. I paid him no mind. "They might be armed."

I kept walking, taking a roundabout course that led me along the broadest wall. That way, I could case out the building, get a sense of what I was walking into.

350

Glancing back at Jeffrey, I saw abject terror in his eyes. He was following along, one hand in a jacket pocket, presumably gripping the gun.

I let my eyes drift downward, but he shook his head. "It's mine," he said, clutching it tighter.

In response, I took a step forward, as if to demand the weapon, but he stopped, jerked backward. He was shaking his head emphatically. It was then I had to make a choice. I could go on like this, or try to wrestle the gun from him.

I looked over his shoulder, thinking about how close my house was from here. I seriously contemplated leaving him to go back home.

"I want to use my gun," he said.

Before I could protest, a loud sound boomed from within the Boogie House. I knelt down, and Jeffrey followed suit.

It didn't sound like a gunshot - it was more solid, like wood on wood - but it convinced me I didn't have time to wander back home. It had to be now, no matter how unprepared I was.

I circled around and approached from the backside. I managed to keep my nerves intact, but Jeffrey shook uncontrollably. I could hear the fabric of his jacket rustling as I pressed myself against the wall.

Pausing briefly at the front corner of the building, I peered around and looked for any sign of human life. Seeing none, I stepped around and readied myself for the big reveal.

The front door was empty; I could see that from my position against the wall. I don't know what I had expected, but it wasn't this. My pulse quickened, and an equalizing surge of adrenaline pumped through me.

"Bullen," I bellowed, "if you're in there, just know I'm stepping inside. Don't shoot. This is Rolson McKane."

And then, just like that, I went into the Boogie House.

* * *

351

It took a few moments for my eyes to register what I was seeing.

Ronald Bullen was strapped to a chair, side-by-side with Janita Laveau. There was a third empty chair next to them.

"Figures," I said. I felt the cold of a gun barrel being placed against the back of my head.

Fourteenth Chapter

"I'm not a crack shot with a pistol, but at this range I could make our guests living Pollack paintings," Jeffrey said. "Play nice and sit in the chair beside Emmitt's mother."

I did as I was told. Jeffrey held the gun against my temple as he made me tie my feet together and then tie them to the chair. I then had to stretch my hands behind me so he could tie them together. Once this was done, I had no chance of getting out. I tried various tactics from action movies, but they only rubbed my wrists raw, so I gave up.

Jeffrey tiptoed along one wall, reached the end, turned around, and repeated the process. His face was clenched in its usual frightened state. He looked on the verge of tears.

"Oh, man, this all escalated. So. Quickly." He punched a rotten board, but it didn't break. "How'd I get here?"

Bullen tried to speak, but a filthy length of cloth had been stuffed in his mouth and secured with duct tape. He was on death's door but hadn't crossed over. He had the look of a quilt patched together with human skin.

I turned to Janita. "You all right?" I whispered. She nodded, but it was clearly a lie. Her face was dotted with bruises and one eye was swollen. She was not gagged but didn't speak, either.

Jeffrey's back was to us, and he was talking to himself in that way that only someone who is deluded can. I leaned forward. "Bullen," I said. "You all right?"

Bullen's eyes remained fixed on Brickmeyer. He nodded, but this, too, was an unfortunate gesture. His nostrils were coated in dried blood, each eye purple with deep, harsh bruises.

Jeffrey spun around. "Uh-unh," he said. "No planning. Can't have anything interrupting this, can we? This part has to go well for the whole business to work out properly."

Something, a blur of some kind, flickered in my periphery, but I ignored it. Or tried to. Jeffrey hadn't seen it, or couldn't see it, so I wondered if I had, either.

It was then I caught a slight whiff of gasoline. Jeffrey smiled lopsidedly, fake and disturbing, before crossing the length of the juke joint and pulling out a giant red canister.

He held his nose to the opening and said, "Yep, that's the stuff." He shook it once, and pungent gas sloshed out, covering his right hand. The younger Brickmeyer sniffed his knuckles and shrugged before heading back in our direction.

The process began with Jeffrey dribbling gasoline around us. He stopped after a few rounds and placed the canister on the floor. "I've got two of these," he said, "Just in case it don't get hot enough in here."

He coughed once and spat on the floor. "You know, you should be glad your phone cut out back there at the Laveau place. A couple more seconds with the detective, and I'd have killed you right there. Wouldn't have wanted to, but that's the way it is."

I tested the waters with Jeffrey. "Janita's got nothing to do with this, Jeff. Let her go. Deal with Ronald. Deal with me. He kidnapped Emmitt, and I'm the one who investigated the case."

"Why would I care about that?"

"Because it would have eventually led me to you, wouldn't it?"

Jeffrey's face turned bitter. "You and he, the two of you, were

354

going to ruin our family. And she," he said, flicking his eyes toward Janita, "was just as bad as my old man. She wouldn't have accepted her son. She wouldn't have wanted him to be with me. So she's got to participate in this with you, I'm afraid."

"Are you afraid, Jeff?"

"No," he said, avoiding eye contact. "I've got it all figured out. Bullen kidnaps the both of you, brings you here in order to get you to talk about my father - to frame him - but what he doesn't count on is two local cops figuring it out just in time to stop it all."

He paused, listening, and then said, "Oh, and here they come now."

The sound of brakes outside. Two doors slamming. Feet crunching on dead twigs. I was unimpressed with the two uniformed officers who stepped inside: Owen Harper and Ricky Walton. Owen looked like he'd swallowed a cat whole, but Ricky couldn't have been happier to see me strapped to this chair.

"What's with the fire?" I asked.

Jeffrey glared. "Once Bullen figures out he can't get information out of you, he decides to kill you. He shoots you both in the head and sets the place on fire to destroy the evidence, but Owen and Ricky here show up and kill him in a shootout just as the Boogie House grows too hot for the bodies to be salvaged. It all fits with the picture the LJPD will paint of Ronald Bullen. Story over."

He tried to smile, but his nerves wouldn't allow it. "Oh, and speaking of narrative, that reminds me."

Brickmeyer's hand emerged from behind his back with the pistol. He had put it up to do the thing with the gasoline. I saw it, really, for the first time then. It was Bullen's gun and not his. He fumbled with it for a moment, trying to cock the hammer, and then he aimed and fired at Owen Harper.

The bullet caught him in the chest. Undoubtedly, Jeffrey was going for a headshot but had missed. Owen stumbled back, surprised, and fell against the entranceway, a jagged red circle forming at the entry point. "Hey!" Ricky screamed. "That wasn't the deal."

"He would talk." Jeffrey said. "Got it during the firefight. Simple as that."

Ricky stared, standing stock-still at the feet of his dying partner. His hand had gone to the hip holster, his fingers unsnapping it instinctively. Framed by the doorway, he almost looked heroic. Almost.

"Relax, officer. I'm not going to shoot *you*. I just can't have this coming back to me whatsoever. Okay, now let's get on with it."

Ricky continued to regard Jeffrey skeptically, even as Jeffrey returned to the canister. The hand remained fixed on the butt of his pistol. Jeffrey's (or rather Bullen's) gun had returned to its former position, in the back of his pants.

Brickmeyer hefted the can above his head and dumped gasoline all over Bullen, who struggled against the ropes and screamed deep within his throat, the sound of man aware of impending death.

My attention was drawn upward. My mind had produced another hallucination, this time hovering just above Brickmeyer's head, spreading out like a bat readying itself for flight. I glanced at Ricky to see if he was seeing it, too, but he no more registered the black haze than he did his partner moaning at his feet.

The smell of gas hit me instantly. Droplets of the stuff spattered my face. In all the commotion, I tried to dislodge my hands from the tape, to no avail. Janita remained still and quiet, as if she'd accepted the situation's inevitability.

When Jeffrey stopped pouring, the room became quiet, save for Bullen's exhalations. He sputtered and grunted, trying to keep the gas from going down his nose.

"Asshole kept a file on my father the entire time he worked for the LJPD," Jeffrey said. "Wanted to ruin him because of a decades-old land dispute. Can you believe that?"

No one replied. Even Ricky regarded him suspiciously.

"He was *obsessed*," he continued. "The pictures he showed you, McKane, were ones he himself took. Psycho. You know why he kidnapped Emmitt in the first place?" He leaned over and spat in Bullen's face. "*Desperation*. Somebody found his little file and destroyed it. Thanks, Ricky. He thought it was over. And then he happened upon me and Emmitt together. It gave the sick bastard motivation for one last-ditch attempt to ruin my dad. But it didn't work, did it? Did it, motherfucker?"

Jeffrey took a step back. He breathed with a force that made me think he was hyperventilating. "My God. What am I doing?"

There was a brief moment when I thought he might call the whole thing off. But then he got that look in his eyes again, and it all recommenced.

He turned to Ricky. "Shoot him."

Jeffrey stepped away from the three of us but kept his gaze fixed on the cop. "Jesus. You know, Bullen, I dreamed last night that I'd burned you alive. I just put a lighter to your face and watched it go. It was so real. I woke up seeing things. I want to, but I can't do that. I'm not a monster. Not like you. Ricky, shoot him."

Ricky glanced from Bullen to Jeffrey to me and then back to Jeffrey. "I can't do that, J," he said, stuttering. "I can look the other way. That was our deal. But actively taking part is beneath even me."

"Taking part? Taking *part*? You're already taking part. You're *here*, aren't you? This will save the police department. The only way it can even function is with my father's help. Without him, it would fall completely apart."

"That's why I'm here," he said. "My job's all I got."

They glared at one another for a moment. "Fine, give me the gun. I'll do it myself. It's just got to look real enough that you can cover it up."

They exchanged pistols, and Jeffrey took the time to figure out how to use it before approaching Ron. "Dad sure will be relieved about this."

Then I had an idea.

I leaned over. "Forgive me," I whispered to Janita. I felt the slightest nudge of approval. I dreaded what I was about to say, but it was a last-ditch effort.

Jeffrey raised the pistol, aiming for Bullen's forehead. His finger trembled on the trigger.

"Maybe that's why your father killed himself," I said, blurting out the words in a single breath.

He turned to me, face twisted up into something quite inhuman. The black smudge surrounding him continued to grow. "What'd you say?"

"You think that picture in the paper is why he stuck his head underwater and didn't come up? I do."

"Shut up."

I didn't bother to think about what I was saying. As long as he let me talk, I was safe. "I do. I think he was ashamed. Ashamed before he found out and even more so once he knew for a fact that you weren't just ineffectual but something he couldn't approve of."

Jeffrey's face became jagged, uneven. "McKane, I'm warning you. I'll kill this one and then work on Laveau right in front of you. Make you watch."

I ignored him, plowing forward. "You know that phone call I made?" He didn't respond, but I kept going. "What I didn't tell you is that your old man is dead. Was found today, while you were out and about, planning this little coup. I bet your cell phone isn't on, is it?"

He was incredulous. "Stop it. You're lying."

"Check with your accomplice over there. Certainly he's heard about it by now. Ask him."

Brickmeyer straightened up as if a cold finger had grazed his neck. His whole body went rigid, and he dropped the gun to his side. "Liar!" he said, finally. "Fucking asshole liar. Call this asshole a liar, Ricky. Tell him how full of it he is."

"Jeff," Ricky began, taking a step forward. "He-"

"No! It's not true," he said. He was shouting. "It isn't. McKane convinced them to stage it all, to get someone to make a mistake."

Ricky stepped forward, searching for sufficient words. "I saw him, Jeff. He's gone, man. Just do what you got to do, and let's get the hell out of here. Your family's gonna start looking for you soon."

Jeffrey didn't quite begin to cry at this, but his face twisted up into a horrible expression, and he began to make these half-hiccup, half-sobbing sounds.

"It's all over," I said. "There's nothing left to protect. Killing us won't do any more for your father than letting us go. Please, Jeffrey. Listen to reason."

He raised both hands to his face and quietly broke down for a moment. Seconds dragged by. Once his shoulders stopped moving with the weight of his grief, he leveled the barrel of the gun on Ronald Bullen and shot him three times in quick succession.

Bullen gurgled in his throat and thrashed violently. The first bullet got him in the chest. Brickmeyer hadn't held the gun tightly, so the second and third shots went higher. The second pierced his shoulder and the last clipped his head. It wasn't enough to kill him instantly, but a quarter of his skull disappeared in a spray of blood.

I was in shock. The smell of smoke and blood and gasoline were making me sick. I didn't even turn my head to watch Jeffrey splash the walls with gasoline and set them on fire. I smelled the result, and I heard the crackling of wood as the place went up. Old as it was, it wouldn't take long for the whole building to be reduced to ashes.

He returned to his spot in front of us, his eyes burning holes into me. "You're next, asshole," he said, yelling in order to drown out the screaming and groaning and destruction.

I've always thought the saying "staring down the barrel of a gun" was kind of strange and dramatic, but it was the most apt description my mind could muster. The darkness inside the barrel was more terrifying than any night in the Boogie House.

And just before the pistol bucked in Jeffrey's hand, I saw a nearly-invisible coil wrap itself around the younger Brickmeyer's arm, like a python tightening around a victim, and somehow it filled me with a sense of grim, knowing comfort. Jeffrey Brickmeyer had no idea what he was doing to himself.

The gun erupted in flame, emitting a cacophonous roar, and for a moment I thought my stomach had caught on fire. I felt my blood and life seep out and stain my shirt. Janita was screaming at the top of her lungs. The same word, repeating, *nononono.*

In the midst of this, something happened.

A small fire had begun to spread up Jeffrey's arm in a coiling pattern, very much like one of my visions. It was entirely unnatural, and he had not yet noticed it. But he would.

The next moments passed in some kind of slow motion. Jeffrey raised the piece to finish me off, when another shot was fired. I was losing blood at a pretty rapid clip and felt the shock draining consciousness from me. The room was growing dimmer.

It wasn't Jeffrey's gun that had fired.

I managed to hang on to see what happened next. Jeffrey spun around, giving me a head-on view of the Boogie House's entrance. I half-expected Ricky to be the second gunman, but Ricky lay in a heap in the doorway, blood streaming from his broken and twisted nose. His kneecap had been blown away. The man in his place had a gun trained on Brickmeyer, and he was guaranteed not to miss.

About that time, the darkness took me somewhere else, perhaps for the very last time.

Still, I had never been so happy to see Deuce in all my life.

* * *

I might as well have had my eyelids sewn shut, because everything was a black, inky color. Something like drowsiness overwhelmed me, and I slid off into a dreamlike state, like the mast of a sinking ship disappearing into the deep.

A shock hit me, and my eyelids popped open. This time, the darkness wasn't quite as impermeable. I was upright. I was trying to walk, but the ground sank beneath my feet. I struggled to keep above ground.

In the distance, a silhouette approached, disfigured in a supernatural way. As the shape approached, it became whole, and I saw that it was not Emmitt Laveau but my mother, who was clad in her burial dress. Her arms were crossed, a baby swaddled in a cream-colored blanket against her chest. She smiled sweetly, as if only an afternoon had passed since I'd seen her.

She had never been so beautiful. We were walking along a darkened path, and I had to pull my feet out of the ground to keep from sinking into its depths.

"You are the spitting image of your father," she said. "Put a white border around you, and it would resemble a picture I once had."

I had imagined this moment for thirty years, and not once had it included talking about my father. "We're different," I managed, gazing stupidly at her face. It had grown blurry and insubstantial in my memory, and seeing it now retouched all of the indistinct parts. The small dabbling of freckles on the bridge of her nose. Her long eyelashes. The intensity of her eyes.

She seemed unfazed by my comment. She said, "He was angry, and you are troubled."

"He was a murderer. Cold-blooded. I'm *nothing* like him. He killed" - and I nodded at the baby hidden under the blanket - "*his* father."

She tilted the blanket in my direction, and the cloth unraveled to reveal an empty bulge, not air exactly but, well, *something*. The absence of something. I nodded, trying to understand, but my mother only smiled, looking older each time I looked at her.

"He wasn't alone."

"I know."

"You don't care about that anyway. You want to see something else. That's why you're here. It isn't to catch up with me."

"I wish there was something to catch up on, Mama. I'm not sure you'd be proud of me."

"Oh, but I am. I see what you're doing right now, and I want to help. It's the least I could do after, well, you know."

"It wasn't your fault."

"I cheated on your father, and I knew him, understood how he would react. I hoped against hope for that baby to be his, and all the while I knew it wasn't."

"Nobody deserves what we all went through, except him."

The light flickered, and my mother stopped walking. "We don't have much time, Rolson," she said. "I wish there was more. But there will be. Someday."

"Have I always had this ability? To speak with the dead?"

"Who said this was real?"

"It has to be real."

Her face became soft with an uncanny light. "It's somewhere in between."

"I wish I could feel something right now. I don't even have the urge to reach out and curl your hair, the way I used to when I couldn't sleep. I can see it - your hair - and I think I could just run my fingers through it, but I don't have the slightest desire to."

"I'm sorry, Rolson. It wouldn't work. We can't just hold hands and wander down the dark path. It just isn't allowed."

"Why didn't you come to me before?"

"You need me."

"I've always needed you."

"Follow behind, and make sure to keep up. This isn't going to be pleasant."

With that, she turned and resumed walking. We were no longer standing at the edge of the flickering orange backdrop but rather descending a winding road, black on all sides. I wiped at my eyes, veiled in an almost tangible darkness, and found that we were cascading a steep hill beset on all sides by barren, contorted trees, rough and tangled and savage as the animals I imagined living among them. All of this was a wasteland, eroded and without life, and the longer I peered at it the more indistinct it became.

She moved effortlessly down the path, looking as though she were floating, and I struggled not to sink. I knew where we were, somehow, but my mind could not articulate it. And yet, despite my vague self-awareness, I was determined that I was lost and said so many times, though my mother ignored my pleas.

I should have known I wouldn't be able to keep up, but even I was surprised in a detached way whenever I spilled headlong into the muck and dirt of the path. By the time I reached my feet again, I was truly lost. My mother was nowhere to be seen, and in her absence there seemed to be no path at all, let alone a clear one.

A flash of what might have been lightning cracked the sky, illuminating the jagged landscape around me. I found myself not on a crooked, steep path, but just outside the Boogie House. Only, its walls and ceiling weren't ablaze.

Without warning, a voice so raw it sounded like it had been rubbed with sandpaper called out. "Hello?" it said, and I squinted in the darkness for its source. I saw a dim light strike the back of a young man's head. It was Emmitt Laveau's, and it bobbed once, twice, and a third time before lifting all the way erect.

He sat chained to the old, rusted, disintegrating bar, his breath rasping in his throat. "Is anybody there?" he called, turning his head so that he faced me straight_on. His eyes passed through me with such intensity that I looked away.

"Hello?" he continued. His voice was full of fear and pain. "Can someone hear me? I thought I heard somebody. Can someone help me, please? Please? PLEASE!"

The last iteration seemed to rip something deep in his throat, but it didn't completely silence him. He continued whimpering shallowly, tilting his head forward in order to cry.

Even in the darkness, I saw what a bad state he was in. He'd been beaten within several yards of his life, and when he raised his face again, I saw the welts and cuts and bruises more clearly.

"I'm here," said a voice somewhere nearby. "I've got you, Emmitt."

It was Jeffrey Brickmeyer.

I stood in the doorway and watched.

Laveau stopped crying long enough to show that he recognized Jeffrey. He smiled, and then he broke down again, but the tears were different somehow.

"Oh, Emmitt. Oh my God," Jeffrey said, kneeling next to him. "I can't believe this. Oh my God."

Jeffrey knelt, if a bit timidly, and placed both hands on Emmitt's shoulders. He kissed him, first on his swollen forehead and then on the lips, holding it for a few moments before pulling away. Then he placed his face in the crook of Laveau's neck and sobbed. Finally, Emmitt said, "It's okay, Jeff. Now that you're here, it's okay."

With his face still resting there, in the crook of his neck, Jeffrey nodded. When he pulled away this time, Laveau's eyes maintained a kind of grim focus.

"Okay," Emmitt said, "We've got to hurry. Any minute now, two big-ass men are going to show up. So listen. Stop crying. Listen, look for something around here sharp enough to cut through the tape. Once you get me out of here, we're gone. We can hop in your Beemer and hightail it out of town. That sound good to you, Jeff?"

Jeffrey nodded, but it was half-hearted. When he finally spoke, his voice was weak and watery. "I can't, Emmitt. You know I can't do that."

"Why not?"

Jeffrey paused, as if gathering words that, no matter how he assembled them, would not come out right. "I'm one of his closest advisors, and he's making a run for the Senate this time, the U.S. Senate, and-"

"The hell with your father's career, Jeff," Emmitt countered.

Jeffrey hesitated. His eyes met Emmitt's, and Emmitt screamed, a pained, angry wailing. "*Look* at me, Jeff. Look at me. Goddamn your father, Jeff. He's getting me killed here. Just let go."

Jeffrey swayed on his knees, whispered, as if unconvinced himself. "My father's...not responsible."

Emmitt completely broke down at this. "He's got you pegged, that's all. He knows how to manipulate you. Jesus, he's the reason I've been kidnapped. Somebody wants to get back at your father. How do you think he knows about where I am? Why do you think he told you?"

Jeffrey suddenly stood up. "You lie."

"What do I have to lie about, Jeff? I just want to be with you, with or without your father's acceptance. I could give a shit about that. I just want out of here *right now*. Help. Me."

"My daddy's a good man," Jeffrey said.

From my perspective, I could see Emmitt fighting against the eventuality of his tears. His bottom lip quivered and widened into a heartbreaking approximation of a smile. His eyes bore knowledge of what was about to take place, and he struggled to resign himself to it.

Jeffrey screamed a half-scream, half-growl, and slapped Emmitt, which resounded like a gunshot. Then he backed up and waited for a reaction. Emmitt didn't give him one. He rested his chin on his chest and cried quietly, almost sweetly, despite the situation.

"Please, don't," Emmitt began. "Jeff, please. I'm begging you."

This time, Jeffrey punched him. He had aimed for the back of his head, and stumbled backward after it. The punch was weak, without purpose, but it landed nonetheless. "*You stop it!* There's nothing I can do. I can't disobey my father. He controls everything I do. He controls *everything.*"

Emmitt raised his head and said, "He didn't control us. That happened without his say-so."

"That's different. You know that. I hid it from him, and look what happened."

"What happened?" Emmitt said this flatly and evenly. "What happened? Nothing. Nothing has happened. Yet. He's found out. The men who took me told him, and so now he knows. So what? He can get over it, or we can run away. Personally, I say to Hell with your father."

Jeffrey punched Emmitt so hard that he himself screamed in pain. The rage in the young Brickmeyer had reached a crescendo. I could feel it in the air. I stepped forward, intending on doing, well, something. It felt pointless, even as I approached.

I went right through the both of them. I didn't feel anything, didn't possess either of them, the way they do in the movies. In one side and out the other.

And I didn't stop, either. I just kept on going. I went through the window on the opposite side of the building and followed the path I had chased H.W. Bullen down that first night.

I didn't stay to witness what happened next. I couldn't. I had seen the end result. That was enough. The state of Laveau's body was far worse when I later found him, and I didn't want to see what kind of malice would be visited upon him.

Instead, I waited down the path a ways, leaning against a pine tree, anticipating Brickmeyer's return. Sure enough, minutes later he appeared in a sliver of moonlight, running unevenly toward me. He was crying openly, forever a child. His vehicle lay at the end of this particular row of pines, and when he passed me, he reached into his pocket and pulled out a jangly set of keys. Something dropped to the ground.

I knelt down. The key fob. It was the key fob I thought had belonged to one of Brickmeyer's henchmen or to Brickmeyer himself. It had been Jeffrey all along. He was Emmitt's true killer.

The taillights of Jeffrey's BMW lit up, and moments later it disappeared, kicking up dust in its wake. I stood there in the darkness, alone and bewildered in this purgatory.

So. Hmm. He loved Emmitt Laveau, or at least pretended to love him so that Emmitt, kind and as gentle as he was, became convinced that they were in love.

And maybe that was true. Maybe Emmitt Laveau saw something really special in Jeffrey, and maybe he drew that out in the private moments between them. Thinking about that for even a moment usually cuts the question of "How could he possibly..." right in two.

Those private moments are what grant us love, and they are also what blindfold us to reality, whatever subjective truth is out there.

But the third member of their relationship was clearly who Jeffrey loved, and even the desperate cries of a worn and broken lover could not convince him otherwise. Standing in the sunshine of someone else's affection could not cast off the shadow of his father's influence.

"Where to now?" I asked aloud. The wind picked up in a sort of response, but that was all I got.

Some pine needles drifted down to me, and I anticipated them landing, but they passed on through. Everything seemed to pass on through. I stepped away from the tree where I pretended to lean and walked slowly down the pathway, admiring the sad, haunting beauty of the trees, leading me down toward the place where the land met the highway.

It was where I would wait, because I had nothing better to do. Hell, I had nothing *else* to do. I certainly wasn't going to trek back up to the

Boogie House.

I waited down by the roadside for a few minutes before beginning to babble to myself. Soon, the babbling turned into a wailing scream. "Laveau!" I screamed, and then realizing there were more than one, said, "Uncle K. Help me out of here. I. Need. A. Way. Out."

Nothing happened. The breeze blew. I screamed. The darkness remained. That was it.

When I was done screaming, I sat on the ground and stared at the dirt. I closed my eyes. My mind wasn't exactly at its clearest, and the more I concentrated, the more aware I became of a distinct pain in my abdomen. At first, it felt like a pinprick. Then the sensation deepened, becoming a throb. I kept my eyes closed, waiting. Wondering. It was all I had left to do. I silently implored the old man to help me, expecting him to appear in the darkness and lead me to whatever occurred after this. Was it Hell I had to look forward to, or was I subject to this for the rest of eternity, to occupy the junction between memories and dreams?

Two loud bursts punctuated the darkness, and I opened my eyes. Gunshots. They seemed to have come from somewhere above me. I rose and hurried out into the open air beyond the trees, staring into the cloudy sky. I craned my neck up and spun around several times, looking for my exit. I didn't see anything, but the world around me had changed. I didn't feel as aloof or distant as before, and the pain in my stomach was becoming unbearable.

The sky changed colors. Clouds swirled into vast, twisting shapes, and I felt the first beads of rain on my forehead. I soon found it difficult to stand, and I dropped to the ground, going first to my knees and then landing face-down on old pine straw.

I opened one eye and felt excruciating pain. A cough welled inside me, and though it hurt to do so, I let out a rasping series of hacks. I raised my head, feeling it throb, and knew it wasn't a dream.

I was *outside*, lying in the dirt. The Boogie House itself had all but collapsed. If before it had looked like a face made of fire, now it resembled a funeral pyre. The fire leaped up and licked the sky, and though there was nothing overtly supernatural about it, I thought I heard music under the violent chaos of the Boogie House's final moments.

I watched it burn, trying to make sense of things, and then the pain swelled, and though I tried to fight it, I succumbed to an uncomfortable sleep. I would be told later it was because of all the blood loss, that I shouldn't have been awake at all, that I had probably imagined all of this in the first place.

But I hadn't. I knew better.

The sensation of bouncing up and down knocked me out of my unconsciousness. I felt numb and weak and tired, and I grunted in dismay. I heard a familiar voice say, "I got you, man. Just hang on. Just make it 'til we get to the car. I'm going to make sure you live through this."

"Deuce," I said, and then was out again. This time, it seemed, for a good long while.

Epilogue

Very often, you are not your own life's hero. As hard as I had fought to solve Emmitt Laveau's murder, turns out Deuce was the real Samaritan. On seeing my missing phone calls, he had gone to the one place that seemed to be drawing me perpetually to it. He disarmed Jeffrey Brickmeyer and left him bleeding there in the Boogie House while he dragged out the survivors.

Ronald Bullen bled to death on the way to the hospital, in the back of the ambulance. Several bullets from his gun were found in the bodies of Lyle Kearns, Red Tyson, and H.W. Bullen. It's still not clear if these murders occurred before or after Jeffrey Brickmeyer kidnapped Ronald. He was given a low-key funeral. No one but the preacher and gravediggers attended.

Leland Brickmeyer's death was ruled a homicide, though no physical evidence was found on the premises and both the maid and landscaper admitted to seeing no one at the house at the time. I doubt if a warrant for Uncle K will ever be issued, and I still wonder what he saw in his own dreams that made him carry out the murder.

And as for Jeffrey Brickmeyer.

When visiting me in the hospital, Deuce became clued in to what I had known all along. "I shot him once, and rather than come running

371

out into the open air, he went flailing towards the back of the building. Suppose he thought he'd find a window leading out back. But he didn't. I dragged you and Janita and Owen outside and went back in to see if I could find his body. But I can tell you it wasn't there. Whole place burned up, and yet they still ain't found the man's body, not a trace of it. No tissue. No clothes. No bones. No nothing."

Staring up at him from my hospital bed, I did not reply. I saw his mind working on something he wasn't quite ready to deal with, and I wasn't ready to let him in on everything I knew.

With a sad, confused expression, he said, "Something unearthly went on there." It was the truth, and I let the silence linger some more. "Can I tell you something else, Rol?"

In my heavily-medicated state, I could only nod. It was one of the few beneficial things about being shot. I didn't have to explain nearly as much as everyone else wanted me to.

Deuce almost seemed embarrassed at what he said next. "I'm hoping the medication will erase this from your memory, because I don't want it getting out, but here goes. The other night, when I shot him, and I was cutting the duct tape off all of you, it wasn't Jeffrey Brickmeyer's legs that carried him to the fire. It was something else."

I nodded, trying to convey that I understood. He ignored me and kept talking. He said, "I remember, I was working on your tape, holding one of your hands away from the knife blade so I wouldn't accidentally slice off a finger, and I looked up to see two smoky figures perched on Jeffrey, one on each shoulder. Dragging him toward the fire, him fighting it the entire time. I know it sounds like I inhaled too much smoke. You think I'm crazy?"

I shook my head.

"Good," he said. "Then let me tell you the most fucked-up part. It wasn't smoke at all, but, well, shit, I don't know, *spirits* or something. Smoke with human faces. God, this sounds so stupid. Looked like two old fellas used to live here, I guess. Anyway, they dragged him off into the fire, him kicking and screaming, and, I've got to be honest, it looked like - to me - the fire wrapped around him like two arms and made him disappear. Janita didn't even register that she'd seen it. And once I let go of your hand, I didn't see anything out of the ordinary, either."

He laughed uncomfortably. "Hell, maybe I did inhale too much smoke. That'll be our little secret, won't it?"

I nodded, and he stood up. "Fine, good, Rolson. You go on and get better. I'm going to get on finding you a new lawyer. Seems like your buddy Clements has skipped town. Maybe he had something to do with this whole situation."

He got up, stretching his back, and headed for the door.

There was one mystery I did need to ask him about. "I lent you twenty bucks last week. I ain't asking for the money, but how bad is it, Deuce?"

"I can't tell yet," he replied. "I'm always hoping for my luck to change."

And, with that, he left.

* * *

The Boogie House burned to the ground, as expected. The fire department tried to put it out, without much success. Even with all the recent storms, the juke was a collection of burnt embers before anyone could do much to stop it. All that remained was the tin roof, and even it was severely scorched.

On digging out the foundation, in an effort to get rid of the memories as much as the building itself, some human remains surfaced. Two adult males, both of whom had been shot in the head and stuffed into pine boxes, were pulled out and sent off to labs for testing. It is believed the two skeletons belong to the club's former owners, who had disappeared under mysterious circumstances years ago. Detective

373

Hunter told me the man wanted in connection with the murder was Jarrell Clements.

* * *

A suicide note left behind by Jarvis Garvey confirmed his involvement in the death of Terrence Birrell, naming both himself and Clements as accomplices. My discussion with Clements had sent him into a manic state, and he'd called Jarvis to warn him. It set a whole chain of events into motion.

Jarvis, in the years following the murders, had grown penitent and was almost relieved that the truth might actually, *finally* come out. Clements didn't share his sentiment and demanded he keep quiet. When Jarvis responded that, well, no, he'd just go along with whatever happened, Clements became incensed and told Jarvis *he*'d be the only one to go to jail.

Apparently, he didn't believe his own hype. The authorities tracked Jarrell Clements to a ratty hotel just outside Memphis. Riding a pretty harsh drunk, he'd left a sloppy trail behind him and was dragged forcefully to the waiting cruiser.

* * *

I got out of the hospital and went to court. Deuce found me a young lawyer fresh out of school who practiced near Dublin. The judge, given all that had happened, sentenced me to the bare minimum for my DUI. By then, the whole story had reached the public, and I was considered a somewhat mysterious celebrity.

While spending a single day in lock-up - the bare minimum - I decided a change of scenery might be good for me. I had sucked about every last drop of juice out of Lumber Junction, and the contemptuous looks others had given me in the wake of my DUI had been replaced by bizarre and frightened stares, so it was not a stretch that I pack everything up and put the house on the market.

During that period, I went to Vanessa's funeral drunk on beer and high on painkillers, and I made it through the whole graveside service without breaking down. I placed a rose on the coffin before it was lowered and hugged her parents on my way out.

The memory of that day remains more blurry than the dreams of the Boogie House. Drinking no longer affects me adversely, though I've promised myself I would try sobriety out, complete with the AA chip she had brought home from her first meeting. I'd accepted Van's death as a wound that would eventually scar over, rather than heal.

I'm a different person, I know, but life is like a stone in a river. You don't notice the waters taking the edges off until they're all smooth. I'd like to say this has fundamentally changed my life, and I'm on the other side of the darkness, but I can't say that. It's just too early to tell.

I'm not over Vanessa, probably never will be. Don't know I'll ever be at peace with how things ended up between us. But I did some things right. I just didn't do all the things right, and I'll have to live with that, too.

Over the course of the week where I boxed things up, threw things away, boxed things up again and then unboxed and subsequently threw them away, I found the collection of things Van brought with her, including a small, silver briefcase. I fiddled with the locks for a few minutes but was in too much of a hurry to crack them open. I resolved to open it as soon as I could, and the potential contents kept me occupied when it was hard to think of her.

Janita Laveau, without her uncle to keep her tied to this town, moved on. She went to Louisiana to live with a distant relative. Apparently, she and I'd had the same idea. I got to speak to her once, but I was so high on meds I couldn't quite get any words out.

I wanted to apologize for not helping. I wanted to let her know that I had done nothing, that she had placed her faith in me for no good reason. But I suppose she got what she needed out of me, and not for a bad purpose, either.

It is something I still think about. I played a part in this investigation, but I was nowhere near the hero I thought I might become. I'm the same person I was before, only now I realize I might be a broken man, as well.

Curiously, a dog started hanging around the house about then, coming first within viewing distance and then occasionally working its way toward the front yard. It was timid and old and probably feral, so anytime I showed any interest in it, the damned thing would run off into the woods for hours at a time. I put out fresh water and some leftovers everyday until finally, with me peering secretly through the blinds, it ambled up and began to eat. It ate slowly at first but then gulped down the food and water and then licked the bowl. It would still bolt whenever I showed my face, but I expected that to only last for a little while.

Finally, the dog came to trust me, and I sort of adopted him. He was old and ugly, but it made me happy to take care of something. Took my mind off of things. On the first afternoon he let me pet him, I came out onto the front steps and sat down, slowly stroking his coarse and tangled fur.

I stared into the distance, peering at the trees across the way. It was a cloudless, windless day, and at some point I thought I heard the sound of an acoustic guitar. I continued to pet the dog, but my whole body went cold.

Moments later, I heard the engine of an old beater, and a teenager in his daddy's truck roared by, an old blues song blaring on the radio. I smiled and waved, and he kind of acknowledged me.

I went back inside and poured out every ounce of booze in the house while the dog watched. Tired and weary, still building my stamina back up, I took a long nap. I did not dream.

Made in the USA
Lexington, KY
21 February 2016